For Pauline, Sharon, Erin, Zoë, Irene, Abigail,
Amanda, Lorina, Brenda, and Sally.
You are all women of vision, which is
just another word for 'Seer.'

Contents

Prologue: Ascent

Long shafts of sunlight broke through the morning mist and turned the town of Elysir golden. As the town's folk opened their doors to start their day, they peered into the streets with trepidation. Roof tiles littered the cobblestones in shards. Clay pots lay in pieces, their flowers long since lost to the storm. In tight knots, housewife muttered to housewife—never had she seen such a tempest, not even among the red-sanded *leveches* from Afrik. Ominous it was, when the storm struck—as a witch was about to burn.

Unlike their wives, the men of the town put on a stoic front, but inwardly, they worried the storm was more than it appeared. In the *plaza mayor*, two pillars stood bereft of heretics, their kindling untouched, as if to point taunts at the god. Sooty streaks snaked up the Solarium's front, as high as the golden dome. The priests insisted arsonists were to blame, but the temple looked as if it had been struck by lightning. In any event, it was the prudent man who paid his temple tithes and minded his own affairs.

A practical, pragmatic lot, were the people of Elysir. It never occurred to them that the mist lifting from the morning cobblestones was a soul ascending to heaven.

)L(

Odd, thought the soul as it rose on warm banks of air. The night before, it had been a storm so swollen it had completely emptied itself of rain. There had been a reason for that, but now, it couldn't remember what it was. It didn't matter. The view below was breathtaking. A town curled in on itself, like a cat snoozing in the sun. Beyond, the land stretched into rolling hills and pierced the sky in sharp peaks. *I was afraid of heights once,* the soul remembered. *Why, I wonder?*

As it tried to recall, black and white spears shot towards it from out of the clouds. The soul gasped in surprise. Storks! The birds barrel-rolled and tickled him with their wing tips, their black eyes sparking with mirth. The sea appeared between banks of mist, resembling beveled jade. A solid wall of cumulus closed in. The birds soon gave up their game of tag and flew with intent, their wings beating strongly as they bore the soul even higher. Their feathers glimmered and turned molten. With a final push, the soul rose above them, sensing their parting. The storks tipped their wings in a final salute and slid away into the haze.

Goodbye! the soul called after them wishing they hadn't gone.

It finally floated to a gentle stop. It was alone now in a strange landscape of boundless light. Or perhaps *alone* wasn't quite the right choice of a word. There was no one to see, but there *was* a sense of presence, of something—someone—who was near and distant at the same time, as if the space *itself* was the person—separate, distinct, and yet...not.

Alonso, said a disembodied voice.

Alonso froze.

Come back to yourself.

With sudden clarity, Alonso realized where he was and who the voice was. Fear shriveled him into his old form. He clutched his face and crumpled to his knees. He waited for the blow that would smite him from his miserable existence, send him screaming to a burning hell forever. No one was more faithless than a fallen priest. No one more jealous than a wrathful god.

Instead, he heard a sigh, the sound of patience enduring eons. *Love is never misplaced, Alonso,* the god said.

Alonso wanted to weep—from relief, from fear—he wasn't sure which. *Forgive me,* he sputtered.

Why? What have you done?

The words filled him with terror and hope. Was it possible he had been wrong about the god? That Sul was not the vengeful deity he had always thought he was? Misrepresenting the god was sin enough, yet... Sul's question begged an answer.

He had done nothing wrong, apparently. Except forsake his priestly vows and his faith, shift his devotion from a god to a girl. That had been the worst sin of all. He had fallen in love. Yet according to Sul, love was never misplaced.

Alonso's fear fell away like a tattered cloak. If Sul meant those words, then the god knew his greatest desire—and tolerated it. *Please,* he begged, *send me back. I must go back. She needs me. I must go to her.*

For what seemed an age, Sul didn't speak.

If love is never misplaced, how can I be wrong? It was unnerving to be confronted with nothing but white light. It would be so much better if a divine figure stepped from it to engage him.

The glow remained steady but within it, there was an undercurrent, a hesitation, as if Sul considered ramifications.

Please! Alonso insisted.

I can send you back, but you can't share her body as you did before. It will mean constant suffering. You will experience death, over and over. Perhaps worse things.

I suffer without her, Holy One. I've died three times. How can any more deaths matter?

He felt an infusion of warmth.

Very well. You shall have your wish, Alonso. But remember, if mortality ever becomes too great a burden, you will return to me. And when you do, it will be forever.

Thank you! Alonso closed his eyes and pressed his hands to his lips in gratitude. Forever was beyond understanding. He would be with Miriam now. Already, the god's brilliance was fading.

Without warning, the divine light winked out as if a door had closed. For a moment Alonso floated in blackness, and then mortality pierced him through. The pain was keen; the god's absence left a gaping wound. He choked and tumbled from heaven, an angel shorn of its wings.

But the pain lessened as he thought of Miriam.

I am coming back to you, love, he whispered, his heart pounding.

They would never be parted again.

Tor Tomás, Grand Inquisitor for the Holy Father Church and Confessor to Their Majesties, Felipe and Maria, slammed his hands against the armrests of his chair and lurched to his feet. "I don't pay you for feeble excuses, Captain! I pay you to flush them from whatever god-forsaken hole they're hiding in!" He was bare from the waist up, save for a thick bandage about his ribs. On his left side, a fresh stain of blood seeped through the gauze. He glanced down at it in horror. The scar on his face stood out in stark relief, a pale bolt against angry red. "Now, see what you've done!" He glared at the captain.

"Forgive me, Radiance!" Captain Morales's lips were white with fear.

"Well, don't stand there, gawping! Get out and find them!"

Morales spun about on his heel, narrowly missing Umberto, Tomás's valet. The near collision almost cost the aging monk his fresh supply of bandages. Umberto mouthed a curse. Impatiently, Tomás splayed his arms for his chamberlain, reminding Fra Francisco of a chicken at the market.

The Papal Nuncio hid a smile beneath his hand. These three were more entertaining than a play.

Tomás caught him. "What are *you* smirking at?"

Francisco's smile vanished. "Me? Why, nothing, Radiance. I was just taken with..." he gazed wistfully after the retreating captain as if he were a dainty he might pluck from a tray, "all the comings and goings around here. We aren't used to such a flurry in the Holy See."

Tomás eyed him balefully. "I find that hard to believe."

"It's true. Life is simpler in Roma. We don't concern ourselves with such...initiatives."

"You should. Witchcraft is a growing evil."

"Is it? We've had a few burnings in Italia, but most of the time, they're nothing more than trumped up charges of neighbour against neighbour. I mean, really—a midwife with a knowledge of herbs? Where's the danger in that? It hardly seems worth the effort."

"I'm not talking about midwives. The Diaphani are a race of poisoners and sorcerers. The man who stabbed me was under the influence of a Diaphani witch."

"Really? How...alarming."

"It wasn't alarming! It was demonic!"

"Oh, of course, it was! Forgive me! I'm sure your wound pains you greatly. But I understand you already had her tied to a stake? And she escaped?"

"She summoned a storm so powerful, it doused her kindling."

"I see. And the fire in the nave?"

"Caused by the same witch and her lover."

"Hmmm. No doubt we have underestimated the threat. I shall advise His Holiness immediately."

"Isn't that what you're doing?"

Tomás pointed at the letter he was penning. Francisco glanced down at it. "Uh, no. This is a missive to a friend."

"Give it here."

"But, Radiance, it's nothing, a trifle!"

"No correspondence leaves these walls without me seeing it first. For all I know, you've been ensorcelled."

Francisco spread his hands in surrender. "I assure you, I've had no dealings with witches."

"We shall see." Tomás waved Umberto in his direction. The sour-faced monk shuffled toward him, snatched the letter from his hands, and then hobbled back to Tomás like an ill-tempered dog.

"Read it," Tomás ordered. Umberto pursed his lips and squinted. His lips moved slightly as he read the words.

"Aloud, you fool!"

Umberto probed a molar as if it pained him and began anew, his voice a wheedling rasp.

> "Dear Pantalone,
> The weather here in Elysir is dreadful! Nothing but rain, rain, rain. I can't tell you how much I miss you, but I do. So far, nothing to report, but I hear the dramas of Miguel de Saavedra are excellent. I may have to travel to find them. Until then, tweaks and tickles, my boy! You know where! Send my love to Columbine.
> Yours, Lechie."

Tomás raised an eyebrow. "Lechie?"

Francisco reddened. "A nickname...for Arlechinno. It's a role I used to play—"

"And Pantalone and Columbine?"

"The same. They are parts from the Italia Commedia dell-arte. Pantalone is...a friend. Columbine, too. We were all actors before I took my vows. Really, Radiance. This is most embarrassing!"

"I am sure it is." Tomás smiled smugly. "But I need to know with whom I'm dealing."

"You know with whom you're dealing! I am his Holiness's envoy, his Papal Nuncio!"

"His Holiness chooses odd emissaries for his interests."

"That depends on what you consider odd."

They regarded each other for a long moment. It was no secret this Pope preferred the company of talented, young men. Tomás's tastes were even more deviant than what passed for normal in Roma if the rumours Francisco had heard were true. He spread his hands. "I am here on the Holy Father's command. I am to keep him appraised without burdening you further. Even your own Majesties have granted me their permission, Radiance."

"I have not been negligent in keeping them informed."

"No, but you have piqued his Holiness's interest. If the Diaphani are as great a threat as you claim, he will donate funds to further the Crown's cause."

Tomás indicated to Umberto that he should return Francisco's letter to him. Francisco received it with grace and tucked it into a red-lined sleeve.

"Do you tumble?"

The question caught him off guard. The Grand Inquisitor's tone was the same as if he asked him if he ate infants.

"Acting isn't tumbling, Radiance, but as Arlechinno I have carved a cartwheel or two."

"Show me."

He was still testing him. It was tiring, but expected. "In my position, that would be undignified, don't you think?" He smiled at him indulgently. His role as Papal Nuncio protected him—for now.

Tomás glared as if he might wrest his secrets from him through intimidation alone. Finally, he gave up the attempt. "I must rest. Leave me." He dismissed him as if he were a troublesome flea.

"Certainly, Radiance." Francisco rose gracefully. "I will return to the suite you so kindly provided. Shall we meet again for Vespers? Break bread afterwards, perhaps?"

"I am not attending."

"Oh, of course. Your condition prevents you. How thoughtless of me. Very well, I will see you on the morrow." He bowed, glad for an excuse to escape. He felt Tomás' hard gaze on his back as he headed for the door. When he reached it, he turned and smiled a faint goodbye. Then he closed the door softly behind him.

His rooms were not much larger than two monks cells adjoined. The message was clear: Tomás loathed having him here. If he were too comfortable, he might stay longer. As he entered the antechamber, he noted attempts had been made to return his belongings to their original places. Tomás's spies would have found little, save for what he had left for them to find. The ruse with the letter had served the same purpose—misdirection. Perhaps a bit obvious, but if Tomás assumed he was stupid, so much the better. It was always better to give your hosts something to believe. He reached for his weathered riding cloak and settled the cowl over his head. As he left the Solarium, the temple bells tolled three. It was still raining.

He took his time, tarried here and there to scrutinize his surroundings in case Tomás had instructed he be followed. That didn't appear to be the case. Eventually, he found his way to a saddler's shop and paused at the doorway to watch the man at his work. After a brief moment, he entered the shop, explaining that his journey from Roma had been grueling. One of his stirrups had come loose, and did the saddler, by chance, have a new one recently arrived from Madrone? He held out a silver *linare*. It was worth ten times what the stirrup cost.

The saddler blinked at him like a mole caught in the light. He nodded and plucked the coin awkwardly with his left hand.

It *was* possible that the man was left-handed, but as he worked the leather, he had favoured his right. *Good*, Francisco thought. Pantalone had come through. Columbine's spy network was in its infancy, but the faction that supported her had managed to establish a covert mail service in Esbaña, all for the purpose of keeping track of where he was and if he was successful in his quest. The saddler was theirs.

Francisco gave him the missive. "I'll be back in a few days, to see if the stirrup's arrived." He had no intention of returning. Tomás would not remain long in Elysir, of that he was certain. His letter to Pantalone, Columbine's contact in Madrone, had said as much.

I may have to travel to find them.

It would take time, but Pantalone would pass along word of his progress to her. In the meantime, he prayed for Columbine's safety. With that bloody half-sister of hers reversing all the reforms and leaving a trail of beheadings in her wake, his *Gloriana* was in grave danger. He would have to find those who dabbled in the hidden faith, convince the Diaphani it was in their best interests to save her—and themselves.

Chapter Two: Choque Cultural

It was the utter silence that finally roused Miriam. The scrape of hooves against tunnel rock, the weird echoes of her people passing blindly through inky chambers, the whimpering of tired, thirsty children, the wailing of hungry babes—all gone like a distant dream. The unnatural quiet crashed in on her and brought her fully awake. With a start, she came to. The scrap of skirt she clutched turned out to be her own fingernails carving deep moons into her palm.

With a gasp, she extended her hands into the stygian darkness. The sudden movement made her dizzy. Her vision prickled, creating a warp and weft of afterimages that should not be there. The knowledge of what must have befallen her made her tremble. She let out a small cry.

Gods! I'm lost! I've wandered away from the Tribe. They'll never find me! She must have fallen into a daze while walking, must have let go of Nadia's hem without realizing. She had lost track of them, and they of her. The hunger and thirst of the past few days had made them stupid.

She took a step forward, a cry for help dying on her lips. Perhaps they weren't too far ahead, perhaps she could catch up with no one being the wiser. She took another ragged breath to steady herself. The last thing she wanted was to confirm that Joachín had been right.

What do you mean, you're bringing up the rear? They had stopped at an underground spring, the last water they would drink before reaching the end of this maze. He had been presumptuous, irritable with her lack of compliance. He had taken on the mantle of leadership and had assumed his authority over her. It didn't help the rest of the Tribe accepted his role without question.

What I said. I'm as responsible for the Tribe as you. If you lead, I will be last, so no one is left behind.

So no one is left...? He had stared at her as if she had taken leave of her senses. *Forgive me,* he began, turning to the Tribe for support. *I don't mean to suggest any of us is unimportant. But she*—he had emphasized *she* while stabbing a finger in her direction—*is our matriarch. If something happens to me, then Miriam must lead.* The Tribe nodded, the protocol, understood. He pointed to his side, as if to summon her like a dog. *Your place is behind me, Miriam.*

Ephraim, her dear father, had given up dictating to her when she was thirteen. She wasn't about to let Joachín de Rivera tell her what to do, even if he *was* their newly appointed patriarch.

My place is where I say it is. I decide where I go, not you, Joachín. Her jaw had hurt from clenching it so hard.

Be reasonable, Miriam. He couldn't have said a worse thing; it made her more determined than ever. *You've been cut, you've lost blood. With that slice across your throat, you're at greater risk than the rest of us.*

He meant the shallow knife cut the Grand Inquisitor had given her in their near capture in Elysir. She forced herself to keep from fingering her neck. *I'm fine. It's healing.*

Even so, Iago will bring up the rear. Iago was Joachín's sixteen-year old cousin. Other than Joachín and Ximen, he was the only other surviving male.

She stared him down. *No, I will be last. Everyone who has a horse will continue to lead them. The rest of us will keep our hands on their flanks or on the clothes of the person in front of us.*

For a tense moment, he looked as if he might grab her bodily and set her atop his stallion. Luckily, he didn't. *Fine*, he said, louder than necessary. *We will do as our matriarch demands.* He had said *demands* as if suggesting she were a shrew. Maybe she was. As she took her place at the end of the line, his expression had been tight, closed. He had refused to look at her. His dismissal failed to bring her the satisfaction she thought it might.

Why, oh why, had she argued with him? Pride was why—that same old demon. She had had to maintain her independence, to establish her place among the Tribe as much as he did. She could take care of herself *and* them. She didn't need to be treated like a child. On the other hand, if she had done as he had said, she would not be in this predicament.

There was no help for it but to choose a direction and to pray it was the right one. The path fell slightly to the left. She couldn't be sure, but she thought they had passed a section like that at one point. If the ground sloped, maybe it meant they were coming to the end of their journey. Of course, the caves might descend into the heart of the mountain before climbing again. She shivered. Best not to think about that.

She fumbled her way along, toeing her foot along the path. There was some comfort in blindly keeping her fingers to the wall. After about twenty feet, it curved abruptly. She didn't remember it doing that, so she stopped. Cool air brushed against her face. What caused air to flow in caves? Connecting tunnels? Gaping pits? She didn't dare lose contact with the wall as she edged her way along.

She went another ten feet and began to feel confident again before disaster struck. Her foot slid out from beneath her into thin air. Had she been on a level surface she might have prevented herself from toppling, but there was nothing to grab. She lost her balance and fell. With a shriek, she flew through black space. She landed almost immediately onto her stomach. The impact knocked the air from her lungs.

The fall terrified her; she lost her nerve. She pushed herself up from the ground and started to sob, a horrible sucking noise that sounded halfway between a moan and a rasp. Her chest hurt. She had scraped her nose. The air was stale and tasted of dust. She had ripped the filthy monk's habit half-way up her thigh. She wasn't hurt other than a scratched face, a sore hip, and wounded pride, but could she possibly feel any more miserable? She could. She might die of thirst before she clawed her way out of this hell hole. She should have called out for Joachin the second she realized she was lost. Who knew how far he and the Tribe had travelled since then?

Crying raggedly, she crawled on hands and knees to the base of the ledge. Frantically, she felt her way to the top. She had fallen about five feet. She was lucky she hadn't suffered a concussion. Even if she could pull herself over the lip, there was nothing to hold onto, nothing to prevent her from sliding back down into where she was.

"No!" she whimpered, striking the edge with her scraped hands. It was too much. She sat down in a heap and wept in frustration. She was crying so loudly she didn't hear the crunch of a boot on stone.

"Miriam!" A familiar voice cut through her sobs.

She let out a wail before she could stop herself. He had come! Joachin had found her. Of course, he had.

"Gods, are you hurt?" More cautious steps. He was nearer now, perhaps by several feet. "Don't cry. I'm here. I'll get you out. It'll be all right."

"There's a d..ddd...dddrop! Be careful. I just fell down it...." She hated how pathetic she sounded, how useless she felt.

Another step. Gravel rattled down the side of the decline. "Ximen warned me about it. We're all here. Iago's got my arm and Zara has his. We've made a chain for you."

I'm sorry. The apology died on her lips. She couldn't say it. It meant total defeat.

"I'm right here, at the lip." His voice was warm, reassuring. "Give me your hand."

She sniffed. "I can't see you." She sounded as if she were whining. She was. She reached into the black void, not knowing where his hand was, but desperate for his touch.

Strong fingers wrapped around her wrist. Her gift as a *sentidora* flared into life. Joachin. What he was feeling overwhelmed her. First and foremost, he was relieved; his terror assuaged—he had been beside himself with worry, fearing she might be dead. Then came the justification and the guilt. She *should* have listened to him. He had known best. He should have forced her behind him in spite of the scene it would have caused. And finally, desire—that underlying sexual tension that lay between them like a flame, no matter how much she tried to snuff it. Joachin believed Lys had ordained they be together. He wanted that, even if she hadn't yet accepted it.

His hand tightened. "I'm going to pull you up. Can you help yourself?"

I'm not completely...!" She bit off the retort. At the moment, she *was* helpless. If she answered him like a surly child, the Tribe would think even less of her. He strained to lift her up.

"There. I have you." He pulled her protectively into the crook of his arm. She clung to him for a moment, ashamed for needing to be there. His fear evaporated. He was calm and in control. She was with him once again, where she should be. "Back the way we came," he called over his shoulder. Slowly, the Tribe withdrew like a snake retreating into its hole.

When they made their way back to what sounded like a large cavern, Joachin didn't question her as to how she had become separated from the rest. The horses nickered in the darkness, glad of the returned company. Without a word, she took her place behind him, and the Tribe resumed its march. She burned with embarrassment, thankful no one could see her face, nor she, theirs.

)(L)(

After several more hours, the horses became restive. As they snorted, a draught of fresh air curled past her, carrying a hint of green. *Goddess help us, are we finally getting close?* she wondered.

"We've made it! Ximen says the exit is just ahead!" Joachin's enthusiasm echoed weirdly about them.

"Praise Lys," someone whispered. It sounded like Luci, his aunt. A chorus of voices agreed with her.

As the Tribe hurried forward, the darkness lessened. Miriam could see Joachin in front of her, with Ximen at his side. As they rounded a corner, they were blinded by a sudden shaft of light. Fidel pranced and pulled at his reins. She stepped back to avoid being trampled. Behind her, everyone who held a horse experienced the same thing. The beasts sidled and stamped, anxious for their keepers to free them.

"Let them go!" Joachin released Fidel. The stallion bolted and the mares followed after. Women and children coughed in the dust.

At the cave's mouth, Joachin allowed everyone to pass so he might account for them. Miriam waited with him, not to be outdone. It was the first time she had seen his face in three days. His beard had grown thick. His eyes were dirt-rimmed but they shone with pride. He had brought them safely through. As Zara lumbered past them, he waited until she had passed before extending a hand to Miriam. He seemed to think it was only fitting that they finish this last leg of the cave trek together.

She ignored his hand. "I can manage."

His expression fell. He pressed his lips tightly. Whether he did it out of hurt or dismay, she didn't know. Now that they were out of danger, the last thing she wanted was to be close to him. She was all too aware of the mutual attraction they held for one another, simmering beneath her control.

She studied the trail snaking to the valley below. It was mostly scree. The Tribe was half-way down. Joachin stepped past her, his expression noncommittal. She didn't need a touch to confirm his frustration. She tossed it off and straightened her shoulders. She *would* be last, after all.

Hitching up her ruined monk's habit, she studied the terrain. The worst drop fell at a sharp angle and then leveled to a manageable pitch. As she stepped carefully, shale skittered down the slope. After the humiliation of the caves, she would *not* fall. The rock presented a bit of problem. The soles of her feet had toughened over the last few days, but unlike the cave floor which had been mostly smooth, these stones looked sharp. She would have to be careful.

It helped to see where she was going. When she finally reached the bottom of the slope, Joachin had mounted Fidel. He refused to meet her eyes. Iago sat astride a bay and didn't look at her, either. An awful suspicion struck her. The Tribe was hungry. They had no weapons with which to hunt. "Where are you going?" she demanded.

Joachin ignored her.

"Tell me you aren't riding off to rob some poor farmer."

He shrugged. "Fine. I won't. Let's go," he told Iago. He kicked Fidel with his heels.

She caught the horse's reins. "No, Joachín! I won't have it!"

"You won't have it?" He glared down at her as the horse pranced. "I am patriarch, Miriam. I do what I think is best for our Tribe. We're hungry. I need to take care of it."

A week ago, the Inquisitional Guard had slaughtered all of their men at the Womb, save Iago and Ximen. Undoubtedly, Tomás searched for them, now. "And if the Guard comes upon us while you're gone? Is it your plan to come back to more dead bodies?"

A lance of pain cut through his stunned expression. She had gone too far, she had reminded him of all the deaths he had caused. For a moment, no one spoke. Finally, he straightened in the saddle to collect the tattered shreds of his pride. "I doubt if anyone has the temerity to touch you, matriarch," he said. "They wouldn't dare." He yanked the reins from her hands. Beneath him, Fidel pranced, impatient to be off. He swung the horse about and galloped into the trees. Iago charged after him.

A sea of dismayed faces confronted her.

"So," she said, sensing their lack of support. "He leaves us to run off on a fool's errand."

Casi, Luci's twelve year-old daughter, frowned, not understanding how Miriam could miss something so obvious. "No, Miriam. They've gone off to steal."

"Hold your tongue, Casi." Luci glanced away.

"But they have, Maré. I wish they'd taken me with them. Riding in, grabbing things. Iago gets all the fun."

"I don't know about the rest of you, but I'm for a bit of a wash." All eyes turned to Zara. "Five days in those caves, and I can't stand my own stink." She laughed at herself. As one, the rest of the women followed her to the stream or busied themselves with children. Even Ximen refused to meet Miriam's eye.

"We are in danger!" Miriam insisted, as they retreated. The last thing they needed was an angry farmer alerting the inquisitors of their position. Judging by their avoidance, they sided with Joachín, trusting he would provide for their needs without getting caught.

She stomped away from the camp to take a moment for herself. How could she be their matriarch when their ideas of what was appropriate differed so much from hers? They would have to change. She would demand that they act with integrity in all matters. It was the only way to stay safe. She was their leader as much as Joachin, appointed by both Anassa and Lys. She would insist on how they must behave, even if she had to cross Joachin to do it.

Three hours later, Joachin and Iago thundered back into the camp. A large sack hung from Fidel's flanks. Joachin leapt from the stallion to pull the bag free. Iago carried a smaller pouch. They tossed both sacks onto the grass. The Tribe drew around, curious to see what they had brought.

"What's in the big one?" Zara hovered over it, clasping her hands.

Joachin smiled. "Take a look and see."

She pulled open the neck of the sack. A red haunch appeared, complete with a cleft hoof. "A ham! He's brought us a ham!" Zara cried. The Tribe crowed with approval. Zara grabbed Joachin by the ears and kissed him soundly on the cheek. "Oh, you wonderful, wonderful boy!"

Miriam stared at the smoked haunch as the women withdrew it from the bag. It bothered her Joachin had stolen it from some poor farmer's smokehouse. Meat was dear in the winter months. As hungry as she was, she didn't think she could eat it.

The children whimpered hungrily, crying with impatience. Her mouth watered in spite of herself, as Iago carved up portions. He offered the first cuts to her and Joachin. Her stomach rumbled, but she shook her head. Other than the mule she had taken when she and Ephraim had escaped from Granad, she had never stolen anything in her life. Joachin glanced at her sidelong and waved the meat aside.

"Let the children eat first. Then the rest of us. The matriarch and I will eat last."

She let out a slow breath, furious to be put in such a position. If she refused it, she would upset the Tribe, convince them that she found them wanting. The ham was trouble—the farmer would soon discover it missing. She suspected it wasn't the only thing Joachin had taken.

Iago paused, looking as if he might question the deferral, but he accepted it with good grace. He made the rounds to Ximen and the women and children. By the time he approached them a second time, she was able to eat a little, if only reluctantly. If anyone noticed, they didn't care. Over the next hour, the Tribe gorged themselves on seconds and thirds.

"This is so delicious," Zara said, patting her belly, "that I almost forgot the other bag." She pointed at it. "What else did you bring us, boys?"

"That," Iago said proudly, "was Joachin's idea. He grabbed them at the last minute."

"Can I see?" Casi pounced on the sack.

"You can, but the top thing is for Miriam."

She stiffened. He *had* stolen something else. Why did it have to involve her? Casi plunged her hands into the pouch and withdrew a lumpy ball of russet. "Oh," she said disappointedly. "A dress."

Miriam set down her meat. "No."

Joachin frowned at her.

"Why? Don't you like the colour?" Zara cocked an eyebrow.

She bristled. "I don't like that it's *stolen*, Zara! I can't wear a stolen dress!"

Joachin shrugged, deflated. "Well, you can't go around looking like a monk. If you're worried we'll run into its previous owner...."

"That isn't my concern! Stealing is...it's just wrong! You've deprived some poor unsuspecting farmer!"

"Fine. Don't wear it." He dismissed the dress with a wave. "We'll figure out something else."

For a few moments, no one said anything. Zara retrieved the dress from Casi. "If the matriarch doesn't want to wear it, *I* will."

Everyone stared at her.

"It's too big for her, anyway. She can have my old dress."

A stunned silence fell. Zara outweighed Miriam by seven stone. The widow's weeds would fit her like a sack.

"Besides," Zara added, winking at Joachin. "I'm done with looking like a widow. I might find me a man in one of the towns. Why not be festive?"

Tiny grins sprouted on everyone's faces, save Miriam's.

"There's more in here." Casi pulled out a pair of boots, three blankets, several coins, and a skillet.

"The boots are also for Miriam." Joachín said quietly. He refused to meet her eye.

"Well done, Patriarch! You've thought of everything!" Zara clambered to her feet. "Excuse me. I need to change my clothes." She headed for a gorse bush.

"This is good, Joachín," Luci said, as she pulled the blankets from the sack. "The children can huddle under these tonight."

Casi shook her head. "Not me. I'm nearly thirteen."

"Even so, you will sleep with Toni and Tessa."

"I don't want to, Maré. Tessa kicks."

"She won't, if she's warm."

Five year-old Tessa stuck her tongue out at Casi. Casi returned the favour. Both mothers admonished them. Miriam had the distinct impression everyone was filling the moment with chatter.

Zara reappeared from behind the gorse bushes, looking as if she were ready for a *fiesta*. The women murmured in approval. The dress fit her perfectly, but it also made her look like a frayed red hen. She preened and promenaded toward Miriam as if she were walking down the grand *avenida* in Madrone. "Here you are, Matriarch," she said, stopping before Miriam and sniffing disdainfully. She held out her old black dress. "Tie a rope around your waist. It'll fit."

Miriam felt the blood rush to her face. It was clear Zara and the rest found her wanting. She accepted the weeds in silence. She couldn't condone what Joachín had done, but the worst of it was, he had planned ahead. She couldn't travel with them dressed as a monk. Zara's dress, smelly and worn, was the only option. "I'll wear it in the morning," she said stiffly. She would wash it in the stream, and then hang it to dry once everyone was asleep. There was no point in insulting Zara further.

"Good." Joachín clapped his hands as if the matter were closed. "Let's get some rest. We need to leave before daybreak."

"Never stay long where you've committed a theft," Iago said.

"Never stay the *night*, if you can help it," Joachín corrected, "although I'm sure we'll be safe." He glanced at Miriam. "The farm we visited is over an hour's ride away. We aren't likely to be discovered. We didn't see any sign of the Torch Bearers when we were passing."

"Visited." Miriam set her hands on her hips. "Such a quaint word when one really means *robbed*." She stared him down and everyone else in turn. "Funny, how those who break the law, minimize it."

Joachín looked away. No one else met her eye.

She strode away to seek some solace beneath a lone oak at the edge of their camp. The Tribe knew she was right. At least they had the decency to look guilty. A small victory, but it failed to satisfy her as much as she had hoped.

Chapter Three: A Failed Attempt

The owl was a handsome specimen, nearly two feet in length, with fierce, imposing brows and striated feathers of brown and cream. Even dozing, it maintained a certain dignity of which Alonso approved. He had come upon it in snoozing in a pine tree, not far from where Miriam and the Tribe had camped. Sul had told him he could no longer share Miriam's body as he once had, but the god had said nothing about becoming lesser beasts. He would much rather be a man, but in the meantime, he wouldn't mind becoming an owl. Sometimes the goddess Lys was depicted with one, sitting atop her shoulder. Owls were a symbol, the mark of a seer.

He had made Miriam a seer once. Why not again?

Stop daydreaming, Alonso, he chided himself. *Pleasant fantasies won't bring you together.*

He regarded the owl for a moment, wondering how best to attempt a possession. Was there a way to seep into the bird's pores, to occupy its flesh? Did he have to synchronize with its heartbeat, or was it only a matter of occupying the same space? Then, there was the whole question of spirit. Every living thing had a soul. Would the bird tolerate the intrusion?

He girded his will, knowing he might be in for a fight.

Forgive me, old man. He settled upon the sleeping owl like an invisible cloak. *I promise, I won't abuse the privilege.*

For the briefest of moments, there was a sense of soft feathers, stiffer quills, and then solid, wiry flesh. Then he was in, he shared its body, he animated the owl. A surge of alarm struck him like an unexpected plunge into cold water. Alonso found himself half-submerged in the stream, knocked from his perch as if he were no more than a bad dream of fleas. With a furious screech, the owl snapped its great wings open, took to the air, and determinedly flew away. Sputtering from shock, Alonso gathered his wits and floated back to hover over the stream's bank.

So much for that, he thought, mentally drying himself off. Apparently owls weren't good candidates for possession.

You will suffer death over and over, the god had said.

Not a happy thought, but a clue. Maybe his next attempt should be with something less...hale and hearty.

In any event, it was time to return to Miriam, incorporeal or no. Hopefully, she had managed to eat some of the *jamon* that low-life thief Joachín de Rivera had stolen. Poor girl, the rascal upset her so much, she could hardly eat. She needed someone to take proper care of her, someone who met her needs, someone who clearly understood the difference between right and wrong. *The sooner I can let her know I'm back, the better,* Alonso thought.

The forest disintegrated into smears of brown and green. He reappeared beside her where she sat beneath an oak at the edge of the camp. The Tribe was ignoring her. She looked so miserable he couldn't help but set an arm about her shoulders.

It made her shiver. He had no more presence than a cold breeze. He dropped his arm.

I will find a way for us, my love, he said.

Miriam sighed.

Alonso sighed, too. As much as he wanted to stay with her, there was little point until he succeeded in his task. He floated off into the trees, in search of a suitable host.

Chapter Four: Emotional Turmoil

In spite of the danger of telltale smoke, Joachin allowed a small
fire as the Tribe bedded down for the night. They had become
acclimatized to the core temperature of the caves. The night's chill
proved a challenge. He refused to allow any of the women to stand
watch, preferring to assign that duty to Iago and himself. Miriam
wasn't sure whether it was because he didn't trust them to do a proper
job, or whether he needed to remain in charge.

As the moon rose, she left her oak and headed for the stream, taking
Zara's dress. Joachin noted her departure but said nothing as she
disappeared among the trees.

The horses nickered as she approached, but they soon returned to
their dozing. She knotted the monk's habit about her knees, stepped
into the water, and gasped as the icy cold hit her legs. Her feet turned
numb. She ignored them and set to work.

Some of the dress's stains resisted her efforts. She rubbed at them
furiously, but the cold soon forced her to abandon the attempt.

Shivering, she clawed her way back up the steam's bank. She tossed the dress awkwardly onto a gorse bush.

Thoughts of the fire tempted her. She wanted to return to it to get warm, but it was the first time in weeks she had been alone. Sometimes, it was better to be cold and miserable, than an outcast among a crowd.

She sat on the grass and hugged her knees, making her habit form a rough tent. Her teeth chattered. She couldn't stop trembling. It reminded her of the time Alonso had warmed her with his presence the night they had found Gaspar. Such a horrible tragedy, but Alonso had been there to help her through that loss. *How I miss him,* she thought sadly. Now there was a man of principle, a man who knew what was right and what was wrong.

Where was he now? Had he gone to a distant paradise at last? She fervently hoped so. Why did people have to die at all? Death seemed a cruel thing for the gods to create, to give life and then to snatch it away, taking those who were loved best and most.

I will always love you, Alonso, she told him, staring at the stars through the trees' canopy. Her eyes smarted. She took a shuddering breath and knuckled her tears away. She would *not* cry. Ever since they had left the Womb, she had contained them so none might see. Her grief was too precious to share.

"Come back to the fire. You're cold."

She turned. Joachin stood there. How had he come up behind her without her knowing? Why did people always intrude when one wanted to be alone? "I'm *fine!*"

"You're not. You're shivering." If he had seen the tears, he said nothing of them.

She turned away. "I'll come back in a minute. Why aren't you keeping watch?" She threw the reminder at him like an accusation.

"I had Iago take over." He settled onto the grass beside her as if he had no intention of leaving. His shoulder brushed hers.

She flinched. Why couldn't he just go away? She was too spent to deal with him now. Suppressing her grief had cost her more than she liked to admit. They said nothing for a few minutes. "What do you want, Joachin?" she asked at last.

He didn't reply right away. "To talk," he said finally. "I...I want to smooth things over between us."

She shrugged. "You are what you are, and I am what I am. We don't look at things in the same way."

"I thought you might see the sense in the dress."

"I see it. I just don't like how you came by it."

"If it helps you to know, he was drunk. We found him passed out with wine jugs littering the floor beside him."

"Who?"

"The farmer."

"And you think that makes stealing from him any better?"

He shrugged.

"What about his wife? Where was she?"

"I don't know. She wasn't there."

Miriam pursed her lips in distaste.

"I need you to forgive me."

He was solemn, earnest. Despite the handsome face his plea was that of a penitent choir boy. How could she deny him? And yet his words were empty. "What does it matter, Joachin? You won't change no matter what I say. If you see the need, you'll steal for the Tribe again."

"I don't think your anger with me is really about that."

She stared at him.

"I think you still blame me for all the deaths of the Tribe. For the loss of your father."

She glanced away. The pain of that was still keen. But he had been forced to confess because of a tattoo. "I told you I forgave you for all that, back at the Womb."

"And for not being him. Your priest."

She closed her eyes to shut out the thought of Alonso. Other than the night she had told the Tribe that Alonso had been the one who had made her a seer, she had never spoken of him again.

"I wish I were him." Joachin's voice was fraught with longing. "I think maybe you loved him in the way a woman loves a man. Except—

he wasn't a man, was he? He was a ghost. But even if physical loving was impossible, I think maybe you still loved him with all your heart."

He had guessed most of it, but not all. She would never stop loving Alonso. And they *had* found a way to love, although not physically. Their shared sexual energy had brought her to an ecstatic peak. Maybe her anger with Joachin was a way to keep him at arm's length, to stop him from affecting her the way he did. He made her feel as if she were betraying Alonso. It was a terrible thing to lose someone you loved. "It's hard not to love someone who shares your every thought, Joachin," she said, remembering.

A flicker of pain crossed his face. There was no point in being unkind. "Alonso knew me like no one ever has. He was a good man, honourable and kind. He paid the ultimate price and sacrificed himself for me. How can I not love him for that?"

"He sacrificed himself?"

She nodded. "The storm that shook Elysir the night I was going to burn? Alonso became that storm. He thought it was the only way to save me from the fires. In doing that, he accepted the permanence of death. He's gone forever, now." It occurred to her that Joachin had also done what he could to rescue her. He had torched the temple and had freed her from the stake.

Joachin let out a slow breath. "Well, I suppose once you've loved someone, you never really stop. Your priest was a lucky man. To know you like that. He had an advantage I never did."

A smile touched her lips. Alonso had seen Joachin as having the advantage.

"What is it?" Joachin matched her smile.

"He didn't like you."

His eyebrows rose. "He didn't? Why not?"

"He...." Why had she let that slip? She couldn't tell Joachin that Alonso had been jealous of his physicality. That he had sensed her hidden attraction for him. Joachin stared at her intently, his eyes probing. Did his tattoo heighten his ability to sense lies of omission? "I don't know."

"I think you do. What aren't you telling me?"

She glanced away. "Like I said, 'I don't know.'"

He grinned. "I think you've just told me a fib." He poked at her shoulder. She jumped. "He was jealous of me, wasn't he?"

"No!" The truth made her heart pound.

"He was!" His delight struck her like a beacon. "Why would he be jealous of me unless he felt your attraction for me? You said you could hide nothing from each other. He didn't like me because *you* were attracted to me, weren't you? *Aren't* you?"

She stood abruptly.

He sprang to his feet. "I'm sorry. I shouldn't have pushed you into a corner like that. It was wrong. Let's talk about something else."

She took a deep breath, distracting herself from him by reaching for Zara's dress. It was still sopping.

He slipped in front of her to prevent her from leaving. "You're a *sentidora*, yes?" He changed topics as easily as he might switch hats. "Why didn't you tell me this before?" She crossed her arms to hug herself. He was impossible. "You're my confessor, now?"

"No, but we should be open with one another. For the Tribe's sake."

The Tribe was not his real reason, but she wasn't about to argue it. They had just come from an awkward topic of conversation. "When should I have told you, Joachín? When we were stumbling through the caves? When you rode off to steal that ham?"

"No, but maybe tonight, while we sat around the fire. How does it affect you? I've never known a *sentidora*. I can only surmise."

She felt much better now that they were on solid ground. "It's a blessing and a curse. With one touch, I know how people are, physically and emotionally." She moved to step around him.

He intercepted her. "So, you feel what others feel. But this happens only when you touch them?" He crossed his arms as if to reassure her. From his expression, she could tell his mind was working furiously.

"Yes. Clothing protects me. Otherwise, I'd be bombarded. "

"Which would be awkward. It would be like me, dreaming everyone dreams. Maddening. So, when I touched you before, you reacted to my...presence?"

She was sure he had been about to say *desire* but had changed his mind. She didn't like where this line of inquiry was going. She set a hand on her hip. "It's not as if I'm so affected that I have no will whatsoever."

"Of course not. But you *are* affected."

"Yes. For better or worse."

"In that case, we must protect you from the *worse* as much as possible."

She glanced up at him, wondering about his intent. He was suddenly closer to her than before. He still kept his hands to himself, but he didn't have to. Her breath quickened. He was handsome man, respectful of her wishes but determined to meet his own. If she gave him even the smallest bit of encouragement, he would kiss her. She had no doubt he would do it very well. He knew she found him attractive. Her lips parted in spite of herself.

Taking it for a cue, Joachín leaned in.

"I can't!" She pushed him away. Her fingers burned where they connected with his skin. The loss of control, the idea that her own passion might outweigh her good sense, terrified her. It didn't matter the goddess had ordained they be together, that Joachín thought they should be, too. How could she discard Alonso so quickly?

She bolted for the camp.

How dare you try to seduce her! I'll...I'll kill you!

Alonso threw himself at Joachín. A small whirlwind of leaves lifted about Joachín's feet, distracting him momentarily from Miriam running down the path. He frowned in annoyance and then trudged after her. Feeling frustrated and powerless, Alonso watched them go.

How was he to thwart Joachín de Rivera? Owls weren't good candidates; their wills were just too strong. Maybe a rabid rabbit or a menacing mouse? Gods! The situation was impossible!

I don't need to kill him, he realized, once he calmed down. *I just need to make Miriam aware of me. Of course, it won't be the same for us—how can it be? But she still loves me, and that's what counts. That's why she was so upset just now.*

Reassured by this reasoning, Alonso drifted back to the camp. For the rest of the night, he kept watch over her, at times frantic, at others,

The Tattooed Seer

furious that he couldn't prevent Joachín de Rivera from approaching her, should he choose to do so, again.

Fortunately, Joachín left her alone.

Chapter Five: Developments of Another Avian Sort

Francisco's eyes flew open. Grey light seeped in through the window. His back ached. The bed had been full of lumps, the worst he had slept on in months.

Gods, but these Esbañiards are sticklers. In Roma, he had never been expected to attend Matins or Lauds, but here, it was eight offices a day. Three hours of sleep wasn't much, but he had to remain above reproach. Maintaining appearances was crucial.

He threw on his habit and boots, and then headed for the stairwell expecting the peals of Prime to ring at any moment. Instead, a crash of footfalls met him as he reached the main floor. Black and white habits rushed past him in a blur. Luster monks in brown milled in groups or hurried away on some purpose.

He grabbed one fellow by an elbow. "What's happening?" he demanded.

"Let go! I have to...!" The monk's eyes widened in recognition. "Forgive me, Stellar! I must see to the Grand Inquisitor's carriage, make sure he has enough provisions for the journey."

"Why? Where's he going?"

"A bird's come from Marabel. Captain Morales claims he's detained a band of Diaphani, there. The witch who escaped us from Elysir may be among them."

"Where is the Grand Inquisitor?"

"In his chambers."

Francisco released him and plowed his way through the bedlam in the hall. Everyone seemed to be running in different directions.

Since the door to Tomás's suite was wide open, he walked in without invitation. Umberto was winding a clean length of bandage about Tomás's chest. He cursed his lateness. Had he arrived a moment sooner, he would have seen the tattoo.

He fluttered his hands as if the effort to make his way through so many people had left him exhausted. "Heavens, Radiance! Such a lot of excitement this morning! I understand you've received a message from Marabel? Something about the witches who've eluded you, thus far?"

Tomás's face, which had soured upon seeing him, curdled even more. "You are well informed," he replied.

"Oh, not at all! One of your monks told me. I asked, fearing it might be your health taking a turn for the worse. How are you feeling this morning?"

"Impatient to leave." Tomás knocked Umberto's hands aside.

"Surely, you're not riding in your condition?"

"No. I'm going by carriage."

"An excellent choice. Why don't I arrange breakfast for us on the road? Perhaps some biscuits with that *jamón* you Esbañiards are so famous for? And one of your fine *tintos*, I think? Why not be comfortable along the way?" He grinned hugely, as if his high spirits might infect his host.

For a moment, Tomás looked as if he might refuse him the company, but one did not dismiss the Pope's Nuncio without rejecting the Pope himself.

"I'll see to it! I won't be a moment!" Francisco spun about on his heel before Tomás could change his mind, Pope or no. It would take them at least half an hour before they departed, long enough to dispatch a note to Pantalone, who would send it on to Columbine in Inglais.

Leaving Elysir for Marabel, he wrote.

Chapter Six: Plans and Dreams

It wasn't so much that Joachín ignored her, as that he busied himself with other concerns—they mustn't leave any trace for the Torch Bearers to find, which horse would bear more than two riders, who would carry the blankets, pork, and pots? Once those details were settled, he, Iago, and Ximen discussed travelling to Marabel. It annoyed her they excluded her from their planning.

"Why Marabel?" she challenged as Joachín announced their plans. "I thought we were going to avoid the towns. The Torch Bearers will have a contingent there."

He gave no hint of how their encounter from the night before might have affected him. "I have a business contact in Marabel. We might be able to interest him in investing—"

"Investing in what?"

"In us. He's wealthy and has connections throughout Esbaña. He may already have an interest in the New World. I'll ask him to cover our passages aboard a ship. In return, we pay him off by working for him when we get to wherever he wants us to go."

"What would we do?" She suspected it would be something illegal.

"I don't know, Miriam." He sounded tired. "Maybe raising cattle or growing sugarcane. He'll tell us what he needs to have done."

She wasn't the only one who raised an eyebrow. Joachín read the hesitation on the Tribe's faces.

"It may be hard, but it will be honest work," he assured them. He glanced at Miriam for support. "Which is what you want, yes? We only work long enough to pay back what he lends us to get to Nueva Esbaña or wherever. Once we've paid back the loan, I see no reason why we can't turn our hands to our own interests. What might we do?" He snapped his fingers and pointed at Luci, his aunt. "You and Guillermo traded in indigo, yes? Some of you women are weavers and dyers. There's a new dye I've heard of that creates a true red. It's a closely guarded crown secret, but if we discovered it, we could establish a business where people buy the dye from us. Or, even if we never learn the secret, we could still make a healthy profit growing and manufacturing cotton. The import taxes from Esbaña to the New World are horrendous. Why should the colonists buy goods from Esbaña, when they can buy them more cheaply from us?"

Miriam suspected there were laws in place to prevent that very thing, but she kept it to herself. All around her, the women were nodding, looking hopeful. Even Iago and Ximen bore huge grins.

"What do you think?" Joachín asked, growing excited by the prospect he had painted. "We are determined. We are together. We can do this!"

All about her, small conversations broke out about the pros and cons of dealing in cotton or wool or hemp. The women were enthusiastic. Joachín had offered them hope. As much as it annoyed her to admit, Miriam knew it was a good plan, even if they never discovered the secret of the red dye. As for the legality of colonial trade, she suspected the local authorities would turn a blind eye. It was much the same in Granad when she had needed hard-to-come-by herbs for her pharmacopoeia. No matter where one went, there was always a thriving black market. Even she hadn't been above using it which made her question her own motives momentarily, but then, taking advantage of black market goods wasn't really stealing. Who knew Joachín would have such a keen business sense? On the other hand, who might better understand the value of goods than a thief?

There was still the problem of getting into Marabel without drawing unwanted attention.

"I'm not sure yet how we'll enter the town," Joachin replied after she voiced that thought. "It may be we don't all pass through the gates. I'll gauge the level of threat once we get there."

She wasn't happy with his choice but what else could they do? If they wanted the help of his investor, they had to risk going into Marabel. She didn't have any better ideas to offer. No one seemed to think seeking employment from one of the farms on the way to Qadis was a better option.

"Let's saddle up," Joachin said. "The sooner we get there, the better. We're not far from a main road. From what I saw, it doesn't look well-travelled. I think we'll be safe. Iago, bring up the rear and keep a look-out."

Iago nodded and the Tribe dispersed to their horses. It soon became evident that she had no choice but to ride with Joachin. Everyone else had found a partner. Joachin extended a hand to help her mount. She girded herself, afraid the moment their hands met, their attraction might spin out of control, but nothing of the sort happened. His desire was still there, but it was subdued—as if he had set it away on a shelf. He kicked Fidel in the ribs, and they were off.

The forest passed and they soon found themselves trotting down a dusty road. As the morning lengthened, her fear of being with him dwindled, but guilt still pricked. Instead of fearing possible pursuit, her mind kept returning to him, how his muscles rolled beneath his shirt as he rode, how his sweat dampened his backbone and ribs. His scent wasn't unpleasant. It reminded her of dusty earth spattered by rain, of herbs, like rosemary and dill. Her stomach rumbled. Was she so weak she could react to him like this? So fickle she could forget Alonso so soon? It seemed she was. She hated herself for it.

"There's something I want to tell you."

Joachin startled her from her reverie. It was the first time he had spoken to her since they had set out. "Last night, I had a dream."

She frowned. "A dream?" Oh! He meant a prescient one of the future. He was a Dreamer. "Of the Tribe?"

"No, it was more personal. It was of us."

She flushed.

"It isn't what you think, although I'd welcome any fantasy of you. No, I dreamt we had a son."

Her mouth fell open in surprise.

"You'd just given birth to him. He was beautiful, with a mass of black hair and a strong pair of lungs. Zara was midwife. She handed him to me. I cradled him in my arms."

Her sense of reality spun out of control. "Why are you telling me this?"

"Because I need you to know I take you seriously." He paused, as if trying to find the right words. "I'm not after a casual dalliance with you, Miriam. I can have that in any town. No, you need to know we have a future together and that I'm dedicated to it. I think that's why you ran away from me, last night. Because you thought I was trifling with you."

She swallowed. "You must have imagined it."

He shook his head. "No, it was a true dream. We hadn't named him yet, so I can't tell you what we'll call him. It was a hot day. There was a bright sun outside, with palm trees swaying beyond the window. The only thing I don't know is when this will happen. I'm guessing—in a year or two."

She was at a loss for words. That he should dream of their future and in such an intimate way was beyond imagining.

Beside the road, the woods opened into a small, shadowed clearing. A stream wove past it on its opposite side. Joachin called a halt so the Tribe might grab a bite and freshen up there. They had little chance to speak after that. She slipped from the horse, glad to escape Joachin and his revelations about their future.

The children were hungry. The women clustered about the sack with the pork. She had no stomach for it and wandered down a path beside the stream, thankful for the respite.

At the water's edge, she washed her face and then studied the nearby plants. In a dry sandy spot, a familiar bush grew. She crushed a few of the spiny dark leaves and sniffed them appreciatively. Their pungency lifted her spirits. Rosemary was both a culinary and healing herb, good for easing hurts and calming the mind. Brides also wore it in their headpieces, but she thrust that unsettling thought aside. *Maybe all I need is to feel useful,* she reflected. Her first week as matriarch had been a failure.

Further upstream, a bulky lump passed among the tree trunks. Zara's new dress made her stand out. With a crow of delight, she plucked a plant up by its roots.

What had she found? If they shared a common interest in herbs, it might help heal the breech Miriam felt growing with the Tribe. She made her way over to the potion-maker. "What have you there, Zara?" she asked.

Zara held it out for her to see. Long brown pods dangled from a sturdy stem.

"Oh! Faba! The beans are good for shaking palsy," she said. It was a lucky find. The plant was hard to come by.

"That, and other things." Zara's lips twitched with humour. She tucked the plant into her bodice and smoothed down the bulge.

"Other things?" The beans had only one use, as far as she knew. Ephraim had schooled her, passing along everything he had learned in Zaragoza, a medical college of much renown. "I don't think so. Mind you, we didn't keep them as part of our regular stock. Papa only asked me to buy them occasionally."

"Well, if he used them, I doubt if he'd tell you." Zara smiled. "Or maybe he prepared them for someone else."

Why was she being so patronizing? Faba beans increased blood flow which was beneficial for palsy. What else did one use them for? Unless...Ephraim had never shared the sexual concerns of his patients with her—he had dealt with those himself. Sometimes men needed help with...blood flow. And sometimes, they wanted longer dalliances....

"Why do we need an aphrodisiac on hand?" she demanded. Would she never stop being infuriated by these people?

Zara's smile fell. "You're young. It's only to be expected you don't understand such things."

"Age has nothing to do with it! I know what's right and what isn't! We don't need to be suppliers of...sexual enhancements! What's next, Zara? Whoring? Is that how we'll make our way in the New World?"

Zara's eyes flew wide and her mouth fell open. "How dare you?" She drew herself up to her full height.

"I...I am sorry. I shouldn't have said that. I didn't mean it."

"It's a good thing you don't." Zara set her hands on her hips. "No one tells *me* what to do, *Serina*. I do what I please. If you're to be our matriarch, *you* must be the one to change!"

Miriam bristled. "I will insist on what's right!"

"You'll do better to practice tolerance. We aren't perfect. You think it's wrong for us to steal. *I* think it's wrong for children to starve." She shook the faba plant at her. "This will bring us money, no matter what I decide to do with it." She swept away, as affronted as a duchess with a flea.

Miriam watched her go. Her head was starting to ache. She took a moment to compose herself.

When she returned to the camp, Zara stood in private conversation with Joachin. His brows lifted in interest. He muttered a few words of approval. Zara squeezed his arm and winked.

Miriam avoided Zara's gaze as she made her way to him. "Can you stow this in your saddlebag?" she asked.

"What is it?"

"Rosemary. Good for aches and pains." Her head hurt. She should have taken some herself. It didn't help to see Zara whispering among the others.

"I understand you and Zara shared some words."

Miriam made a face. "I see she was quick to tell you about the faba."

"She did. Don't be too hard on her. I need to be aware of these things. About what's going on with the Tribe."

"What is she going to use it for?"

"The faba? I don't know."

"It should only be used for shaking palsy."

"Then perhaps that's how she'll use it."

He was doing his best to placate her. For some reason, he did. As they mounted up, she felt the Tribe's hard gaze upon her back. Joachin nudged Fidel from the trees.

"Back!" he shouted as suddenly, reining the stallion about. "Get back! Ford the stream and take the horses as far as you can into the trees!"

Miriam stared down the road from the direction they had already come. She couldn't see anything beyond the turn, but a steadily growing rumble assaulted her ears. Riders were approaching and at speed. Her heart skipped a beat and then started to pound. Without a doubt, she knew it could only be Tomás and his army of Torch Bearers. They had finally found them.

The next few minutes were terrifying ones. Joachín managed to get everyone turned around. The Tribe crashed heedlessly into the stream, up the far bank, and into the trees. They had barely found cover before flashes of black and white swept past them, galloping hard for Marabel. Bringing up the rear was an ornate, unwieldy coach, bearing an emblem of a tree, a lamb, and a cross—the Inquisition's coat of arms.

Chapter Seven: Access Denied

"Where are they?" Tomás demanded.

"In the hold below, as you ordered, Radiance," Captain Morales replied curtly.

The man *did* cut a fine figure, Francisco thought, but the temptation to dip into those waters would have to wait. Witches, finally! He fell into step behind Tomás barely able to contain his excitement. Captain Morales barred his way. "Only the Grand Inquisitor is to attend."

Francisco tried to step around him, but the man was a wall of steel. "I'm the Papal Nuncio!" he sputtered. "The Pope's representative! I'm supposed to be there!"

"Sorry. Grand Inquisitor's orders."

"There must be some mistake. Radiance!" Francisco called after Tomás. "Tell your captain to allow me to pass!"

Tomás disappeared around a corner beyond hearing.

Francisco fumed with frustration. They had ridden all this way without stopping, and he had had to endure Tomás's ill temper the whole time. "So what am I to do, then? Wait until your master is good and ready to share his findings with me?"

"I'm to escort you to your room."

Something unpleasant, like an eel slipping through muddied waters, passed behind Morales's dark gaze. Francisco blinked in surprise. Had Tomás ordered the captain to kill him? Unlikely. It was too soon after his arrival in Esbaña and would create a fuss in the wrong quarters. But if he wasn't about to be assassinated, then what? Tomás wanted him out of the way, but distracted rather than discarded.

A dalliance. Gods, could it be? Morales wasn't of the right persuasion. On the other hand, the captain was enough of a toady to do whatever he was told.

"I shall write his Holiness about this!" he replied indignantly. "Is my room fitted with velum and quill?"

"I can provide them for you, if it is not."

"Am I allowed to wander Marabel at will?"

"I am to accompany you, to see to your needs."

So Tomás *had* ordered him to comply! "Then perhaps you should escort me to my room, Captain." He pursed his lips in a moue and glanced at him sidelong. Let the captain think him a dandy and a fool.

They walked side by side without speaking, passing a stairwell that led to the dungeon level before coming to a richly appointed wing. Eventually, they came to a carved door of Moori design made up of interlacing stars. Morales pushed the door open wide.

The suite was opulent, a far cry from his miserable quarters in Elysir. Tomás meant to distract him in any way possible. "Surely, this is the Grand Inquisitor's suite," he said.

"His rooms are further down the hall." Morales's tone was flat. "Is there anything more you need?"

From his expression, Francisco knew the captain sincerely hoped not. How much had Tomás offered Morales to play the prostitute? Or had he threatened him with worse? Francisco strolled into the room, "I *do* wish his Radiance would have allowed me to accompany him." He turned sharply. "Have you seen the witches, Captain?"

Morales stood uncomfortably in the doorway.

"Here, don't stand there. Come in. Let's talk." A flagon of wine waited on the table. "May I offer you some wine?"

"I'm on duty."

Which meant the wine was likely doctored. "You refuse a cup, yet you promise me...diversion." He shook his head resignedly and poured a cup. "It's all right, Captain. I understand you're only doing your duty, but I'd still welcome conversation."

Morales crossed the carpet and sat stiffly in the chair Francisco indicated. Francisco swirled the wine as if appreciating its colour and took an appreciative sniff. "Tell me about yourself, Captain."

"There's little to tell."

"Oh come now. A handsome man, like yourself. Surely, you've seen action."

"Some. On the border between Esbaña and Franca."

"Ah, yes. Terrible business, that. We heard about it in Roma. Were you injured?"

"I took a spear to the side."

"Oh, my. Did you scar?"

Morales nodded and glanced at the wine wistfully as if hoping Francisco might drink it. Francisco set down his glass. "Excuse me, a moment. I'm uncomfortable. This is getting hot." He unclasped his riding cloak and headed for the bed, as if intending on leaving it there. From beneath a fold in his hood, he retrieved a tiny pouch and cupped it in his left hand. "I find scars very attractive. I don't have many. My battles have been of a different sort." He returned to his chair. "May I call you by your first name, Captain?"

Morales nodded.

"What is it?"

"Rodrigo."

"Rodrigo! Such a strong name. It means famous or powerful ruler. Did you know?"

Morales shook his head.

"Are you married, Rodrigo?"

"No."

"I didn't think so. It's hard to keep a wife, especially when one is constantly on the move."

Morales nodded, shifting uncomfortably.

Francisco leaned into his ear, as if to share a confidence. "I know why you're chaperoning me," he whispered. Morales met his gaze. "You've been told you must do whatever's necessary to keep me occupied. I find that tempting and revolting at the same time. I'm not a vulgar man, Rodrigo. I don't believe in crossing swords with anyone unwilling to meet me on...the same battlefield."

Morales swallowed.

"I'll retire to my bed—alone. I know we're not the same kind. But there is one thing I would ask, before you leave me."

"What is that?"

"That you grant me a kiss. Just one, so I might dream of what might have been between us."

Looking as if he were steeling himself, Morales nodded.

Francisco grabbed him hard on the thigh. As the captain gasped in surprise, Francisco jammed the tiny pouch onto his nose and held it there in a tight grip. Morales's first inhalation was enough to stun him. After another few seconds, he slumped into his chair. Francisco pulled the sack free and stood well away from the pale blue powder as it floated on the air, a blend of burundarra, belladonna, and other hard-to-come by opiates.

Once the dust settled, he knelt beside Morales, who stared at him slack-jawed. "Where are the witches being held?" he demanded.

Morales's mouth worked. Spittle dribbled from the sides of his mouth. "Dun...dungeon, low'r fl...oor."

"How many guards has Tomás stationed there?"

"Thr...ee."

"Have they been told to stop me?"

"Don'...know."

"Who's in charge of the Solarium when Tomás isn't here?"

"Sol Ben...Benavid...." He garbled the rest.

"Sol Benavides, yes. Will he also witness the questioning?"

"Don'...know."

"This is what you'll remember from tonight. We sported, all night long. You submitted to my wishes and hated every minute of it. Neither of us left this chamber. You'll tell Tomás this in the morning.

If he orders you to kill me, you'll tell me first. You won't remember being drugged, and further, when I do this—" he snapped his fingers before Morales's eyes "—you'll do what I say, tell me everything you know, especially about the witches. Do you understand?"

"Yesss."

"When you can move, you'll undress and climb into that bed. Then you'll fall asleep immediately."

Francisco wiped Morales's nose with his sleeve. The blue powder disappeared. There was no point in leaving things half done.

He slipped from the room, thankful the hall was empty. Other than Morales, Tomás hadn't ordered anyone to stand guard. When he reached the stairwell, he encountered a number of monks. Unaware of Tomás's wishes, they bowed in obeisance as he passed. He acknowledged them with a blessing and continued down the stairs.

At the bottom, a guard stood at attention but let him pass. He turned the corner and strode to the end of the hall. Two more guards stood before a locked door. He approached them with clasped hands.

"You are to attend the stables," he said quietly. "Harness fresh horses for his Radiance's coach. We've received a dispatch from Madrone. We are to transport the suspects immediately and head for the capital."

It was a brash move. If he were lucky enough, he might even steal the witches from beneath Tomás's nose. *Gods forbid, it actually goes that far,* he thought. Whenever possible, it was better to have a well-thought out plan.

The guards exchanged a glance.

"For the gods' sake, must I show you the royal missive? Go!"

His voice was heavy with authority and they responded to it, too accustomed to do otherwise. He watched them leave. Should Tomás question them later, he would make sure the proper documents were available. Forgery wasn't an issue. He had any number of royal seals secreted upon his person. He stood back from the door, in shadow. Inside the interrogation room, a woman wept. He hazarded a glance through the grill.

Four miserable people stood in front of Tomás, Sol Benaviddo, the high priest of the temple, and a recording secretary. Two men and an older woman clung to each other for support. The fourth member of their party, a girl of about fifteen, stood a distance from them. She was shapely and young, but any attractiveness ended there. Her face was misshapen and her skin, pocked-marked as if disfigured by some horrible disease.

Tomás's voice drifted through the bars. "So, you maintain that none of you have practiced witchcraft, save for the girl, there."

The older man spoke up. "Radiance, ask anyone who knows us. We recently fulfilled an arms commission for the Duke of Milano. The girl was foisted on us...."

"But she is your son's wife."

"He was forced to marry her."

"Who forced you? Did *she* force you?"

"No, our people." The older man lifted his hands for mercy. "We don't associate with them, anymore. We're respectable." The older woman clutched at her son. The girl stared at them stonily.

"Why did they force him to marry her?"

The old man glowered at his son. "He took liberties."

"Were you in the valley when my army slaughtered your people? If so, how did you four escape?"

"There are caves. We passed through them."

Tomás waved at the secretary. "Make a note of that." He turned back to the older man. "But you took the girl with you. Why?"

"She followed us. She insisted on going with us."

"We aren't cruel—" the woman began.

"Shut your fool mouth, Leonora!" the older man barked. He spread his hands to appeal to Tomás. "We are makers of fine weaponry, Radiance! Prince Felipe's armourers have approached us to supply him with cannon. If you imprison us, we can't fulfill his wishes!"

Francisco let out a slow breath. Gods, what a coincidence. Felipe was married to Maria, Inglais's current queen. Esbaña and Inglais were aligned against Franca. If Felipe approached his own weapon makers instead of spending his wife's coin that meant the war against Franca was bankrupting Inglais. Did Columbine know?

Tomás leaned back in his chair to stare at the pock-faced girl. "How did you come by those marks on your face?"

She stared at him sullenly.

The younger man stepped forward. "She cast a spell. It went wrong."

"What was the spell supposed to do?"

"She wanted to kill the woman I was to marry. She invoked a demon. It attacked her, instead."

Tomás shifted uncomfortably as if realizing he shared quarters with a snake.

"She wanted to kill the Medina girl, but it didn't work," the older man added quickly.

"Medina girl?" Tomás straightened. "You mean Miriam Medina?"

The four stared at him. "Yes," the older man said. "She was his intended."

Tomás ignored him and focused on the girl. "So—*you* invoke a demon to kill Miriam Medina. But it didn't work. Either your demon was a weak one, or Miriam Medina is the stronger witch. I'll bet you hate her for that reason."

The girl nodded, her eyes full of loathing.

"Good. You *should* hate her. She is evil incarnate, an enemy of our Father Church. If I were to save you, you must promise me you'll turn from your wrongful ways."

"You're letting us go?" The older man stared at him in amazement.

"Yes, since Prince Felipe has an interest in you. The girl, however, remains with me."

The three clutched at each other in relief.

Francisco watched them in disgust. They would sacrifice one of their own to save their sorry hides. How contemptible. As for the witch, she might be useful. Tomás would soon conclude his interview. It was time to leave.

He retreated quietly and found his way to the stables where he informed the guards they were once again needed to stand outside the dungeon door. If luck was with him, they would take up their posts with no one being the wiser.

It turned out luck was.

Chapter Eight: Babes and Crones

After making sure no other army followed Tomás and his contingent, Joachin cautiously led the Tribe along the road to Marabel. Eventually, they came to the end of the forest. Beyond, the land fell onto a gently sloping plain which had been cleared for orange groves. The sun dipped towards the horizon, turning the afternoon golden.

"You would have us jump from the pot into the coals?" Miriam demanded. They had been having the same argument for over an hour as they rode. Now the Tribe stood with the horses on the periphery of the trees and gazed at the town beyond. "We've just missed being discovered by him, Joachin! It's madness for us all to go there!"

"I'm not saying we should *all* go. Just me—"

"You don't think the Town Watch hasn't got a description of you, too? Why were the Torch Bearers riding at speed, Joachin? The only reason is because Tomás knows where we are! Maybe he heard from that farmer you stole from!"

Joachin shook his head. "Unlikely. If that were true, then Tomás would be combing the woods for us, not riding hell-bent for Marabel.

No, something else has grabbed his attention. I know it makes things inconvenient—"

"Inconvenient?"

"Yes, *inconvenient*, but that's all. The north gate isn't the only way in. I know other routes. I'll go, meet with my contact and arrange—"

"You aren't going alone. How will we know if anything happens to you?" She sought the Tribe's support.

"Iago will come with me—"

"Iago, again! That means you leave us with only Ximen to defend ourselves."

"Then what do you suggest, Miriam?" he asked tiredly. She knew she was testing his patience.

"That *I* go with you."

"You?"

"Yes, me!" She set her hands on her hips as the rest of the Tribe looked on. "At least I have the sense to stop you from doing anything foolish. We'll approach the gate, but stop before we are seen. If I think there's too much of a risk for us, we'll come back and figure out another way."

"All right. And you're correct about the north gate." His concession surprised her. "Since Tomás took it, we should avoid it. We'll slip around to the east gate, instead." A few of the women nodded in agreement. That made sense. "We won't be long," he told everyone. "Stay together and out of sight."

He and Miriam mounted up and set off. Instead of following the road to the north gate, they skirted the forest for about a league before coming upon a second road. It wound across a dusty plain where it dipped before climbing to the other side of the town. Half-way between the forest and Marabel, an ox and cart had stopped in the shade of a cypress. The ox was still yoked to the rig. The driver was nowhere in sight.

Joachin approached the cart cautiously. When he and Miriam were about a hundred feet away from it, a giant stood up beside it. They hadn't seen him because he had been leaning over something in the bed. "In Sul's name!" he shouted, seeing them. "Is that a woman you have with you? We need your help!" With outstretched hands, he ran toward them.

Joachin pulled Fidel up short. A soft cap covered most of the stranger's face, but there was something vaguely familiar about him.

"Gods!" Joachin muttered. "Can it be?"

To Miriam's surprise, he spurred Fidel forward and into a trot.

"She's in labour," the giant said as they drew up alongside him. "I've never delivered a baby before!" Beyond him, a woman lay moaning in the cart. Her skirt was tented between her knees.

"Barto?" Joachin asked in amazement.

The giant stared at him. "Joachin!" he cried, equally stunned.

He was the same guard who had released her from the cell in Granad, the one who thought she reminded him of someone else. How was it that he and Joachin knew each other? Barto's eyes widened as he recognized her. "*She's* the one you had to save?" He shifted his regard between the two of them.

Joachin nodded and frowned. "Yes, but how do you two know...?"

The girl in the cart groaned. Miriam slid from Fidel and hastened to her side. "I'm Miriam," she told the distressed girl. "You are?"

"Maia," she whispered. "My baby is coming."

Miriam set a cool hand to her brow and felt her belly tighten. False labour. The true labour would start soon, but the birth was still a day off. The contraction subsided.

Maia stared at her. "The pain. It's gone!"

"For now." Miriam stroked damp strands of hair from her forehead. "It will return. You'll deliver tomorrow, I think."

Maia's eyes grew wild. "We have to make the gates tonight. I don't want to have my baby in a cart!"

"I'll see what I can do. Rest now." She covered her with a rough blanket and stepped away from the wagon to speak with the men. "She's stable for the moment," she told Barto, "but you'll want to get her settled as soon as possible. You should hurry."

"You'll deliver her?"

She darted a glance at Joachin. He wasn't happy with the complication. "You don't have family waiting for you in Marabel?"

"No. We have no one."

"I see." It was bad enough that they hoped to pass through the east gates without drawing notice of the town's guards, but with a labouring woman in tow....

"I'm responsible for a whole Tribe, now," Joachín told Barto. "We left them in the forest not far from here. We're running from, well, I expect you're running from him, too." There was no need to explain. Tomás would have guessed Barto's involvement, especially with Maia missing. Joachín glanced at Maia worriedly. His brows lifted in surprise. "But...they look like sisters! That might be enough of a distraction! They'll be watching for me, or for me and Miriam alone, or for a group of Diaphani. But the four of us—we don't quite fit. We could say we're family, heading for relatives in Marabel!"

"You get Maia through this, and we will be family," Barto said gruffly.

Joachín and Miriam left Barto and Maia, and returned to the Tribe briefly to tell them of their new plan. Miriam wasn't happy with leaving the Tribe in the woods, but with Tomás at large in Marabel, they were safer where they were.

"I don't have poppy," Zara said, thinking of Maia's needs. "She might need it for the pain." Zara was convinced that Miriam was unable to bring a new life into the world on her own. She and Luci would assist. They would pass through the east gate at dawn without being noticed—there were too many coming and going for the gate guards to pay attention. Joachín would meet them. Miriam was too tired to argue, and it wasted time.

"I'll find it," Joachín assured Zara.

"Lys keep you." Luci hugged Miriam while Joachín and Zara exchanged quiet words. After the faba bean incident, she wished she knew what they were.

The sun was setting, bathing the valley in rose. Barto spotted them and set a switch to the ox. It wasn't long before they approached the gates. Two of the Town Guard were in the process of locking the gates for the night. The guards eyed them suspiciously.

"My wife is in labour," Barto grumbled. "Let us pass."

The larger of the two held up his palm. He swaggered to the cart and yanked the blanket aside to expose Maia. "Looks that way," he told his partner. "Your names?"

Miriam froze. They hadn't discussed aliases, they had been too distracted by Maia and her impending birth. Joachín's tattoo would force him to tell the truth. "For Sul's sake!" she blurted before his look of unease gave him away. "She's about to give birth at any moment, and you stand there, demanding names? Fine! We are the Fernando-Garcías! I am Isabel, she's Rosa, this is Juan, that's Tío, and soon, we will have little Carlos or Carmen, depending! Let us through!"

Joachín turned in the saddle as if to calm her. "They are just doing their jobs, *cielo*."

"Then they should let me do mine!"

"We're trying to reach our parents in the town," Barto explained. "The baby's coming sooner than we expected. We've been travelling all day."

A sergeant-at-arms appeared at the gatehouse door. "What in Sul's balls is going on out here, Jiménez?"

"Latecomers, Sergeant." The beefy guard pointed at Barto. "Says his wife is in labour."

The sergeant strode over to the wagon to glance down at Maia, and then he stared at Miriam. His face gave nothing away, but beneath the unexpressive demeanor, she sensed his thoughts churning. "You two are sisters?"

She nodded, pursing her lips in frustration. Joachín set a restraining hand on her arm.

"Where are you from?"

Barto broke in. "Andor."

"Andor is a long way from here."

Barto glanced at Maia. "She insisted on being with her mother."

The silence lengthened. The sergeant continued to study them. "Very well," he said finally. "Let them through."

The corporal pointed at Joachín. "But what if they're the Diaphani the Inquisition is seeking?"

"These aren't Diaphani. Their faces are too soft."

Miriam thanked the gods for her and Joachín's mixed blood.

"Besides, I know Andor." The sergeant tossed a thumb at Barto. "They're all like that. Big as bears."

Maia let out a sharp cry.

"Get her out of here," the sergeant told them. "Last thing we need is a brat squalling at the gates."

He stepped back into the gate house and the guards waved them through. Miriam waited until they were well out of earshot before speaking to Joachin. He was tense. "What's wrong?" she whispered.

"You lie like a master. I don't know whether that reassures or upsets me."

"I had to say something. You were in no position to do it."

He grimaced.

She prodded him. "I think you're more upset because you hadn't thought about us being questioned in the first place."

"There is that," he admitted.

The market district was nearly empty. The few merchants who remained were packing up their wares for the night. Joachin skirted the square and led them down narrower and narrower streets until they came to a tall Moori gate. As they passed beneath its arches, the character of the town changed. There was less light here. The air became unpleasant, smelling of piss and dung. Vagrants slept on corners or in alleys. Small groups of men loitered on the streets. There was no sign of the Town Watch or Inquisitional Guard for which Miriam was thankful, but she questioned their absence. What kind of a *barrio* was it, where even the town's constabulary refused to go? Granad had its seedier quarter, but none so downtrodden as this. They passed a garishly painted inn that strained at its own opulence. A slovenly, bare-breasted girl watched them from a balcony as they passed. She had mussed red hair and looked spent and worn.

Miriam leaned against Joachin. "We just passed a *bordello*, Joachin. I don't like it here."

"It's all right. Trust me."

She wasn't sure whether he meant trusting his ability to defend them should they be accosted, or that no one would make the attempt. Fortunately, Barto was a deterrent. Only a fool, or a gang of fools, would think to test him. She kept that thought to herself.

They headed along another few streets before entering an alley that looked as if the sun never touched it. Half way down it, they came to a studded iron door set into an imposing stone wall. Joachín dismounted and rang a brass bell beside the door. Peals cut the air and echoed off the nearby walls.

"Whose house is this?" Miriam demanded.

Joachín didn't reply. After a few moments, a small portal set into the door opened. The face of an elderly woman appeared there. The crone was not happy to see them. "What do *you* want?" she demanded, eyeing Joachín.

Joachín bowed politely. "Good evening, *Sera* Olivares. How nice to see you! Is the *Patrón* in?" He presented the picture of civility.

Sera Olivares peered past him. "What have you got there?"

Maia moaned. Barto turned in the seat to comfort her.

"You got someone sick back there?" *Sera* Olivares demanded.

"She's in labour, *Sera*. She needs a place—"

"Labour?" The crone's face soured even more. "Then take her to a hospice! What do you think we run here? We don't give charity!"

"*Sera*, I know it inconveniences you, but I wouldn't ask if it weren't important. You know I don't bother with trifles. She isn't the main reason I'm here. I have a business proposition for the *Patrón*—"

"Who's get is it?"

"I beg your pardon?"

Barto took offence. "Who's *get*?"

Sera Olivares ignored him and rounded on Joachín. "Don't play games with me! Which nobleman's is it? How much is it worth?"

Miriam gasped. Did she think they were selling a child?

"The baby *isn't* the proposition, *Sera*," Joachín replied, refusing to take the insult. "It has nothing to do with my proposal. The child is incidental."

"Well, it *isn't* incidental to me. Go bother someone else." The portal closed. Joachín thrust his hand through it. A squawk came from behind the door.

"Get your hand out or I'll crush your fingers! See that I don't!"

"If the *Patrón* finds another has benefited because you've turned us away, where will that leave you?" Joachín left his hand where it was.

"Same as where I am, now! Remove your hand or I'll smash it!"

"Fine!" He pulled his hand free. He turned to Barto. "I'm sorry. There's no help to be found here. Let's go."

As if his resignation was what she had been waiting for, *Sera* Olivares reopened the window. "What's the scheme?" she demanded.

Joachin faced her. "It involves moving goods to and from the New World."

"What kinds of goods?"

"People."

"Slaves?"

"Free men."

"Hmph. What good are free men if you have to pay them?"

"That depends on the investment."

"What's the pregnant girl got to do with it?"

"She's one of us. I have a team of workers looking to establish a foothold in the New World. We will do anything the *Patrón* requires in return for our paid passage. We can farm, raise cattle—"

"Anything, eh? How many in your group?"

"Twenty-four. Half are children."

She snorted. "Child labour. Very well. Bring that rig through."

"Thank you, *Sera*."

The window clanged shut. Miriam wondered why Joachin bothered to thank her.

"It never hurts to show one's appreciation," he said after she shared the thought. "Especially with the old and bitter."

"Why is she so bitter?"

"She and the *Patrón* lost family after the purge in Sevill. Their wealth protects them here, but they hide in the shadows, like sparrows from hawks."

Miriam found it hard to picture *Sera* Olivares as a terrified sparrow. The gate opened. As they passed into the courtyard, the old woman scowled at them like a harpy in search of a roost.

"Joachin." *Ser* Olivares addressed him warmly as he entered his study.

"*Patrón.*" Joachín rose to clasp his hand. He was glad to have found a moment to wash and shave. Not that Ser Olivares would have minded, but he preferred to meet him looking a bit less disreputable.

Ser Olivares removed the striped prayer shawl from his shoulders and laid it carefully inside a cedar chest, a sign of his trust that he should allow Joachín to witness him do so. Joachín valued that more than any of their prior exchanges of gold. "Forgive the wait," he said. "You've caught me at my devotions. Mother tells me you've brought a ragtag bunch of ruffians with you?" He smiled as they settled into chairs of walnut and damask. "You must forgive her. With each passing year, she finds our situation here all the more difficult."

"Mistress Sarai is correct in more ways than she knows."

Ser Olivares quirked an eyebrow, inviting him to continue. Joachín told him all about the Tribe, of how he had come to be its patriarch. When he was done, the old man steepled his fingers. "We have much in common, you and I." He stared into space as if remembering the past. "I'd forgotten about the Diaphani. Like my people, they are much abused." He cast him a steady glance. "You *do* know that the inquisitors have come to Marabel. They've set up a skeleton force here, at the Solarium."

"We ran into some awkwardness at the gates. Fortunately, we didn't fit the descriptions of whom they were looking for."

"Fortunate, indeed. How can I help you?"

"We need to leave Esbaña. Travel to the New World. Get beyond the Inquisition's reach."

"Even the New World is falling under their jurisdiction. I haven't told Mother yet, but we are relocating."

"Where?"

"Amsterden. The city burgomasters have offered us asylum."

"You'd trust in the Low Countries over the New World?"

"I have no choice. Mother doesn't tolerate the heat. In Amsterden, she'll have the winters to complain about."

Joachín smiled. *Ser* Olivares had described his mother perfectly.

"So, you wish to settle and farm?" *Ser* Olivares continued. "That's a far cry from your usual line of work."

Joachín nodded. "I was thinking of cattle or cane. Of course, with your backing, you would hold the major interest."

"There's a problem with that. I've sent most of my capital on ahead to Amsterden. All I can offer you is passage aboard a ship."

"That's a start. Where is it docked?"

"In Qadis. She's set to sail for Nueva Esbaña on the twenty-first."

Joachín's heart fell. That was only eight days from now.

"Can you make it?"

"We'll have to."

"Good. I'll send word to arrange passage for you on the *Phoenix*. In the meantime, there may be something else you can do for me. I've heard there is gold on the island of Xaymaca. At the moment, Don Lope, Vizconde de Qadis, is staying at the *Crowing Cock*. My contact tells me he has a map of the gold's location."

The Crowing Cock? What on earth is he doing there? Surely he can afford better lodgings...."

Ser Olivares smiled. "He can. But he's as miserly as he is ruthless. We have crossed purposes before, through representatives. He is not aware he has stolen from me. I would like to repay the favour."

"You want me to steal the map?"

"That would be useful."

"And if we go to Xaymaca, to find the mine?"

"It isn't a mine, yet. The natives scratch away at a vein, but from what I understand, the gold is substantial. The Vizconde has just come from arranging investment capital in Madrone."

Joachín smiled tightly. He had heard of the exploits of Don Lope, and none of them good. It would be a pleasure to relieve the vizconde of his money. If it meant helping *Ser* Olivares, so much the better. "How do we reach Xaymaca from Nueva Esbaña?"

"Stay aboard the *Phoenix*. Xaymaca is the second port of call. There's something else, Joachín." *Ser* Olivares tapped his fingers against his chair, a thing he did when the stakes were high. "You've heard of the Silver Fleet, of course."

Joachín nodded. Every Esbañish thief, every Mediterranean corsair, every privateer and pirate who sailed the Great Ocean Sea lusted after the silver plate loaded from Vera Crucia on the Esbañish main. The Fleet sailed for Esbaña twice a year.

"If you learn the sail dates, my Amsterden associates would pay you handsomely."

Of course they would. Anyone with that kind of information would become fabulously rich. But was *Ser* Olivares motivated by more than simple greed? His plans to relocate to Amsterden.... It was rumoured the Low Countries were seeking independence from Esbaña. How better to fund an independent army, than to steal New World silver? If it came to that, it would be better to insist on a share of the take rather than a sole payment. "I shall do my best in both endeavours," Joachin said. "Gold and silver, every man's dream. We should establish code words, so I can alert you of my success." Post by sea was never private.

"Certainly. What strikes you?"

"*El Lince D'oro* for the gold and *El Lince Plata* for the silver."

"*El Lince?*"

"Yes. What my Tribe calls me."

"The lynx. How appropriate. Include a reference to the time and date for the fleet, and that will work well." *Ser* Olivares steepled his fingers and smiled. "And now, let us speak of simpler things. Mother tells me we'll soon hear a baby's cries in this house."

Joachin imagined how *Sera* Olivares had described it. "I expect so. It's kind of Mistress Sarai to accommodate us."

Ser Olivares snorted. "Oh, we both know Mother isn't motivated by kindness. Still, it makes me happy. Wives and children. So removed from a man's world, yet the foundation of everything we do."

Joachin nodded. He was right. Miriam and the Tribe meant everything to him.

That most important member confronted him later as he was tiptoeing past the birthing room. He had hoped to elude her, but neither luck nor labour saved him. "You're going out?" Miriam demanded, looking incensed. "At this time of night?"

"I have business to attend to, for *Ser* Olivares."

"What kind of business?"

His hand drifted to his truth tattoo. He couldn't lie to her, but he didn't have to admit everything, either. "It's a small thing. How is Maia?"

"Sleeping fitfully. I'm hoping she won't start her real labour until morning."

From inside the room, Maia moaned. Miriam turned at the sound.

"You'd best see to her." Time to make good his escape.

"Wait! You didn't answer my question!"

"Go! She needs you." He fled down the stairs. Even *Sera* Olivares didn't hear him as she tallied sums on a ledger in a parlour off the hall.

Exiting the house, he didn't bother with the gate but climbed over the wall, landing on cat's feet in the alley. Leaving the civilized way meant asking *Sera* Olivares to unlock the gate, and he didn't want to annoy her further. As he made his way along the dark streets, the locals eyed him, judging, calculating. Whenever he caught their eye, he acknowledged them with a nod and a grin, the message clear: *try me and it will cost you.* No one did.

He soon came to the *Crowing Cock.* The red-haired prostitute no longer leaned from her perch, but a man paused inside her candle-lit window to draw the curtains. He wore a short, pointed beard, a style popular among the nobility. In front of the *bordello*, two liveried guards loitered beside an ornate coach. Joachín ignored them and strolled into the inn.

The place was half-full. A few of the regulars glanced up as he entered, but they soon returned to their drinks. He found a corner table with a good view. A wide staircase led to the upper level.

From the kitchen, a barmaid entered, bearing a tray of mugs and ale. She was dowdy and heavily-set, her hair tied in a messy bun. After setting the mugs before three men at a distant table, she approached Joachín to hear his pleasure. He flashed her one of the coins he had stolen from the pig farmer, a silver *linares*, enough to buy a round for the entire bar. "Sit with me a moment, *Serina*," he said, patting the bench beside him. "I want to purchase your time."

Her face purpled. "I ain't no...! You want a whore, go upstairs!" She turned on her heel, but he grabbed her by the wrist.

"Tell me what I want to know, and the coin is yours," he whispered. "First, your name."

She paused, glowering at him. The other patrons bent over their drinks. No one paid them any mind. "What d'you need my name for?"

"It makes for better confidences."

"Nita."

"Good. The nobleman upstairs. Who is he?" It was important to confirm Don Lope was still in residence, in spite of what *Ser* Olivares thought. Important people never stayed in one place for long.

"Calls hisself, Don Lope de Qadis. Has business with the Court or some such."

"I see. And how long does he plan to stay here?"

"How should I know? He don't tell me—"

"Has he paid to stay the night?"

"He has. Don't know about tomorrow."

"We'll worry about tomorrow when it comes." He rose.

"Wait! What about my coin?"

"I have an errand to attend to. I'll be back."

"But you said...!"

"I said I'd pay you when I've learned everything I want to know. You haven't told me all I need to know yet."

"Bah. You ain't nothin' but a liar and a cheat."

He sighed. "I wish that were true. About me being a liar, anyway. I'll be back in the morning."

"As if I care."

Joachin smiled. She was of a type. Like the miser Don Lope was rumoured to be, Nita served only Mammon.

He had in mind to visit a particular establishment known only to a few in Marabel, and of those who did know of it, none admitted to the fact. Its business was of a nature that not even *Ser* Olivares, trader in ill-gotten goods, would touch. There were some wares the old man would not handle, some things he would not do. On the other hand, he never questioned Joachin's methods, or how he came by his merchandise. In some respects, the less *Ser* Olivares knew, the better.

Joachin came at last to another crooked alley. Unlike the narrow street which fronted the Olivares' hidden sanctuary, this one was barely wider than a goat trail and smelled as bad. He made his way down it until he came to a wooden door, unexceptional in any way, except that it looked as if someone in a fit of rage or madness, had attacked it with a knife. Where long carvings didn't score the wood, the door was punctuated with stab marks. The damage was fairly recent. Whoever had visited here had been denied, and they had left behind their fury, for all to see.

Joachin drew in a deep breath. Only fools indulged in what was sold here, and only the dregs of humanity sold it. He would never stoop that low. He tapped lightly on the door and stepped back. From a window overhead, a pale face appeared momentarily and then disappeared as he knew it would. After a few moments, the door opened a careful crack. He could not see the door keeper. Beyond, all was darkness.

"What you want?" asked a softly accented voice. It sounded young and female. Fahdah's girls often were.

"Narjis?"

"No."

So Narjis was gone. He hoped she hadn't succumbed to the temptations of this place, or that Fahdah had sold her, but on the other hand, if Fahdah had, it didn't necessarily mean to a worse life. Even a stable was better than a cesspool.

"I have something to trade with your mistress."

"What is it?"

"Faba." He doubted he needed to explain what the beans might be used for.

"Your name?"

He hesitated. Fahdah knew him by his alias, José of Taleda. His mouth twisted, attempting the lie. It was impossible. "She has known me as José de Taleda." The truth.

"Wait here."

She returned in a few minutes to draw him inside. He followed her down a narrow hallway in darkness until they came to another door which she opened, causing the sudden illumination of ruddy light to reveal who she was. Like Narjis, she was slightly built, with a thick dark braid that dangled down her back and past her waist. Her skin was a tawny dusk. Smoke curled past curtained doorways in finger-like tendrils, beckoning, promising. He didn't have to peer beyond the drapes to know what he would find there. On straw-filled mattresses, men lay in various stages of euphoria, all of them opium struck.

The girl brought him to an unoccupied cubicle and invited him within. The mattress looked as if it had been hastily turned to its cleaner side. He knew she hadn't had the time to rid it of its vomit, an unfortunate side-effect of an overdose. The room smelled sweet and sour at the same time.

"You wish to partake?" she asked, lifting a hand to the waiting brazier.

He remained standing, having no desire to rest there. "No."

Her expression was flat. "Then, something else?"

She was about Casi's age, around twelve or thirteen. It upset him that she was expected to provide any kind of service he chose. "No. I came to trade."

"For what?"

"Dartura." It was possible that Don Lope would recognize the taste of opium, but Dartura had no taste at all.

"How much?"

"Whatever this will get me." From inside his shirt, he retrieved the pouch Zara had given him. Dartura was a rarity and therefore, expensive, but he suspected Fahdah would have a small cache. She dealt in just about everything.

The girl disappeared, and he waited for her to return. He had never met Fahdah in person. Like *Ser* Olivares, the Moresca only worked through intermediaries. She also remained in hiding. It was even possible that there was no Fahdah, any longer. Joachin suspected the Solarium knew of her business, but it was also possible that too many men of importance—priests and noblemen—indulged in her services.

When the girl returned, she handed him a small, folded packet. He unwrapped it as she watched. It was difficult to tell whether the plant material was Dartura. The tiny crumble of brown flakes could well have been any herb. On the other hand, it was said Fahdah valued her reputation above all else. He would have to trust the packet and her.

There was no point in arguing the paltry amount. If this was Dartura, he wouldn't need much.

He felt the girl's scrutiny and nodded. Seeing his acceptance, she lifted her hand to the door to indicate their business was over and he should find his way out.

Back in the stinking alley, his conscience told him he should return to Miriam, but the temptation to act rather than wait, proved to be too much. Besides, if she detained him for some reason, it was altogether possible that Don Lope would be gone by morning. The best time to steal the map would be tonight, after the vizconde partook of his supper. Then to wait for the drug to take effect.

He checked his progress half way to the *Crowing Cock*. He could steal the map, but it would be better to have an accomplice in case anything went awry. Iago was light on his feet and quick of mind. With Guillermo dead...the thought brought him a stab of pain.

He swallowed, caught his breath. He was responsible for Guillermo's death, for all of their deaths, for which he had to atone. It was up to him to take Iago in hand, to see to the boy's future. Iago had done well in helping him steal the ham from the farm—he was a natural talent. The Tribe might grow cane, or cotton, or even trade indigo in the New World, but there was no faster way to profit than theft. Stealing from a miser who dealt in human suffering as Don Lope did, only made the notion sweeter. Yes, he would bring Iago along. It would only take another hour to return to the Tribe and come back with him, hopefully in time for Don Lope to take a late evening meal or perhaps drink a glass of wine. It was possible the old man disdained the Crowing Cock's offerings, but few men refused what was offered for free, especially if they were misers.

It hadn't been too difficult to extricate Iago from Luci and Zara and the rest of the Tribe. Iago had been eager to go, and Ximen, after Zara had questioned whether they would be left completely defenseless, had risen to the occasion in assuring them that under his guardianship, everyone would be all right. Besides, he reasoned, Tor Tomás was already stationed *inside* the town. It was unlikely the Grand Inquisitor would choose to spend the night searching the surrounding countryside. As he said it, his pale glance fell upon Luci.

It was hard to tell but for some reason, Joachin had the impression he was too annoyed with Zara to include her in his regard. She had used an unfortunate turn of phrase - Ximen's too old! - and it had injured his pride.

"How is Maia?" Zara asked, ignoring Ximen who was ignoring her.

"Miriam thinks she won't deliver until tomorrow."

Zara sniffed. "Pray she doesn't. Our matriarch may be our matriarch, but she still needs experienced hands."

"Don't worry," Joachin had added. "We'll be back by dawn to fetch you. Wait for us at the east gate."

And now, he and Iago stood in the shadows of the alley beside the *Crowing Cock.* Behind them lay a dead-end with a garbage heap.

"That's his coach?" Iago nodded at the dark hulk parked in front of the inn. The horses still stood in their traces, shifting uncomfortably from hoof to hoof. Don Lope wasn't such a miser as to deny them their feed. A pile of dirty hay had been left for them. Two henchmen loitered beside it, talking quietly.

Joachin nodded.

"Paranoid, isn't he?" Iago concluded, suspecting as Joachin did, that Don Lope kept his horses in harness so he wouldn't have to pay stable fees. "How do you know he doesn't keep the map locked in there?"

"I don't. But if it's important to him, he'll keep it close by. It's probably in his suite."

"This place has a suite?"

"I expect so. He's a nobleman. He'll want some comfort." He slapped Iago on the chest. "Time to act. Look sharp, like you belong here." They headed for the door.

"Why would I want to?"

"That isn't the point."

"I'm joking. You're saying I should look full of myself, so people think twice about crossing me."

"Exactly."

"Good. Then I'll pretend to be you."

Joachin sputtered. Iago grinned at him lopsidedly. He was teasing him again. Joachin smiled in spite of himself.

The inn was nearly full. They were sized up as they made for a table set in a shadowed alcove near the kitchen. This time, Joachín didn't bother to smile but held each stare as if it were a personal affront until the bearer looked away. Iago followed suit but elaborated on it, occasionally lifting an eyebrow as if to say, *care to dance?* Joachín approved. There was enough attitude there to dissuade any but the biggest fool. He caught Nita's eye and waved her over to the shadowed nook where they stood.

"So, yer back," she said ungraciously.

"Is there a place where we can talk privately?"

"Why? So you can cheat me further?"

"No cheats. You'll earn your *linares* if you tell me everything I want to know, plus perform a simple task."

"Oh, a task now! What task?"

He waggled a forefinger at her. "Not another word, until we can speak without eavesdroppers."

"Come into the kitchen, then."

They followed her to the back of the inn, where a dried out haunch of beef smoked over a banked hearth. Dirty dishes and cutlery were stacked to overflowing on a crude table. Clay mugs littered the brick floor, the shards of several having met their end there. In one corner, a huge barrel lay on its side, tapped and dripping. Above it, jugs of wine lay stacked on shelves. Joachín's stomach grumbled. He ignored it. Business, first.

"This private enough, for you?" Nita demanded.

Joachín ignored the question and posed one of his own. "Is there another way to the second floor of this establishment?"

"Why d'you want t'know?"

"I ask the questions, not you."

She set her hands on her ample hips. "You seem to expect somethin' for nothin'."

"If you want that *linares*, you'll stop balking and wasting our time. Is there a second set of stairs? A servant's route, perhaps?"

"Aye. Through there." She tilted her head to a small entryway that lay off the kitchen.

"Where does that go?"

"Second floor, back of the inn."

"In which suite is Don Lope staying?"

"Double room off the front, with the balcony window. Looks over the street."

"Good. Here is where you earn your *linares*, Nita."

She waited for him to continue. He doubted if he could trust her, but if she managed things as he told her, she would be as culpable as they. Iago shifted from foot to foot.

"I need you to add a special herb to Don Lope's food."

"He's already eaten. Practically threw the plate at me when I went to fetch it. Said he expected better for breakfast."

Damn, Joachín thought. He had been overlong retrieving Iago.

"You thinkin' to poison him?"

"Of course not! I wouldn't ask you to do that. Poison makes for bad business."

"What is it, then?"

"Something to help him sleep." That was true enough.

"Why?"

"He has something of ours," Iago interposed. "Something he stole. We want to get it back."

Joachín was doubly glad he brought Iago along. He couldn't lie to Nita, but Iago was under no such constraint. Nita's eyes narrowed. "What did he steal?"

"A map. Of a goldmine."

Joachín kept his hands at his sides. He wanted to hit Iago. He had divulged too much.

"We were the ones who found it," Iago continued blithely. "He thinks to mine the gold out from under us."

"A goldmine? Where?"

"On the island of Xaymaca."

Nita set her hands on her hips and eyed them craftily. "That'll cost you *two* linares, then. One, fer what y' already owe me, an' another for fixin' his breakfast. Mind you, he dies an' I scream for the Guard. I ain't takin' no blame for no murder."

"We don't plan on murdering him." Iago replied, again too helpful.

Joachín ran a hand through his hair. "Does he take a late night glass of wine?" He needed to bring the conversation back under his control.

"He does, but yer also too late fer that."

"What if you were to take one up to him, say, with the inn's compliments?" Iago suggested.

It was one thing to lie, but the falsehood had to be believable. "No, he would never believe that," Joachín said. "What does he have for his breakfast?"

"Eggs and meat."

"What time does he take it?"

"Couple hours after dawn. He likes his sleep."

He handed her the packet. "Mix this in it. We'll be back in the morning to pay you."

"You'll pay me now." Her glance was steely.

"Fine. One now, for your information and doing what I ask. You'll get the second after we've accomplished our business."

She sniffed, unfolded the packet, and squinted at the contents. "Ain't much here. Do I use all of it?"

"All of it," Joachín confirmed. There was enough Dartura there to put Don Lope out for several hours. She nodded, refolded the packet, and tucked it into her bodice. Joachín gave her the coin. He and Iago took their leave of her then. At dawn, they would fetch Luci and Zara to assist with Maia's delivery. While the women were busy, they would return to the inn and snatch the map. Joachín had hoped to do it under the cover of night, but that couldn't be helped.

"Where are we going?" Iago asked, as they made their way along darker and narrower streets.

"To a friend's. Miriam is there, with another old friend of mine and his pregnant wife. I'm afraid you're going to have to spend the night in the stables." There was no point in distressing *Sera* Olivares further with yet another guest, and he didn't want to think what Miriam would say if she saw Iago. She would know they were up to something, and she would demand to know what it was.

"That's okay," Iago said. "It's warmer than the woods."

Miriam set a hand to Maia's belly. The contractions were quickening. Judging from the light coming in through the window, it would soon be dawn. "Don't worry," she soothed. "Everything will be fine. Just breathe through the pain."

"I...ohhh!" Maia gasped.

"Do something!" Barto said.

"Watch me." Miriam forced the girl to regard her. "I have women coming to help. In the meantime, breathe like this." She demonstrated. Together, they panted, weathering the contraction. It helped.

"You can stay with her for now, Barto," she told him as he stroked his wife's cheek, "but as things progress, I'll need you to go." Most men were only too happy to leave. Those who stayed sometimes panicked and made things worse.

"I've delivered lambs, calves, and foals," Barto said firmly. "I stay if she wants me to."

Miriam considered the two of them. The girl looked to Barto for strength. As long as he didn't faint and stayed out of the way, she would allow it. "Very well," she relented. "Your job is to remind her to breathe. Make her watch you. When the time comes, prop her to push." Hopefully, Joachin would return soon with Luci and Zara. It would help to have extra hands.

Sera Olivares hadn't brought the water and linens she had requested. She excused herself. "I'll only be a moment," she told Maia.

The old woman wasn't hard to find. She sat in her kitchen, eating a bowl of gruel. Did she ever sleep?

"Those fresh cloths and water I asked for? I need them," Miriam said.

"We don't have any." Sera Olivares took a second spoonful and pushed the bowl aside.

Miriam took a deep breath. "Surely, you have some compassion for that poor girl upstairs. It's her first child. She's frightened, and doesn't know what to expect."

Sera Olivares stood abruptly, clenching her fists. Her eyes were rage-filled. "Why should I have any compassion for you when none has been shown to me? You think life is simple! I tell you, the only thing that protects you in this world is coin. Nothing else! Make sure your man pays me in full before she delivers, or I don't care what my son says! I'll set the Guard on you!"

Miriam ignored her. A ladle and pail of water sat on a far counter. She headed for them. *Sera* Olivares gasped at her audacity and stormed from the room. Once she was gone, Miriam drew in a deep breath to steady herself. There was a long history, there. Whatever it was, their presence had sparked painful memories in their hostess.

I suppose I can always take the blankets from Joachín's room, she thought. He still wasn't back. She lifted the pail and carried it to the second floor, turning at a tread on the floorboards behind her. A tall, austere man stood there, wearing a long surplice of burgundy wool. He approached her, carrying a tower of wash cloths. "I hope these will suffice," he said. A faint smile touched his lips. "Forgive my mother, *Serina*. She's unused to guests in this house."

"Thank you. That's very kind." She shifted the pail to one hand and reached for the cloths.

"No, allow me. You are burdened."

She wondered if *Ser* Olivares had overheard her conversation with his mother.

"It's been a long time since we've had a baby in this house," he said happily. "I'm looking forward to it."

"Are you really?" He and his mother were complete opposites.

"Oh, yes. I prefer beginnings to ends. They're like hope and despair, residing in the same house. Do I surprise you?"

His eyes were warm but probing. He didn't strike her as a man who missed much. "No," she lied.

"Perhaps I do, a little. That's all right. I am used to it."

They had come to Maia's door. Miriam took the cloths from him. "Thank you, *Patrón*."

"You'll keep me informed of her progress?"

"If you wish. Once Joachín is back, I'll ask him to tell you."

"Excellent. And when we meet again, perhaps it will be to the sound of a baby's cries." He was quietly enthusiastic.

"Yes." She set a hand on the door. For a head of the underworld, he wasn't at all what she expected. What kind of arrangement had he made with Joachin? Surely, it was illegal. "*Ser* Olivares," she asked, turning abruptly. "What did you and Joachin...?"

The hallway was empty. Had he sensed what she was going to ask? She shook her head in exasperation, hating that she didn't know what he and Joachin were planning. In the birthing room, Maia's face was tight with pain. "She's had two more pains since you were gone," Barto said.

Miriam set the cloths and the pail on a bureau and settled beside Maia. Beneath the contraction, the baby felt vital and strong. *A boy*, she realized, after a moment. *I won't tell them. Let it be their surprise.* She thought fleetingly of the son Joachin had told her they would have.

Feet thumped up the stairs. Miriam glanced out the bedroom door. Joachin appeared at the end of the hall with Zara, Luci, and Casi in tow. The women looked breathless as if they had run from the town's gate. Casi hopped from foot to foot, as excited as a kitten in catmint. Iago appeared behind them.

Why had Joachin let Iago come? Ximen was too old to protect the Tribe. "Why is Iago here?" she demanded, looking to him for answers.

He looked ill at ease. "I need him." As Zara, Luci, and Casi rushed past her, he disappeared down the stairs as if he couldn't get away fast enough. Iago followed at his heels.

"Joachin!" she shouted after him. He ignored her and clattered down the stairs. Maia let out another sharp cry. "It's all right, dear," Zara soothed from inside the room. "I have everything you need right here."

Miriam clenched her fists and returned to the room. "Do either of you know what Joachin and Iago are up to?" she demanded.

Luci busied herself with the birth cloths. Casi sucked her lips between her teeth as if she had been warned against saying anything. Zara settled beside Maia on the bed. "My goodness," she said brightly, "you're doing well!"

"Am I?" Maia asked weakly.

"Yes, indeed! I've seen hundreds of births, and yours is progressing exactly as it should! I don't expect any complications." Zara ducked beneath the sheets and took a quick glance between Maia's spread legs. "Why, I think I can see his dear little head crowning!"

"I...oooh!" Maia gasped. Her gasp turned into a small scream.

"You just let it out as you want, sweetheart!" Zara said, once she subsided. She set her hands to Maia's swollen belly to rub it and shoved Barto out of the way. He stood abruptly, trusting to the master in midwifery who had taken over. "Not long, now!" Zara enthused.

Maia nodded tiredly. Miriam envied the effect Zara had on both Maia and Barto. Luci tucked cloths about Maia's legs while Casi poured her a cup of water. Barto stroked his wife's hair. Her assistants had things well in hand.

Fine, she thought contemptuously. *Don't tell me what Joachin is doing.* She would have it from him later, one way or the other. In the meantime, there was a baby to bring into the light. She set Joachin from her mind and ordered Zara to stand aside in a tone that broached no argument. With a practiced eye, she assessed the baby's crowning and prepared to usher Maia into motherhood.

)(L)(

"Did he eat all his food?" Joachin, Iago, and Nita sat huddled in a dull corner of the inn. Sunrise had come and gone. The Vizconde's coach was still parked out in front. His guards slumped beside it, drowsing.

"I gave him the herb in his eggs, like you said. Then I went up later to get the plate. Food was gone, and he was snoring like I never seen him." She held out her hand for the last coin.

"Not so fast. We still have to get the map," Iago said.

Joachin winced. Even though he had whispered it, talking openly about the map was not something he should have done. The inn was nearly empty at this time of the day, but a few drunks still slept off their drink in a corner.

"Is there a room with a window that opens onto the back of the inn?" he asked, his voice barely a whisper. "Near those back stairs? I don't want one that opens onto the front street."

"End of the hall and to your right. Ula works there, but I can toss her out. Tell her I got to change the bedstraw."

"Good. Do it."

"Pay me."

Iago began to protest, but Joachin set a hand on his arm. "Leave it. She's done her part. The rest is up to us." As he paid her the last *linares*, he cast her a glance that suggested it would be best if she maintained her silence.

She read the threat there. "I ain't no snitch," she said, affronted.

As Iago made his way outside, Joachín followed her into the kitchen and up the servant's stair. When they came to the landing to the upper floor, she pointed at the nearest door. "That's the room you want. Give me a moment to clear it. Stay here and no one'll see you."

"Where's the Vizconde?"

"End of the hall."

Joachín waited on the step. Around the corner, Nita bustled into the room to rouse Ula. "Get up, you lazy *puta*. I need you to sleep with Flora." There was a slap and a yelp.

"Ow! Why? Someone pay for us both?"

"No! Now get out!"

"All right, I'm going! I don't understand the hurry...."

A door slammed. Nita loomed before him and motioned for him to follow her into the room.

The place had a tired, spent atmosphere to it. The lace curtains were torn, the bed recently vacated. Clothing lay strewn across the floor. There were multiple stains on the walls—red wine, candle wax, and other splatters Joachín didn't want to know. The place smelled of dirt and rose water, the last so faint it made him think of flowery ghosts.

I hate brothels. He strode over to the window and looked out. In the shadowed alley below, Iago waited beside the trash heap. He turned to Nita, needing to impress upon her their need for secrecy. "I'm sure I don't have to remind you to keep your peace."

She shrugged. "You paid me well enough." She turned away, as if glad to be shed of him.

He listened to her tramp down the stairs and then he headed for the room at the end of the hall. He paused at the door to listen. Only snoring came from within.

Good, he thought. *He's out cold.*

Cautiously, he cracked open the door. Two bodies lay in the bed. His heart gave a start. Nita, damn her, had neglected to tell him that as well as breakfast, the vizconde had ordered the red-head who had leaned from her balcony the night before to attend him. Had she also eaten the tainted food? Until he entered that room, there was no way to tell.

He should call off the attempt, avoid the girl screaming for the guards, but if she was drugged, when would he have another chance like this? He wouldn't. Don Lope would never allow himself to be placed in such a vulnerable position again. He would hire a taster, or force one of his men to test his food.

Another unpleasant surprise, the vizconde was a much younger man than he had assumed. For some reason, he had expected him to be an aging, gone-to-seed pinchfist. Even naked and snoring, Don Lope looked every inch the conquistador. A dangerous adversary, indeed.

He crossed to the bed on silent feet and considered the red-headed girl. One option would be to choke her, just long enough to bring about unconsciousness, but surely, he didn't need to stoop that low. On the other hand, if she screamed, she would alert the guards.

Without further prickings of conscience, he clamped one hand across her mouth, while the other grabbed her about the throat. Her eyes flew open in horror, but as he didn't choke her, she watched him with wide eyes until she relaxed. Slowly, he lifted his hand from her neck and set a finger to his lips. She blinked and nodded her understanding. He drew in a deep breath. "I am looking for something," he whispered. "I'll make it worth your while if you tell me. A map. Do you know where he might keep it?"

Her glance drifted to Don Lope, sleeping beside her in the bed.

"Don't worry. He's drugged. He won't wake."

Sensing the vizconde's insensible state, she sat upright and shoved his arm away with revulsion. He must have used her badly.

"The map?" It was hard to ignore her breasts. "Or perhaps a casket?" Possibly, the vizconde kept his valuables in such a chest. Speaking of chests, her nipples were very rosy.

She shook her head and touched her throat.

He frowned, no longer distracted. Why didn't she speak?

As if sensing his thought, she opened her mouth to show him. Where her tongue should have been, was only a stub. Some noblemen, especially if they were in the midst of delicate negotiations for a titled wife, would only sleep with prostitutes turned mute. All the better to keep one's reputation intact.

With a curse, he grabbed Don Lope by the throat, wanting to choke the life from him. He pressed his thumbs into his larynx and watched the Vizconde's face redden. Then he released him. The man was filth. Why dirty his hands? Besides, he couldn't afford to kill him now. The town was crawling with Torch Bearers. Whoever the whoremaster of the Crowing Cock was, he wouldn't tolerate the murder of a nobleman on the premises. Nita would be forced to tell.

"I'm sorry for your hurt," he told the girl, meaning it. As tempting as it was to rid the world of the likes of Don Lope, he had to find the map. He wasn't sure how long the Dartura would last, although experience had taught him several hours. He glanced about the room. A wardrobe sagged in a corner. He yanked the doors wide. Inside were dresses and a moth-eaten blanket. He looked under the bed next. Nothing.

The only other obvious place was the small table standing near the balcony's window. He lifted the cloth. And there it was. Nestled between the table's legs was a bronze casket set with garnets.

It took him no time to force the lid. Inside, he found the map on a roll of velum, along with a leather pouch. As expected, the map was labeled *Xaymaca*. Several landmarks were indicated, including three hills in the centre of the island. A strange face—a shield with slitted eyes, a gaping mouth, and a protruding tongue—had been drawn at the base of the highest one. He had never seen anything like it.

He returned the map to the casket and then teased open the mouth of the pouch. Inside glinted six gold lumps. Each nugget turned out to be the size of his thumb.

As he held one up to the light, the girl watched him with huge, astonished eyes.

He crossed over to her and pressed the nugget into her palm. "When he wakes up, he'll blame you. Take this and go." He nodded at the vizconde.

She stared at the fortune in her hand and then at him as if in a dream.

"For your pains," he told her. "Leave Marabel. Make a fresh start."

Without giving her a further glance, he slipped from the suite with the casket and headed down the hall. In Ula's room, he opened the window and tossed it to Iago, waiting in the alley below. As Iago caught it, they exchanged grins. His cousin gave him a thumbs-up and then took off with the casket at a run. As Joachín slid a leg over the window sill, he congratulated himself. All had gone as planned. Behind him, a floorboard creaked. He turned, only to see something round and hard as it took him across the skull. His head burst into pain. Red filled his vision, blotted by black. He slid to the floor and knew no more.

)(L((

"What do you mean *there's been an emergency?* I'm in the middle of one!" As Iago fidgeted from foot to foot, Miriam confronted him outside the birthing room. Inside, Maia gave a loud shriek. The baby was imminent.

"We had some business to attend to at the *Crowing Cock.* Joachín—"

"You went to that *bordello?*" Miriam's voice rose in pitch.

"It isn't what you think. We weren't visiting the girls."

"What then?"

"He's been caught." Iago set the casket into her hands. "This belongs to Don Lope, a vizconde and a terrible man."

She gasped. Quickly, she checked the casket's contents. A roll of velum fell to the floor as gold nuggets spilled into her palm. "Gods! You stole this?" She reached for the roll and stuffed it and the gold back into the chest. "Zara, see to Maia!" she shouted at the bedroom door. "I'll be back! Gods, Iago! What have you done? Pray to Lys they haven't called the Guard on him yet!"

"Where are you going?" Iago chased her down the stairs.

"I'm returning this to the Vizconde and pleading for clemency!"

"You? Wouldn't it be better if Barto and I—"

"Don't think, Iago! It gets you into trouble!"

"He isn't the kind of man you want to deal with, Miriam!"

"It's too late for that! Get out of my way!"

He pulled at her arm. "You don't understand! Joachín will kill me if I let you go there!"

She knocked his arm aside and ignored his pleas all the way to the *Crowing Cock.* "Tell your mother and Zara where I've gone and why," she insisted at the inn's doorway. "As soon as Maia delivers her baby, leave Marabel and find the Tribe."

"But...!"

"No, Iago! I am counting on you to escort everyone to safety. If Joachin and I don't find you by dawn, take everyone and leave. Do you understand me?" She shook him by the arm, her grip like pincers. "No rescues! The Tribe is your first responsibility. If you fail them, I will curse you to eternity!"

He paled, believing her capable of it. She wouldn't, of course, but she needed him to think she could. He turned and ran back the way they had come.

She stepped into the inn's dim interior. It was late afternoon. The place was already half full. Ignoring the cat calls coming her way, she strode through the common room with her head held high. A large woman in a dirty apron eyed her as she approached.

"I'm seeking the Vizconde, Don Lope." She showed the drudge his casket. "This belongs to him. I need to return it."

"I'll take it." The woman held out her hand.

"No. I must return it to him personally. I need to plead for mercy for the man who stole it."

The large woman gave her a sardonic smile. "Well, ain't this a funny turn of events? Come, *Serina*." She stressed the honourific as if it were an irony. "I'll take you to them."

She led Miriam up a wide set of stairs to a second floor balcony which overlooked the tavern, then down a narrow hall.

"The Vizconde's with your man, in there." She knocked on the door. A guard, with a ham-sized fist, pulled it open. In the middle of the room, Joachin lay unmoving at the feet of a dark-haired nobleman who sat at a small table near a window. The Vizconde glanced up sharply as he saw her. As the drudge pushed Miriam into the room, Joachin let out a low moan.

"*Bella* here, says she's got your goods. She's come to trade for her man." Nita pushed her forward.

Don Lope prodded Joachin with a boot as he considered Miriam. "This filth is yours?"

"He's...he is my kinsman." She wasn't exactly sure how to describe their relationship. She wanted to run to Joachin, to check him for injuries. The side of his head was bloody. Bruises were forming on his face and arms. They had beaten him. She stood where she was, knowing any move on her part would be a mistake. Nita closed the door behind her.

"Not your husband or lover?"

"No."

"A brother?"

"No. I've come to return what he stole from you. He shouldn't have taken it. Please, let him go."

Don Lope pursed his lips. "It isn't so straightforward as that, *Serina*. He did something to me that is unforgiveable."

Iago hadn't told her everything. She swallowed. "What is that?"

"He drugged me, so he might steal that casket you are holding." He motioned to the guard to take it from her. "So, for me to let him go is asking a great deal. You've returned my property, but that doesn't address the other injury."

Silence descended. Joachin moaned and lifted his head. Don Lope lashed out and kicked him in the ribs. Miriam stifled a cry. Joachin fell back to the floor like a sack.

"What do you want?" she whispered.

The Don tapped his lips with a finger. "I think—" he eyed her speculatively, "I want double the amount of what is in here." He smiled nastily. "Did you look inside?"

Miriam nodded.

"Then you know the amount of gold of which I speak."

She nodded. With a groan, Joachin staggered to his feet and lunged for him. Don Lope's guards grabbed him before he got close. The bigger one punched him in the stomach.

"What do you say?" Don Lope asked mildly as Joachin doubled over.

"I...we have no way of getting that amount!"

"Oh dear. How unfortunate. Then you leave me no choice but to—"

"I returned your property!"

"Even so." He flicked a finger at one of his men. "Alert the Guard."

"Wait!" Miriam stepped in front of the man to prevent him from leaving. Perhaps *Ser* Olivares would lend them the money. They could pay him back, even if it meant living in servitude for the rest of their lives. "I think I can get it."

"Really? But before, you said—" He was toying with her.

"Our...our *patrón*. He lives here in Marabel. He's rich." She glanced at Joachín. "They have worked together, before. "I am sure he would put up the money."

"Well, if you think—"

"I do! Just let me go, and I'll run to him, plead with him if I must."

"You would beg for this one?" He nudged Joachín with his toe.

"Yes." She knew it was true. "I would."

Joachín lifted his head to lock his gaze with hers. There was something in his eyes, a miserable hopelessness that told her the attempt would be impossible. What didn't she know?

"Very touching," Don Lope said. "But I think *he* will go, and not you. Think of it as my guarantee. If he returns with the money, you're both free to leave."

She nodded, feeling as if she wanted to faint.

"Very good." He nodded at Joachín. "How long will it take him to come back with the coin?"

"At least an hour." Perhaps it would take *Ser* Olivares some time to arrange for the funds. Maybe that was what Joachín was trying to tell her.

"He has half an hour and no more. If he doesn't return within that time, so much the worse for you." Don Lope glanced down at Joachín with disgust. "Toss that trash into the street," he told his guards, "to do as it chooses."

The guards dragged Joachín into the hall. As the door slammed behind them, Miriam held her breath. If she tried to run, the Don would be on her in a second. She tried not to dwell on it.

He settled into a chair by the window and indicated she should take the seat opposite. "A little conversation, while we wait," he said. "For the moment, there is no need for things to be unpleasant between us. Sit," he ordered, with more force than was necessary.

She sank onto the cushions. Through the muslin curtains, she watched as the guards hurled Joachín into the road. He lay bleeding on the cobblestones before managing to rise. The town locals laughed and kicked grit in his direction.

"You see? Your paramour is fine." Don Lope smiled. "I've kept my side of the bargain. Now, let's wait to see if he keeps yours."

Chapter Nine: Rat Poison

Had he a body, Alonso would have kicked Joachín de Rivera as he stumbled down the street. *I could kill you!* he shouted as Joachín lurched away, leaving a trail of blood behind him. *How dare you leave her to the mercies of Don Lope de Qadis?* In the upper circles of Esbañish society, Don Lope was known as a man without conscience and a furious temper. He hadn't hurt Miriam yet, but that was only a matter of time.

There had to be something, anything, he could do to stop it. It was now pushing noon. Most of the locals were in early stages of inebriation. He doubted he could possess any of them to force their wills. Besides, it wasn't smart to operate under the influence of drink. He needed his wits.

The street in front of the *bordello* offered no possibilities, so he searched the alley behind. An old nag stood in the shade, hitched to a post. The only other living things nosing about were rats on a trash pile.

He considered them. A rat might work. They were fighters—vicious and fierce—unfortunately, those tendencies might also thwart him. One had a patchy coat and rheumy eyes. A sick rat wasn't his best bet, but that same debility might work to his advantage. He had to try.

He grabbed it by the heart, anchoring himself to it. His head turned hot, his guts, queasy, but he filled the rat's body—success! Unfortunately, the rat wasn't so ill that it didn't sense his intrusion. It hissed and bit a neighbour on its haunch. Suddenly, he found himself in the middle of a snarling ball of snapping teeth and raking claws. He forced his host away, earning a bite to his flank as they retreated.

Move, damn you! he shouted, prodding his host to the wall. The bite on his hip was agony. The leg felt as if it were on fire. Every movement made him want to stop, double over, and lick at the wound, but need forced him to suffer the pain. There was no time, and Miriam was in trouble. *Climb!*

The rat clawed at the wall and scrabbled up the first brick, then the second. They made slow but painful progress. Alonso was certain at any moment it would lose its hold and tumble, faint and dizzy, to the ground. He held it in an iron grip, pushing it as hard as it could go.

Finally, they climbed over the lip of the roof edging the first floor. His host was almost spent. He allowed it a moment to recover, then once again, they were on the move. They trundled past one window and then another. Finally, they came to the small balcony jutting from the vizconde's suite. The rat collapsed on its belly, panting. Its heart thudded, he could barely see. If he pushed it any more, it would die. All he could do was wait for it to recover.

"Something to drink?" Don Lope indicated the wine on the table. "Don't worry," he reassured Miriam, "Unlike your man with his packet of drugs, I've done nothing to alter it."

Miriam said nothing. Taking her silence for consent, he poured wine into two goblets and handed her one.

"Drink. Tell me about yourself."

He seemed in no hurry to ravish her, if that's what he had in mind. Who knew what a man like this could want? Perhaps he prided himself on being courtly. It was smarter to keep him talking. "There isn't much to tell."

"Oh, I doubt that. A lovely girl like you? How did you come to be with that piece of garbage?"

"It's a long story."

"I'm sure it is. You're not from the streets. If I were to guess, I'd say you were a merchant's daughter."

"My father was a physician."

"Truly? How surprising. Yet you associate with thieves."

"I was hoping I might change him. He shouldn't have taken your goods."

Don Lope burst out laughing. "How like a woman! Let me tell you something about men, my chick. You can't change them or their natures. Don't even try." He dangled the leather bag before her. "Do you know what's inside this pouch? Did you look?"

"Yes. Gold nuggets."

"Yet, you return them to me. I can't decide whether you're an honest woman or a stupid one. Gold doesn't impress you?"

"Gold has its place."

"It does, indeed. This gold is from the New World. Would you like to know how I came by it?"

"Not really."

He laughed again. "For one in such a vulnerable position, I'd think you'd prefer to humour me. I'm going to tell you, anyway."

She remained silent.

"Every nugget in this pouch has been paid for in blood, which affects the colour, or so I am told. I choose to believe it. When blood is spilled, it improves the land."

She stared at him, sickened by what he was suggesting.

"In this particular case, the natives who knew of this vein had been fighting over it for centuries. They fight no longer. My troops are the flower of Esbaña. Of course, Sul is also on our side, as we are bringing the true faith to the heathens."

He waited for her to murmur her admiration. When she didn't, he smirked as if her lack of response was of little account. "I suppose you've studied the map."

"Not really. I wanted to return it to you as soon as possible."

His lips twitched. "How charming you are. You might be lying, but it doesn't matter." He sipped his wine and eyed her over the goblet. His amusement faded into speculation.

She had to keep him talking. "Can I see it?"

His brows rose. "Why not?" With an easy grace, he removed the roll of velum from the bag and spread it on the table between them. An island, entitled Xaymaca, lay like a fresh water pearl upon a vivid blue sea. Several mountain ranges crisscrossed it. Three large peaks sat in the middle—volcanoes, judging from their flattened tops. A strange face was drawn beneath the largest one and labeled *Los Buitres*.

Don Lope pointed at it. "The vein is there, is as wide as my arm, but the terrain is difficult, fraught with floods and mud slides. Still, it's worth mining rather than scratching away at the gold as the native dogs have done."

She ignored the slur. "*Los Buitres*—the vultures. Surely, a name of ill omen."

"It comes from native superstition. They believe a man-eating god lives there. Handy, if you want rivals to avoid the place. As I said, spilled blood affects the land. The gold in this pouch is almost pure."

"How do you plan to remove it?"

"Slaves. Unfortunately, my men were a little too zealous in teaching the natives a lesson. They decimated the population, although I understand there may still be pockets of them in hiding."

A tiny scrabbling came from the window. Miriam glanced through the lace curtains. There was still no sign of Joachin or a rescue party. The noise came again, closer this time.

Don Lope didn't notice. He juggled the nuggets in his palm as if the sight of the gold might impress her. His smiled faded. His head shot up and he glared at her, accusing. "There are only five, here. Where's the sixth?"

Fear swamped her. "I don't know what you mean."

"You think I'm stupid? That I wouldn't know how many were in here? What kind of game are you playing?"

"I'm not playing a game! I don't know anything about a sixth nugget!"

"Do you know what I've done to natives who oppose me?" His eyes were wild. Terror pinned her to her seat. "I've hacked them to pieces, I've sliced open bellies. I've grabbed suckling infants from their mothers and dashed their brains out against rocks. Don't tempt me to do something like that to you!"

Miriam shook. For one tense moment, neither of them spoke. And then panic spurred her, forcing her to bolt. As she ran for the door, he lunged for her across the table, sending plates and goblets flying. She ducked out of reach, missing his fingers by inches. The door was locked. She darted aside as he clawed at her shoulder. The only way out was through the window.

As she ran for it, something small and grey leapt from the windowsill. She didn't stop to see what it was, only to register that it flew past her as she clambered onto the balcony. Don Lope howled from inside the room. The grey thing—a rat—clung to his knee by its teeth. He bellowed and bashed it with his fists, swinging his leg this way and that to dislodge it. As he danced and hollered, she leaned against the balcony's railing. The ground looked a long way down.

Alonso had never liked the taste of blood, but steadfastly held on, only to strike at Don Lope again when he was knocked from his hold. Miriam was through the window. *Good, she's escaping,* he thought. He struggled frantically as hands wrapped about his chest.

He couldn't breathe, his strength was spent. A pain, sharp and immediate, pierced him; he felt his ribs crack and his heart burst. He was too stunned to scream. Bright colour filled his vision as he felt his life spiral like water down a dark drain.

No! he cried in despair, as death claimed him. There was no way to stave off the inevitable. His last thoughts were of the god's words: *you will suffer death over and over, Alonso.* Which meant he would return to Miriam again, but with no way of knowing how or when.

Chapter Ten: Love Knot

There was nothing for it, but to leap from the balcony. Behind her, Don Lope throttled the rat as it attacked him. Below, the local men in the street had seen her. They grinned and shouted for her to jump—Come, *bella*, we will catch you! She swallowed, hoping they would cushion her fall. She stepped over the balcony's railing and leapt, landing on heads and shoulders. The men tore at her as if she were a prize to be won at a *feria*.

"She's mine! I had her first!" A hefty lout clamped her about the waist. She thrust his hands away as a contender clouted him across the head. He staggered as she fell. Two more men grabbed her by the arms.

"Let me go!" she shrieked.

"Hold her!" Don Lope yelled from above. His head disappeared inside the window. Within seconds, his guards would charge from the *taverna* and claim her.

She fought the two who held her. They grinned, enjoying the sport. She lashed out and kicked the one on her right in the shin. He swore and drew a fist to punch her. His partner shouted an alarm as someone yanked her out of the way. There was a flash of metal and a spray of red. In astonishment, she stared as Joachín gutted the brute. Then he pulled the knife free and slashed it across the throat of her second captor before she could blink. More blood spattered in its wake. Barto was nearby, knocking heads like they were puppets. Iago swung a torch to clear the crowd. The locals backed away, unwilling to risk their skins against three madmen. Don Lope's toughs appeared at the *bordello's* entrance.

"Run!" Joachín shouted as he pulled her by the hand. Don Lope's guards were trained fighters, not drunkards brawling in the street. Iago swung his brand to clear a path. Behind them, Barto threw locals into the guards' path as if tossing horseshoes onto a forge.

Joachín drew her down too many streets to count. They lost track of Iago and Barto, but she suspected this was what they had planned. It was harder to chase multiple quarries. As the afternoon wore on, they found themselves in a residential part of Marabel. Eventually, they scaled a wall with difficulty and entered a small, vacant garden. In the dying light, Joachín's head had grown slick. The gash across his temple had reopened. He collapsed against the stone wall to catch his breath. She caught him as he slid down it. "Joachín!"

His eyes fluttered. "I'm all right. I just have to rest."

He wasn't all right. He was nearing collapse. In a dim corner, a fountain burbled. She dipped her hands into the basin and returned to him with a palmful of water. "Drink," she said. "You've lost a lot of blood." His hands shook as she helped him. "We need to wash that cut," she insisted.

He protested, but he was too weak to stop her. As she scooped water over his head, she sensed his exhaustion. There was something else— shame. He had failed her.

"There," she said, keeping her voice light so he wouldn't suspect she knew. "If we wash your face, you'll feel better." She knew she shouldn't fuss so much; it would unman him. He didn't argue, but insisted on stumbling to the fountain on his own so he might swab himself clean.

There was a lone candle shining in the window of the nearby house. Whoever owned the *casa* might soon discover them. They needed to leave. "Do you think Barto and Iago got away?" she asked softly.

He nodded, closed his eyes. "I expect so. We should make our way back."

"In a minute. Thank you for rescuing me, Joachín." It was important to salvage his pride—even if he didn't deserve it.

He winced. "I shouldn't have had to."

"But you did. That's all that matters."

"It was my fault...."

It was, but they didn't need to dwell on it. He had accepted his responsibility. "Shhh. It's done."

They rested for another ten minutes before making their way back to *Casa* Olivares. The water restored him greatly. He seemed to know his way which didn't surprise her. As they walked, she realized there was much she didn't know about him. Her life in Granad had been simple. Until the Grand Inquisitor arrived, she and Ephraim, her father, had lived very well. Joachín, on the other hand, had been an orphan since eleven. He had lived in the streets and alleys of Talede, a hard town. She recalled the icy fury with which he had struck the two who had accosted her. His dispatch had been terrible and quick, but it had also been...exciting.

Never, could she admit this to him. It was bad enough admitting it to herself. As for her need to soothe—there had been more to that than duty. Even from the start, she had found him attractive, had been drawn to him.

Love him or deny him, the goddess had said.

How much longer could she deny what she felt?

But I don't love him! she insisted, as if the goddess listened. What she felt for him wasn't the love she had for Alonso. She glanced at Joachín sidelong. He was a constant distraction. She wanted to draw closer to him, to bask in his warmth. *This thing may not be love*, she reflected, *but it's as potent.*

Never could she let him know.

They came to a passageway so narrow it couldn't accommodate them both. Joachín set a hand to her elbow. The sudden contact with her skin made her catch her breath. He was feeling protective, worried. "What is it?" she asked, glancing past him.

"Stay here while I make sure it's safe."

"Don't leave me." The admission was out before she could stop it. Too much had happened, she didn't want to be alone for even a second.

He glanced at her and reconsidered. "All right. Hopefully, Barto and Iago have collected the women and they've gone on."

She had forgotten about Maia and the baby. "Did Maia deliver?"

He nodded. "Yes. Barto wouldn't have come with me, otherwise."

He peered into the narrow walkway before them. Rough bricks protruded like warts from the wall. He squeezed her hand. She swallowed, too aware he enjoyed being her protector. "Follow me, then. This way leads to *Casa* Olivares. Stay close."

They slipped into the cleft. She clung to his hand. His strength was returning as if her trust in him restored it. They made their way and came to the alley fronting the house. Joachín peered around the corner. He ducked back immediately as someone shouted, "There he is! I saw him!" It sounded like *Sera* Olivares.

He thrust her ahead him. "Go! She's called the Watch on us."

There was a clatter of hooves and the thump of boots on cobblestone. The soldiers couldn't ride into the alley, but they could chase them on foot. As they fled, they heard the sound of metal—swords—scraping on stone behind them. Why had *Sera* Olivares reported them? Miriam didn't have time to dwell on it.

They bolted from the walkway and stumbled into the larger street. Joachín grabbed her and soon they were running around corners and into alleys. At one point he forced her up a ladder, and they skittered along a roof. In her desperation not to fall, she sent a tile hurtling over the edge. As it struck the ground, it smashed into shards. Joachín held onto her tightly. They kept moving.

Finally, he leapt from a stable's roof and onto a stack of hay. He caught her as she fell. For a moment they lay together panting. Then he rose and pulled her into a dark shed, where they were less exposed. They leaned against the wall to catch their breaths and listen for pursuit. There was none. Without warning, he groaned and caught her head in his hands. He kissed her, no longer able to contain himself.

Her legs buckled. The taste of his tongue set her on fire. She didn't know where his lips ended or hers began. She pressed against him, needing him as much as he needed her. Part of her recognized that she was reacting to his desire, but she also wanted this, she wanted him. They had escaped, but they had also come too close to death. Life was precious, and so was he. He fumbled with her dress. She helped him, hating Zara's weeds.

Between kisses, they struggled, pulling at each other's' clothes. When they were free of them, they stared at each other briefly. She swallowed. His body was lean and compact. His tattoo made him look wild, primal. He seemed to think the same thing of her. He pulled her into his arms and burned a line of kisses down her neck, trailing a string of them to her breasts. She clutched his head and held him, attacking him with kisses as well, loving the taste of sweat on his shoulders. The tang of blood from one of his cuts made her pause, turning her momentarily tender. He didn't notice and drew her on top of him, cupping her buttocks with sure hands.

His erection startled her. He was hot and stiff. She gasped, surprised and breathless. His desire inflamed her. And then, for no reason she could discern, he pulled her down to his side. She sensed the thought—it was too soon, too quick. He had to wait.

"No!" she told him fiercely. "Love me, now!"

"Not yet."

She clawed at him, not believing he could resist her. He crushed her mouth and let his tongue do what the rest of him promised. He slid on top of her and rocked between her legs, not entering, but pressing and prodding. She became so frustrated she wanted to bite him.

"I've made a mess of so much, my Miriam," he said, breaking their kiss. The friction against her maidenhead made her moan. She wanted him there, inside, bearing down.

"Not so fast, my love. I have to do this right." He nuzzled her neck and kissed it, cupping a hand between her legs.

"Why?" she gasped.

His fingers found her maidenhead. She lurched in revolt. "Because I want to make sure it's as perfect for you as it will be for me."

He would make her weep with frustration. How could he deny her? She had been with Alonso, but technically, she was still a virgin. She let him have his way and soon found his instincts were correct. She whimpered and encouraged him. With him, she was no longer a woman. She was an animal.

When he finally entered her, she climaxed. She rose and thrust with him, crying for more, wanting him to love her, always. It wasn't like the time she had been with Alonso. How could it be? This was primal, of the flesh. *He's mine*, she thought, as she convulsed. Her body and mind soared, she floated beyond the stable in which they lay. He thrust to his own climax and sent her spinning heavenward a second time—the gift of the *sentidora*, the experience of what others felt. The *little death*, Alonso had called it. Joachín groaned and collapsed in her arms.

There is no past and no future, she thought as she held him tightly. *Only this moment. Only Joachín and me. Alonso is gone, but Joachín is here. Let us stay wrapped in each other forever.*

Chapter Eleven: Long Range Plans

"Don't insult my intelligence! I *know* you're one of her spies, so let's not play at striking pells any longer. You can report to her that I am accommodated to embracing the faith, that I *will* attend the Mass regularly and do whatever else I must to please her." Ilysabeth's brown eyes, normally so dull, blazed with autumnal fire. Her red hair, peeping from beneath her cowl, framed her pale face like a crown.

For a moment only, he was tempted to negate her charge, to continue to pretend with her as he had done for some time.

She rubbed her forehead with a shaking hand. "I am so very tired," she admitted. Her next few words were barely audible. "Almost to the point where I would be done with it."

"Lady—"

"Princess!"

"Princess. I...it sorrows me to hear you say this."

"Does it? Why? Aren't you *her* toad?"

"I am no one's toad."

"What then, Priest? Oh, spare me. You're the Papal Nuncio, brought from Roma to turn me from my father's evil ways. I am sick to the death from the hearing of them. Leave me in peace."

"We have another hour, at least—"

"*Sul's Blood!* Then I shall sleep while you drone on." In a most unlady-like manner, she slumped to her couch, not caring that he remained sitting uncomfortably at her side. It was a position that invited seduction, beyond all ties to sanity.

He looked down upon her with concern. In spite of her closed eyes, she was trying hard to keep her lips from trembling. Beneath those pale eyelids, she was close to tears. In all the weeks that he had been assigned to her, he had never seen her this close to breaking. She had been staunch, spirited, as her father had been, but even here, shielded as she was from the outside world, word must have come to her about the burnings. This show of temper hid what she feared most, that her own death was imminent.

He shifted awkwardly, unsure of what to do. She was beautiful, a thing that had not been lost upon him from the beginning, which was also a strangeness in itself. It surprised him he was reacting to her so. Was that why they had assigned him to her? That they thought he was beyond the reach of her charms? No secret remained hidden forever. They knew he preferred men, but there was something about her that caught him, made him want to clasp her in his arms and promise that all would be well. Did she wield that same glamoury her mother was rumoured to ply? Gods! Lying there, as she was, she was completely at his mercy. The truth of it was, he was completely at hers.

He swallowed. "Perhaps there is something else we might do, Princess."

Her eyes flew open. Those brown orbs seemed to possess the earth itself. She remained where she was, glaring at him and hating. Perhaps she had meant to tempt him. What better way to have him removed, than to accuse him of impropriety?

He cleared his throat. "I wasn't always a priest, you know."

She showed no interest. She didn't even blink.

"Before I took my vows, I was an actor in the *Commedia dell'arte*."

He expected that might spark a reaction, but no. Sul, what an iron will she had. "I used to play the part of Arlechinno. Here in Inglais, you might know him as Harlequin."

She sat up abruptly. The suddenness of her movement surprised him. Still, no verbal response, but at least he had her attention. "I thought...perhaps...that if you tired of the Book of Sul, that is, once we've completed our devotions, it might entertain you for me to perform...."

"You were an actor?"

"Yes—"

"How is it that a Papal Nuncio and priest of Sul was once an actor?"

"It's a long and dull story."

She insisted on hearing it. Of course, he didn't tell her everything. Much of his life had been unseemly. But those deep brown eyes had already witnessed a great deal of violence in her young life. He suspected she guessed more about him than he was willing to say. When he had shared enough to satisfy her curiosity, she demanded that he should bring a mask and cap to play Arlechinno the very next day. She, in her turn, would play Columbine to his Harlequin.

"Surely, it is more fitting for you to play Isabella, Highness. Like you, she is young, and beautiful, and Isabella is a variation of your name—"

"An Inamorata? Don't talk nonsense, Brother Francis. I will play Columbine, a serving girl, for that is what I am." He wondered if she said this for the benefit of any spies listening, for of course, there were others besides himself. "I serve my kingdom," she added smoothly, "as I serve my Queen. It is proper and fitting that I should do so, as deemed by the order of our birth."

"You are much more than a servant, Princess—"

"I am not. For me, Columbine will do nicely."

He considered her with growing respect. All of what they did would be reported to Maria. And Maria, considering how much she hated her royal half-sister, would laugh at how Ilysabeth had been brought to kneel so low.

"Oh, Arlechinno! What fools Isabella and Florindo be!" Ilysabeth warbled, setting a finger to her chin. To his amazement, she winked at him. It passed so quickly he almost missed her doing it. Fortunately, he knew where all the spy holes were, and any of those watching would not have seen it. For some reason, he suspected she knew where they were, too. He should have warned her against a scenario that spoke of those two ridiculous innamorati. It could be argued that she had referenced Maria and Felipe to mock them, but too late, the taunt was out. She had said it.

"Why, not so, Mistress!" he denied, hoping to recover her fumble in judgement.

"Why, yes so, Dunce! Saints preserve me forever from such a fate! Love is a disease that ends only in despair!"

She had turned to him as if to throw that sauciness in his face, her nose inches from his, the consummate actress, a perfect Columbine. Instead of a princess, he saw a fiery seraph, a red-haired succubus who claimed him then and there, body and soul. It stunned him, took his breath away. The urge to kiss her became overwhelming. The last time he had kissed a woman, it had been his mother and he had been eight. Shortly thereafter, his world had gone up in flames. His physical inclinations, whatever they had been, were irrevocably changed. Or so he thought.

The ground dipped beneath him, and Ilysabeth vanished. He woke, wondering what it might have been like to kiss her when a pair of well-honed buttocks hove into view. Reality re-established itself. Rodrigo—Captain Morales was bending over to grab his breeches. They had fallen from the chair where he had dropped them the night before. In his hurry, he tripped over Francisco's habit to reach them.

Francisco drew in a deep breath. His dream of Ilysabeth...an after-effect of the burundarra, no doubt. The blue powder hadn't drugged him as it had Morales, but even to breathe the smallest amount affected one's dreams.

Best let him leave without a 'good morning'. Through cracked eyes, he watched the escaping captain. With false memories of manly love implanted in his mind, Morales would have reached his limit. *It almost makes me want to comfort him,* Francisco thought. He continued to feign sleep, but was still prepared should Morales decide to attack him.

The captain seemed more bent on retreat than murder. As he shut the door softly behind him, Francisco relaxed, but lay where he was, setting both Morales and Ilysabeth aside to review the night before. The Ferraras had been released. He had found their names in the notary's notes. The fool had left them on his desk, out in the open for anyone to find. Rana Isadore remained in custody. He still didn't know where Tomás had hidden her. At four in the morning, he had given up the search to return to his suite to snuggle one-sidedly with Rodrigo. Not a moment too soon, for Umberto, Tomás's chamberlain, had entered their room five minutes later to check on them. The monk held his cresset lamp high, smirked and left, assuming they had partaken of the tainted wine and each other. He would report their dalliance to Tomás.

None of that was important. What was, was he had finally found his witch.

He had to snatch Rana Isadore from Tomás's grasp, convince her to support Ilysabeth's claim to the throne. The best way to do that was to give her what she wanted—revenge against her rival, Miriam Medina.

But...how smart would that be, if the Medina girl were the stronger witch?

If one witch was good, two would be even better. And chances were one would lead to the other.

You're getting ahead of yourself, Francis, he thought. *Outwit Tomás first, and then we'll see what comes after.*

Chapter Twelve: Reunion

Miriam and Joachín slept for a few hours. As the sky pearled, they made love again, but it was lazily done. They were still drunk on their earlier passion. At one point, Joachín traced his fingers over her tattoos. Unlike Anassa's markings which had been works of art, Miriam's were crudely done—first by herself in an attempt to resurrect Alonso, and then when Anassa had shielded her from Tomás.

"Did those hurt?" Joachín propped himself on an elbow and looked down at her.

"No. I was too panicked to notice at the time."

"Guillermo once told me all Diaphani women mark themselves."

"They do." She smiled. "But I never thought I'd be one of them."

He drew a small circle about the tiny arc that lay between her breasts. "This one looks like a little moon."

"It's my birthmark."

"A goddess mark."

She didn't want to think about Lys. His face was a mass of cuts from the beating he had received. To distract him, she drew him into a wet embrace, intent on kissing away every hurt.

An hour later, they agreed it was best to be on their way. They had to find the Tribe, to see how everyone fared. They reassured themselves Barto, Iago, and the women would have escaped, otherwise they would have been held by the Watch. They stopped often to kiss as they stepped into their clothes. A shadow of new beard blurred the cuts on Joachin's face. She marveled at his ability to dismiss his pain. He was smiling, as if all was well with the world. As they walked, she felt sore and tender in disturbing places. It was different for men, she supposed.

He noticed she was having trouble keeping up. "All you all right?"

"Fine."

"It isn't far. Do you want to rest for a moment?"

"No. Where are we going? Surely, not the town gate."

"There's a place where we can climb the wall without being seen. It will bring us close to where we left the Tribe. Hopefully, they've waited."

One foot after the other, Miriam, she told herself. Hopefully, exercise would ease things. She'd been so quick to suggest exercise for others in the past, although not for this particular reason. She thought longingly of the horse they might have stolen from the nearby shed. She smirked. What a hypocrite she was.

"What is it?" Joachin asked.

"Me."

"You?" He threw an arm around her shoulders and gave her a squeeze. "Well, I can't think of anyone more wonderful."

"But I'm not."

"I beg your pardon?"

"Wonderful. I'm...not." How to explain their lovemaking had nearly crippled her? That thievery wasn't so bad an option if it might ease her discomfort? She choked on a laugh and groaned. Joachin stared at her as if she had lost her wits. "I'm a little...uncomfortable this morning."

"Oh!" He grasped her meaning. "Is there anything I can do? If the wall's too difficult, we can find another way."

"No. I was thinking of stealing a horse. Of how it might help." Unable to stop herself, she sniggered.

He stared at her in astonishment and laughed. "You *are* love mad!" He looked immensely pleased with himself. "Of course, it only happens when you've been with a magnificent lover." He set an arm about her waist to help her to walk.

She smiled. "Is that so, Doctor?"

"It is. I have seen it many times."

Her smile disappeared. "So, you've had many patients in the past?" She stopped, set her hands on her hips.

He swallowed, looking uneasy. "A few, but that shouldn't concern you." He set a hand to her elbow to get her moving but failed to budge her.

"Why is that?"

"Because I am also love mad. And only for you. And you should know I'm telling you the truth, because I can't lie."

Appeased, that earned him a kiss.

The town wall wasn't as awkward as she expected. Their escape route lay beneath tall cypresses on either side. Thick branches helped them ascend. By the sun's rise, they were on their way, heading down the road to where they had left the Tribe. By mid-morning, they found everyone huddled around a miserable fire. Iago jumped up with his knife drawn to confront them.

"Oh," he said in relief, setting the blade back into its sheath. "It's you two, thank the gods."

Luci looked as if she hadn't slept. "I was so worried." She drew up to them and hugged them both.

"I told you they'd be all right," Iago replied.

"Did Maia and Barto make it back?" Miriam glanced about the camp. Barto's wagon sat beneath the trees beyond the fire. A tarp, of sorts, covered the rig's top and sides.

"They're all in there, sleeping," Zara said. "It was a tough birth. When the baby came, he came fast. We had to cut her. She agreed to the tattoo, so it's all for the best. They're Tribe, now. How did you two make out?"

"Fine." Joachin glanced away. Miriam refused to meet her eyes, but not before Zara caught her blushing. She hated being so transparent.

"Oh! *I see!*" Zara nodded at the other women as if to say, *I told you so.* Tiny smiles sprouted on everyone's faces like violets in springtime. Miriam held her retort in check. Her people were happy, life transpired as they thought it should. She and Joachin were now a pair. To Zara and the rest, their union confirmed the goddess watched over them.

Joachin was my choice, she thought with annoyance. It didn't help to admit Lys might have been right about them being matriarch and patriarch among other things. Joachin fulfilled her in a way she had never expected. Her passion for Alonso was still strong, but her desire for Joachin was as potent. The demarcations of love had blurred.

"Time to break camp," she said stiffly, ignoring their grins.

Chapter Thirteen: Uneasy Suspicion

Consciousness **returned** **to** Alonso as the sun struck
the rat's bloody and broken body. It lay on a trash heap behind
the *Crowing Cock*. He rose from it abruptly and tried to regain his
bearings. In tight spirals, he turned, a dust devil scattering dirt in all
directions. There was a strong pull to the south. Worry gnawed at
him, like teeth on bone.

She's no longer in Marabel. She's escaped, thank Sul, he thought.

He lifted on the morning breeze and claimed the sky like an eagle
in flight. Soon, the tiled roofs of Marabel passed beneath him in
cluttered disarray. At the town's southern perimeter, cliffs plunged to
a river far below. He soared over it, heading south-east. Far beyond,
the waves of the sea sparkled in the sun.

It didn't take him long to spot the Tribe. They skirted the south
road like ants on a pilgrimage, choosing not to travel openly. He
dropped from the heights and dove for the first pair of riders. Miriam
sat behind Joachín de Rivera. Surely, she could have ridden with

someone else or even handled her own horse, especially after all the trouble the fool had caused.

Alonso floated as close as he dared, not wanting to make her shiver. A faint smile touched her lips. She looked happy, as if the Tribe were on a pleasant outing rather than running from Torch Bearers. Joachín de Rivera also seemed to be in high spirits. Why? They were very...at ease...with one another.

Actually, *at ease* wasn't quite the right description. They looked.... *No*, he thought, dismissing it. *She hates him. She blames him for everything that's happened, and so she should. He's a lowlife, a cutpurse, a womanizer.*

Joachín leaned back to murmur something into her ear. Miriam pressed against him, so she might hear him better. She held him a little longer about the waist than Alonso thought necessary. Joachín gave her hand a quick squeeze.

Alonso froze. *Surely not*, he thought. *All he's managed to do is convince her that he's honourable, somehow. He's made excuses about what happened in Marabel. She'll come back to her senses, soon enough.*

But what to do, in the meantime? If he found a sickly animal nearby, it would take all of his strength to keep up with the Tribe. He would have to wait until they camped for the night. Then he'd find some poor creature to possess and finally be reunited with Miriam.

And when she sees I've come back, all will be well, he told himself.

How could it be otherwise?

Chapter Fourteen: A Dole of Doves

Francisco didn't see Tomás for the rest of the day, but he learned from a gossipy monk that Rana Isadore had spent the night in the Grand Inquisitor's suite. Between Sext and None, Francisco retraced his steps and searched for spy holes he might have missed earlier, hoping to find one that would show him what they were doing. He finally found one in the *garderobe* adjoining Sol Benaviddes' study, plugged with a thin wedge of wood, the end of which had been sloppily painted to match the mortar. Out of paranoia, mean spiritedness, or a want for secrecy, Tomás had evicted the high priest from his own rooms. Which made it handier for Francisco to observe, so long as no one discovered him there.

He retrieved a hidden stiletto from the top of his boot, a tool he found useful for all sorts of situations. A piece of wood still blocked the other end of the spy hole. It would be risky re-opening it, but there was nothing for it; the wood would splinter and fall. If anyone noticed it, his escape time was limited. There were no windows in the *garderobe*, only a short passage that led to the outer room. He couldn't miss this opportunity; the day had yielded no new information. Tomás would not waste time in determining the extent of Rana Isadore's power. He had to know what it was.

I would not want to be Rana Isadore, this day, Francisco considered as he jabbed at the hole.

Ten minutes later, he had managed to poke a large enough opening to see through the wall. At first glance, all he detected was a room with a vacated bed, but luck was with him. Through a far doorway, Tomás and a shrouded woman sat at a table. She could only be Rana Isadore. Either she, or Tomás, had chosen to hide her hideousness beneath a veil.

"When do I get my necklace back?" she asked meekly. Unlike her bold demeanor from the night before, she now seemed cowed.

"When you satisfy my requirements."

"I...I thought I did."

"Bed sport doesn't qualify."

Francisco squinted. Tomás fingered a strand of what looked like oddly shaped beads around his neck. Wait—they weren't beads, but bones. Human?

Umberto appeared, holding a cage of white doves. "Where do you want these?"

Tomás tucked the necklace inside his habit. "On the table."

"Anything else?"

"Refreshments, for afterwards."

Umberto nodded and set the cage down.

"What of our papal nuisance?" Tomás asked.

"Last I saw, he was heading to afternoon Mass. I haven't seen him since."

"You're supposed to be watching him."

"I can't watch and fetch birds at the same time."

"Keep him busy. I don't want him nosing about. Wait. Before you go, make up the bed."

Umberto scowled but said nothing. As he entered the bed chamber, Francisco held his breath. If the old monk glanced up at the wall, he would see the hole. Umberto shuffled about the bed, tucking in sheets.

Just finish and go, Francisco prayed.

The monk picked up the velvet pillows from the floor and set them against the headboard. Then he reached down and pinched something between his thumb and forefinger. Wood splinters. He glanced up and peered at the hole.

Francisco didn't wait for his shout, but bolted from the *garderobe* and into the outer room where he had pried open a window, just in case. He threw his leg over the sill, praying the outer ledge would hold him as he slammed the window shut. He fell out of sight as Tomás and Umberto burst into the room.

Chapter Fifteen: Wedded Bliss

Joachín brought the Tribe to a halt at sunset. The sky had turned pink. They set camp beneath a grove of wild almond trees. A stream gurgled nearby, promising fish. The air was warm, which buoyed everyone's spirits.

"Joachín and I are taking a short walk," Miriam advised Luci after their dinner of almonds and trout. Luci smiled indulgently. Despite the sadness and misery she had endured, she showed remarkable stamina, Miriam thought, like all of the Tribe's women.

"Take your time. Don't hurry," Luci said.

"We're going to see if we can spot the sea." She hated that it sounded like an excuse, but that's what Joachín had suggested. If they were able to spy the ocean, they'd have a good idea of how far they needed to go come morning.

Zara wagged a finger at them. "If you're gone more than two hours, I'll come looking."

Joachín waggled a finger back. "Don't you dare, Zara."

"We won't be long." Miriam found Zara's assumptions embarrassing. She grabbed Joachín by the arm to haul him away, and then reconsidered. She didn't want them to look too familiar. He caught her fingers anyway and kissed them.

"They all know," he whispered. "Don't let it bother you."

"She always presumes...."

"And what she presumes is right. Let her be happy for us."

"We *are* going to look at the sea, aren't we?"

"Unless you'd rather do something else."

"No!"

He chuckled, squeezing her. "I'm only teasing, *cielo*. Our private life is our own, as much as we can keep it."

They had come to the brow of the hill. He drew her to the top. A few stars had come out, and further off Miriam thought she saw the roll of sluggish waves.

"There. See them?" He wrapped his arms about her and smelled her hair.

She nodded, content. "At times like this, I feel as if the Inquisition is a thousand leagues away. Maybe we'll escape Tomás, forever."

"That's a good hope. I like the idea of starting fresh, of travelling to a new land."

"I like it, too." She snuggled into him, basking in his warmth. "Do you think it's as beautiful there as it is here? This is a lovely place."

"I wanted to show it to you."

That surprised her. "Really? Why?"

"This was one of the places where I dreamt of you, before we met. You were in Batos, running from the Torch Bearers."

"You dreamt that, here?"

"Not here, exactly, but under one of those almond trees."

"Have you had any dreams of us, since?"

"Not since the one about our son."

The thought of having his child no longer disturbed her, but the fact that he hadn't dreamed any more true dreams was worrisome. She was no longer a functioning seer. Without his dreams, they travelled blind. "Why haven't you had any more, I wonder?"

"Because all of them have come true." He kissed her. The moment lengthened. She considered taking Luci's suggestion. There was no need to hurry—they had time. If they slipped away now, Zara would never find them.

Joachín broke their embrace. "Time for us to get back."

"Why?" The abrupt departure of his kiss left her dizzy.

"Because we have to return to the camp."

"But...we just got here!"

"I've planned something."

He would say no more of it, even when she pestered him. By the time they returned to the camp, the Tribe had formed a semi-circle around the fire. Ximen stood before them. Everyone was grinning hugely.

"Go on." Joachín pushed her toward Ximen.

She frowned at him, not liking surprises. "What is this all about?"

Ximen beckoned her forward, his pale eyes gleaming in the dusk. "I have a request, Matriarch," he said, as she approached him.

"Oh?" She glanced at Zara, wondering what new demand she had made. The potion-maker shook her head. Luci covered a smile with a hand.

"It is a solemn thing. Not to be entered lightly," Ximen said. "We grieve that your father, Ephraim, can't be with us to grant his blessing. Therefore, consent lies solely with you. Earlier today, the Patriarch approached me."

Joachín had spoken briefly with Ximen when they had stopped to water the horses. She assumed they had discussed where they would camp for the night.

"He wishes to declare his love for you and to formalize your relationship in marriage. I am happy to accommodate him, if you agree. Joachín de Rivera Montoya, step forward."

Her mouth fell open. Behind her, Joachín removed his shirt.

"You have something to say?" Ximen prompted.

"I do." He walked up to her with his shirt in his hands, as if it were a poor and humble gift. "I say that the Goddess of Love ordains we be together as husband and wife. If she decrees it, we must obey."

"You wish to marry me because Lys ordains it?" Miriam set her hands on her hips. Where was his confession of love? Deep down, she knew her brusqueness was only to cover her embarrassment, her invasion of privacy in a public setting.

"Lys knows our hearts," he replied, unruffled. "She gives us not only what is best, but what we also desire. She knows we can't do her will if there is no sweet return."

"If she will have me," he continued, addressing the Tribe but not taking his eyes from her, "I promise to love Miriam, to serve, and protect her, to be Patriarch to her Matriarch, to lead the Tribe at her side for as long as we both shall live. I will be true to her, and to her, alone. I will be husband to her, if she will be my wife."

Instead of the traditional roses that would have been sewn there, his shirt was discoloured with blood. Those stains were more precious to her than rubies set in gold. He dropped to one knee and knotted it tightly about her hips. "Will you do me the honour?" he asked. His voice broke. To her surprise, he looked tense.

Did he actually think she might say no? She loved him—of course, she did. Now that he had confessed his love publicly, she knew it to be true. It wasn't what she had felt for Alonso, but it was love, nonetheless. Perhaps passion was as individual as the people who felt it. "Yes," she replied, her voice catching. "I will. And you do me the honour, too." She pulled him to his feet and kissed him soundly, no longer caring who watched.

The Tribe burst into cheers.

Chapter Sixteen: Ardillo

Alonso couldn't decide whether the squirrel was sleeping
or hibernating. He didn't think the latter; the weather was too
warm. Perhaps the creature was old. It breathed slowly; its heart beat
haphazardly. Dusk was falling. Red squirrels were supposed to be
active at night, weren't they?

Becoming a squirrel wasn't the perfect solution—he wasn't sure
what was—but it would have to do. Miriam would recall their night in
the Womb when he had spoken to her about riding a squirrel from
tree to tree. The branches had swayed crazily. The ride had left him
breathless. The creature would charm her—it wasn't a filthy rat. As the
squirrel, she would see he had returned in a moment.

The Tribe was cheering about something. In the midst of all of their
suffering, they still found something to celebrate. He was glad for
them. Perhaps later, he would find out what it was.

Wake up. He prodded the squirrel. The creature stirred a bit, but it
was so sleepy it drifted off. He pressed himself into the limp body,
and then hung on tightly to its heart, expecting it to react. Instead,

he found himself wrapped inside a snug squirrel blanket. And that blanket had no inclination to move.

What is wrong with you? He hated to torment it, but he had to make it leave its nest. He imagined the talons of a great horned owl, narrowly missing its back. The squirrel twitched and gasped. It bolted awake and fell from its perch, but caught hold of a lower branch. He envisioned the owl again. Blood rushed to his head as the squirrel fled down the trunk. Now that he had awakened it, he saw why it slept. Every joint of the poor thing ached.

They were three-quarters of the way down the tree, when its front legs gave out from beneath it. They tumbled to the ground and landed badly on a root, where the squirrel wedged a front paw beneath its chest. Alonso pulled at the offending foot. The squirrel whistled in pain. They had sprained it in the fall.

There was a crunch of leaves. Something huge leaned over them. It had mammoth legs and scarecrow hair.

"Are you hurt, little squirrel?" Casi Montoya reached out a hand to pick them up. The squirrel lacked the strength to stop her.

There was dancing. Miriam followed Joachin as best she could. The Tribe sang and clapped for them before taking their turns. Sparks rose into the night sky. After several hours, she drooped with exhaustion and happiness. She wanted to be alone with her husband. They needed to sleep. At least, for a few hours.

"We've made a tent for you." Luci pulled her aside as Joachin took a turn with Zara around the fire. She pointed at a rough tent they had constructed from bent willows and quilts.

"But you need the blankets for the children!"

"They'll be fine. It's your first night as a married woman. You and Joachin need some privacy."

She continued to protest, but Luci refused to listen. Even Maia, nursing little Grimwald, insisted that Miriam enjoy their first night.

"Barto will keep the fire going until morning." She held her baby close. "It's our gift to you. I wish we could give you more."

Joachín joined her. "Best to be gracious about it, *cielo*. They won't have it any other way. Come on. It's time we bid everyone a good night."

A chorus of well wishes followed them. To Miriam's surprise, Zara looked wistful, as if caught up in the romance of the moment. Joachín lifted the corner of the blanket that served as their door. She ducked inside. He crawled in beside her and let the tent flap fall.

For a moment, they sat in silence, listening to their people. Someone laughed—Iago, it sounded like. Their Tribe was happy. Their marriage had been an opportunity for joy.

He stroked her cheek with a tender finger. She turned to him and slid her arms about him. As he kissed her, they fell onto the quilts. His kisses inflamed her, but she knew she wouldn't last.

"I'm sorry," she murmured. "With everything that's happened—I have no energy left. I wish I did, my husband, but I don't."

"We've only been married a few hours and already, you tire of me?"

"Of course not!"

He kissed her forehead. "I'm only teasing, *querida*. I'll wake you in a few hours."

"Not if I wake you, first."

"I'd like that. And it will be better then, too. All those listening ears will be asleep."

She choked. "They wouldn't! Would they?"

"Of course, they would. Zara, especially. I can't decide whether we should be as quiet as mice or put on a show."

"You aren't serious." She looked at him worriedly.

"When it comes to you, I am always serious, *cielo*."

"Oh, you." She poked him playfully in the chest and turned on her side.

He chuckled and nuzzled her ear. "Sweet dreams, my Miriam," he whispered. Snuggling against her, he pulled her close.

"You, too," she replied, happy that his arms were around her and feeling more contented with life than she ever thought possible.

"You'll be cozy in this sack," Casi promised Alonso. He had had no energy to fend her off, nor did he want to use his only weapons available—his teeth and claws.

"I've put some nuts and grass in there for you, so you can eat," Casi said. "I'll get you water in the morning."

The damp cage closed in on him as she pulled the drawstrings tight. Then, thinking better of it, she loosened the neck a little. "So you can breathe," she whispered. "Don't run away, okay?"

The least of my worries, he thought.

He suffered a moment of vertigo as she lifted the bag into the air. It was stuffy and lurched like a leaking raft. His poor paw throbbed. The squirrel licked it, which made them both feel a little better. Surprisingly, the squirrel was no longer terrified. It saw him as a nest mate. His lack of fear in their shared accommodation comforted it. Perhaps he should give in to its need to nap. When everything was quiet, they would have more strength, they could force the sack's opening, or chew their way out. After that, he would find Miriam, wherever she slept.

And then—it would almost be as before. Whenever they touched, he would live in her mind, and she in his. He would turn her back into a seer. He could leave the squirrel's body periodically to search for the Guard. They would grow old, together. He would stay with her until she passed.

And when death becomes too great a burden for you, Alonso, you will return to me.

Not without my Miriam, he thought, closing his eyes.

Joachin contented himself with watching Miriam snore. She would be mortified if he told her, but the sound pleased him. She made a soft buzz like a happy bee. He shifted his weight slightly. She rolled onto her back. As her breathing leveled out, he cuddled next to her and marvelled that she lay there.

You have one hour, wife, and then I wake you with kisses. He nuzzled her neck and breathed into her hair.

Sleep didn't come right away, so he settled onto his back and made plans. They had seven days to reach Qadis. Providing nothing went wrong, that gave them time enough to work somewhere for a day, so they would have a bit of coin for the New World. Pray to Lys *Ser* Olivares had arranged for their passages aboard the *Phoenix*.

Herradur was the closest village to them from here, but not a good choice. Inez was there. Rufio, the whaler he had beaten, also. Old dalliances never appreciated new wives, nor new wives, old loves. Best to avoid Herradur, altogether.

Bacalao was further along the coast. If they didn't waste time, they could make it in a day. It would be no lie to tell Miriam it was better to head there. It also put them that much closer to Qadis. Hopefully, *Ser* Olivares had made the necessary arrangements in spite of the conflict with his mother. What had happened to set *Sera* Olivares off? He suspected it had to do with money. She had assumed they would pay her for the trouble and bother they had caused with Maia.

He closed his eyes and envisioned the New World. Once they had money, they could lease land and farm. Grow cane or keep cattle like the *hidalgos*. And of course there was the gold. He regretted losing the map. Three tall peaks in the middle of the island with a strange mask depicted near the largest. Was *Los Buitres* a name or a curse? Best to discuss it with Iago and Barto in the morning.

He drowsed in a no man's land for a time, and then he began to dream, but the dream was unlike any he had had before. Two scenes vied for prominence. They shifted back and forth, like alternating veils. One took precedence, and then the other.

In the first dream, his hands were in chains. A naval officer bawled at him to move. He held a whip and shook his fist—any more stalling, and they'd all earn the lash. He followed a line of black men up a gang plank, their destination, a slave ship.

In the second scene, a mob screamed about a pyre loaded with kindling. Tomás towered from a pulpit above the crowd. Miriam was pushed through the throng. This time, it was she who staggered beneath chains.

The scenes flitted back and forth, each a terrible nightmare. He was in chains and then she was.

What does it mean? Are these both fated, or only one of them? Lys provided no answers. A shriek broke his nightmare. He started awake.

Miriam was huddled against the side of their tent. Something brown and scrawny had crawled into her lap.

He slapped the vermin aside, and then grabbed his boot to strike it before it could bite her.

"Joachín! No!"

He pummeled it beneath his heel.

She shoved him aside and held the small, inert creature to her breasts. "Why did you do it, Joachín? Why did you kill him?" she wailed.

He stared at it, mystified. A squirrel. The thing trembled once and then went still. "Because it was attacking you! You were screaming!" He reached to take it from her. She leaned away from him, holding it close. She buried her face against it and wept.

He stared at her, stunned. What was the Tribe to think? She had screamed and pleaded with him on their wedding night.

"Alonso," she whispered, cradling the bloodied mat to her cheek.

There was no chance of making love to her now. They spent the next hour talking about what had happened.

"He's come back, Joachín. Or he would have if you hadn't...." She looked as if she were about to cry again.

He pinched his nose. She had said Alonso was gone. He had turned into a storm. She had grieved. Weren't dead men supposed to stay dead? "I don't understand."

"I don't expect you to. I don't understand it, myself. But it *was* him, Joachín. I felt him the moment he touched my hand. I cried out in shock."

"Perhaps it was only a dream."

"It wasn't a dream. I'd know him in any form."

He had managed to finally wrest the squirrel from her. As carefully as he could, he had set it outside their door. What did it mean? He doubted he would like it, once he knew.

"Alonso! I am so sorry!" She set her fingers to her lips and stared at the top of their tent.

Her belief that Alonso might still be with them in spirit was disturbing. "You think he's up here?"

"I don't know. Maybe."

"Miriam, that's unsettling. I can't have you talking to him whenever we're together. I'll feel as if a third party is watching us, listening."

"He loved me, Joachín, and I loved him."

"I know, but you're my wife, now. You're supposed to love me."

"I do. But have you never loved anyone else?"

For a fleeting second, he thought of Inez. "No. Well, my mother, of course."

"But you've had *other* women."

"Yes, but I never loved them."

"So, you slept with them but never loved them."

Dangerous territory. Not where he wanted to go. "It's different for men."

"How is it different?"

"This isn't something I want to discuss at the moment. You're my wife. That should count for something."

"It does, but I'm trying to make a point with you, Joachín. What would it be like if one of your past loves turned up? Wouldn't you be torn between her and me?"

"No. I wouldn't."

"But what if she were hurt? Or she needed you in some way? You'd never abandon a woman in need. Alonso is back, Joachín. What do you expect me to do?"

"Say you love me more."

For a moment, she said nothing. Then finally, "I can't."

He turned from her, hurt to the core. How could she say such a thing? This was their wedding night. He hadn't expected to be usurped by a dead squirrel. He was glad he had killed it. Given the chance, he would do it again.

"But I *can* say I love you differently."

He glanced at her sourly. "How?"

She caught his hands with hers. "You are my fire, Joachín. My hearth. You're warm and passionate. I love how immediate you are. You excite me. You make me think anything is possible. Alonso, on the other hand, was like water—life-giving, refreshing, pure. Like rain, he blessed everything he touched. I'm not surprised he turned into a storm."

"So I don't bless you?"

"You inflame me. You make me burn brighter."

He was tempted to point out that fire and water didn't mix, but kept that to himself. Best to get them off the topic of Alonso, entirely.

"My fire's burning, now. Let me light yours." He drew her close.

She stiffened. "Joachín, I don't think I can."

He flopped onto his back. "You think he's here? Right now?"

"I don't know."

"You're a *sentidora*. Search for him. It shouldn't be a problem for you."

"You're angry."

"I'm also trying very hard to be patient."

"All right, I'll try."

He waited with bated breath. Gods forbid Alonso was floating around them in the ether. Let him stay dead.

"No. I don't think he's here."

"Good." He nuzzled her neck.

"Do you think he'll come back?"

She was staring at the top of the tent, again. He exhaled slowly. "I don't know." He took a deep breath, the sound of patience. "If it were me, nothing would keep me from you, *cielo*."

She turned to him, grateful. "Thank you, Joachín. I can only imagine how hard for you this must be."

You have no idea. He was stiff and erect. She still had her damn dress on. "It is, but I love you."

She melted. With a tiny smile, she pulled her dress over her head and tossed it into a heap beside them. For a moment, they drank in their nakedness and then fell into each other's arms.

Marrying a *sentidora* definitely had its benefits, he decided later. Judging from her reaction to him, she felt exactly what he did, after all.

Chapter Seventeen: Rubbish Heap

Francisco limped in to the nave, cursing under his breath. He had found Rana Isadore, but his near discovery by Tomás and Umberto annoyed him, especially when it was so soon within the game. *Am I getting old?* he wondered. His knee hurt where he had clipped it on the window's ledge. It continued to throb dully during the Mass. After Vespers, he made a point of arguing the finer points of the sermon with the attendant monks, to test them. They would remember his ill temper and assume he had been present the whole time.

Alibi firmly in place, he changed his clothes and sought out Umberto an hour later to inquire after Tomás's health. "I haven't seen the Grand Inquisitor all day. Is he well?"

Umberto nodded, his eyes sharp.

"And Rodrigo...I mean Captain Morales. Is he anywhere about?"

"If you require him, I can have him attend you." Umberto's smirk suggested they believed his sexual tastes ran to the masculine. Good. Tomás would use that to his advantage and fail.

"That isn't necessary. I'm sure the captain has many tasks to which he must attend. But, perhaps, you could tell me where I might find him?"

"Stables, most likely. Or the garrison."

"Of course. And they are...?"

"North side of the temple."

"Thank you, Umberto. And please pass along my regards to the Grand Inquisitor."

As Umberto turned to leave, Francisco noticed a damp patch on the front of the chamberlain's habit which had been previously hidden by his sleeves. It was hard to tell against the black, but it looked as if he had tried to wash the spot clean. An innocent stain perhaps, but more likely, not.

He headed for the stables. The convenient thing about them was that they were also in the vicinity of the temple's rubbish heap, his true destination. He had a suspicion of what he might find there.

He walked down a wide hall that passed the refectory and large kitchen, ignoring the monks who toiled there, and then into a narrow corridor leading to the Solarium's north end. Ensuring no one was about, he pulled off his habit to reveal a dirty jerkin and hose beneath it, and then clapped a floppy hat onto his head. To anyone encountering him unexpectedly, he would look like a rag picker, searching for food.

He slipped through an outside door and entered a three-sided courtyard. Before him rose a hillside of trash. The place smelled abysmally, but he stomached it and clawed his way over moldering bones, rotten fruit, and broken crockery. Rats hissed at him and skittered out of reach, choosing to flee rather than fight. On the far side of the garbage heap, he found what he was looking for.

In a burlap sack, six doves lay. Their necks had been broken, their breasts stained crimson from a bloody tattoo.

He had seen such a glyph before. *Stregas* in Italia used such glyphs on red hens to scry for lost items. The blood was dribbled into a bowl of water, where pictures were said to form.

Were Tomás and his new witch using it to find Miriam Medina? Had they located her, using the birds?

He would have to abduct Rana Isadore to find out.

Chapter Eighteen: On the Road to Bacalao

Miriam and Joachín rose late the next morning. When they finally left their tent, the day was warm and the sun was hours into the sky. The Tribe had snuffed the fire, although it still smoked. Luci handed them bowls of porridge. "It's no longer hot. I didn't expect...."

"It's fine. Thank you," Miriam replied.

Joachín said nothing but winked in his aunt's direction.

"Everything all right between you two?" Zara strolled up to them. "We heard a scream last night."

"We had an invader." Joachín lifted the bowl to his lips.

"Oh?"

"I took care of it. Nothing to worry about."

"How did the rest of you fare?" Miriam asked, wanting to change the subject. She avoided Zara's probing gaze. "Were you warm without the blankets?"

"Fine," Luci said. "Although Casi was restless. She was up and down all night. I worried she had a fever. It wasn't that. She won't tell me what's put her out of sorts."

Barto and Maia approached the group. Maia held little Grimwald in a snug pouch. "*Goig sigui el tu*," she said, smiling at Miriam.

"It means *may joy be yours*," Barto said. "In Andor, we say that to newlyweds on their first morning."

"Thank you," Miriam replied. "And to you."

"We also have a custom of stealing the bride, but Ximen didn't think that was a good idea."

"This isn't hill country, my friend," Joachin said.

"No, but it's great fun when it isn't your bride." Barto grinned toothily, reliving fond memories.

They heard a wail. "*Ardie!*"

Everyone turned. Casi clutched a small rag of fur. Miriam and Joachin exchanged a look. She had found the squirrel. Iago reached for it, but she refused to give it up. "No!" she protested. "He's mine! Oh, Ardie! What happened to you? Why did you run away?"

Luci walked over to her. "This is what kept you up last night?"

"I caught him, *Maré*. He was sick. I was going to make him better!"

Luci reddened. "How many times have I told you not to touch sick animals?"

"How about if we bury him, Casi?" Intervening, Joachin set a hand on her shoulder.

"No!"

"Ardie's gone, Little Cat. There's nothing we can do."

"I don't want to put him in the ground. I want him in a tree. We can hang him in a little bed, like we did for *Paré*."

Joachin's face fell. Miriam came to his rescue. "Squirrels like to bury things, Casi. They bury nuts so they can find them in the winter. Maybe Ardie would like that."

Casi turned the thought over in her mind and then nodded glumly. She and Joachin dug a small hole at the base of the tree where she had found Ardie, and then covered him with earth while Ximen said a few words. After that, everyone mounted up. The road fell steadily. In the distance, the sea blazed in the sun.

Joachín squeezed Miriam's hand where she had set it about his waist. "Thank you."

"Her words hurt, I know."

He nodded. "I still feel responsible for Guillermo...for all of them. If I could undo their deaths, I would."

"Lay the blame where it belongs. At Tomás's feet."

"But if I hadn't gone to the temple...."

"We all make mistakes, love."

"I make big ones."

She gave him a squeeze. "Then let me guide you, Husband. Listen to me, and I'll keep you straight." She shielded her eyes against the glare. It was hard to tell, but it looked as if a cluster of buildings dotted the coast. "There's a village down there. Is that where we're headed?"

"No. We turn off at a crossroads."

"But isn't the village closer?"

"Herradur's a hamlet. We're better off travelling to Bacalao. There will be better opportunities to make money there."

"Honest employment, I hope."

"Of course. We can't afford trouble."

"Thank the goddess for that." She leaned against him and enjoyed the breeze in her hair. He wasn't exactly tense, but there was something in how he sat that made her think he was avoiding things. "Is there some other reason you don't want to go into Herradur, Joachín?"

His reluctance was so strong, it actually repelled her.

"A fight. I don't want to talk about it."

She was tempted to press him for details, but their lovemaking the night before had been wonderful and the morning pleasant. Why spoil it? She wanted to be a good wife. Sometimes, a husband needed privacy. Let her start their first day as a married couple honouring that.

The late start that morning meant they wouldn't make it to Bacalao before the gates closed for the night, so Joachín led them to a sandy cove not far from the town. As the Tribe descended a hill thick with juniper and cactus, they noted fishing boats at anchor on the water. Other than those, the bay was vacant—no locals lingered on the beach. The Tribe gathered driftwood and set camp on the sand. Overhead, palms waved in the evening breeze. Miriam hugged herself, not because she was cold but because the view awed her. She had never been this close to the sea.

"Do you think the New World will be like this?" She gazed over the sunset flecked waves. Joachin had come up behind her and encircled her in his arms.

"Most of the islands are tropical. Xaymaca will be like this, but with more flowers."

"I'd like that."

He plucked a sand daisy and tucked it into her hair. "There. Now you're an island girl."

"This island girl's hungry."

"I'll see what I can do about that."

He waved at Iago, Barto, and Ximen. Soon, the four men were up to their knees in surf, casting lines made from unraveled blanket wool and crudely whittled hooks. As they fished, the women picked thistle. Miriam had never eaten the heads, but Luci assured her that once boiled, they were succulent. Casi found a wild lemon tree.

"Good girl!" Luci said. "Now we have flavouring for the fish!"

"Assuming they catch any," Zara added wryly.

Miriam regarded Joachin in the waves. He looked happy, invigorated by the sport. She rubbed her arms against the cool breeze. She should be content, but a curious lump had settled in her throat.

Alonso. He had come back as the squirrel. He'd also been the rat that had attacked Don Lope; it was too much of a coincidence to think otherwise. If he was able to come back twice, he would return to her again. She would have to make sure she didn't panic when he did, that Joachin didn't send him back to the land of the dead.

Joachin whooped. They had caught something.

The dog was old, her white coat dirty and matted. She shook her head as if plagued by fleas. Alonso had seen such dogs. Shepherds used them to herd sheep in the mountains between Esbaña and Franca. How had such a beast, more suited to the snows of Andor, come here? Clearly, she had been abandoned, or perhaps she was lost. This one panted in the shade of an oleander bush.

Hello, old girl, he said, hoping she might sense him. At times, dogs barked for no reason. Old wives claimed they saw ghosts.

Either the beast didn't hear him or she didn't care to respond. She lay on her side, panting. He touched a haunch. Immediately, she lifted her head and growled. He removed his hand. If the dog bit him, he'd be affected by her fear. *You need water. I know where you can get some.*

The dog eyed him and lay back down in the dirt.

How did you come to be here? he pressed.

A picture formed in his mind—a caravan rumbling over hot gravel, horses stamping, dust rising in clouds. A wagon disappearing down a long road. The dog was tired and anxious because she hadn't been able to keep up. Finally, she collapsed beneath this bush.

Alonso tamped down his disgust. He knew of noblemen and commoners alike who treated their animals like property. They abandoned them when they lost their value. He had never condoned such a lack of remorse.

I know of another pack, he said. *We can go there.*

The dog wanted her own pack.

I understand. But you won't last long without food or water. If you let me take you there, we can eat and drink.

She rose on sore feet, a tentative assent.

I'll have to ride you. I don't have a body of my own.

The image of a horse flowered in his mind.

Yes, like that. Except you'll carry me inside.

She pictured a bitch with a pup in her teeth.

Something like that. Without waiting for her permission, he settled into her. Her heart was strong, but her eyes were failing. Her paws throbbed. In several spots, they were worn raw.

This way. He nudged her in the Tribe's direction. He winced as she stepped on a cracked pad.

The Tribe sat around a fire. Under the palms, sparks floated into the darkening sky. Ximen had caught the largest mackerel. Joachin, Barto, and Iago accused him of unfair advantage.

"How did I do that?" he asked as everyone ate their fill.

"Magic," Barto said darkly, tossing a bone into the fire. "Your white eyes see where the fish are. How else?"

"I'm a Rememberer, Barto, not a seer. If you think I have any advantage over you, I admit, I do." He pointed at the calm water. "I know where the fish are. They're in there."

Maia burst out laughing. Miriam smiled.

"In any event, the mackerel is good." Joachin took a bite. "Let's see who lands the biggest one in the morning."

"I don't think Ximen should be allowed." Iago glowered. His fish had been the smallest.

"Fine," Ximen said good-naturedly. "I'll sit on the beach and watch you work."

"Why can't us women fish?" Casi asked.

"You?" Iago glanced at her scathingly. "You're no woman."

"Am so! You're just afraid I'll show you up. I bet Miriam can catch as many as Joachin."

Miriam held up her hands. "Spare me. If I did, I'd hear no end of excuses."

Joachin smirked at her. "You think you can best me?"

"In some ways, yes. In others, it's a draw." She blushed, unable to keep a small grin from escaping. Everyone chuckled. Zara guffawed.

Joachin made a show of stretching languorously. "I am tired after so much fishing and eating. It's time we turned in." He held out a hand to her. "Coming, Love?"

She nodded, avoiding everyone's eyes.

"'Night, everyone," Joachin said as they held hands. They left to a chorus of farewells.

As he led her away, she knew sleep was the last thing on his mind. "Where are we going?" she whispered, feeling her desire rise.

"There is a sheltered cove, up ahead. I've left a blanket there."

He had planned ahead? She wasn't sure which aroused her more—that he had done so, or that they had no tent to cover them.

"But won't someone see?"

"The Tribe won't spy on us."

"But what if a fishing boat goes by?"

He regarded her soberly. "If it does, we'll have to be very still, hardly moving. It's dark. We'll blend in with the sand. If anyone glances our way, they'll have a hard time seeing us. On the other hand, once the moon rises, we might cast shadows. If we sweat, our bodies will gleam. Hopefully, no one is out there. But if they are, we'll have to take our chances."

Her heart pounded. The idea of making love with Joachín on a deserted beach with the moon shining on their bodies made her breath catch. But even more arousing was the idea that they might be seen, that she would let him take her in the open. She knew the heights to which he could send her. He would provoke her so much that she wouldn't care who watched. She might even welcome voyeurs. Let whoever wanted to see watch how they coupled, note how she claimed her pleasure, whisper at what a wanton she was.

On her back, on her knees from behind, she would be an empty well he would fill completely. They might satisfy each other many times before the dawn.

By the time they found their blanket in the hidden cove, she was tearing her dress from her body. She was so heated with desire that she threw it into a heap and fell onto her back.

He was stiff and ready. They did without foreplay. As he brought her to climax, it occurred to her that he had planned things to occur in just this way. In claiming her, he challenged anyone who might be watching them as well.

The moonlight made everything stand out in sharp contrast. The dog's dull vision made travelling difficult. She wasn't easily frightened by the bats or the odd bird they spooked, but it bothered her she had no depth perception, particularly when they encountered sharp rock. Alonso had taken her as far as she could go. The cliffs surrounding the cove were too steep. Her feet hurt.

The Tribe had camped a short distance from where they were. *This way*, he prompted.

She whined. Her paws bled.

I know someone who will take care of you. It's just a little ways. She'll bathe your paws and wrap them, give you water and something to eat.

The prod for information was laced with pain.

A girl. She likes dogs. He wasn't sure of that, but he suspected it was so.

The image of a fair-haired child, wearing a bulky dress and overlarge boots intruded on his thoughts. He had no idea who she was, but he knew well enough the dog did.

Not her. Another girl. She will help you.

After twenty minutes, they came within sight of the camp. Embers burned in the sandpit. Bodies snored beside it. The dog whined and shifted from paw to paw; she wanted to go down to the people but the sand invaded her cuts. She collapsed into a heap of pale fur and licked a paw as Alonso left her. Disembodied, he floated over desert shrub and into the camp. Casi lay beside Luci, staring at the stars. Miriam was nowhere to be seen, but he would find her later, and then he would deal with that bastard, Joachín de Rivera. What did it mean that Miriam was sharing a tent with him? Surely, it could only be a tribal custom, a symbolic pairing, where the Tribe acknowledged them as Matriarch and Patriarch, if only in name. He would get to the bottom of it as soon as he was reunited with Miriam, but first things first. The dog needed care, especially if she were to be a longer-lived host than that poor squirrel had been.

Casi, he said, settling beside her. *I have a pet for you.*

She made a face. He caught a fleeting image of Ardie, the squirrel. He sent her a picture of the dirty rug lying beneath the palm. *She isn't far. I bet you could find her.*

Casi glanced at Luci. Carefully, she lifted the corner of their blanket and sat up.

"Where are you going?" Luci didn't crack open an eye.

"I have to pee."

"All right. No exploring."

"I won't, *Maré.*"

So it wasn't an all-out lie, Casi attended to business before responding to Alonso's prompting. Once she was done, he hovered beside her. *Over here.*

She hesitated. Luci had warned her not to explore.

You're not exploring. You're checking the camp.

Iago's supposed to do that.

He's asleep. He isn't supposed to be, but he is. In the morning, you can tell him he neglected his duties.

Casi brightened. It dawned on him she didn't sense his suggestions as coming from outside of herself. That was strange, but he had no time to dwell on it. When she was within ten feet of the dog, she stopped short. *What is it? A wolf?*

No, Casi. A dog.

Wolves aren't white. It's too big for a fox.

The dog whined.

"Oh!" she said aloud. She took a few tentative steps toward it. "Are you all right, puppy? You won't bite me, will you?"

Alonso settled into the beast. This time, the dog hardly noticed his presence.

"Are you lost? What's your name?" Casi hunkered down beside them. "You're white, except you're all dirty. Can I call you Blanca?"

The dog dropped her head onto her paws. She was so bone-tired, she could barely keep her eyes open. Casi settled her hand onto her brow.

"I'll take care of you, Blanca. I bet you'd like some water. Wait here. I'll get some."

Alonso closed his eyes and listened as she scooted back to the camp. A short while later, she set a bowl of water beneath Blanca's nose.

The dog rose awkwardly and drank. The water refreshed her. Pleased with the outcome, Alonso left both girl and beast. Casi would do what she could to ease Blanca's hurts. It was time to find Miriam.

For some reason, she was in a cove not far from the camp. He drifted her way, not in a hurry. He wanted to savour the moment, to watch as she wandered along the beach in the moonlight thinking about him, or she sat on a piece of driftwood, listening to the waves and wishing he were with her. It was strange she chose to be alone, but he thought he understood why. They were two balls from the same skein of yarn. They both needed solitude. Night was one of the few times he had had to himself as a High Solar. She would take the night air and find some breathing space, allow herself some time away from the Tribe.

It all made sense, especially if she had been forced to spend time with that Joachín de Rivera.

And if she's sleeping, I can watch over her. In the morning, I'll follow her back to the camp and infiltrate the dog. When Casi tells her about me, she'll reach out to pet Blanca. And the second she does, she'll see I have returned. We'll be together once again.

Would she be overjoyed? Or would it be too much of a shock, as the squirrel was? He hadn't counted on scaring her the way he had. And then, with de Rivera pummelling him to death as if he'd been a snake seeking warmth—at least, that death had been quick.

She loves me. I know she does. It was hard, being severely restricted as he was. He wanted to be a man, to hold and protect her, to love her as they had once done. But that wasn't to be. Still, being a dog might be the next best thing. No beast was more loyal. He wondered how long Blanca might live. She was old, but perhaps she had a few years yet. They would cope. The important thing was, he was back.

He passed the last outcropping of rock like a breeze upon the beach.

And there, in an alcove of rock, barely hidden from anyone's view, Miriam clawed at the sand and whimpered like a bitch in heat as Joachín de Rivera thrust into her.

A howl, so sharp and agony-filled that it might have come from shattered dreams, broke the night's peace. It was followed quickly by a scream. With a cry, Miriam pushed Joachín away. "What was that?" she whispered, staring past his shoulder to the camp. Fear doused passion, leaving her dazed and anxious.

"Gods...." Joachín grimaced. He was still erect.

"*Cielo*, Are you hurt?" She glanced down at his member with concern.

He winced. "I'll live."

"I'm so sorry, love! But that howl went right through me! We should see if the Tribe is all right!"

"I don't think I can get up."

Voices rose and fell, magnified by the water. The Tribe was discussing something heatedly, but they no longer seemed upset. Whatever had bothered them was gone. Miriam wasn't convinced. "That sounded like a wolf."

"I don't think there are wolves around here, *cielo*." Despite his earlier distress, he was recovering quickly. "The Tribe is fine." He burned a trail of kisses down her neck and slid a hand between her thighs. And then, he made a suggestion. There was something erotic, he murmured, about their coupling, especially with wolves nearby. It wasn't likely, but it *was* possible. In another moment, they wouldn't be able to stop themselves. They were like wolves in heat.

The thought of it turned her wild.

Chapter Nineteen: Francisco is Almost Left Behind

It had seemed strange that Umberto should be so solicitous as to bring him a goblet of mulled wine before he retired. After the monk left, Francisco allowed a drop of it to settle on the tip of his tongue. Beneath the strong spice, the taste was bitter. Opium. How unoriginal. He tossed the contents out the window. Tomás wanted him out of the way, which meant they were travelling soon. Maybe tonight.

If he didn't drink the wine and followed them, even by seeming coincidence, they would know he was on to their ploy. He couldn't be so obvious.

He left his suite and strode down the hall, intercepting a monk who seemed surprised to see him. "Could you ask Captain Morales to come to my quarters?" he asked.

After a brief hesitation, the monk nodded.

"Fra Umberto was kind enough to bring me mulled wine. I know the Grand Inquisitor is indisposed, but I'd like some company. I thought the captain might like to join me in a cup before I turn in."

"I'll see if I can find him."

"Please do. Tell him I'll expect him shortly."

He returned to his room and doused all the candles save for one near the door. He had only a little of the burundarra mix left. It was a precious blend and hard to come by. He shouldn't have used so much the first time. It would have to do.

Ten minutes later, a sharp knock came at his door. He opened it and invited Morales inside. The captain smiled pleasantly. There was no reason he should smile, unless he looked forward to what he was about to do—murder, Francisco suspected. Before he could make a move, Francisco clapped the small pouch of burundarra to the captain's nose. Morales choked and fought him off, but he held him firm. The captain relaxed. The fire of vengeance faded from his eyes.

"What orders have you been given about me, Rodrigo?" he whispered into Morales's ear, still holding him tight.

"Kill you."

"I figured that. What are Tomás's plans?"

"Rr...ride for Ante..anqarra."

"Why?"

"Witch says...other witch is there."

Antequarra was forty leagues away. It would take them all night to travel. "What will Tomás tell the Papacy about my disappearance?"

"Stabbed while...givin'alms to th' poor." A dull smile spread over his lips.

"That isn't funny."

Morales sobered.

"This is what happens, Rodrigo. You think you've killed me. You stabbed me and tossed me into the Rio Gemilla. But I'm not Francisco. I'm your first cousin. You promised your aunt you would look out for me. I've just joined your ranks. You need to supply me with armour and a horse. Keep me out of the Grand Inquisitor's way. Do you understand?"

He nodded.

"Who am I?"

"Raúl...my," he sighed, "...my *primo*."

"Yes. Go and get what I need. Meet me at the trash heap near the stables."

Francisco released him. As soon as Morales was gone, he removed his habit to reveal new garb, that of a labourer. He snuffed the last candle, and slid through his open window. The next while would be difficult. With no more burundarra at his disposal, he wasn't sure how long his hold over Morales would last, or when he would be in a position to locate more. It would have to do.

Some time later, Morales, believing him to be Raúl, had fitted him in the rank of private and assigned him to the supply wagon, the lowest job given to the greenest of recruits. Francisco cursed his own effectiveness. As the drayman, he was beneath Tomás's notice, but the cart would often fall behind. When the troop rode out of sight, the captain galloped back and threatened him with extended watch if he didn't keep up.

"The horses can only go so fast, Rodrigo! What do you expect me to—"

Morales clouted him across the head. "Don't call me Rodrigo, you idiot! Refer to me by rank!" His horse stamped and snorted beside the wagon. "By Sul, if you ever speak to me like that in front of the men, I'll beat you senseless! You're an embarrassment, Raúl! I don't care what *Tia* Carmen says!"

Francisco flushed hotly but he had no choice but to take Morales's abuse. In real life, he outranked him in their equivalent circles. If Ilysabeth ever took the throne, he would surpass him in military standing as well. This is what came from acting without a thorough investigation beforehand—a novice's mistake. Gods, what bad luck that *Tia* Carmen had a simpleton for a son! Quite possibly, the captain was also acting out of suppressed rage, as if he retained a memory of what truly occurred. Francisco wished his ear didn't hurt so much.

"What did you say? I didn't hear you, *Privado!*" Morales lifted his fist to strike him again

"*Sí, Capitán!*" Francisco shouted as he ducked.

"When we stop, unload all the supplies."

The order wasn't necessary, but Francisco played along. "I'll do my best, sir!"

"See that you do." Morales reined his horse about and galloped after the retreating contingent. At the head of the troop, Tomás's carriage rumbled over a moonlit hill.

They rode all night, giving him plenty of time to think. And what he thought about mostly, was Ilysabeth.

Pray to the Gods, you're still safe, my Princess.

It had been four months since he had last seen her. The memory of it was indelible, as if the gods had scribbled him in to play a small but important part within a larger history, an epic, upon which worldly events turned. Before he had met Ilysabeth, he hadn't been particularly religious. Fate and rich patronage had turned him from an actor to a priest. But now, he embraced a new faith, and at its core was a queen.

Several months after she had been removed from the Tower, and he as her Confessor along with her, he had come upon her crying silently in the garden at Hartfield.

"Francis," she whispered wretchedly, while leaning against an oak as if she had no more strength to hold herself up, "She has summoned me to appear before the Privy Council. She has finally made up her mind, but it's all a ruse. I'm terrified she'll have me killed along the way. It will be made to look like an accident. What can I do?"

She was so miserable and so vulnerable that it filled him with the deepest longing—to protect her, to shield her. That he loved her was no longer in any doubt. But his passion was not a sexual thing. He didn't desire her physically, so it sprang from a deeper source. To say his devotion was only due to her glamoury only demeaned her.

There was a way, he had been toying with the idea for some time, but it would damn her more surely than any weak charge of sedition and planned reginicide.

"If I may speak frankly, Princess," he began.

She gave a futile little laugh. "Oh, it hardly matters what you say. I am to leave within the hour."

"This may make a difference. It is rumoured that you, like your mother, are a witch."

Her eyes blazed. He suspected she took his accusation as a betrayal. As downcast as she was, she had not expected to hear that.

"Bear with me. Whether you are, or whether you aren't, isn't the point. I suspect there *is* some magic in you. You've addled me well enough." He held up a hand to stave off forthcoming protests. "But *if* you are so accused, why not seek out that which will surely damn you? There are a people known as the Diaphani, a race of witches. They are being hunted by the Inquisition in Esbaña and elsewhere—"

"I know what they are."

"If I were to offer them sanctuary on your behalf, I am certain they would be grateful. And that gratitude, translated into power, might be what is needed to set you on the throne."

She studied him for a long moment, her gaze searching. He had wondered at the time if she were silent because to bid him to go and do as he suggested would surely earn her the axe.

After a moment, he acknowledged her refusal to reply. Her gaze was guarded, mistrusting. Even after these months, she didn't believe him. He hardly blamed her. There had been so few in her life she could trust.

"I will accompany you to Londres. They are unlikely to kill you enroute, especially with your Confessor who is also the Papal Nuncio on board. They don't have enough evidence to convict you—I know this for a fact. But you must remain strong, Princess. They will try to break you, get you to admit to things which they will twist to use. I know you are clever and will look to yourself. Lys's protection, that you do."

Her eyes widened slightly at his invoking of Lys. As a representative of Sul, he had no business appealing to the goddess.

"From Londres, I will leave you and travel to Esbaña to seek them out. I will find the witches for you, Princess. I will win them to our cause."

The palace guards had arrived to escort her from the garden. She was informed her carriage was ready. No more words passed between them, but he could tell from her demeanor, from the way she carried herself and by the flush of her cheeks, she had decided to believe him. He had given her hope.

Ilysabeth. His princess, untouchable, unreachable, formidable, yet so vulnerable. How was it that a man such as himself, who bedded both men and women as circumstances required, should love her as he did? He adored her, worshipped her. The 'lys' in Ilysabeth hadn't been placed there for naught.

Chapter Twenty: Seer's Best Friend

At sunrise, the sea turned a shell pink. Waves scalloped the sand in gentle arcs. A ribbon of cloud unfurled across the pearling sky. In spite of the glorious morning, Miriam couldn't shed the feeling that something was wrong. She untangled herself from Joachin's arms and reached for her dress.

"They're fine." He snagged her by the elbow to pull her back down.

"Joachin, I won't rest easy until we know for sure."

He surrendered. "Are you still worried about that howl from last night?"

"It wasn't normal."

"It was an animal of some sort, nosing around. If it caused a problem, we would have heard."

"Still, I'll feel better once I know." She pulled her dress over her head. He sighed and reached for his pants.

As they approached the camp, the Tribe greeted them with smiles. Even Ximen, as blind as he was, acknowledged them with an awkward nod. She wondered how far his understanding of past events extended. The idea of voyeurs had been exciting, but now, it bothered her, especially if Ximen was party to what they did. Their love life was Joachín's and her own business.

"Sleep well?" Zara stirred a black pot over a crackling fire.

"Never better," Joachín replied.

Zara handed him a bowl.

"What's this?"

"Mussel soup. I was up with the tide, collecting them. Unfortunately, that's all that's in it, except sea water and kelp."

"Sounds like you're trying to convince me."

Her mouth dropped in surprise, and then she poked him in the shoulder. "Oh, you! You don't need *that* kind of help."

He winked at her and gulped.

Miriam accepted a bowl. "Was there some kind of disturbance last night? We heard a howl."

Zara made a face. "Casi has a new pet. It wandered into the camp last night. Filthy beast, half dead by the looks of it. I don't like dogs, much."

Miriam glanced to where Zara pointed. A mound of fur lay on a sandy blanket. The beast looked like a dirty white bear. Its four paws were bandaged with blue rags—from Casi's dress, it appeared. The dog watched them for a moment and then looked away. "A dog?" she asked. She had never seen one such as this.

"Demon, if you ask me," Zara said darkly. "Noisy thing scared me half to death. Woke me up, howling right over me! Set Maia's baby to squalling, I can tell you."

"It looks like a Great Pyren."

The women turned inquiringly to Joachín.

"Breed of mountain dog. He's a long way from home if he found his way here."

"She," Zara corrected. "Not that I care. Casi's already named her."

Casi emerged from the bushes on the hill with Luci behind her. Seeing them, she waved madly, paused to hug the dog, and then ran up to them. Luci followed at a more leisurely pace.

"I've a new dog, Joachín! Come and see her! Her name is Blanca." She grabbed him by the hand.

He let himself be towed. "She looks hurt."

"She cut her paws. *Maré* and I bandaged them."

Miriam frowned. How could they transport a dog? The only place to put her was in the cart, but that was Maia and the baby's place. Joachín was of the same mind. "If her paws hurt, she won't be able to walk, Casi," he said carefully.

"She can ride in the cart with me."

He glanced at Maia and Barto.

Barto shrugged.

"It's fine with me," Maia said. "We can make room."

The four of them approached the beast on the blanket. The dog seemed depressed. She had set her muzzle on her paws, as if the effort to lift her head was too much. Greasy smears encircled her eyes, reminding Miriam of tears. Did dogs weep? Blood seeped through the rags on her feet. *Of course, she's depressed,* Miriam thought. *She's old, hurt, and lost. Who wouldn't be?*

Iago drew up to them, looking worried. "I expect you heard her last night. I don't know how she got past me. I hope she didn't bother you."

"No." Miriam refused to meet his eyes.

"Here I am, Blanca." Casi wrapped her arms about the dog's ruff. Blanca didn't move, but lay in her arms like a dull lump. "I've brought new friends to meet you. Pet her, Joachín. On her head like this." Casi demonstrated. "She's nice."

"Hello, old girl." Joachín reached for an ear.

Without warning, ten-stone of snarling dog set upon him in a flurry of teeth and claws. The women screamed. Joachín lifted his arms to fend her off. Blood bloomed across his shirt. He tucked in his chin to protect his neck as Blanca lunged for his throat. Barto drew his knife. Miriam threw herself across the dog and clawed at her scruff. A bolt of recognition shot through her.

She dug in her fingers hard. "Stop it, Alonso!" she cried. The maelstrom of his fury sent her mind spinning in circles.

I hate him! I'll kill him! He took you! His voice hammered in her head.

He had seen them together. *Come away!* she pleaded. *If you don't, they'll kill you. I won't be able to stop them.*

The fire went out of him. Blanca collapsed. Miriam, Joachin, and the dog lay in a sorry heap, unmoving. The Tribe waited breathlessly, not knowing what to do. Barto stood poised to stab Blanca, his knife at the ready.

"It's all right," Miriam said. She didn't dare move, knowing that the moment she did, Barto would strike. "The dog is fine, now. She was possessed." She held up a hand to stave off protests. "I'll explain in a moment. For now, no one touches her. Don't worry. She won't attack again." She rose gingerly, watching Barto carefully. When she was sure she had convinced him, she hauled Blanca from Joachin. Both he and the dog looked dazed.

"Who is Alonso?" Barto still held his knife.

"I'll explain later." The dog was an empty sack, as if all the life had been drained from her. No one moved, although Casi looked as if she wanted to. Miriam knelt beside Joachin to pluck his shirt from his wounds. Both of his forearms were a bloody mess. A row of punctures scored his left shoulder. Despite the blood, no major arteries were severed, thank the gods. He struggled to sit. "I'm all right," he insisted.

"Lie still for a moment." She set a hand on his chest to keep him from rising. "Wait until your breath comes back. Can someone see to his wounds?"

Zara frowned. "You won't tend him?"

"I have to deal with this, first." She snagged Blanca by the ruff and pulled her away.

Casi stepped forward. "Where are you taking her?"

"Into the trees."

"I'll come, too. She trusts me."

"This isn't Blanca, Casi."

"Casi, come here." Luci yanked her protectively to her side.

The Tribe watched silently as Miriam dragged the dog away. She kept her hand deep in the folds of Blanca's neck, but it wasn't the dog she touched. When she closed her eyes, Alonso limped at her side, leaning against her like a warrior returning from a crusade. His blonde hair was dirty, like Blanca's fur. He was scowling. Through his anger, she sensed his thoughts. She had betrayed him. Her faithlessness had pierced him as deeply as a sword.

She wanted to cry and laugh at the same time. He was back! Alonso, her love, her twin, the other half of her soul! She drew him into a small glade framed with oleander and cacti. Blanca collapsed into the dirt. Miriam dropped to her knees, wrapped her arms about the heavy neck, and pressed her face into the matted fur. She closed her eyes. In her mind, she nestled into Alonso's neck.

Alonso, she whispered, holding him. *Forgive me! I am so very, very sorry! How was I to know? I thought you were gone from me forever. I never meant to hurt you. Joachín and I....*

Do you love him?

He threw the question at her like an accusation. She couldn't lie. She had been weak to give in to the desires of the flesh, but her passion for Joachín had flowered into something more.

Gods. You do love him.

I'm sorry.

You're not!

He knew her completely. It was impossible to hide.

Why couldn't you have waited?

Alonso, what was I to do? You died—three times! I thought the third time was the last. How could I know it would be any different? That after sacrificing yourself, you could return? What do I know of the afterlife? Nothing!

You wanted me to come back.

I did! But I didn't think it was possible! How did you do it? Did you make an arrangement with the gods?

Something like that. She caught a flash of a brilliant, white light. There was something within it—a presence so compassionate it filled her with wonder. Alonso's face glowed as if some of that holiness still radiated from it.

I turned down Sul for you. He stared at her, his blue eyes spearing hers. *Do you have any idea what that means, Miriam? I turned down our Creator because I thought a better paradise awaited me with you! And He accepted my rejection! I thought you loved me! That's the sense I had of it when we made love that one time. If I hadn't felt it, I wouldn't have come back. Do you think I like being a dog? Or a squirrel? Or a rat?*

Of course you don't.

I can't be a man for you. I can't live inside of you like I once did—that way is closed to me. All I can do is animate near-dead animals and relive some of the old life that was ours when we touch. But I told myself, any road to you would be worth it. So I return, and I find you fornicating with that...that bastard....

Joachín isn't a bastard.

You think I enjoyed watching him take you like that? And you, liking it?

That was private, Alonso.

It isn't private, anymore!

We are married. Joachín is my husband.

I SHOULD BE YOUR HUSBAND! Me! I'm more worthy of you than him!

There was no point arguing. His jealousy needled her like cactus tines. She didn't blame him for feeling the way he did. Had their positions been reversed, she would have felt the same. Tears pooled in her eyes. *I do love you, Alonso! I will always love you! Nothing will change that. Joachín is...there are times I don't agree with what he does. You and I are more of a kind. Can't you be happy that we are together, once again? If you love me, you will put up with Joachín. He will have to put up with you.*

Can you keep it platonic? Not share yourself physically with him?

Don't ask me for that, Alonso.

Meaning you won't.

I will spend time with him and time with you. When I'm with him, I ask that you respect our privacy, as the rest of the Tribe does.

So that's what I am now—one of the Tribe.

You are more than that. You know it.

So I am to endure you fucking with your lover.

The obscenity stung. There was no way to satisfy his frustration.

Fine. I can oblige, he replied tartly. *Do something else while you're occupied. The last thing I want to see is you and him together.*

I'll spend time with you, too.

Yes, and we know how that will be. Cozy chats by the fire.

It would kill her now, if he left her. Yet his continuing presence with her might be too painful for him to endure. *Does my love no longer satisfy you, Alonso?* she asked softly.

He didn't reply. He wanted more, wished he might have what Joachín did. There was no easy solution, but he would stay. She loved him so much for it. She glanced at Blanca's paws and winced. *Those must hurt.*

He shrugged.

The dog doesn't seem to mind you.

She's old and tired.

I'll have to explain her behavior to the Tribe. Can I tell them you are sorry you attacked Joachín?

He laughed bitterly. *Say whatever you like. I'm sorry I didn't kill him. It seems I have little choice but to suffer him now. It remains to be seen if he can tolerate me.*

He'll have to. For the Tribe's sake.

Don't expect him to. My guess is he'll leave the minute things get difficult. Just like he did the last time.

She ignored the barb and hugged him. *I'm so glad you're back, Alonso. I love you so much.*

He grimaced, but her expression of love seemed to mollify him. *I suppose I can still be useful. Thank Sul you managed to get away from Elysir. How did you escape?*

Joachín started a fire in the Solarium and cut me free from the stake....

Him, again. Where is Tomás at the moment?

I wish I knew. We know the Guard is searching for us in the cities. We're heading to Bacalao. It's small and hopefully safe. Joachín has arranged for a ship in Qadis to take us to the New World. I'm worried about going there. It's a big enough port that it won't escape Tomás's notice.

Then the first thing I need to do is to find him. Learn of his plans.

She sagged with relief. Not knowing where the Grand Inquisitor was, was a source of continual tension.

Not to worry, mi ama. Now that I'm back, I'll never leave you unless this poor old girl can't carry me. When that's the case, I'll find something else. Things will get better. You'll see.

She didn't doubt it. Alonso would keep her informed. She might even be able to see through him again as a seer. *He's still so beautiful,* she thought. *He looks like an angel.* She wanted to kiss his handsome face. She kissed Blanca's ear, instead.

We'll have to see what we can do in my new form. Experimenting might take a good deal of your time.

She flushed, not sure whether he referred to seeing or kissing. It bothered her. She was a married woman, now. *We should return to the others,* she said.

They headed back. Ximen was explaining something at length to the Tribe. All faces turned to them as she and Alonso reappeared. Casi claimed Blanca. As Miriam let go of the dog's ruff, Alonso vanished. It was as he had said. They could only communicate when they were in direct contact.

"There have been questions," Ximen began.

Joachin was on his feet. Zara had bandaged his arms with what looked like the remains of his shirt. Miriam slid a hand about his waist. "Are you all right?"

He glared at the dog. "No, thanks to *him*."

They knew.

"I've told them as much as I understand," Ximen said. "That the dog carries the spirit of the High Solar, Alonso de Santangél."

"He isn't mad, is he?" Zara eyed Blanca nervously. "I don't know about these things, but it strikes me that dying three times does strange things to one's head."

Miriam stifled an awful desire to laugh. "I don't know much about it either, Zara. I was a *clara vidente* because of Alonso. He might be able to make me a seer, again. If we know where the Torch Bearers are, we can avoid them."

Everyone nodded at this unexpected boon.

Iago remained unconvinced. "Then why did he attack Joachin?"

"Alonso regrets doing that." She was thankful she didn't bear a truth tattoo. Anger sparked in Joachin's eyes.

"Blanca isn't Blanca?" Casi asked anxiously.

Miriam went to her. "Blanca is still Blanca, but she needs special care, Casi. The High Solar—you remember him? He was with me when we saved you from the snake."

"Oh, *him*!"

"Yes. He's inside Blanca now, in the same way that he lived inside me, except, sometimes," she shot a look at Joachin, "I'll need to be alone with him to discuss what he's learned. Most of the time, he won't be with Blanca. Instead, he'll be checking on what the Torch Bearers are doing."

"So he attacked Joachín but Blanca didn't."

"Yes. I'm sorry about that."

"Let me understand this," Barto rumbled. "That dog is still a dog, but more than a dog." Miriam nodded. He turned to Maia. "I told you she was a witch."

Maia looked embarrassed.

"Well, she is. No offence," he said, seeing the disapproving looks rise among the Tribe. "Where we come from, all our wise women are witches. They have pets, familiars. Like the dog, there."

"It *is* unusual, but not unheard of," Ximen said. "Four hundred years ago, one of our people had an owl that liked to foretell the time and date of everyone's death. It wasn't much appreciated."

"I can imagine." Luci looked askance.

"What happened to the owl?" Casi asked.

"It foretold its own death and died."

"I never liked owls much," Zara said.

Bacalao wasn't far, but Joachín wanted to get to the gates before the noon crowds. Because it was late fall, seasonal workers poured into the town, looking for employment. He said little to Miriam as they broke camp. She wondered if he would speak to her as they mounted up.

"How is your shoulder?" she asked once they were astride Fidel.

"Fine." He snapped the reins. The stallion shied, surprised by the sting. She caught Joachín around the waist. He felt as unyielding as iron.

"Can we talk about it?"

"What is there to talk about? He returns from the dead. You run off with him instead of taking care of me. It's obvious where your heart lies."

"I love you, Joachín."

"Yes. But you also love him. Who's next? Some old goat I don't know about? Tell me, so I can prepare for it ahead of time."

There was no point arguing with him. He wasn't ready to talk sense. They rode for a few minutes without speaking. Tall cypresses paralleled the road, sentinels standing at attention in the breeze.

"If he attacks me again, I *will* kill him. I don't care what he means to you." He stared straight ahead.

"He won't."

"We are Matriarch and Patriarch. There is no room for another in that pairing."

"Alonso is here to help us."

"No, he's here because of *you*. Don't try to convince me otherwise."

"I wasn't trying to."

"Let me also remind you of something, Wife. I may be your husband, but I'm also *El Lince*. He's a dog to my cat. If he tests me again, he won't survive my claws."

She shivered. Joachin was deadly with the knife. He would keep that promise, she knew.

Chapter Twenty-One: Bodega

At noon, they stopped near an estuary that emptied from the
hills into the sea. A reedy marsh framed the shoreline. The water was
brackish but fresh enough to satisfy the horses. Bacalao was an hour's
ride away. As the women cooked the noonday meal, Miriam slipped
away to speak with Alonso.

Casi sat beside him in the wagon. "How is Blanca?" Miriam asked
her.

"Her paws aren't bleeding any more. I rinsed out her bandages."

"Thank you for taking good care of her, Casi. Would you leave us
for a moment? I need to speak with Alonso."

"He's really in there? To me, she's just Blanca the dog."

"He's really in there."

"If you say so." Casi kissed Blanca on the head, hopped from the
cart, and ran to the women. Miriam settled beside Alonso. From
across the camp, Joachín shot them a dark look. As he turned away, a
heron lifted from the marsh and took flight.

A cat to my dog? He thinks pretty highly of himself. Alonso's legs dangled over the wagon's edge where Blanca's paws drooped. It was an unsettling image, the man superimposed upon the dog. Blanca had diminished, as if Alonso's spirit outshone hers. He no longer looked grimy. His white gown was spotless and his blonde hair almost too bright to behold. She wondered if he reflected the sun's noon-day light. A glow shone all about him like a corona.

You eavesdropped on us when we were talking?

I don't stay with the dog. I was with you some of the time you were riding. I've also been scouting ahead. So far, we're safe.

Good. I was wondering–

If we can see together. Yes, let's experiment.

He vanished. His departure left her cold, as if the sun had slipped behind a cloud. Blanca whined in complaint. She had gripped her too tightly.

Well? Suddenly, he was back, as bright and as immediate as day.

Nothing. Despondency claimed her. *It isn't like before, Alonso.*

No. Sul said it wouldn't be. We'll just have to manage as best we can.

But how will I see for the Tribe?

I'll come and go. Report what I've learned. But you'll have to check with me often.

What if I don't check when I need to?

Then I'll howl.

She laughed. That would work. She wrapped her arms about Blanca's neck and buried her face in her fur. *I'm so glad you're here.*

Your husband isn't.

A shadow fell across them. Startled, she glanced up. Joachin stood there, glowering. She released her hold on Blanca. "Time to go," he said flatly. He turned on his heel and headed for Fidel.

He refused to talk to her as they rode. Despite her attempts to draw him into conversation, he remained stonily silent. Soon, vineyards appeared on the landward side of the road. The vines were still in leaf, but there was no sign of fruit, evidence the bodegas were busy pressing grapes.

"Maybe we can ask about work at one of these places?" She pointed to a low, chalk-coloured building in the distance. It sat half-way up a hill, trellised with vines. A stack of barrels sat beside it, apparently another winery. The breeze carried the scent of ripe must.

Joachín didn't reply.

She bit down on her frustration. "Stop being childish," she said finally. "You have to speak to me some time."

The only response she received was the creak of the wagon's wheels.

"Why are we going to Bacalao? Won't it be more dangerous, there? Especially if Tomás has sent a contingent to find us?" She poked him in the ribs. "Joachín!"

"We're under a time constraint," he said tightly. "We need to make Qadis in five days. If we don't, the ship sails without us."

"I wish you'd told me that before."

"You were busy."

He could have mentioned it as they rode. "Alonso doesn't *have* to be a problem—"

"He *is* a problem."

"He's an advantage. He'll scout ahead, advise us of any threats. He'll search for Tomás. See what he's up to."

"And when he isn't doing that, he's as close to you as breath."

"I've told him my private time with you is private. He promised he wouldn't interfere."

"I'll bet he wasn't happy about that."

"He wasn't. He asked me to forego our lovemaking."

"He *what?*"

"I told him I wouldn't. He's accepted it. The last thing he wants is to see us together."

"Let him watch! I'll show him what he's missing."

"He knows. He saw us last night in the cove. He attacked you today because he was mad with jealousy."

She couldn't see Joachín's face, but she suspected he was smiling. It wasn't a nice smile. "I know how hard this is for you, Joachín."

"Yes, well. We'll see how *hard* it is for whom." He squeezed her thigh. She shivered, guessing what he had in mind.

An hour later, they crested a hill. Bacalao came into view. Three walls, with squared off towers, framed the town. The fourth side lay open to the sea. Numerous masts pierced the sky, mostly from lateen-sailed *dhows* from Araby, but there were a few large galleys and three-masted *naos* among them.

Blanca began to bark furiously. Joachín glanced contemptuously at the dog.

"Gods, Joachín!" Miriam cried, pointing ahead. Alonso was trying to warn them. The town's gates were opening. Flashes of black and white riders appeared there. "Those are Torch Bearers! They're coming this way!"

He reined Fidel about and galloped at the Tribe behind them. "Back!" he shouted. "Turn around!"

"Where do we go?" Barto shouted. Beside him, Maia looked terrified and held onto little Grimwald tightly. Casi clutched at Blanca. The dog still barked as if it meant to wake the dead. Luci grabbed Casi, afraid she might lose her over the wagon's sides. Iago and Ximen galloped up to meet them.

"What's wrong?" Iago demanded.

"Bearers! At the town's gates! We have to go back. Pray to Lys we haven't been seen!"

"But there's no cover!"

"There's that copse of trees at that last bodega we passed! Hopefully, they won't come that way!"

They thundered back down the hill as fast as they could go. Dust billowed in clouds behind them. A smaller, rutted trail led off the main road and ended at the stand of willow and ash they had passed. Joachín ushered the Tribe into the trees. They caught their breaths and waited.

Five minutes passed.

"Maybe they went a different way?" Miriam whispered. She stood with Joachín beside Fidel.

"I'll go see," he said. He reached for the saddle's pommel.

She stopped him. "There's a better way." She indicated Blanca. Without a word, Casi gave up her place. Miriam set her hands on the dog.

Alonso appeared before her. *We were fortunate. They've gone north. To Anteqarra, I think, but I'm guessing. We can't go to Bacalao. They'll have* told the Town Guard to keep watch. We may not be so lucky evading them next time.

I'll tell Joachín. Was Tomás with them?

Not that I could see. That doesn't mean he wasn't. He may even be staying in Bacalao. I'll see if I can find him. For the time being, it's best we stay where we are.

In these woods?

No. At the bodega. They're pressing grapes at the moment. They have some workers, but they could use more.

But that doesn't make sense, Alonso. If we stay here, the Guard could discover us at any time!

You're at greater risk if you move, now. A smart bird knows when to go to ground. Have you ever pressed grapes?

No.

Get ready to stain those pretty legs. A few of the girls are already hard at work. They say a woman's skin enhances the flavour.

What about Joachín and the men?

Heavier work. There are always barrels to be loaded for the market.

I'll suggest it.

Come to me, tonight. Hopefully, I'll have more answers.

She removed her hands. The Tribe regarded her silently. "We're safe, for the time being," she told them. "The Bearers have gone north, although there may be a partial contingent remaining in Bacalao. Alonso says we should stay here until he has a better sense of their movements."

"What if we ride after nightfall?" Iago put the question to Joachín.

He seemed to be of the same mind as Alonso. "A patient cat waits until the time is right. Everyone stay here until Iago and I come back. You two, watch the road." He nodded at Barto and Ximen.

Miriam followed him but he stopped her. "In this place, its only men who speak to men," he told her curtly. He turned on his heel and set off for the bodega. "Besides," he called over his shoulder, "you're the only one who can talk to that *dog*."

His exclusion struck her momentarily speechless. Incensed, she started after him, ready to insist she was matriarch, but Ximen intercepted her. "This bodega belongs to an old *morisco*, *Sera*. He won't acknowledge you. It's cultural. Best let the patriarch handle it."

How did Ximen know? Once again, she was taken aback by the depth of his ancestral knowledge and memory. For that matter, how did Joachín know of the customs here?

"The overly large sun façade on the gate," Ximen murmured, guessing her thought. "Only those accused of a lack of piety would display one."

On the bodega's outer gate, a huge woodcut of Sul hung. Multiple rays emanated from it like the legs of a gigantic spider.

Let us not be flies in a web, she thought as Joachín strode up the hill.

The old *morisco* who owned the bodega refused to allow dogs on the premises, Joachín announced. Alonso would have to stay with the horses. She wasn't pleased about that, and even less happy when Joachín took pleasure in it. The gate opened to reveal an old man standing there. Although he was copper-skinned and dressed as a farmer, Miriam found it easy to imagine him in a turban and silks. A fountain bubbled and gushed in the courtyard. Stacks of barrels extended beyond it into a cave.

Ximen, their spokesman, set a hand to his heart and bowed. "*Ser* al-Ma'din," he said.

"Friend Ximen." The old man returned the courtesy. "Once again, you honour this house."

To her surprise, Joachín stepped aside to present her to the old man. "Allow me to introduce my wife, *Ser* al-Ma'din."

"A pleasure," the old man said, regarding her as if she had suddenly appeared in their midst. "Welcome to this house, *Sera*. Your beauty graces it like the most exquisite rose." Joachín stared her down, as if warning her not to respond. She frowned. The rest of the women drew up behind her and waited.

An elderly woman appeared in the house's doorway. She wore a pale scarf over her head and a robe of misshapen cotton. Like *Ser* al-Ma'din, her eyes were as sharp as her nose.

"My wife will show you to the women's quarters," *Ser* al-Ma'din said mildly.

"Women's quarters?" Miriam turned to Joachin in dismay.

"Excuse me a moment." He set a hand to her elbow to usher her aside.

"He means a *seraglio*, Joachin! Harem quarters! What's to stop him from locking us in or worse?"

"He's old. Your virtue is safe."

"It isn't my virtue I'm worried about! What if he calls the Guard?"

"He won't do anything to draw unwanted attention to this place. They are what they appear to be—old *moriscos* who, despite appearances, still keep to their ways. We can't go past Bacalao at the moment."

"I'm going to talk to Alonso. Maybe he's learned something."

He grabbed her by the arm. "If you leave now, you'll insult them."

"You worry about appearances, rather than our safety?"

He let his breath out slowly. "Indulge me. If you want to consult with Alonso later, I won't stop you."

"Unless they lock me in."

"They won't lock you in."

"You don't know that."

"If they do, I'll break down the door."

"Fine." She still wasn't happy about it. They returned to where the *Ser* al-Ma'din's waited.

"If you would have your wife escort my wife and women to their quarters," Joachin said to *Ser* al-Ma'din, "I would be most appreciative."

"Fatima will show them the way." *Ser* al-Ma'din waved them off as if they were nothing more than a herd of goats. "Tonight, after the day's toil, we will dine. Are there musicians among you, *Ser* Ximen?"

"We are not what we were," Ximen said. "Some of us can still sing. Our Patriarch, however, is an excellent dancer."

"Fatima says I torture the *oud*. Let us see what Sul provides."

"You. Come." Fatima al-Ma'din beckoned to Miriam. She disappeared into the house as if expecting the women to follow. A wall of hot steam struck them as they entered the dwelling. Three large copper pots sputtered near a far wall. The first had been set over a low fire and resembled a hammered kettle with copper tubing spiraling over the top. The second was a large onion with a smaller spout. The third had a large drum with a lip at the bottom.

"An alembic!" Miriam pointed to the first container. "You're distilling wine!"

Fatima surveyed her with interest. "You know *saca*?"

"I've never made sherry, but my father was a physician. We distilled alcohol for medicinal purposes."

Fatima nodded. "For perfumes, also. Same process, but not many flowers this time of year."

"I could help."

"No. Work for Fatima, only."

"What are we supposed to do, then?" Zara wasn't happy with their situation.

Fatima eyed her as if she were a heifer ready for the market. "You stomp," she said.

"No, higher! Tuck your hems into your waistbands!"

The girl who addressed them looked as if she thought them all fools. She was attractive in a sharp-edged way, but she had a cagey look about her, like a fox eyeing hens. Her blouse was spattered with red, her legs exposed to mid-thigh. "You crush the grapes like this. The finer the mash, the greater the juice. Understand?"

What was there to understand? It wasn't a difficult concept, Miriam thought.

"I am Inez," the girl said loftily. "This is Anita." She nodded at the plump blonde beside her. "What are your names?"

"Madelaina," Miriam supplied.

Casi's eyes widened in surprise. Luci and Zara introduced themselves in turn as Estrella and Luna. Casi said nothing, but looked as if she were trying to decide on a name.

"So, Madelaina, from where do you hail?"

"Here and there."

"Your men down there—some of them don't fit with the rest of you. That big one, especially." She meant Barto.

"He and his wife have recently joined us. They're from the hill country, up north."

"And him?" She lifted her chin to indicate Joachín.

"Taleda, I believe."

"I knew a man from there. Are you married?"

Miriam straightened. "As a matter of fact, I am. That's my husband you just pointed out."

Inez said nothing for a few moments. "What does he call himself?"

Miriam frowned. She hadn't asked, *what is his name?* but what he called himself, as if she expected an alias. "José," Miriam supplied, using the name she and Joachín had decided on earlier.

"A common name, José." Inez swung her leg over the rim. "Work the crush until you can no longer feel the grapes. *Ser* al-Ma'din will collect the juice shortly. Then dig out the dregs. There are shovels over there." She indicated three spades resting against a wall.

"Where are *you* going?" Zara demanded.

"To help Fatima with the evening meal. With you here, we have a crowd to feed."

"How long do I do this?" Casi puffed as she stamped.

"'Til sunset," Inez replied airily.

"We'll have this finished long before then," Zara said.

"Oh, I thought it was obvious. After you're done with this batch, the men fill the vat again. You'll be at it for another two hours." She strolled away, pausing to shake her hair free from her kerchief.

"She gets the honey, and we get the comb," Zara muttered darkly. She regarded Anita. "How long have you been at this?"

Anita held up four fingers.

"Four hours?" Zara asked in astonishment.

Anita shrugged and kept stomping.

By the time two hours were up, Miriam was exhausted—all of the women were. She had seen Joachín a few times. He and the men had hauled grapes, lifted the crush into the vats, and hefted barrels onto wagons bound for Bacalao. Ximen had been excused. He and *Ser* al-Ma'din spent the afternoon discussing the intricacies of *saca*. Once again, the Rememberer's memory made him an asset. Miriam learned this second-hand, after chancing upon Joachín in the courtyard.

"How are you?" he asked.

She glanced up from the fountain where she had paused to take a drink. Her hair was a sticky mess and felt like straw. His expression didn't help. He looked conciliatory. At least he was no longer angry. The hard work must have soothed his temper. "Wonderful. Can't you tell?"

"I didn't know this is what they'd have you do. We'll leave in the morning."

Inez appeared in the kitchen's doorway. She didn't look as if she'd spent much time over a hearth. She wore a fresh blouse and had tucked a rose behind her ear. "Hello, José," she said.

Joachín stared at her, as if dumb-struck. Miriam glanced between the two of them. Did they know one another?

"We are old friends, José and I," Inez explained. Her gaze settled back onto Joachín. "Too bad you didn't stay in Herradur, José. Things became...unpleasant after you left."

Joachín swallowed.

"You were right about Rufio. He *was* a brute. And Pepe. He threw me out." A thin smile touched her lips. "I hope you'll dance for us, later." She glanced at Miriam. "He's a wonderful dancer."

Miriam frowned. "Yes, I *know*."

"Oh, of course you do. I keep forgetting he's your husband. How long have you two been married?"

"Three days."

"Is that all? Well, I must go. Fatima needs me to oversee the meal." She regarded Joachín. "Perhaps we can talk later, José. About old times."

"I...if you wish."

"I look forward to it."

"Inez, wait." Miriam stepped forward to confront her. Inez arched an eyebrow. "I thought you said the men and women were segregated, here."

"Only at night, Madelaina. At the evening meal, we women eat on one side of the room and the men on the other. Fortunately, the al-Ma'dins don't expect us to conform to their ways completely. They tolerate conversation, among other things."

"Other things?"

"Dancing. I look forward to seeing you dance tonight, José. Until then." She disappeared into the house.

Miriam turned on Joachin. "So *that's* why you didn't want to go to Herradur."

He avoided her gaze.

"Admit it!"

His face worked against the inclination to lie. "Yes."

"You were involved with her?"

"I wouldn't call it *involved*."

"What would you call it then?"

"A mistake." He turned on his heel and left the courtyard before she could pry any more details from him.

Chapter Twenty-Two: Veiled Threat

Blanca panted beneath the wagon. She had drunk the water Casi had left, but she was thirsty again which meant Alonso also suffered. It seemed the longer he spent with the dog, the more susceptible he was to her complaints. Coming and going made little difference. Blanca's pains were his own. The dog was also pining. In spite of Casi's ministrations, she longed for the blond girl he had seen in her memory. Dogs were loyal creatures. They never forgot their first loves. *We have much in common, you and I,* he told her sadly. *Perhaps one day, we'll find your mistress. In the meantime, I expect Casi will come with food. If you get too thirsty, bark. I'll be back, shortly.*

He left her and drifted toward Bacalao, searching for any sign of Tomás. There was none. As far as he could tell, the contingent had left for destinations north, but that still left the Grand Inquisitor at large. *Hard to kill the snake when you can't find its head,* he thought, recalling the old proverb.

He floated over sloping hills, bare except for vineyards and parched olive groves. The trees cast long shadows. The sun was setting. In the distance, white villages appeared. He weighed the potential of each. Anteqarra was the only one big enough to support a castle, which is why he suspected Tomás would be there. After the *Reconquista*, the priests had converted many of the Moori strongholds into houses of Sul. Tomás liked his comforts; if he were anywhere nearby, it would be there.

The fortress at Anteqarra commanded his view. A blocky and imposing structure, its granite crenellations protruded like teeth from the top of each wall. A golden dome had been erected over the keep's roof, as out of place as a glass eye with molars. Alonso dropped towards it and passed through thick walls.

In the nave, an Orb hung, suspended by ropes and pulleys. Several monks fed the eternal flame. Bells rang for Vespers. Priests shuffled from dormitories, scriptoriums, or the refectory in solemn procession. From the stables, a troop in black and white livery marched as if called to war. Were they the same contingent he had seen, riding out from Bacalao? Of Tomás, there was still no sign.

He headed for the next most likely place, the High Solar's quarters. If Tomás's comfort meant taking away someone else's, that was where he would be. Most Solariums followed a similar lay-out even if the building was once a Moori stronghold.

Alonso found him in the fortress' largest suite.

Instead of his robes of office, Tomás wore a caftan of blue and gold— Sul's colours, but a far cry from protocol. His head and feet were bare. He lounged on a divan and munched dates. Opposite him, a veiled woman sat in a chair. She was also dressed in gold and blue, but her face was completely hidden. They looked like two chess pieces from the same side of the board. *Who is she?* Alonso wondered. Between them, a bowl of water sat. A Luster monk approached them with a cage of white, fluttering doves.

The cleric set the birds on the table. Neither Tomás nor the strange woman spoke.

"Will you require anything more, Radiance?" the monk asked.

"No. Leave us."

The monk bowed and left.

Tomás regarded the woman sourly. "This time, I want specifics. Vague descriptions, like *near the sea* aren't enough."

She said nothing but watched the birds. When Tomás began to look impatient, she told him, "I want to find her, as much as you. She stole my happiness."

Tomás sucked on a date and spit out the pit. "Ah, the pain of unrequited love. He gave you up without a qualm. I'm surprised you haven't conjured something to punish him."

"It's not him I would harm."

"You won't harm her, either. You'll hand her over to me."

"And when I do, what will you do?"

"That's my business. I don't keep you to ask questions. Get on with it. Let's see how successful you are."

She reached into the cage and caught one of the doves. She held it steady and set a dagger to its breast. It struggled, sensing its fate. With a sharp thrust, she pierced it through, and then carved a bloody tattoo across its jerking body. She held it over the basin. Blood dripped, staining the water red.

She cut the remaining birds in succession, dropping each corpse at her feet like the pit of a date. Tomás leaned forward to watch the scarlet water. The scar on his face shone palely against his flushed skin. The girl also peered into the bowl to watch.

They remained silent for a time.

"Well?" he demanded.

"She's close. See how the blood curdles? The patterns are stronger. I see dark, round objects...."

"Not boats, again."

"No. They sit on fields with dull soil—"

"That sounds like—"

"Wait. There is a courtyard. Rivera is with her."

"Joachín de Rivera?"

"Yes. And another woman who is speaking to them. I don't know her."

"I don't care about her! If you can see that kind of detail, why can't you tell me where she is?"

She continued to stare at the water. "It's gone," she said at last.

"What do you mean, it's gone?"

"The vision is over. The water has clouded."

"You said it would work."

"I need more blood—"

"I'll use your blood, next time!"

"Killing me accomplishes nothing," she said tonelessly. "You want to see more, you'll have to provide a greater sacrifice."

"Like what?"

"Something larger. Maybe a dog or a cat."

"Hmph. She's bloodthirsty, this goddess of yours."

"She has turned from me."

"Then she's not much of a goddess, is she?" He lifted his caftan. Beneath it, his penis stood erect. "Come here."

She didn't move.

"I said, 'Come here.'"

When she didn't, he grabbed her wrist and forced her to straddle him. He held her firmly around the waist and began to thrust. "I find your tolerance amusing," he said as she grimaced in discomfort. "It means you'll suffer anything, no matter what the cost. I like that. We have a lot in common, you and I."

He pumped harder. When she sat there like a dull lump, he snarled in frustration and rammed her like a lance, nearly dislodging her from his lap. Finally, she cried out in pain. Red bloomed across her face veil. She had bit her lip.

"Better." He subsided only slightly. "You need to show me more enthusiasm. Think of it as motivation...for finding your replacement."

Alonso had had enough. Rape and blood magic were the worst kinds of blasphemy, crimes against the natural order. If the Tribe remained too long at the bodega, Tomás would find them the next time they tried.

Who was she, this witch? There was something familiar about her. Tomás hadn't removed her veil, which meant he preferred things that way. Why?

Pondering it, he rose through the ceiling. It was time to return to Miriam.

Unaware that another also shared his distaste, Francisco stepped away from the suite's door, where he too had been eavesdropping. It was time to pen a quick note to Pantalone and Columbine, to let them know where he was and what he had found. Pray to the goddess, Ilysabeth was still safe. The only thing that comforted him was the thought Pantalone would have sent a depressing letter to Marabel, if she were not. Even in this backwater, news of her death would have reached here. It was a risk to send a letter, but with luck, Tomás was too busy with Rana Isadore to intercept it.

Chapter Twenty-Three: Confession

The **meal** **consisted** of a first course of melons with pomegranates, followed by bread and oil, and finally goat and onions in gravy. As Miriam expected, Inez was foremost among the servers. After giving *Ser* al-Ma'din his fill, she served Joachin next, lingering near him and making conversation. By the time the platters arrived for the women, there wasn't much left but rinds, scraps, and bones.

From the women's side of the room *Sera* al-Ma'din waved aside the poor leavings. "A believer eat one intestine, a *kafir*, seven."

Casi frowned at the old woman. "What does that mean?"

Luci hushed her.

"It mean," *Sera* al-Ma'din said loftily, "that true follower sup like sparrow. Unbeliever sup like pig."

"I'm a true follower, then," Casi said despondently. She looked at the onion Luci had given her.

"Take." *Sera* al-Ma'din scraped her meager meal onto Casi's plate. "Children not follow rule." As Luci murmured her thanks, Miriam couldn't help but wonder what motivated *Sera* al-Ma'din more:

setting a good example for the infidels or bestowing a kindness on children. Casi cast a grateful gaze at the old woman. "Lemon sherbets for dessert," *Sera* al-Ma'din added, thawing a bit, "but only if you eat all food."

"I will!" Casi assured her.

"Good." *Sera* al-Ma'din gave her a rusty smile.

"You're very kind," Luci said. "She's famished after all the hard work she did today."

Sera al-Ma'din frowned slightly, as if not understanding. "Hard work?"

"She worked in the vats with us. She's not used to it."

"She stomped? Who say she do that?"

"Your worker—Inez, told her to take her place."

The old woman pursed her lips. "Tomorrow, she help me. Chickens to feed, goats to milk. You like that, child? Follow old woman around?"

Casi nodded with her mouth full.

"Then, as Sul wills. Come, we bring sherbets."

"Did you use magic to make them?"

Sera al-Ma'din smiled indulgently. "Am I djinn? No, child. We have ice cave. You see tomorrow, if you like."

"Can I *Maré*?"

"Of course. Just make sure you don't get in the *Sera's* way."

Miriam watched as Casi skipped behind the ancient *morisca* like a pet ferret. "She seems to have taken to Casi," Miriam murmured to Luci.

Luci nodded. "She doesn't approve of the rest of us much, but she seems to have a soft spot for children."

"Where is the rest of their family? I'm surprised they don't have sons and daughters to help them run this place."

Luci shrugged. "Who knows? Esbaña likes *moriscos* about as much as it likes us."

On the men's side of the room, Inez filled Joachín's cup. He lounged with the other men on cushions strewn about the floor. He took what she offered, thanked her brusquely, and tossed it back.

"What are they drinking?" Luci asked. "I don't think we've had any of that."

"Sherry," Miriam replied.

Zara leaned toward her. "That Inez has intentions towards Joachín."

Miriam made a face. "They know each other."

"What?" Luci and Zara stared at her.

"Joachín and I had words. That's why we didn't go to Herradur. He wanted to avoid her."

"Then why is she here?"

"I have no idea."

"They've had a prior...association?" Luci asked.

"Assignation, is more like," Zara said.

"He hasn't admitted it, but I trust him."

"Shhh," Luci whispered. "She's coming this way."

As if reluctant to leave but finding no other reason to stay, Inez headed in their direction. As she passed them, intent on reaching Anita and the other workers, she lost her balance and swayed. Unexpectedly, she plopped down beside Miriam, looking faint. Perspiration dotted her brow.

"Are you all right?" Luci asked.

Inez glanced at Luci's unfinished plate of goat's meat. Her lips trembled. "Fine," she said. She rose abruptly and half-walked, half-ran to the kitchen.

"Is she drunk?" Zara asked.

"I'm not sure." Miriam watched her go. Inez hadn't smelled of liquor. But if she were ill, it was hard to be sympathetic.

Half an hour later, after the men had drunk more sherry and the sherbets were served, Inez reappeared as if nothing untoward had happened. She joked with the other workers who sat apart from the Tribe. When *Ser* al-Ma'din appeared with his *oud*, she applauded loudly. Iago accompanied him with a drum. Ximen, always a surprise, stood and sang a long and drawn-out call to prayer.

Miriam stared at him in amazement. "How does he know what to sing?" she asked Zara.

"He knows everything. He's mingled with the Moori in the past. He picks what he needs from ancestral memory."

"But how does he keep it all in his head?"

"He told me once it was like opening a door. You choose the right one and take what you need. When he's done, he closes it."

"An unusual talent."

"Not so strange as talking to the dead."

Miriam smiled and thought of Alonso. She would have to excuse herself soon to see what he had learned.

Ser al-Ma'din stood and addressed Ximen. "It has been so long since I have heard that. No matter what our race, we are all worshippers of the Great Sul. Your song is an expression of that, no matter how strange it seems to foreign ears."

Miriam looked over the gathering. Clearly, Ser al-Ma'din was covering for both himself and Ximen, in case any of his workers thought to report them. She didn't think anyone here would accuse them of forbidden practices, but appearances were deceiving.

"And now, more *saca* to celebrate!" he announced loudly. He looked as if he already had too much.

From across the room, Sera al-Ma'din lifted an eyebrow. "More saca, Husband?"

"Yes, Wife, more!" His tone warned her not to argue. Under normal custom, the Moori never touched alcohol, but the converted al-Ma'din's partook and sold it to the infidel. Perhaps by indulging, he hoped to defuse any challenge that he failed to follow the true faith. Ser al-Ma'din lifted his glass high. "To Sul!"

"To Sul!" the men responded. They tossed the contents back.

"Again!" Ser al-Ma'din waved at Inez and Anita to refill the glasses.

Sera al-Ma'din made a face and left the room.

The company relaxed. This time, the men sipped the sherry as if they had permission to enjoy it.

"So, tell me," Ser al-Ma'din asked, turning to Ximen. "Where is Hector Cortez? He was one of my best customers. I would fill his *vardo* to the brim."

Joachin's expression fell. Miriam wasn't sure how many glasses of sherry he had had.

"He is dead, my friend." Ximen said sadly.

Joachin downed the rest of his glass.

"Dead? How terrible! I am sorry! I didn't know!"

"We all are."

"What happened?" He waved Inez over a third time. "Again. I never tell Fatima, but *saca* offers me solace."

"Torch Bearers," Ximen said.

Joachín ran a hand over his eyes and left it there. Miriam rose to go to him. Zara pulled her back down. "Let the men work it out," she whispered.

"Perhaps, a dance, Joachín?" Ximen suggested.

Ser al-Ma'din looked shocked. "Surely not, if you grieve. Dance is for joyful occasions."

"That is where we differ, *Ser* al-Ma'din." Ximen gave Joachín a long glance. "When we Diaphani grieve, it is the best time for dancing. What we don't express in words, we say with our souls. Dance for us, Joachín," he prompted softly. "Express what we've all held in, so tightly and for so long."

Joachín took a ragged breath and nodded. He set his glass upon the floor. The crowd made room for him. He refused to look at anyone. For a long moment, he stood there, just staring at his feet.

"A *Guiridilla*, I think," Ximen whispered to Iago. "He'll set the tempo." Iago nodded. They waited.

Joachín glanced up abruptly. To Miriam's alarm, tears had streaked his cheeks. "This is for Hector," he mumbled, "and for Tavio, his son."

She wondered how much he had had to drink.

His face twisted. "For Guillermo, my uncle, and for Donaldo, the best guitarist there ever was." His voice broke. He shook his head to clear it. "For Jaime and his bride Kezia, for Lorenzo...." He named every member they had lost, bitterly, painfully—some sixty-two names in all. She was in awe that he remembered them all, when some of them she could barely recall. *How terrible his guilt is,* she realized. He was close to breaking; his shoulders shook. He would not meet her eyes. How had he kept his grief hidden for so long? He took a deep, shuddering breath and composed himself. "For all the deaths of my Tribe, for my family, for all the loves lost." His voice faded to a whisper, but no one missed the last three words, dropped like roses into a grave: "This...small...thing."

He closed his eyes and lifted his arms. He held them tightly, as if fending off a specter—Death, she knew. For a moment he was agonizingly still, and then he slumped, dropping into a wide arc with his leg extended, around and behind, a vortex for all of the sadness in the room. He swept up the grief and clutched it to his chest, embracing it. With another turn, he released it, and let it go.

His feet set a slow beat. He moved stiffly and unseeing, a soldier on a march. Soon, his heels added to the tempo, but the martial element remained. Miriam felt as if he moved through time, as if every aspect of his expression was one of inevitability and suffering, yet somehow, he conveyed the strength to go on. She imagined him at war, on the losing side of a senseless battle. Suddenly, he struck a pose as if to say *enough*. Everyone held their breath, wondering what he would do next.

With intense concentration, he closed his eyes again and his feet began to move. His face tightened, grew hard. Now, he fought Death, pummeled it, his feet struck harder and faster; they became a blur, his timing so convoluted and rapid that if not for his virtuosity, Miriam would have lost track of it. He spun, spiraled, a tempest. His feet never lost the beat. All about her, the Tribe began to clap, matching his passion with their cries. Against the drum, Iago's hands vanished as he kept up the pace.

With one final leap, Joachin pounded his fist to the floor, an imaginary knife in his hand. Then he rose and stabbed the invisible blade into his chest. His face contorted, he pulled it free and tossed it aside. The message was clear: grief is terrible, but through those who live, the dead go on.

Beside her, Luci was weeping openly. Behind her, Zara wailed. Through tear-stained eyes, Miriam stared at Joachin and clutched at her heart. She stumbled for him, wanting to comfort him, but everyone seemed to be of the same mind. People surged past her. She paused, knowing she would find time to be with him later. She would ease his grief in the best way she knew how. No *seraglio* would keep them apart.

To her surprise and dismay, Inez stood beside her, as if she too, had wanted to console Joachin, but common sense prevailed. "There are some things," she said, "that can never be taken from you." She glanced at Miriam. "He dances like that. Like he believes it."

Miriam nodded. "Yes. He reminds us of it."

"He is...." Inez swayed.

Miriam reached for her. "Are you all right?"

"Don't touch me."

She stumbled away. Miriam watched her leave for the kitchen and then she forgot about her, wanting to reach Joachin. He beckoned to her to join him. She pushed her way through the well-wishers, needing to be at his side.

Shortly thereafter, they removed themselves from the crowd. Joachin seemed as anxious to be alone with her as she was with him. Before they fell under *Sera* al-Ma'din's watchful eye, he pulled her from the dining hall. Torches flickered in the courtyard. Joachin drew her into the cave. They stumbled down a dark aisle of barrels. The smell of grape floated heavily on the air. By the time he pulled her around a corner, the light had disappeared.

He drew her down into warm straw. "I am so sorry," he moaned, tucking his head into her shoulder.

"There's nothing to be sorry for," she whispered.

"There is. I have made so many mistakes...."

"Not important. Only this moment, only you."

He kissed her.

Their lovemaking was short, intense, and passionate. Their kisses were few, discarded to the intensity of their need. Miriam held him as if their time together was precious, as if Death floated above them like a vulture. As briefly as it had begun, their love-making ended. She cried her joy, her loss. Moaning and depleted, Joachin slumped beside her.

"I'm afraid." His voice broke. Her shoulder was wet. He was crying again and not hiding it.

"What are you afraid of, Love?"

"Of losing you."

"You won't lose me."

"I've lost everyone. The Tribe, my mother. I can't stand it if I were to lose you."

"That won't happen. I won't let that happen."

"What if it does?"

"Then we'll find each other, again. What is this about, Joachin?"

"Nothing that makes any sense. I love you, Miriam. I love you more than life itself." He hid his face in her hair.

Had he dreamed of a future that boded ill? "I love you, too. Have you had a—"

His lips found hers, stopping her from asking the question.

An hour later and after making love again, although not as desperately as they had the first time, they crept from their hiding place. They passed through the empty courtyard. He walked her to the kitchen, but she hesitated before entering. "I should see Alonso," she told him. "I'm not sure if Casi remembered to feed Blanca. I told him I'd check with him to see if he's learned anything."

"I'll take you." He set a hand to her elbow.

"You won't like it when I put my arms around him."

"Do you have to?"

"I have to touch him to communicate. It's the only way."

"All right." He sounded resigned. "I'll wait for you by the gate."

"I need to get food for Blanca."

"Allow me. If you go in there, *Sera* al-Ma'din might catch you and insist you head for the *seraglio*. If I go, she's more likely to indulge me."

"Fine. I'll wait."

She watched him go and stood in shadow beyond the doorway. The night was sultry, the fountain burbled, she longed for a bath. When Joachin didn't return after five minutes, she headed for it and splashed water on her face and arms. Then hazarding a glance to make sure no men were about, she rinsed her legs. Joachin appeared as she dropped her skirt. He held a bowl of meat scraps in his hands.

"What kept you?" she asked.

"I ran into Inez."

"What did she want?"

"To talk. I said you were waiting."

"What did she want to talk about?"

"She didn't say. I didn't ask."

They headed for the gate. "I don't like her, Joachín. She thinks she has a connection with you."

"I met her in Herradur. Her father was a whoremonger. She turned out to be no better a pimp than he was."

"Then why is she here?"

"I don't know, and I don't care."

"She needs to remember you're my husband."

"Yes. And Alonso needs to remember you're my wife."

She smiled at him ruefully and retrieved the bowl of scraps. It was better when they weren't arguing. Love-making had a lot to do with it. She gave him a quick kiss, content in the knowledge that he watched her as she picked her way down the hill.

Chapter Twenty-Four: Rivals

Where have you been? Alonso stood beside her as they leaned against the wagon. Blanca panted at his feet. *I barked myself hoarse and no one came! Not even Casi!*

I'm sorry. I didn't hear you. There was music and dancing. She flushed guiltily. There was no need to tell him about her time with Joachin.

Tomás is in Anteqarra. That's where the contingent was bound when we saw them leave.

Anteqarra? That isn't far.

Not only that, he has a pet sorceress with him. I couldn't see her face. She wears a veil. They've been trying to find you through blood magic.

A shiver of fear ran up her back.

She sacrificed six doves and dribbled their blood into a bowl. She described the courtyard here and mentioned you and Rivera.

She saw us?

For all I know, she made it up, but the coincidence is too great to ignore. I couldn't see a thing in the water.

We have to leave. Now. In the dark, there's a chance we can skirt Bacalao undetected.

She left him to run back up the hill. At the gate, Joachín stood with Inez in a circle of torchlight. She was doing most of the talking. Joachín listened, but he looked upset. Neither of them noticed her. Joachín shook his head. The breeze carried his voice down the hill. "Impossible."

"It isn't." Inez sounded angry. "Deny it if you like, but it changes nothing." She walked backed to the house.

Miriam drew up to him. "Deny what?"

He turned, startled by her voice. He flushed hotly. "She...she said some things I find hard to believe."

"What things?"

"They don't matter. She's lying. What did Alonso tell you?" He ushered her through the gate.

"He said he found Tomás."

"Where?"

"In Anteqarra."

"Then we need to leave."

"Yes. That's not all. Tomás has a seer in his employ. They're using blood magic to find us. She described our location."

"Gods! If that's the case, they could be on their way! I'll round up Iago, Barto, and Ximen and speak to *Ser* al-Ma'din. With luck, we can sneak past Bacalao. Get the women. I'll meet you at the horses in a few minutes."

He gave her a quick kiss on the cheek. She ran to the house.

As she expected, the kitchen and distillation room were empty, but fortunately, the door to the *seraglio* wasn't locked.

She opened it to find women sleeping on the tiled floor. The Tribe took up one corner. She shook Luci awake. From the far side of the room, Inez sat up on her pallet and watched.

"We have to go," Miriam whispered. Luci nodded and roused Casi.

"What is it?" Zara looked dazed.

"I'll explain when we reach the horses," Miriam said. "Help me wake everyone."

"Torch Bearers?" Luci asked.

"Not yet. Soon, possibly."

Without another word, Zara rose. In moments, all the women had collected their things and were on their feet, heading for the door.

"But I was going to help feed the chickens!" Casi complained to Luci. "I promised!"

"You can't. We're in danger."

"Chickens aren't dangerous!"

"Hold your tongue and come."

Before Miriam knew it, they had passed through the various parts of the bodega and had reached the outer gate. Below them, Joachín and the men were loading small casks onto the wagon. Blanca stood to one side, looking disgruntled.

Miriam ran down the hill to Joachín. "Why are we taking the sherry?" she demanded.

"This is our payment. *Ser* al-Ma'din doesn't carry coin. We'll trade them in Qadis." He cinched the barrels with a strap.

"What about Maia and the baby? Where will Alonso sit?"

"I traded part of our earnings for another horse. Casi and Luci will ride it. There's still room for Maia and the dog in the wagon."

"What are *you* doing here?"

Miriam turned. Zara had confronted someone on their periphery. She squinted against the torch light to determine who it was.

"I'm coming with you."

"No, you aren't. That's my horse you're grabbing."

Miriam frowned at Joachín, and then headed for the two women. "What's going on?"

"*She* says she's coming with us," Zara said.

Inez stood there, refusing to relinquish the reins. "I'm in danger, also. I have to go with you."

For a tense moment, no one said anything. Miriam felt the blood rush to her face. She fought for control. The compulsion to slap Inez was overwhelming. The nerve of the woman! All she wanted was to be with Joachín. "You're not Tribe," she said tightly. "No one invited you."

"I *am* Tribe."

"According to whom?" Zara looked askance.

Inez ignored her and regarded Miriam with calculating eyes. "According to your law." She nodded at Ximen. "I asked him. At supper, when I served him."

Everyone turned to the blind man for explanation. Ximen stood as still as death. Miriam wondered if he were trying to recall the conversation. Unlikely. Ximen forgot nothing.

"He told me that any woman who carries the blood of the Tribe *is* Tribe. I carry José's blood. His seed is in my belly. I am pregnant with his child."

People gasped. Miriam stared at Joachin as if he had punched her. Inez smiled, enjoying the news.

Miriam paled. "Is this true?"

His silence was answer enough.

"How could you do this to me, to *us?*" she shrieked.

He came to life. "Don't believe her. She's lying."

"Did you sleep with her?"

"One night, only. Before I met you. Over two months, ago!"

She couldn't speak. She yanked the reins from Inez and handed them to Zara. Dumbfounded, everyone watched her without speaking.

"Where do I ride?" Inez asked, as if things were settled.

Miriam curled her hands into fists to keep from clawing at her face. Somehow, she found her voice. "If you think to steal my husband, you are sadly mistaken. I will honour Tribal law—for now. But when I have proof you have lied about this, I will cast you from the Tribe myself. Keep away from me and keep out of my sight. I have never cursed anyone, but there's a first time for everything."

Inez shrugged at the empty threat.

"I will ride with Ximen," Miriam said, ignoring protocol. "Iago, double up with Casi. Luci, you will ride with...Joachin." His name was bile. "As for you," she turned to Inez, "you will ride with whomever is willing to take you."

"*Puta,*" Zara muttered.

Miriam didn't correct her. She headed for Iago. Wordlessly, he gave up the reins as she mounted. Ximen sat behind her. She waited stonily as the Tribe figured themselves out. No one wanted to ride with Inez. Finally, Joachin had to determine who her riding partner would be. It turned out to be Nadia, the only choice. Of them all, she was the most tolerant, or perhaps, the most meek.

The ride from the bodega was cool and dark. The moon had set by the time they headed out. The sky was black. Clouds occluded the stars, promising rain. For a time, Miriam welcomed the chill. She felt colder than the night.

Had he known? Was this what he and Inez had been discussing when she had come upon them? Had he been in the habit of bedding anyone he could before he met her? Was she just another one of his women?

I dreamed I held our son in my arms.

A pain too sharp to bear pierced her to the quick. It wasn't their child he had dreamt of, but Inez's. Her throat closed. Her eyes smarted. She had been a fool to believe him, to trust him. And now, this—a dream of what might have been, stolen from her.

Unless she was pregnant, as well.

She stiffened. When had she last bled? With a start, she calculated the days. She was late. Panic spread through her like a weed taking root in her chest.

Behind her, Ximen shifted uncomfortably.

He sensed what she feared. In comparison, the burden of his ancestral memory made her gift as a *sentidora* a frail weight. She reined in her anxiety, forced herself to become calm. Even with the pain of this latest betrayal, she had the wherewithal to choose Ximen for a riding partner. She would take advantage of that decision now. He leaned into her as if expecting the question.

"Is the baby Joachin's?" she asked over a shoulder.

"I don't know."

"But you would have seen them...." It wasn't a pleasant thought. "If she carries his child, wouldn't you know?"

"I won't know until she delivers. When the baby draws its first breath, it steps into the present and sheds a past. If I see that first breath, it's Tribe. If I don't, it isn't."

How confusing. How was a present breath any different from a past one?

"Time is a stream," he said, as if hearing her thought. "The present moment is the clearest, the sharpest. Anything that occurs in the past softens."

"So, if the child is Tribe, you'll sense both its present and its past."

"And only the present, if it isn't."

"A half-blood makes no difference?"

"No. I've been able to see you and Joachin as clearly as anyone."

It was a pity he couldn't look in on Inez's history to see if she had been with anyone else. "Your talent must be a burden at times."

"It changes one."

After half an hour of riding, the torch lights of Bacalao came into view. From the tower closest to the water, a great light shone, a beacon for passing ships. Joachin swung the Tribe beyond its reach in a wide detour. Miriam hoped the town guard watched the water more than they surveyed the terrain. Before them, dark hills rose to a headland. Miriam glanced over her shoulder. Far to the north, torches bobbed along a distant road. Riders, heading for Bacalao. The Guard on their tail, it had to be.

She urged her mare forward. Joachin had to be told.

"He already knows." The wind snatched at Ximen's voice. Ahead, Joachin urged Fidel into a gallop. Every rider behind him followed suit. Behind her, the cart rumbled like thunder. Miriam cursed the casks of sherry they had accepted as payment. If they broke from the bouncing of the wagon, they were a danger not only to the cart, but to Maia and little Grim. She also worried about Alonso and Blanca.

They pounded over the hill and flew down the far side. The lights of Bacalao winked out, as well as the torches approaching the distant crossroads. Her own mare was foaming at the mouth. Spittle flew across her cheeks. Finally, Joachin drew them into a small clearing, surrounded by thick scrub.

He ordered them to stay put, and then spurred Fidel back the way they had come. The Tribe waited anxiously. After fifteen minutes, he returned.

"I don't think they saw us," he said. Fidel's flanks streamed. "We are safe here for a few hours, but we need to leave before dawn."

Wordlessly, the Tribe dismounted. The horses were wiped down, blankets were laid out, and children bundled into them. No one thought to ask if they could light a fire. In small clumps, women curled onto their sides, sheltering their little ones. Iago and Joachin passed a few words. Iago nodded. Joachin clapped him on the shoulder and glanced over to where Miriam stood. His expression pleaded. He wanted her to forgive him.

She turned away. She didn't want to see him, didn't want to acknowledge his existence. What he had done hurt her beyond measure. Inez had created a gulf between them, made worse by the child she carried. Miriam was well aware of him as he strode past her to keep watch on the crown of the hill. She hardened herself, chose a place beside a gorse bush where she might sleep alone and undisturbed.

Heavy paws padded toward her. Alonso sought her out. As the dog dropped beside her, he appeared. He lay against her side, with his head propped on an elbow. He regarded her with concern. *How are you?* he asked.

Heartsick was how she was. She suspected he was going to remind her that he'd been right about Joachin all along. She didn't want to hear it, even if it were true.

Then I won't say it.

Were those Torch Bearers? Did we outrun them?

Yes, on both accounts.

It occurred to her someone should tell Joachin. He needed sleep as much as the rest of them. But she couldn't approach him. Not yet.

Let him be. Alonso sat up. *He'll keep watch, no matter what anyone says.*

She wasn't sure whether that was a censure or a compliment. She wished they were done travelling. The sooner they reached Qadis, the better. *I am so tired of being chased, Alonso,* she said bitterly.

You should sleep. Tomorrow, you'll feel better and we'll be one day closer to the New World.

Yes. Anywhere is better than here. But would Joachin be part of that new life? Of that, she was no longer sure.

To make matters worse, something gushed from between her legs. Her monthly time had come. She was not pregnant with their child.

Joachin hunkered down to watch the bobbing lights dance their way to the gates of Bacalao. Behind him, the Tribe lay hidden in shrubbery and darkness. Despite the lateness of the hour, the riders were admitted without confrontation. No one but the Inquisitional Guard or the king's personal retinue wielded that kind of authority. He breathed a prayer of thanks to Lys for protecting them. They had managed to ride past without being seen.

He ran a hand through his hair and thought of Miriam.

The look she had given him when Inez had accused him, it had been terrible, the shock and hurt plain upon her face. He had betrayed her, *again.*

He clenched his fists and released them, stretching his fingers to loosen them. Inez was lying. He was sure of it. The babe was someone else's, not his.

You can't know for certain, his conscience accused. *You lay with her. It's possible.*

But if that were so, why did he feel the wrongness of it so deeply in his gut? Was he reacting to a lie? Did his tattoo give him the ability to detect falseness in others? He'd always been good at that, had always prided himself on sensing a falsehood when he heard one. But when she had told him that the child was his, the tattoo had *burned,* for gods' sake! He had flinched from the pain of it. What was that, if not a sign?

He rubbed his stomach. There was no way to prove it unless Ximen confirmed paternity, one way or another.

He straightened. He would find out. Once his watch was over, he would speak with the Rememberer. He would set things right with Miriam. She would know the truth and forgive him. As for Inez, he'd....

What would he do, if Ximen confirmed her claim? He could no more abandon her than cut off his right arm. Liar or not, she was in a delicate condition. What kind of a scoundrel tossed a pregnant woman to the hills to fend for herself? He couldn't do it. Impossible.

And Inez knew it, had sensed that about him from the start.

She's playing me like a guitarra. Surely, once Miriam calms down, she'll see the quandary I'm in.

On the other hand, maybe Miriam wouldn't.

Her words echoed in his mind. *If I learn you've lied about this, I'll cast you from the Tribe myself.*

She wouldn't understand. Compared to his lynx, Miriam was a tigress. By far, the more dangerous cat.

He clawed at his hair. There was no solution. If the child were his—which he doubted—Miriam would blame him. She condemned him anyway for sleeping with Inez. If the child wasn't his, Inez was still pregnant. He couldn't abandon her. Either way, he was still caught.

Gravel crunched behind him. He glanced over his shoulder. Inez paused, as if unsure how to approach.

Deflated, he turned his back on her to watch the road.

His dismissal didn't daunt her. She settled onto the grass beside him. After a moment, she asked softly, "Is it so bad that I carry our child?"

The question ignited his annoyance. "Under the circumstances, yes." Maybe she would go away if he was blunt and told her the truth. Not that he had any other option.

"When I told Pepe, he threw me out. He said he had no place for squalling brats."

His truth tattoo didn't react negatively. It was an honest admission. He shrugged. "So, none of you girls ever get pregnant?" He knew the answer to that.

"When they do, they take care of it."

He could ask her to abort. Zara would help. But he didn't like the idea, mostly because it made life easier—for him.

"I don't want to get rid of it," she said. "No one has ever loved me except my mother, and then you, that one night. I will have my baby, José. I will love it, and it will love me, even if you don't."

Against his better judgment, a tendril of sympathy unfurled for her in his heart. He could well imagine how she felt. Pepe, her father, had been a brute, no better than Rufio the whaler, who he had beaten the night they had been together. Love was not a commodity to be found in Herradur.

"When I learned about the baby, it made me happy."

His tattoo flared.

"That isn't true." He glanced at her, sidelong.

"Of course, I was also upset, as you might expect. You were gone by then. But I can't think of a better man with whom to share my life."

"I'm sharing my life with someone else."

"If I'd gone with you when you asked, that wouldn't be the case."

He wasn't sure about that, but he wasn't about to argue it either. He doubted Inez had faith in the gods. Suggesting that the goddess had ordained his life with Miriam would make no sense to her. "Miriam is my wife now. I'm sorry you are pregnant, but it changes nothing."

"She isn't a good wife. If she was, she'd be with you now. She'd forgive you your sins, accept you for who you are. Does she accept you, José? My guess is she doesn't."

She was very close to the mark. There were things Miriam disliked about him—his thieving, in particular. "It's Joachin," he said.

"Joachin. I wondered if you had told me your real name."

"I apologize for misleading you."

"Don't. I expected it. You could murder the Pope of Roma, and I'd still accept you. We are of a kind, Joachin. You and Madelaina? Not of the same coin. I know her type—always judging, always thinking she's better than everyone else. Me? I understand you. You'd be happier with me and the baby. I'd make it my business to keep you that way."

"You should go, now."

"Perhaps. But that doesn't change what she is or who you are. And I'd never leave you, Joachin. One day, she will. I would die for you. Remember that."

He stared over the black hills. Inez made her way back to the circle of bush that shrouded the Tribe. He wished he was a thousand miles away, across the Great Ocean Sea, with his wife at his side.

The night was cold. A wind whipped about his shoulders. He welcomed it, even though it froze him. It was penance. More torch lights appeared at the town's gate. Riders spilled through, heading east. He half stood, half crouched, ready to shout a warning. Fortunately, they kept going and were soon lost in the distance. Iago came up from behind him. "Where are they going, do you think?"

For a moment, he didn't reply. The bodega lay to the east. "I don't know," he said uneasily, "but we are very lucky we left when we did."

"You should get some sleep."

His watch was over, but he couldn't leave. The riders might return at any time.

"Go, Cousin. My eyes are as sharp as yours. Besides, the dog will alert us."

He didn't like it, but Iago was right. He was exhausted. He nodded and made his way down the hill. He headed to where Miriam lay beneath the trees. A pale lump lifted its head in the darkness.

Blanca exposed sharp teeth and growled, but he knew full well it was Alonso he confronted. For a moment, the two rivals regarded each other, their loathing mutual. The ruff along Blanca's spine stood up on end.

"You think you can sleep with *my* wife, and I won't have a problem with it?" Joachín objected.

The dog stared him down, its black eyes challenging.

Joachín curled his lip. "Enjoy it while you can, *chilito*. It won't last, this dispute between her and me. And when it ends, you'll be outside the tent, pining."

He made his way to a lonely spot. Blanca watched him without moving.

Sleep was not long in coming for Joachín. Despite being on edge, the world faded into dream. He stood on a familiar street. Miriam cried in fear as half a dozen members of the Inquisitional Guard charged toward her. She bolted in the opposite direction, only to be confronted by more of them pounding around a corner. From out of nowhere, Tomás appeared. "Catch her!" he shouted. Miriam kept fading in and out. At one point, she looked as if she wore a different face. Who...?

The scene wavered, grew indistinct, and then he was the one being confronted, but by soldiers in naval regalia. A tall, black-haired captain stood at the edge of the vision. He couldn't quite make out the stranger, although he was certain he had heard his voice before. "Take him away," the man ordered.

A sudden sense of vertigo, and the dream shifted a third time. Miriam, surrounded by Tomás's troops again. She screamed as the thugs bore down upon her.

"No!" He reached for her.

The dream shattered like ice. He sucked in a breath and opened his eyes to a starless sky. His heart thudded in his chest. He was chilled to the bone.

What did it mean? He knuckled his eyes, hoping to make the dream sharper. Once again, the visions had been superimposed. Was he seeing two possible outcomes? How could that be? Wasn't the future set?

He had long had his suspicions about the future. Perhaps what he saw were only probabilities if they maintained their present course.

What if they avoided Qadis altogether? In his half of the dream, the dock guards wore regalia similar to the town's port authority. It wasn't the same as he remembered, but it was close enough. If they didn't go to Qadis, they would have to find another way to the New World. That would take weeks. The fastest way was to board the ship that waited for them. On the other hand, if they stayed in Esbaña, the likelihood was high that Miriam would be caught.

His half of the dream hadn't said he'd been apprehended by the dock guards. He might escape. The tall, dark-haired stranger was the key. If he watched for him, he might avoid capture altogether, unless it was a question of either-or. Either he broke free and Miriam didn't, or it was the other way around.

They would have to chance it. The *Patrón's* ship was the fastest way. If he didn't board the *Phoenix* with the rest of the Tribe, at least he would have the comfort of knowing Miriam was safe, no matter what his own fate might be.

Sometimes, it was better not knowing.

There was no point trying to sleep. Dawn was still an hour away. The more distance they put between themselves and the Guard, the better. He had to get the Tribe moving. He brushed the grit from his clothes and set off to awaken his wife.

Chapter Twenty-Five: Vow

Rana Isadore sat before a mirror and considered the pockmarks on her face. She couldn't bear to wear the veil at the moment; her welts itched. She had thought they might spend the night in Anteqarra, but Tomás decided she had seen grape vats in her prior viewing. She shouldn't have been so forthcoming. He had forced her to scry again as soon as they had arrived in Bacalao. He had made her throttle several cats. They had scratched her hands to shreds, but the blood was enough to finally pinpoint the bitch. The Tribe was lodged at a bodega, owned by an old *morisco*, not far from here. She had been so tired, so overwhelmed by Tomás's abuse, that she had let it slip.

They're my people. I don't want to hurt them. I only want to hurt her. Rana stared at her face and grimaced. Her brow was permanently swollen, her cheeks ridged in scabs. Her eyes were two black beads set above an ugly snout. *A pig's face,* Angél had told her. The taunt had hurt, but he was right. She was a monster. She didn't blame him for turning her over to the Guard. She would have done the same.

She fingered the bone necklace about her throat. Tomás had finally given it back, partly as a reward for telling him where the Tribe was, but also to show her she held no power over him. In Anteqarra, he had draped it over her breasts as he raped her to prove that point. Rana glared at her reflection as if Miriam stood before her in the mirror.

You're the cause of all this. Anassa, her *puri*, had wrongly bequeathed the necklace to Miriam, when she, Rana, was the rightful heir. After the Guard had torched the Womb, she had insisted to the Ferraras that they return to collect the chain from Anassa's corpse. She had cut her grandmother's little finger from her dead hand. Anassa's knuckle now graced the chain. But even that remnant of grandmother's power was not enough to spark the magic to life.

The necklace isn't meant for you.

Rana started. The voice had come from nowhere, closer than breath. It didn't sound like her dead *puri*, so it had to be an older Ancestor. She dared not think it might be something greater. *Who are you?* she challenged. When the voice didn't reply, she dismissed it as a prick of conscience.

She'll answer for all of it, she promised herself, touching the strand of knuckles at her throat. *For Puri's death, for Paré's, and all the rest. For taking my place as matriarch, but mostly, for stealing Angél.*

She eyed her reflection in the mirror and grimaced. Then she pinned the veil into place. Her vagina still hurt from Tomás's brutalizing. She lay down on her cot and closed her eyes, too tired to blow out the candle.

Chapter Twenty-Six: Inferno

His lower back ached. A bruise was forming. The one chance he had had to sneak into Rana Isadore's chamber was lost; Morales had discovered him creeping up the stairway to the second floor as they were about to ride.

"Where the blazes are you going, Raúl?" the captain bellowed. "Come down here, at once. We're leaving! I can't have the Grand Inquisitor see you bungling about!"

He had received the customary clout over the head. That was becoming a bad habit.

"I swear, if I have to warn you again, I'll send you mewling back to your mother!" Morales yanked him down the stairs. To add further injury to insult, he set a heel to his backside and sent him sprawling out the door.

Riding the nag the captain had given him didn't help either, nor did the worn excuse for a saddle. At the head of the line, Morales rode at Tomás's side. Francisco gritted his teeth against the pain and set his mind to working out a plan. Kidnapping wasn't his usual style, but he might have to risk it if Rana Isadore were to help Ilysabeth assume the throne.

The moon rose, illuminating banks of mist that lay in thick shrouds over the countryside. The land was releasing its sullen dead. Sixty years before, the ground had been drenched in Moori blood. They were riding forth to question old *moriscos* and possibly do worse.

The Guard rode hard up a hill. On its lee side, a bodega appeared, nestled amid rows of black vines. Those who lived and worked there slept. The building shed no light.

Not for long, Francisco thought grimly.

"Open up! In the name of the Grand Inquisitor!" Captain Morales stood with his hands on his hips as if refusing to dirty his hands on the Moori gate. An ornate Sul Star had been set upon it, as if the owners hoped to convince the world of their devotion.

No one appeared to grant them entry

"Secure the periphery," Tomás ordered, dismounting. Morales waved off a dozen riders. They broke from the contingent to surround the estate. Francisco remained at the rear of the troop.

From beyond the gate, an old *morisco* appeared, holding a lantern aloft. He squinted at them. "Is there something I can assist you with, friends?" he asked.

Morales confronted him. "Are you the owner of this establishment?"

"I am."

"Are there Diaphani on the premises?"

"I...."

Tomás yanked open the gate. "Arrest him. He'll lie. They always do." He pushed past *Ser* al-Ma'din. The rest of the troop followed him into the courtyard. Two guards clapped hands on the old *morisco*.

"I protest!" *Ser* al-Ma'din cried. "We've broken no law!"

Tomás ignored him and addressed Morales. "I want every corner searched, every cave explored. They'll flee us like rats from a fire."

Ser al-Ma'din spread his hands for and mercy. "Great One, I didn't know they were criminals! Had I known, I wouldn't have let them stay!"

"Ignorance is no defense," Morales told him.

"We are isolated, here! We don't know what's happening in the cities!"

Tomás turned on him. "Then that is your undoing, old man! *Where are they?*" His vehemence startled Francisco. Tomás looked to be on the verge of losing control. The scar across his face had turned livid.

"The men are in the sheds and the women in the *seraglio*! But they are only women and children!"

"Harem's quarters?" Tomás turned to Morales. "Take the men there. If you locate Miriam Medina or Joachin de Rivera, bring them to me at once."

Morales motioned to the Guard to conduct the search.

"Wait!" Tomás pointed directly at the group of men with whom Francisco stood. His belly dropped into his boots. If Tomás recognized him.... He lowered his head to hide his face beneath his helmet. "You men," Tomás said. "Gather wood. As much as you can find. It's a cold night. We should have a fire." He smiled nastily as he headed for the doorway leading into the house.

Francisco wanted to grab his horse and run, to ride all the way back to Bacalao where he would take Rana Isadore hostage, but Morales would have none of it. In the bedlam created by women roused from their sleep and men knocked into senselessness, Morales took it upon himself to turn his *primo* into a soldier. Francisco became his appendage, his third arm. He was forced to throw men into the *seraglio* and hold them at bay by the sword. In a daze, he stacked straw against the walls and doused it with oil. As the torches were tossed, he relived every excruciating moment when, as an eight year old, he had watched his mother, accused of being a *strega*, burn. While Sera al-Ma'din screeched curses, Morales held him close, as tightly as a lover. People shrieked as the fire quickly spread. The only thing that kept him from charging into the inferno to save them was to remember Ilysabeth. He was useless to her dead. As he and Morales fled like cowards, the last thing he saw was the old *morisca*, Sera al-Ma'din, as her robes burst into flame. Her screams still echoed in his ears.

The ride back to Bacalao was a nightmare. The contingent, having raided the bodega before setting it afire, drank and tossed bottles all the way back to the town's precincts. Tomás indulged them, although Francisco noted the Grand Inquisitor did not partake. Half way there, Morales, too drunk to have the capacity to sit astride his horse, ordered him to lead, while he rode second saddle behind him. He clapped his gloved arms about his waist and whispered into his ear, his voice a slur.

"Remember, when we were boys, Raúl? When I was eighteen and you were twelve? Remember?" He laughed crudely.

Francisco nodded, terrified that if he lifted his head too high, Tomás would recognize him. The Grand Inquisitor rode at their side. Tomás smiled coolly, as if party to their intimacy, but he kept his eyes ahead on the dark road.

"When we get back, you should come to my room. For 'nother... drink. We can talk ov...over old...times."

"Of course, Captain. As you wish." He had no intention of accompanying him.

"It's a...good night. Burned the dev...devils out of their...beds." Morales lurched dangerously behind him. He caught Francisco by the arm.

"You're...a good boy, Raúl. You...did well."

He felt sick. They had set an old woman on fire. In all of his days as an agent for both the Papacy and for Ilysabeth, he had never, ever, done such a detestable thing. He hated Morales, loathed the entire Esbañish army, despised everything the Inquisition and Grand Inquisitor represented. He would never be able to atone, never wash that stain of death from his hands. He had done to the al-Ma'dins what they had done to his mother.

Morales's head fell against his shoulder. He was asleep.

Half an hour later, Tomás drew the contingent to a halt. They were still five leagues from Bacalao, but Tomás could ride no further. His knife wound ailed him. Looking spent, he called for a break. The troop dismounted, many of the men still drunk. Morales roused and slid from the back of their horse. He landed in a heap.

"Help me, Raúl...." He waved a paw in Francisco's direction.

Francisco dismounted and helped him up.

Morales draped an arm about his shoulders. "S'get out of here...." He waved at the trellises of vines beyond the road.

Francisco kept his head down, too aware of Tomás watching them.

"You may as well use the time to help him walk it off," Tomás said testily. He eased himself onto a patch of grass. All about them, men stumbled or collapsed, depending on their state of inebriation. Horses browsed.

"Over there." The captain pointed down a row of grapes.

Francisco took him that way, glad to be out of Tomás's sight.

"Old times," Morales mused. He released Francisco to become a dark hulk lumbering down a row. He laughed loudly and pulled them around a corner. He fell into the grapes.

I could kill him, now, Francisco thought, staring down at him. *It would be easy*. There was still the problem of heading back, retrieving a horse, and abducting Rana Isadore. *Difficult, but not impossible.*

"C'mere, *primo*." Morales wrapped a hand about his calf and tugged him to his knees. Francisco fell awkwardly on top of him.

"Li'l Raúl. 'Member when we were boys? What we used to do?"

Before he could stop him, Morales grabbed him hard and kissed him, forcing his tongue down his throat. Francisco choked. How had he not seen? Outwardly, Morales had despised him, hated him when he was a priest. But under it all, Morales preferred men. He just wasn't willing to acknowledge it consciously or display it in a country that celebrated *machismo* above all else.

He and the captain had murdered a helpless old woman, just as his mother had been. They had burned a dozen more. And Morales wanted to celebrate it by reliving old times with cousin Raúl.

Fine. Coitus was a tool. So was a knife.

Francisco cupped Morales by the crotch. The captain groaned, pulled at his breeches so they might have sex unencumbered. Then he froze.

"You're not Raúl!" Morales glared at him, the shock of recognition overriding his drunkenness. "You're...that priest! Guards!"

Francisco stabbed him in the heart.

"It's all right!" he waved his hands at the soldiers who had come lurching up the row of grapes to answer the captain's call. He laughed feebly and set his palms on his knees to catch his breath. "It was only a snake. I killed it. Scared the hell out of us!"

From behind him, the captain's legs stuck out from beneath the vines. The guards stopped abruptly.

Francisco walked toward them and nudged a thumb in Morales's direction. "He wants more *saca*."

"There isn't any." The guard in front spoke.

"There better be, or he'll have our heads."

A second guard nudged his companion in the side. "Emilio has some. I saw him hide it in his saddlebag."

"Let's get it." Francisco waved at the captain. "Leave him for now. He can barely walk." He grinned.

The guards shrugged and waited for him to catch up.

"Raúl, isn't it? I heard you're his *primo*?" The bigger guard spoke.

"What of it?"

"Nothing." The guards shared a look and smirked.

Francisco stared them down. They glanced away and refused to meet his eye. Good. They thought he and Morales were lovers. Let them think that long enough for him to escape.

In moments, they were back at the camp. He headed for the horses. Tomás still sat on the grass nursing his side.

"You there," Tomás pointed at him. "Help me up."

Francisco set his boot in the stirrup and addressed the first guard. "See to him. I have to take care of the captain."

"I said *you*, not him!" Tomás struggled to his feet. "How dare you ignore my direct command? I'll have you flogged for insubordination! Dismount at once!"

The only way of escape was to rein the horse in Tomás's direction. He kept his head down, but from his elevated position, it was impossible to hide his face. Tomás gasped as he saw him.

"Stop him! I know him! He's a Papal spy!"

"He was with the captain!" one of the guards shouted.

"Gods! Where is Morales? Don't let him get away!"

Francisco spurred the horse hard and the great beast bore him away. In seconds, there were sounds of pursuit as the guards took up the chase. His heart thudded in his veins, excitement washed through him in a flood. Most of the guards fell behind, one slipped from the saddle entirely, but the one who had asked him his name, the biggest one, closed in. Maybe he held his liquor better than the rest.

He allowed his charger to slow, not enough to suggest that he meant to engage his enemy—a fool's choice to show his hand too soon—but enough to make him think he was gaining. Behind him, the pounding hooves grew louder. From out of his peripheral vision, he watched as the guard withdrew his sword from its scabbard. He held his breath and forced himself to stay where he was.

The guard shouted victory. The sword whistled home.

And struck thin air.

Francisco ducked as far as he could as the sword cut above him. He clung to the pommel and pulled hard on the reins, causing his mount to spin about. As the horses screamed and collided, their impact jarred his assailant loose. Francisco kicked him hard under the chin, knocking him to the ground. Before the man could rise, he leapt from his mount and speared him through the throat.

He didn't wait to watch the light die in the guard's eyes. He had no time to waste. The others would be on him in a minute. As he mounted up, he thought of taking the guard's horse for Rana Isadore, but dismissed it as quickly. Lately, he had made too many mistakes. There was no way he could return to Bacalao to fetch her, now. He would have to watch from a distance and wait for an opportunity to present itself.

Chapter Twenty-Seven: Blood Ward

They broke camp before sunrise. Ignoring Joachin, Miriam asked Maia if she could take her place in the cart. She wanted to be with Alonso so they could watch for pursuit. Joachin endured her snub and said nothing.

They avoided the main road. Joachin led them onto higher and broader outcroppings overlooking the sea. In the pre-dawn light, they followed narrow trails that meandered along wind-scoured slopes. The way became difficult to follow, but it meant leaving little in the way of tracks.

Far below and out on the grey water, the surf roared. Breakers rolled in and crashed against the cliffs. Stone arches fell from the land to the sea, bridges that dipped into a dark unknown. Alonso floated in and out of her awareness. Miriam's throat closed. She found it hard to breathe. She feared for the old *moriscos* and what their harbouring of the Tribe might have cost them.

If only Anassa was with us, she thought. *She would know what to do, how to protect us.*

She caught her breath, startled by a sudden insight. Anassa, her old mentor, had known about wards. She had kept the Tribe safe the night Rana had called the *hymenoptera* into being.

Blood magic might be used against blood magic.

Joachín lifted his fist to signal a stop. Barto drew on the reins. All about her sherry casks lurched, threatening to tip, but she didn't notice. Instead, she jumped from the wagon to seek out the one man who might advise her. Ximen wasn't able to confirm the paternity of Inez's child, but he remembered every event involving the Tribe.

She didn't care if she bled herself dry. She would carve as many tattoos as were needed to keep Tomás and pet witch at bay.

"That won't work," Ximen told her. The impending sunrise stained the horizon a mottled red. The Tribe had gathered about them to listen to their talk about wards. "First of all, the Grand Torch Bearer didn't know we were at the Womb until the Patriarch...." He looked uncomfortable and avoided Joachín's eyes. "Well, that's neither here nor there. The Womb is a sacred place," he continued, "with natural shields. Anassa used sage to strengthen them, but we have none of that here. Nor would it be effective against the Guard. They already know approximately where we are. Especially since their own seer tells them."

"What if we target her?" Zara suggested. "Not that I'm good at it, but there must be a few among us who can cast an effective curse." She glanced around. "Don't tell me I'm the only one whose tried it."

Ximen waved the suggestion aside. "If she's already in the Grand Torch Bearer's employ, she'll have enough talent to ward herself from those things. Besides," he added, "I don't like to stoop to that level."

Zara glared at him. "She is tracking us, Ximen! If she pinpoints us, that devil will hunt us down and burn us like tinder! It's hardly up to you to tell us what we might or might not do!"

"I meant no insult, Zara."

"There must be something," Miriam said.

Ximen met her gaze. "There is. But it isn't pleasant, and it *is* painful."

"I'll do what I must."

"It not only involves you, although you'd be the nexus. It requires every woman here to cut herself. And you, Matriarch, will be carved many times." His eyes grew distant. "It's an unusual glyph. It's only been used a few times, and the last was over six hundred and thirty-two years ago. Our men were being wiped out. Our women faced enslavement by the great Ghengis Ghan."

"Let me do it." Joachin stepped forward.

Ximen shook his head. "You can't, Patriarch. Your role is to protect us physically. This battle is on the etheric plane where energies engage, attack, and deflect. Women have always been the stronger in such conflicts. They are the ones with the true power. The Church knows and fears it."

"What do we do?" Luci's expression was taut.

"Every woman carves her right palm with this sign." Ximen scratched a curious mark into the dirt. It looked like a snake, swallowing its tail.

"Me, too?"

Ximen studied Casi for a moment. "No, I don't think so."

"Why not?"

"You haven't crossed the threshold into womanhood, yet."

Casi scoffed. "What difference does that make? I'm a part of this Tribe. If I can help, I will."

"Very well," Ximen said. "If a girl is close and willing, it should be allowed. It'll hurt, though." He eyed her dubiously.

"I've outlived a viper's bite. One little cut on the hand won't compare to that."

Ximen smiled at her faintly and then glanced at Barto and Joachin. "We'll need a sharp knife."

"Do I participate, as well?" Maia stepped forward. Barto set a hand on her shoulder and looked grim.

"You're not of the blood. However...."

"What do you mean, she's not of the blood?" Zara rounded on him. "I delivered that baby and set a tattoo on her, Ximen! Maia is like my own daughter. She's Tribe! Of course, I can't speak for you, *carina*, it's up to you and your man, but if it were up to *me*—"

"It's up to the Matriarch, actually."

"I think," Miriam began, "that Tribe is as much about loyalty as it is about blood." She glanced at Joachin, her intent clear: *maybe you didn't betray me with Inez, but it feels like you did.* It infuriated her Inez stood beside him.

Inez surveyed her loftily. "I have both loyalty *and* blood." She cupped her belly with a hand.

"In succession, each of you must cut the matriarch after carving yourselves," Ximen said. "When you press your blood into hers, the bond becomes a shield, nearly unbreakable. By enduring this on behalf of the Tribe, our matriarch protects us. Once it's done, she'll be able to buffer us through intention alone. We men will also be protected by association."

Miriam was glad her anger snuffed her fear. "So this will keep us hidden from her prying, all the way to Qadis? See us safely aboard the *Phoenix* to the New World?"

"It should. There's only thing that can break it."

"Which is?"

"A stronger, darker spell. I'm not sure what that might entail."

Inez glanced at Miriam and smiled. "Let's get on with it."

The multiple tattoos were to form an interlinking chain across her belly. They had no ink, but Ximen assured them that if the cuts were broad enough, scarification would result. Joachin's knife would accomplish it. Miriam shed her dress and stood shivering in the breeze. The women formed a wall about her; the men retreated behind a finger of rock. Zara was the first to step forward. Luci and Casi shifted to accommodate the breach. As the sun broke the horizon, the potion-maker lifted the knife and flinched as she sliced her own palm. Then, gingerly, she carved Miriam, apologizing all the while. The cut burned, but what bothered Miriam more was the warm trickle of blood that dripped from it. Zara hadn't cut deeply— Ximen had impressed upon them that that wasn't necessary—but, still, being carved by someone else made it worse. As she clamped her teeth together and winced, Zara murmured in sympathy. Then she set her own bleeding palm to the cut.

At her touch, Miriam's talent as a *sentidora* spun out of control, reacting to Zara's blood. The potion-maker's immediacy nearly slayed her. She felt as if she were a cave and Zara, a landslide that choked every space. The sensation passed quickly, but she understood Zara in a way she never had before. Zara was not just a good-hearted, but lacking-in-morals, busy-body. She was as solid as iron, with a dedication to the Tribe to match. Every man was her husband, she was mother to every child. It came as a shock to realize if not for Lys's intervention, Zara would have followed Anassa as matriarch.

"Thank you, Zara," Miriam whispered, amazed by her strength.

Something passed behind Zara's glance—appreciation, a gratitude someone else recognized her worth. She must have sensed something of the kind in Miriam. "Anything," she whispered, her jowls trembling.

Luci followed Zara, and then Casi and the rest. As each woman scored her palm and Miriam's belly, Miriam was struck anew. Luci's compassion knew no bounds. For a brief moment, Miriam thought she stared into the eyes of Lys. Luci mirrored an aspect of divinity that always accepted and never condemned. With Casi, the experience was fluid—she was a river, or perhaps a stream. She rushed and bounced over every boulder of adventure, pausing only briefly to reflect on the eddies of life. Miriam found her a balm. She and Alonso had saved her from the viper. In coming so close to death, was Casi's joy in living the result? Miriam decided if she ever needed rejuvenation, she would seek out Casi and sit by her side.

Finally, Inez stood before her. She sliced the glyph into her hand without flinching, and then watched the blood crease her palm. She regarded Miriam shrewdly, assessing, judging.

Miriam met her stare. They studied each other silently, two lionesses hunched over the same piece of meat. Miriam however, was the more blooded. Her legs were streaked in red. Scarlet smeared her waist, burning and itching. She felt as if something was trying to gnaw her in half. Inez had yet to touch her. She could still refuse it. But Inez's tattoo would complete the chain.

Inez's nostrils flared. For a moment, Miriam thought she was going to stab her, but Inez hesitated. *She's afraid!* Miriam realized with a flush of victory. Inez's brashness covered her fear. She had never witnessed a rite such as this. *If she thinks I'm capable of enduring these cuts, she'll think I'm capable of anything.* "Are you going to cut me," she asked tightly, "or must I show you how?"

Inez didn't move, except to press her lips together. Miriam grabbed her hand and set the point against her side. Inez grimaced, swallowed. Miriam lifted her hand away, freeing her to do what was necessary.

She held her breath and waited. It was altogether possible that she had misread her, that Inez would gore her instead.

Inez's face twisted. She took a sharp breath and slashed the final circle. Miriam gasped. The knife cut more deeply than necessary, but fortunately, not so deep as to sever muscle. During the instant it took her to do it, Inez slapped her hand against her side.

The unnecessary force made Miriam stagger. All about her, women cried in dismay. Miriam didn't hear them. Instead, Inez's blood mingled with hers, sucking her into a maelstrom. Angry memories spun about her like fists. Inez's world was one of war. Every hand that reached had to be struck away, every blow, dodged. In the eye of this storm, a soft light flickered. Inez's baby. Joachin's, as well.

No! This child could not be his. Inez had imposed this upon them. The fetus was an innocent, although its mother was not. Miriam reached for the quavering light, not willing to miss the opportunity to know for certain. This was what Inez was afraid of; that Miriam would finally know the baby's father.

Too late, a flood swept her away. The magic took its effect, the chain was done, the Tribe's influence passed through her in a tide. She was no longer a lone presence, but one of many. She fell to her knees.

"Gods!" someone shouted. Hands lifted her from where she had fallen. Inez stood back as the women pushed past her.

"Is she all right? What happened?" Joachin stepped out from behind the finger of stone. The men appeared behind him.

Zara turned on Inez. "What did you do?" she demanded.

"Nothing! I cut her, like the rest of you!"

"If you hurt her...!"

Miriam moaned. Luci gathered her into her arms. "She's all right, I think. She just needs air. Step back, the rest of you. She's in shock."

"Are you all right?" Zara thrust her way past Luci.

The weight of so many pressed upon her. She had no desire to sit up. She felt more connected to the Tribe than ever. Her talent as a *sentidora* had also increased; she sensed their presence without having to touch them. As she focused on each woman, their outlines blurred, as if they were covered by an invisible blanket. She drew in a deep breath. The effort helped, the weight subsided. "I'm...I'm fine. A little faint...."

"Get her cleaned up. Give her something to eat."

"Sterilize her cuts with sherry!" Ximen called from the rock spur. Joachin strode towards them.

"Patriarch! You have no business here!" Zara barred his way. "We're not done. Go back until she's decent."

Miriam smiled wanly. As strange and misplaced as it was, Zara *did* have a sense of propriety.

"Don't stand there! Off you go!" Zara shooed him.

"Casi, follow Joachin and bring us the liquor," Luci said.

Casi trotted after him. "Look, Joachin! I got my first tattoo!" She extended her hand and showed him proudly.

Chapter Twenty-Eight: Flight

Rana stared at the blood curdling in the bowl. The image of Miriam being cut by a strange woman dissipated. Red threads floated where the vision had been.

She knocked the dish to the floor. The bowl broke into shards. She was too frustrated to move, too furious to call for Tanya to clean up the mess.

She rubbed her temples through her veil.

A ward, it had to be, and powerful magic. She had never seen a chain of tattoos like that before. How had the bitch known to use it? And how had the Tribe become aware of her spying?

Do they know it's me? she wondered. Part of her considered Miriam might, but logic suggested she would have only sensed her intrusion. The spell wasn't that specific. Perhaps the Tribe guessed Tomás would attempt something of the kind.

Through an arrow slit, she stared at the brightening sky.

Miriam had asked Ximen, "This will protect us all the way to Qadis? See us on board the *Phoenix* to the New World?" Obviously, the *this* was the tattoo. She had been fortunate to hear those plans. The Tribe was heading for the port. Judging from the terrain, they were five days out. She would have to consult Tomás' maps to confirm.

It didn't really matter if they blocked her. She knew where they were going.

Her door opened. She turned, expecting Tanya with her breakfast. Instead, Tomás stood in the doorway.

She caught at the necklace about her throat. For a moment, he said nothing, only paused to regard the damning evidence at her feet—three dead hens, bloody water, and a broken bowl. He had forbidden her to scry on her own. He needed to control everything.

"I hope you saw something worthwhile," he said softly. His pupils were huge and dilated. He stank of burnt flesh. What had he done?

"I...I did!"

"What did you see?"

"I saw them. I know where they are."

He floated through the door, a demon without legs, his robes creating that effect. "Yes?" He paused, mid-way. She remained where she was. He liked fear. She wondered if he smelled hers.

"They're heading for Almerida."

"Almerida? Now why would they head east when they've been heading west along the coast?"

"I don't know. I...I watched them ride into the rising sun. Maybe they think you'll make that assumption."

He was across the room in an instant. She had seen his tattoo for speed a few times, when he had removed all of his clothes. He was deathly afraid of assassins ever since Joachín de Rivera had stabbed him.

He grabbed her by the hair and swung her about. She felt as if her scalp were being ripped from her skull. She cried out in pain and tripped over his feet. He held her suspended over a dish shard, the sharp point at her eye. "You're lying! Don't think I won't cut that ugly face and make it better!"

"They're going to Almerida! I'm telling you the truth!"

"If you're lying, I'll stab it out! I don't need a seer with two eyes!"

"I'm not lying!" She began to cry.

He yanked her up by the head and threw her to her bed. "You disgust me," he said.

Her head pounded. She felt sick. To her relief, he didn't order her to spread her legs and offer herself to him. Instead, he headed for the door. "I have to sleep. In a few hours, you'll scry again to make sure, and then we ride for Almerida."

She slid to her knees. "Thank you, Radiance." The expected response. A mistake not to give it.

She listened for his footsteps to fade before she cupped a hand to her cheek. A new lump was forming there. Her heart pounded with fear and hope. She had been given this chance, a few hours. If he lied to test her, it didn't matter. He had never threatened her with the loss of body parts before. He had to be nearing the end of his patience. Or perhaps something had caused him to lose it.

She limped to the door and peered out.

Tanya huddled against the far wall. Rana pulled her into the room and shut the door. "Bring me a bird. A messenger pigeon."

"I don't know if the keep has them—"

"Of course, it has them! Bring me one, and pack provisions. We're leaving."

"The guards will stop us."

"I will deal with that."

"They won't let me take a horse."

Rana dug her nails into her arm. Tanya yelped. "Tell them the Veiled Woman needs dogwort, a hard-to-come-by herb. If they pester you, keep repeating it. Pretend you're in a trance. If you confuse them, so much the better. That's what we want."

"We?"

"Yes, we! Do you want to stay here? We'll have a better chance if we go together. If you breathe a word of this to anyone, I'll kill you."

"He'll know."

"He *won't* know, unless you take too long about it! He's not a god, for bloody sakes. Do what I say if you value your life!"

Tanya bit her lip and ran.

"The bird, first!" Rana hissed after her.

She closed the door softly and headed for the small table that served as a desk. She retrieved the velum and quill she had requested earlier. In as tiny a script as she could muster, she wrote:

> Dearest Angél,
> In five days, the Tribe boards the Phoenix in Qadis. They go to the New World. I don't want to go with them. Come to me. I'll wait for you at La Casa Gallina, an inn not far from the docks. I think you know it. I love you—Miriam.

Ten minutes later, Tanya returned with the bird. Taking it, Rana sent her off to fetch the horse. It wasn't difficult to imprint the pigeon with Angél's location. It was simply a matter of marking the bird's head with spit, making the proper glyph and focusing on who and where. After tying the message to its leg, she tossed it to the winds. She watched as it became a white speck against the ruddy sky. Tolede was two days away. Angél would come to Qadis. He would believe the note because he wanted to believe it.

And when he comes, how do I fix things? She had never been much of a planner. Her way was to act on instinct when the moment felt right. With Tomás riding around in circles, the Tribe would flee in safety. Angél would come to Qadis. She would find a way to entrap Miriam Medina. And then....

For the first time in months, Rana laughed.

And then...she would tell her own dear husband the bitch was dead.

"What's going on here?" Rana set her hands on her hips. Tanya stood uselessly to the side, repeating the litany, *She needs dogwort.* Two of the keep's hostlers held the mare by its reins. "We release no mount without the Grand Inquisitor's say-so," the tallest one said.

"Well, *I* have his say-so. You're wasting precious time. I have things to do for his Radiance this morning. He needs dogwort. If you don't allow us to collect it from the nearby hills, he'll be displeased."

"I never heard of dogwort," the second mumbled.

Rana glared at him, knowing her regard from beneath the veil unnerved most men. The Guard whispered about her, although not with the same coarse comments they used when they spoke of Tanya.

"You've never heard of it," she said softly, "because it is used in sacrificial rites." She tilted her head slightly in Tanya's direction. Tanya, thank the goddess, didn't notice. The hostlers shifted uneasily. "If one of you would rather take her place, that's up to you."

The moment lengthened.

"Fine." Rana grabbed the reins. "We'll be off, then."

The bigger of the two hostlers barred her way. "I'm not sure I can...."

Rana lifted her veil quickly. Her gaze burned into his. He drew in a sharp breath. "I don't think you want to stop me," she suggested.

He shook his head and kept his hands at his sides, not wanting to make contact with her. She mounted without his help.

She indicated Tanya. "Put her behind me. She hardly knows where she is."

They set Tanya astride the horse. "Should we tie her to the saddle?" Now that the big one assumed she had power, he wanted to be in her good graces.

"No. Open the gate."

They rushed to do her bidding. Rana jammed her heels into the mare's ribs and the horse bolted. In moments, she and Tanya were through the gate and charging down the coastal road for Qadis. The wind whipped about her veil and cut into her hair. She laughed aloud. She was Diaphani, as free as a gull. Tomás would never catch her again. But their escape had been easy, perhaps too much so. Had he allowed it to happen? Did Tomás think she would lead him to the Tribe? As the dust churned in clouds behind them, her back prickled. It felt for all the world as if someone watched their escape as they ran.

Chapter Twenty-Nine: The Cork Wood

Joachín pushed the Tribe across the headlands as fast as they could go. After allowing the women to wrap their hands to protect their cuts and assist Miriam, they mounted their horses and were off. He had been tempted to insist she ride with him, but common sense dictated she was better off in the wagon, braced by the sides. That Alonso shared her company couldn't be helped.

"What's ahead?" he shouted over his shoulder to the Rememberer. He wasn't familiar with this part of the coast. Perhaps Ximen knew of a sheltered cove where they might spend the night.

"There's a cork forest about five leagues distant," Ximen said. "It isn't frequented much...the locals prefer the lower slopes. I think we'll be safe."

"And from there, how far to Qadis?"

"A half-day's ride. One, if we have to travel with care."

Joachín nodded. Ximen felt the same way he did—to ride with speed if they could but with caution, if necessary. He would speak with

Miriam to see which one she wanted. She would have to talk to him about that.

How had things become so difficult between them? Alonso was a complication. But so was Inez.

The child wasn't his. He was sure of it. He could practically taste the lie; it was metal on the tongue. Given time, he would convince Miriam of it. He felt her absence as if he had lost part of himself. She was the blossom he wanted to crush to his face, to breathe her in and never let her go. Why was happiness so fleeting? Why did something always interfere?

He would check on her later, insist on examining her new tattoos. It was his place to be concerned about her, no matter what she said. Nothing should come between them. She had promised that. Could he accuse her of breaking that vow? Probably best not to.

The land sped by. They topped a rise. To the south, the cliffs framed the coastline, surf frothed at their bases. Beyond, the land fell, surrendering to the sea. Clumps of desert scrub appeared, breaking the dull, red earth. A league distant, another hill rose, dotted with black twigs.

Ximen pointed. "Cork-oaks. The land dips into a valley. The wood I told you about."

Joachín nodded. It would be good to dismount and set camp, perhaps hunt for supper. And then, once everyone was settled, to make peace with his wife.

If one expected good things, they had a tendency to happen. But making love to Miriam was probably too much to hope for.

Miriam clung to the sides of the cart. With every bounce and jerk of the wagon, her new cuts flared with pain. The sherry didn't help. It was sticky, although it sterilized the tattoos.

Are you all right? Blanca leaned at her side, but it was Alonso she saw.

No.

Should I make the dog bark? Should we stop so you can tend yourself?

She shook her head. They needed to get somewhere safe. Hopefully, they would stop soon. *Have you managed to get a fix on Tomás?* she asked instead.

Last time I checked, he was sleeping. I'll check again.

He vanished, leaving her alone with Blanca. Ahead, Barto manned the reins. The wagon bounced over a large rock throwing her against the cart's side. She winced, bit down on her lip. Barto glanced at her from over his shoulder. He frowned—his way of asking if she were all right. She waved his concern aside. He turned back to watch Maia, who rode with Carlotta, in front of them.

Miriam slipped a hand beneath her waistband to check her bandages. In a few places they were soaked in blood, but the warding tattoo had been worth it. They rode beneath a cloak. She sensed every member of the Tribe. Ximen had said the men were connected through bloodlines. Joachín was linked through Luci. She felt him most of all. Every member felt right, except for the taint that was Inez.

She's lying about Joachín. The more she thought about it, the more it made sense. Joachín had been with Inez—she wasn't happy about that—but it had happened before they had met. At the moment, he was miserable. His despondency rolled off him in clouds. *I need to get beyond this,* she thought, *to put it behind us. If I don't, Inez will only make things worse.* Not that Joachín would allow himself to be tempted by her. Surely, he was stronger than that.

He has his faults, but he loves me. She had her faults, too—her temper, for one. She would have to forgive him. She would rise above this, show Inez there was no place for her between them. *I feel so much better,* she thought, although her torso still burned.

Tomás is in a rage! Alonso blurted. Miriam jumped.

I'm sorry for startling you, but he is! He squeezed her fingers. The pressure was no more than a puff of air. *His pet sorceress has run away! He's turning Bacalao upside-down looking for her! We're better off than we thought! She can't find us, and he can't find her!*

She studied their linked hands. Did his enthusiasm give him more substance?

We have a chance! He shook her hand, excited by the prospect. It seemed that her hand hadn't moved at all. Was this an effect of the new bond? *We'll escape, Miriam! We can sail beyond his grasp to a new life!*

I hope you're right, Alonso. Can you get a fix on his sorceress?

I don't know where to begin. I suppose I could fly about the countryside looking for her.

She dismissed it. *No, if she's gone, Tomás is the bigger threat.*

Unless he finds her again.

Let's pray he doesn't. She smiled. *I can't wait to tell Joachín.*

Joachín? A line creased his brow. He looked at her accusingly. *You sound as if you've forgiven him.*

I haven't, entirely.

Good. He doesn't deserve your forgiveness. He's a degenerate.

A thought occurred to her as she considered him. Had Alonso ever been with another woman? Men kept secrets, especially priests. Perhaps Alonso had had a woman or two.

He looked at her, askance. *I can assure you, I have never impregnated anyone. If I had, I would have honoured that bond, as any decent man should.*

He seemed overly defensive. Which didn't answer her question, but she let it pass.

On either side of the road, wind-bent pines appeared, stooping like old men. The road rose and fell. Her stomach growled. It had been some time since they had eaten. Joachín led the Tribe into a copse of cork. The trees stood like abandoned warriors, shedding their armour of bark.

"We'll camp here for the night," he announced. He motioned for Iago and Barto to join him. They meant to hunt. She eased herself from the wagon. The women scurried about, gathering firewood. Inez didn't bother, but made her way to a nearby stream. Blanca watched from Miriam's side.

Considerate of him, Alonso sniffed, *to put everyone else, first. I know where my considerations would lie.*

The words stung. She had hoped Joachín would glance her way, that she might let him know things were all right between them once again. But he had ignored her instead. *Blanca needs water,* she replied.

She avoided Inez at the stream bank and set off to find a secluded spot. Although her cuts still burned, the water soothed them. She regarded the line of bloody circles ringing her hips. The chain was ugly, but it worked. Perhaps it was stronger than anyone knew, maybe it had actually manipulated events—how else to explain Tomás's sorceress escaping him so quickly? She dabbed gingerly at the glyphs. Once they healed, she might have them inked. Anassa's tattoos had been elaborate, works of art. She could see why many of the women decorated those they wore on their bodies. *Turn the chain into a ring of roses, perhaps?* she wondered. The original cuts would still be there, but there was no reason why they couldn't be beautiful.

Now you are thinking like a true matriarch.

Her head shot up. There was nothing to see but the stream frothing about her knees and the cork wood on the bank. *Lys!* she demanded. *I want some answers!*

The water rushed by. The trees creaked in the breeze. As usual, no voice of the divine feminine responded. Lys had returned to her game of hide and seek. Miriam let out an exasperated sigh. The goddess only spoke when it suited her. She manoeuvred people like pieces on a chessboard. It was annoying to be her pawn.

And yet, her conscience posed, *why should she speak to you at all, if you order her? How is she any different from you?*

The question made her uncomfortable.

Is your life so bad? You've survived. You're the leader of a Tribe. You have important work to do.

The thought was so immediate, she wasn't sure she had thought it. It had been in her own voice, and yet.... She bristled.

My life isn't great! Tomás seeks me, my father and half the Tribe are dead, my husband's ex-mistress carries his child–potentially! And now, You...!

She stopped. How strange only a month ago she hadn't believed in the gods. It was no longer a question as to whether Lys was real. She was–infuriatingly so.

Frowning, Miriam reached for her dress. Next time, she wouldn't be so quick to demand answers. The timbre of the goddess' first comment had been almost praiseworthy. As if beautifying herself was something in which Lys approved. Why would the Mother of the All concern herself with such trivialities?

Unless they weren't trivialities. Maybe Lys saw her adornment as an acceptance of her role. Mothers, by their nature, were intrusive. Although she was sure Lys would prefer to think of it as *involved*.

Miriam smiled. Maybe it wasn't so bad being the focus of a goddess's interest. She hardly remembered Inara, her own mother, but she would have welcomed her care.

Joachin, Barto, and Iago returned an hour later with nothing to show for their efforts; their hunting expedition had been a failure. In the meantime, Luci and Zara had found a few patches of wild onion. It wasn't much, but with water from the stream and a few herbs, they had concocted a cold soup. As the men dismounted, Casi ran to Joachin to tell him the news.

"The Grand Torch Bearer is in an uproar? The sorceress has fled?" Joachin glanced across the glade to Miriam for confirmation.

She nodded.

He sputtered. "But...that's wonderful news!" He broke into a huge smile and laughed in relief. Unwilling to contain himself, he crossed the camp to capture her hands in his. His touch sparked her own elation, but she yelped at his jostling. "I forgot!" he cried, letting her go. "Your cuts. Did I hurt you?"

"I'm fine. They're healing."

He set a cautious arm about her shoulders and waved at the Tribe. "Start a small fire. Tonight we eat hot soup, but tomorrow morning, we mustn't linger." He ushered her away as the women began the preparations. Inez watched them. Joachin didn't notice.

"Am I forgiven?" He led Miriam beneath a huge cork-oak. "You're speaking to me, again. I can only hope."

"Yes, you're forgiven." She leaned against him. "I've decided I don't believe her, either. Whatever happened between the two of you happened before we met. I don't think the baby is yours."

"I wish there was a way to prove it."

"I came close. When she cut me, our blood mingled. I almost touched the child's light."

"Light?"

"Soul might be a better word. I was about to test it, but the ward swept me away before I could confirm things."

He gazed at her earnestly. "I know I hurt you. I'll do whatever I can to make it up."

"Will you send her away?"

He hesitated.

She knew he couldn't. It wasn't in his nature to turn away a woman in need, even if that woman was a lying *cerda* who imposed herself on others. Where Joachín was weak, she would be strong. "It's all right. I'll endure her...for your sake."

He stared at her gratefully.

"But only until she has her baby. After that, Ximen confirms paternity and they can be on their way."

He pursed his lips.

"She's a problem, Joachín. She'll try to break us apart."

"You know she won't deliver for months. She'll have to come with us to the New World."

"She will. But once we're there, it will be no problem for her to find work. There will be many opportunities."

He gazed at her reverently. "You are amazing. I don't know any woman who would endure this. I love you so much. Will you come to me, tonight? Can I cradle you in my arms and keep you warm?"

She was touched by his yearning. "You can, but carefully. My tattoos still hurt. Too much...exertion...will aggravate them."

"I'll be gentle. I'll cover each link with kisses."

She smiled, liking the idea. "Then kiss me, now." She met his lips.

After a few moments, she broke their embrace. "We should get back," she said. From across the glade, Inez watched them, envy raw upon her face.

Joachín was too happy to notice.

As the sun descended, the Tribe ate the remainder of the soup, the best they could manage. According to Alonso, Tomás had left Bacalao. He had split the Guard three ways. One third rode north to Anteqarra, another, east to Almerida. But his escort headed west, on their way to Qadis.

"I'm not happy about this." Joachín set his hands on his knees.

Iago glanced at the sky. "We should be all right. It's a cloudy night. If he comes this way, he won't see our smoke."

"Is he getting close?" Joachín turned to Miriam. She set a hand on Blanca's head. Alonso sprang to life.

No, he replied, *but you'll have to be careful once we approach the town gates. They're being watched.*

Miriam passed along his warning.

Joachin shrugged it off as if it went without saying. "There are other ways in."

Don't tell me he plans on making us crawl through the sewers.

Be nice.

Why? He's a rat, with a rat's ways.

She rose, not in the mood for his jealousy. She loved Alonso, but she loved Joachin as much. It was a difficult situation. Her marriage required commitment.

"Where are you going?" Joachin asked.

"I want to check my cuts, again." Her fingers wriggled in the secret language she had taught him. What she really needed was to relieve herself, but she didn't want to share it with the Tribe.

"Oh," he said. He turned his attention back to discuss plans with the rest of them. Blanca remained where she was, having little choice. Casi hugged her tightly.

The evening was cool, although not so cold as on the headlands overlooking the sea. Miriam took care of herself and washed her hands. A twig snapped behind her.

She knew who it was without turning around. "What do you want?" she asked tersely.

Inez's face was unreadable in the dark. "To talk."

"We have nothing to talk about." She climbed the bank and tried to avoid her. Inez barred her way.

"We do. You need to know he asked me to leave with him."

Her common sense screamed at her to pay no attention, to keep walking, but what she said was too tempting to ignore. "What are you talking about?"

"The night Joachin left me in Herradur? He begged me to go with him."

Miriam curled her lip. "You're lying."

"It's true. My father ran a brothel. Joachin wanted to take me away from that life. He said it was only a matter of time before they turned me into a whore."

"They succeeded."

"I'm no whore! I ran away to Bacalao because Joachín was right! By then, I discovered I was pregnant with his child."

"I'm not listening, anymore." She sidestepped her.

Inez intercepted her. "He didn't love me like a whore. He made love to me like I was his beloved. I had never climaxed with a man before, but I did with him. He showed me what love is. He taught me passion, and I gave it back!"

"He may have lain with you, but he never loved you."

"You weren't there."

"He pities you! Can't you see that? That's why you're here! He's too good of a man to turn you away!"

Inez's expression turned ugly. For a moment, Miriam thought she was going to strike her. She waited, ready to dodge. *Hit me, and I'll hit you back*, she thought.

"You think you know so much." Inez sneered. "I know him like I know my own skin. He isn't for you, Madelaina. He's a liar and a thief. He may be taken with your pretty face, but in the end, he won't live up to your expectations. When that happens, he'll come back to me. I accept him for who he is."

"You should know something, too," Miriam replied. "The old man who advised you on tribal law? He'll confirm the baby's paternity once it's born. And when he proves the child isn't Joachín's, you'll go."

"That won't matter. There is a belief among the fishermen of the Costa del Cobra. A woman only catches when she loves and is loved. I love Joachín, and he loves me. If he really loved you, you'd be pregnant, too." She smiled nastily.

"An ignorant belief. You're delusional." She had had enough. She brushed past her to return to the camp.

"Remember that, next time you lie with him!" Inez shouted after her.

She fled through the trees. She hated Inez in a way she didn't think it possible to hate anyone. Babies were conceived all the time. Love had nothing to do with it. But Inez's words had struck home.

Later, when Joachín approached her to join him beneath a blanket on the grass, she rebuffed him. He hadn't lied about Inez, but he hadn't told her everything, either. She suspected he had asked Inez to run away with him. He was protective of women. His love-making was also a source of masculine pride, that he could satisfy any woman with whom he lay. Inez's revelations hurt because they were true.

She lay beneath a thin blanket and shivered in the darkness. He had been hurt by her rejection; he hadn't understood why. *Just go*, she had said. *I still need time*. Now, all she had was a cold blanket for comfort. Across the camp, Blanca wriggled out from under Casi's elbow and padded towards her.

The dog slumped at her side. Blanca's warmth permeated her back and legs. The faintest brush of a ghostly arm wrapped itself about her shoulder. She turned from Alonso, not wanting him to see the tears in her eyes.

I'm here. Don't cry, Love, he whispered.

Chapter Thirty: Unfortunate Pairings

For a moment, Joachin stood where he was, not knowing what to say. Everything had been all right between them. They had talked. Miriam had said she would come to him that night. When she hadn't, he sought her out, only to be rejected—no, *repelled*—as if he were the lowest louse alive.

Hurt, he stared across the camp and met Inez's eyes. She nodded at him and looked hopeful, but he was in no mood to talk to her. That was the worst possible thing to do. What had she said to Miriam? Whatever it was, he needed to make it right.

He glanced Miriam's way. She lay on the hard ground with her back to him. He rubbed his neck, heartsick. He needed air, to get away.

He stalked from the camp and passed the wagon where the sherry was kept, grabbing a small jug, which he had stowed for his personal use. He needed a drink and deserved one. He had made mistakes—that much was true. But why did he have to keep paying for them? How was that fair?

As he drew up to Fidel, he stroked the horse on its neck. The stallion nickered. One of the mares nibbled at his sleeve. Joachín unstoppered the jug and took a swig. The sherry was sweet and made him purse his lips.

"I think," he told Fidel, wiping his mouth, "it's better to be a horse. Much more straightforward." He took another drink and regarded the mares. "None of this women business. You girls don't care if your man sees another."

He took another swallow, and then another. The sherry warmed his gut. He settled onto the stream's bank to drink.

An hour later, he plugged the jug with its cork and set it clumsily on the grass. He needed to sleep. He slumped over and the ground claimed him.

At first, the dreams didn't come, but then he slipped into the same one he had had twice before. Once again, the images faded in and out, one atop the other: either he was being arrested by the Naval Watch or Miriam was being cornered by the Inquisitional Guard. Fear for himself gave way to fear for her. It upset him to see her attempt to flee and be cornered. These weren't dreams. They were nightmares. Surely, if Lys sent them, she would show him a way out. But how?

"Miriam," he whimpered as she cried out in fear.

"Here," a voice said.

Miriam rolled on top of him. It felt like her, except...he couldn't quite see, her hair was in his face. Had she put on weight? It didn't matter. He wanted to hold her, to love her.

"I love you," he mumbled, setting his arms about her. He wished he hadn't drunk so much. She'd said they couldn't make love, her cuts were still healing. But her fingers fumbled at his breech strings. He swallowed as her hand encircled his penis. It lay in her palm like a dead lump. "Miri," he muttered, "I don't think I can...."

She hiked up her dress.

Alonso's entreaty made her want to cry more. Everything seemed impossible. Joachín hadn't lied—he couldn't lie—but his omission felt like one, even if he hadn't consciously made it. She wasn't his first woman. Inez hadn't been his first, either. But her words rang with a hurtful truth. Joachín *had* asked her to run away with him. And if they had run away together? How different her own life would be.

Don't let him upset you.

Her chest ached. It was hard to breathe. Alonso nestled closer.

Let me help you.

What could a ghost do? She wasn't sure, but Blanca's warmth soothed her. Once the turmoil in her heart settled, she became more aware of him.

When I was young, he said softly, *my mother used to tell me stories before I fell asleep. My favourites were mostly about pirates and knights errant, but there was one that always struck me as special and different. It was about a boy who fell in love with a water sprite. Of course, I never admitted to my brothers I liked it. But when Madré and I were alone, I would ask her to tell it. Would you like to hear it?*

She felt so small, like a little girl. She wasn't sure she wanted to hear a children's tale, but she wasn't sure she didn't not want to hear it, either. She sighed. Alonso took it for assent.

Once upon a time, there was a young man who liked to sing. He had a very good voice, and his favourite place to compose ballads was beside a babbling brook that ran beside his parish chapel. One day, as he sat singing by the water, a beautiful girl broke the water's surface to listen. He had been sure an otter swam by moments before, but now, there was only the girl. She had glossy black hair and eyes as green as lily pads. He stopped singing as soon as he saw her.

'Don't stop!' the girl told him. 'You have such a wonderful voice!'

He was so astonished such a creature would take an interest that he sang to please her. And as he sang, a strange thing occurred. Some would say she cast a love spell upon him, others that the spell was already cast, but his heart blossomed. He felt at one with the stream and the sky. And the source of his passion was the nymph.

'Come with me,' she implored as he finished, holding out her hands. For twilight had come upon them. The bells were calling the faithful to Vespers. The young man knew his choir-master expected him to sing. He also knew that if he tarried he would be late and lost forever.

'How can I?' he asked her. 'You're a sprite—I can no more live in your world than you can in mine.'

'Love transcends all barriers,' she said. 'Either you reach for a new life or stay in your old one.'

And as she smiled, his heart soared. But he knew going with her meant his death. It meant leaving his family and his chapel behind. It meant trusting they would find a way to be together, for always. He wasn't sure it was possible.

'Which life do you choose?' she asked.

And as the sun set, the young man made his choice, knowing it to be best.

Miriam waited. Which one did he choose? she asked finally, feeling impatient that he hadn't finished the story. She turned to her side to face him.

Alonso lay beside her, closer than breath, filling her view like the sun. She lay in the arms of a shining angel. Those who beheld such perfection were struck dumb. She couldn't speak. His blue eyes claimed her, held her captive. She was a white dove, flying in an azure sky. For a moment, she couldn't breathe.

He had told her this story to make something clear. If she wanted to, they could find a way. The heat of his ardour confirmed it. More than anything, he wanted what Joachin had—to be her only love again, and to love her like a man.

He hadn't finished the story because he was waiting for her to finish it.

Did he expect her to die? Would he end her life so she might be with him? She rejected the idea, fought panic with logic. She loved Alonso, he loved her. He had sacrificed himself to protect her. Death wasn't what he had in mind. What then? Did he want to couple with her, as an animal with a human? Gods! The idea was revolting! He was potent—he had to be, in order to survive the way he did, but his love burned too hot.

His face contorted. No! Great Sul, you think I would want to...?

I can't! She rolled away from him and stumbled to her feet. Perhaps that wasn't what he wanted, but she couldn't deal with him right now. She felt overwhelmed by him; perhaps being in the state he was, his intensity was hard to endure. She felt small, too fragile a vessel to contain him. She wanted Joachin; his physicality grounded her. Did Alonso's energy have anything to do with how upset she felt? She stumbled her way to where she last saw Joachin. He wasn't there. She suffered a moment of loss and stared about the camp. She could barely make out the bodies sleeping beneath the trees. The moon drifted behind a cloud. Where had he gone? Perhaps he had sought solace with Fidel. He sometimes did that when he wanted to think. A nicker caught her attention. The horses were picketed near the stream. Something was disturbing them.

She ran down the short path to the water. The moon appeared, lighting her way. The horses watched her approach. Not far from them, a couple lay in a crude embrace. The woman straddled the man. Her skirt was about her waist. His hands were on her bare thighs, but they kept sliding off.

Miriam froze.

Joachin and Inez. Together.

In one fell stroke, they had reduced her to a joke, a fool who believed in the sanctity of marriage. She was the dirt on which they grunted, the grit beneath their feet. That they should couple so close to the camp, and in clear view of anyone passing, told her she was nothing.

Inez turned her head ever so slightly. Miriam caught her look of victory as she glanced her way.

She had planned this! Her humiliation gave way to rage. Joachin was drunk. The jug beside him was a dead giveaway. He didn't know what he was doing.

Miriam threw herself at Inez, taking her by surprise. Inez struck at her to fend her off. They tumbled from Joachin and clawed at one another, two cats fighting over territory.

Chapter Thirty-One: Success and Failure

"Get me food."

Tanya rifled through the saddlebag and produced a squashed loaf of bread. She handed it to Rana.

Rana glowered at her from the stream bank. "That's all you brought?"

"We were in a hurry," Tanya said breathlessly. "I was afraid he'd awaken."

"He didn't. Give it here."

"Where do we go tomorrow?"

Rana took a few bites. "Qadis."

"But won't he go there?"

"He might. I'll have to check. Did you bring a bowl?"

Tanya nodded and retrieved it. Rana gave what remained of the loaf to her and wiped her hands on her skirt.

"We've nothing to sacrifice," Tanya stopped chewing as Rana regarded her without speaking. "You don't mean *me*!"

"I need some blood."

"Use your own!"

"Don't be such an infant. If I don't learn which way Tomás is heading, he'll catch us. I need to scry. Once we get to Qadis, I have friends who can help us."

Tanya's chin trembled

"You'd rather he find us? If he does, he'll hurt you more. A *lot* more."

Tanya screwed up her face getting ready to cry.

Before she could blink, Rana pulled her knife from her blouse and sliced Tanya on the forearm. Tanya gave a small scream and cupped her arm to her chest.

"It's done. Set your arm into the bowl. You're getting blood all over the place."

Tanya stared at her in horror, but she did as she was told. Rana added water, turning the bowl pink. Tanya looked near to fainting but Rana held her firm. They squatted on the stream bank.

Rana nodded. "That should be enough. Now, don't bother me. I need to concentrate." Resentfully, Tanya wrapped her arm in a slip of cotton from her underskirt.

Rana set the knife into the water and cut the proper glyph. *Show me Tomás*, she willed.

The surface of the water quivered and then separated into light and dark forms. Tomás was astride his horse, riding hard. His face was stiff with anger. His cloak billowed behind him like a sail; the Guard rode at his back.

Where is he? she demanded.

The view expanded. Tomás and the Guard pounded down the main road. The moon cast a pale light behind them, they were travelling west. To their right, a shelf of rock rose to a headland. Beyond it lay the sea.

Rana grimaced. It couldn't be helped. She and Tanya would have to move cautiously, leave no trail, and remain out of sight.

Show me Angél, she directed next. The water shifted. Angél Ferrara sat at a table with a candle at his elbow. In his fingers, a shred of white.

He has my message! Rana caught her breath in excitement. The bird had flown faster than she had hoped. With luck, he would leave for Qadis the next day. She drank in the planes of his face, the crush of his dark beard against his cheekbones. *I still love him,* she thought. It didn't matter how much time had elapsed or that he had saved himself by giving her to Tomás. Maybe she wouldn't tell him that she would be the one responsible for Miriam Medina's death. Only that she was dead. *I'll find a way to make you love me, again,* she promised. *Once she's out of the way.*

She watched as he stood, expecting that he would retire to his bed. Instead, he strode from the house. The water clouded. She was sure he had headed for the stables. She and Tanya would have to hurry if she wanted to meet him in Qadis.

Now, for the Medina bitch. She forced her will on the water. With luck, the shield the Tribe had set would only be active while they were awake. Some wards weakened during sleep.

She waited with bated breath. When the water refused to coalesce, she clutched her necklace and concentrated with a will. To her satisfaction, the surface rippled and churned. An image fluttered, but then it settled into stillness. She cursed in frustration, but the bowl remained a placid lake.

She knocked it aside. Bloodied water flew everywhere.

"What?" Tanya whimpered. "Does he know where we are?"

Rana was too angry to answer.

"Did you see the Grand Inquisitor?"

Rana stalked away. She needed to calm down, to think. There had to be a way to break the ward. She would have to do that, in order to find Miriam Medina.

Chapter Thirty-Two: Ultimatums

Rough hands pulled her off Inez. Iago held her securely. She fought him to let her go. "Let me at her!" she screamed, lunging at Inez.

"Matriarch! That's enough!" Ximen blocked her view. She reached past him to claw at her rival. Barto had hold of Inez. Joachín lay at their feet, the gap in his breeches open, his half-erect penis exposed.

"Cover him up," Ximen said in disgust.

Without a word, Zara knelt.

"No, I'll do it. I'm his aunt." Luci jerked his breeches shut, her face tight with anger.

"Let me go, Iago," Miriam ground.

He didn't. "You need to calm down, Matriarch."

"She needs to answer for what she did! He's my husband, Ximen!"

"He was mine before you came along!" Inez spat. Barto shook her. "Stop that, you!"

"Joachín, get up!' Luci ordered.

Joachín blinked at her in confusion.

Luci glared down at him. "Do you have any idea what went on here?"

He tried to rise. His elbow gave out from beneath him and he tipped over. "Was kissing my wife." He gazed up at Miriam adoringly. "S'wonderful."

"It wasn't wonderful! That *wasn't* Miriam, Joachín!"

"Course it was. Who else would it be?"

"You were with Inez!" Miriam yelled.

He looked flustered and eyed her blearily. "Miriam, by th' gods, I thought...."

Luci hauled him to his feet. "You stink of drink. How could you do this with the Grand Torch Bearer on our heels? I can't believe you'd risk us this way!"

"I missed my wife." He reached feebly for Miriam and failed. Luci held him back. He gazed at Inez. "She said she was...you." He gaped at Miriam.

"She *said?*" Fury throttled her once again. "I want her out of here!" she sputtered. "I want her gone! I am matriarch! We will do as I say!"

Inez's eyes narrowed. "Force me out, and none of you will like the consequences. I know who searches for you. I will find him. And when I do, I'll tell him everything. What your plans are, about your arrangement with the *Phoenix*." She would sacrifice every one of them out of spite.

"Not if you're dead." Miriam said.

For one breathless moment, no one said anything. Everyone was in shock.

"Good! Give her a knife," Inez challenged. She glared at Miriam, her eyes full of hate. "I dare you. Gut me like a sow and murder the child I carry. Stain your lily white hands. You think Joachín will love you after that? He won't be able to stand you. He'll wonder if he ever knew you. You won't be his precious *princessa* anymore."

An icy certainty closed in on Miriam. Inez was right. She had threatened her out of rage, but she couldn't kill in cold blood, no matter what had transpired between them. Inez had called her bluff. Even if they abandoned her in these hills, the likelihood was strong she would find Tomás. And when she did, she would tell him everything she knew.

"You'd turn him in?" Miriam demanded, eyeing Joachín. "The so-called father of your child?"

"It's you who risks him, not me."

She wanted to slap her. Joachín broke the moment by vomiting at their feet. Luci gasped in dismay and stepped back. He fell into his own sick. Inez shrugged Barto aside. "I'll leave you to think things over, while you clean him up." The crowd gave her a wide berth.

"Let me go, Iago," Miriam said. She knelt beside Joachín and swabbed his face. She wanted to hit him but didn't. Tomorrow, she would ride with him for Qadis. They might not speak, but the point had to be made. He belonged to *her*. Inez would ride with Barto as a prisoner, whether she realized it or not. Alonso would keep watch.

Alonso. She winced, remembering how they had parted. She wasn't the only one who had been hurt this night.

Later, when there was time, they would talk. She would say she had been overwhelmed, she had acted in haste. What else might she have done? In an animal form, what more did he expect? That she should leave Joachín and the Tribe? That they should find a way to restore him into human form? She still loved him, she would always love him, but their situation was impossible.

She hauled Joachín to his feet and supported him beneath a shoulder. Luci propped him up from the other side. They staggered and walked him back to his blanket. Blanca and Alonso were nowhere to be seen. Miriam settled beside Joachín, feeling as if they were a thousand leagues apart. She fell into an uneasy sleep and dreamed of dogs becoming men.

Chapter Thirty-Three: Telepath

Miriam's rejection hurt him far more than he cared to admit. He didn't realize how much until he came to his senses and found himself floating over Blanca who padded down a moonlit road, far below. Alonso closed his eyes and tried to tamp down his pain. Miriam's rebuff had sent him reeling out of body.

She thought he had wanted to have sex with her; of course, he hadn't meant they be together that way. He only meant to broach the subject so they might consider future possibilities. Certainly, he wouldn't remain a dog. *She loves me. I feel it whenever we're together.* She hadn't trusted his sense of propriety. How could she think he would want such a revolting thing?

What *was* possible? That they find a corpse he could animate so they might make love to one another? That he possess someone nearly dead or terribly old? That was as bad as remaining a dog. Next time, he needed to have a plan.

Sul had warned him, but he hadn't known what the god had meant at the time. *Remember, Alonso, if mortality ever becomes too great a burden, you will return to me. And when you do, it will be forever.*

Forever was a long way off. He wasn't so burdened, yet. But the fact Joachín de Rivera could act upon his love for Miriam in a physical way was a heavy drain.

You knew what was coming, he told himself. *You knew she would seek him out and spend the night with him. You acted in haste, and now, look at where you are. You've upset her, and now, you're drifting away, over a starlit road.*

Where was Blanca going? Why wasn't Casi watching her?

He dropped from the heights and settled into the dog's old bones. *C'mon, old girl. We have to go back.*

There was a fleeting sense of longing, but it was suppressed by thirst and the acknowledgement of sore paws. The dog turned back the way she had come. Luckily, she hadn't strayed too far. They stopped at the stream to lap some water, and then they re-entered the camp.

The place smelled of vomit and alcohol. The stench rolled off of Joachín de Rivera in clouds. The lout was snoring and sleeping it off. Miriam lay beside him on a bed of grass. How could she prefer that bastard to him?

He wanted to bite him. Blanca growled deeply in her throat. Alonso ignored Joachín and turned away. On the far side of the compound, Casi lay beside Luci. Casi was light and effervescent, even in sleep. Her energy was exactly what he needed. He sighed as he slumped at her side.

A small hand reached out and petted Blanca's head. Casi's caress was more than he could bear. Remorse and hopelessness claimed him. Blanca gave a low whine.

"Don't be sad, Alonso," Casi whispered.

He froze. She had called him by name. *You...you're aware of me?*

She nodded.

How...?

She shrugged. *I hear you. At first, I thought Blanca was talking to me, but dogs don't talk. Leastways, not like people do.*

Amazement filled him. Not only was she aware of him, but they were able to converse, mind to mind. *How long have you been able to do this?*

I'm not sure. I think I've always been able to, but it got stronger after we cut Miriam.

There had been a hint of it the first time he had prompted her to find Blanca. She had responded to him as if his thoughts were her own. Had that link been forged when he and Miriam had saved her from the viper? *Can you hear other people, as well?*

She nodded. *I don't like it much. It's noisy. It's better when everyone sleeps. Then I don't have to work so hard at blocking them out.*

He could well imagine it. In the midst of the Tribe, she would be bombarded by their thoughts. *How do you cope?*

Humming helps. Or pretending. Today, I imagined a tree house. I made it out of reeds. I want to build it in the New World.

Can you see me?

No, I just hear you.

A telepath, then, and on the cusp of adolescence. Tribal belief held that gifts bloomed around that time.

What's adle...essence?

Not a topic he wanted to broach. *Ask your mother.*

Maré's sad. I don't like bothering her.

Sad?

She misses Paré. I miss him, too. Sometimes, she cries in her sleep, and then she dreams of him. She stops crying then, because she's happy.

He had been so involved with his own affairs that it hadn't occurred to him that the women of the Tribe still grieved. They hid their sadness beneath patience, resilience, and cheer. Surely, they weren't all despairing. *Is Zara sad, too?*

Yes, but she's sad in a different way. She likes Ximen. She thinks he'll never want her.

That was a revelation. He couldn't help himself. *Does Ximen think about Zara, too?*

Not really. He thinks about the Tribe, or about the past, or about his wife who died. She was pretty.

Alonso drew in a deep breath. The dog exhaled it with a shudder. Even Blanca missed the blond child. Too late, he let the thought slip.

It's okay. I know she does. Casi hugged Blanca tightly. The dog grunted. *But she also loves me. She wouldn't be Blanca if she didn't.*

From the mouths of babes.

I am not a baby!

No, of course you aren't! I didn't mean it in that way. In the morning, you should tell your mother about your gift.

I was going to.

Your talent is very powerful, Casi, but not everyone should know about it. There are people I don't trust.

Who?

He hesitated.

Joachin? You can trust him!

I'm also concerned about Inez. She may hurt Miriam.

Casi's grip on Blanca's neck tightened. *I don't like her. She better not.*

So, you'll only tell your mother about your ability–for now?

Okay. But I bet she'll tell Joachin and Miriam.

There was no way to avoid it, but Luci was no fool. She would limit who was aware of her new talent. Fine, he replied, knowing he was on solid ground. Together, he and Casi would make a formidable pair. He would watch for the Tribe and she would listen. He wondered how far her ability extended, if outsiders were susceptible.

I don't know, but I'll find out! The prospect excited her. *Secrets! I'll learn them all!*

You may, but some you may not want to hear. Joachin flitted through his thoughts again. *If you ever hear anything that upsets or confuses you, tell me right away.*

I will!

You should sleep, now.

Okay. She gave Blanca a hug. *Tomorrow, I'll spy on Inez.*

Good. And Joachin, too.

Joachin? Why?

So we can surprise him! Tell him we know where he's taking us, before he does! Won't that be fun?

She giggled. *It will! I can't wait to see his face!*

Me neither. Goodnight, Casi.

He kept his gaze fixed firmly on the stars, admiring their beauty until she was soundly asleep.

Chapter Thirty-Four: Reconciliation

The dawn was grey. Joachin stood beside Fidel and stared out over the water. Whitecaps dotted the sea. At the base of the cliffs, the surge crashed against the rocks, scouring them clean. Miriam rubbed the gooseflesh from her arms as she approached him. Fidel tossed his mane and shifted from hoof to hoof, unhappy with the damp and the cold.

"I'm sorry," Joachin said, sensing her there without turning. "If you want to leave me, I don't blame you."

"No one's leaving anyone. I thought you might need some willow for your head." She held out a chewing stick.

He stared at her without speaking and then captured her in his arms. His face twisted with pain. "Last night, I don't think I was able to...." He let the thought hang. "Gods. I can't believe I'm telling you this. Still, I have to say it. I thought she was you, but I don't think I was able to fulfill—"

"Don't." She set a finger to his lips. "Don't mention her, don't breathe her name. She's a *puta* who deserves nothing but our contempt. I won't have her come between us."

"I love you, Miriam. I'd never knowingly deceive you. You must know that."

"I'm a *sentidora*, remember? I know." She drew away from him slightly. His breath was awful. "I tried to clean you up last night, but you should wash your face. It might help you feel better."

He looked down and plucked at his shirt. "I'm disgusting."

"Yes. You are."

They made their way back to the cork wood and the stream. They had come to an ox bow which formed a deep pool. She watched as he knelt to scoop water over his face and neck. Finding the effort futile, he somersaulted headfirst into the water.

He came up sputtering, shook the water from his hair, and sent a spray of droplets flying her way. "What do you think you're doing?" she laughed, stepping back.

"What does it look like I'm doing? I'm trying to be less revolting." He scrubbed at his arms and his shirt.

"Well, you've drenched me in the process! A fine riding partner you'll make! I'll never get dry."

He stopped scrubbing. "You're coming with me?"

"Of course. With whom else?"

"I...oh, Miriam!" He clawed his way back up the bank. Water streamed from his clothes. He grabbed her and then dropped his hands so he wouldn't soak her further. "I'll make everything up to you! We'll get to the New World, I'll work hard, I'll find us gold. I'll mine it with my own hands, if I have to! I'll build us a house. We'll have a fine farm. And children! Dozens of them!" He stopped suddenly, realizing he had said too much. Inez and her baby were still a wedge. Miriam smiled wanly. Her new tattoo burned. Her lower belly still hurt from her monthly cramping.

"Let's get moving," she said.

Qadis, he explained as they walked back to the camp, was situated on an isthmus, half a day's journey away. Their ship lay on the port's far side, where the Rio Guadaquir emptied into the sea. A shanty town with warehouses and pens for livestock extended beyond the town's walls. Outside of Portugel, Qadis was the largest stopover for goods arriving to and from the New World.

"What do you mean, we aren't going into Qadis together?" she demanded as he put forth that thought. She stared at him unbelievingly.

He met her glance squarely. "I've been thinking about it. If we all go together, we're too recognizable. From the al-Ma'dins at their bodega, Tomás will know to look for a Tribe of women with only four men, one of whom is blind. I don't like it, but if we go separately, we'll have a better chance of slipping past him. We can meet at the ship. On this side of the port, the women harvest shellfish. The sea gate is left open for them during the day. If you wade through the shallows and scoop shells into your skirts, you'll blend in. No one will think you're anything but harvesters. From there, it's a matter of finding the docks. The sea walls extend a distance from this side of the town. Tomás will have to spread his men too thinly along the walls to watch for us. He can't be everywhere at once. I think he'll narrow his efforts and watch the gates."

"I don't like it, Joachín. I don't want us apart."

"I don't like it either, but there's no other way unless we go through the sewers. No captain in his right mind would let us board a ship in that state. And the horses won't tolerate it."

"You've been through them?"

He nodded. "After a lucky streak at gambling. The fellow who lost to me thought I'd fixed the dice."

"Did you?"

He smiled wryly and rubbed his tattoo. "Of course. I won't be able to do that, again."

She made a face. "So, how do you plan to go?"

"We'll chance the gates."

"But you can't! You said that's where Tomás will focus his efforts!"

"We are four men among hundreds. We have to sell the horses, anyway. This time of the year, the locals bring their stock to port."

"You won't sell Fidel, surely. I thought we were taking the horses to the New World."

"I hate to do it, but we need coin to establish ourselves. The sherry won't earn us enough. But you're right, I'd rather not sell Fidel if I don't have to." He stroked the stallion on his nose.

"I still think Tomás will notice you. Ximen will stand out."

"Don't worry, we'll figure out a way. Sometimes, you have to wait to see what presents itself."

She wasn't convinced. As they re-entered the camp, she glanced at their Rememberer. The old man's white eyes would give him away. But what if they disguised him as a woman? He could walk through the shoals with them. As an old man, he would have his pride. They would have to persuade him, somehow.

Chapter Thirty-Five: Circus

The thing was he couldn't keep trailing Tomás all over the countryside in order to ensnare Rana Isadore. Cover was limited. Tomás would discover him sooner or later.

Francisco watched the keep from a small copse overlooking Bacalao. As he considered how he might fashion a grappling hook, Rana Isadore and her maid burst from the main gates on a horse. His mouth fell open as they galloped for the hills.

How, in heaven's name, had they managed that? Had Rana used magic to manipulate the guards? If so, she wasn't kidnap-able. But that made no difference. His course was now set.

He spent the next several hours tracking her and her maid. There had been a quiet moment when they had stopped at a stream to water their mount, but as he was about to approach, Rana Isadore pulled out a scrying bowl. He had been so intrigued by the process the moment was lost. They mounted quickly afterwards and rode west, the gods knew where.

Of all the possible places to approach her, he never would have guessed what fate finally presented. *Well, Francis,* he told himself as the two women picked their way down a narrow trail, *it's time to brush up on your old tricks.*

)(L((

"What *is* that thing?"

From their rocky viewpoint, Tanya pointed at a large grey beast chained to the ground. It had four thick legs, a long nose, flappy ears, and a stringy tail. It shifted from foot to stumpy foot. Occasionally, it plucked straw from a stack or tossed it aside. All about it, tents sprouted, like mushrooms following a rain.

"An elephant." Rana dismissed it with a wave. "They use it to draw crowds."

"They?"

"Whoever owns it, you fool. That's a circus down there. Have you never seen one?"

"No."

"It's on its way into Qadis. We can join it, become one of their acts. Then, as soon as we pass through the gates, we leave."

"But what will we do?"

"I'll scry. You're my assistant. You'll tell the master I can read the future."

They made their way down a narrow, twisting footpath that brought them to the base of the cliff. The smell of caged beasts and manure was pungent. Their horse nickered nervously.

"How will I know him?" Tanya didn't take her eyes from the elephant.

"He'll be the biggest man here. Look for someone with better clothes and good boots. He'll have black, shiny ones. Refer to me as *Serina Magia.*"

"*Magia?* Is that wise, all things considered?"

"*Serina Adivina,* then."

"What about me?"

"You don't need a name."

"Yes, I do!"

"Then *sangre*, for blood."

Tanya's mouth fell open. She stepped away from her as if stung. "I'm not going unless you promise not to cut me, again!"

"Fine, I promise. It doesn't matter. The circus has birds. The sooner we make arrangements, the sooner we eat."

"I didn't think you could read the future. I thought you only saw the present."

"So, I'll make it up!" Rana wanted to slap her. Tanya was driving her mad. She watched impatiently as the girl sidled past the elephant, keeping well out of its reach. Soon, she was lost amid the clutter of tents. Rana waited impatiently. Ten minutes later, Tanya was back, clutching her chest for breath. "It's as you said! He's a bull of a man. He carries a whip and wears black boots."

She wasted her breath on trifles. "What did you tell him?"

"That you read fortunes. He said it's all trickery, but I said no, you had the gift. I told him you needed a chicken. He laughed and asked if you were making soup."

She itched to strike her. She kept her hand at her side. The last thing they needed was for the master not to take them seriously. "Just shut up and take me to him."

Tanya led the way. As they passed the elephant, a group of men appeared from behind a line of tents, hauling a large cage. Inside it, a tiger paced on heavy paws. Their horse reared. Rana clutched the reins tightly.

"Go back! The other way!" A man waved them off. The tiger roared, a guttural, high-pitched sound. Tanya bolted between tents; Rana jerked the horse after her, only to come face to face with a stack of cages holding bears. The horse snorted and pranced, not liking the bears any better than the tiger.

"Oh!" Tanya gasped. The animals squinted at her, as if the sun hurt their eyes.

"May I offer some assistance?"

The question proved too much for Tanya. She shrieked, seeing who had addressed them. The jester was tall and thin and dressed in motley. He ignored Tanya and stared at Rana intently.

"The *maestro*." Rana held his gaze, even though her veil shrouded her face. "We are looking for him."

"This way." He swept in front of them. She wondered if he did hand springs. He was very light on his feet.

They made their way past a second line of tents. People glanced from their doorways as they passed. Most were dressed no better than serfs and a number of them were malformed. A hunchback warded himself against the evil eye as they passed. Beneath a ragged canopy, two twins slept, conjoined at the chest. Tanya clutched at her sleeve. Rana threw her off. She wondered if the circus lay under a curse.

Soon, they were heading away from the tents.

Rana frowned. That wasn't right. Where was he taking them? If they walked any further, they would be beyond the circus's periphery, near a picket where horses were kept.

"Hoy, there!"

She turned. A midget hailed them. He was no bigger than a child and dressed like a majordomo in a livery of black and gold. "What are you doing?" he demanded. "What do you want?"

Rana frowned, not liking his tone. She turned to question their guide. He had disappeared.

"Where...?" Tanya asked.

"Be quiet," Rana told her. Whoever their guide was, he had motives of his own. *I knew there was something strange about him*, she thought. "We're looking for the *maestro*," she advised the dwarf.

"Why?"

"We have business with him."

"We were *invited*," Tanya added.

"You're going in the wrong direction. His tent is this way."

They followed the dwarf to a tent, which was larger than the rest. Creatures out of myth—unicorns, griffins, and a Minotaur—had been crudely painted on its walls. A great dragon curled about the entry, as if guarding a cave.

Rana tied their horse to a post and brushed the road dust from her skirt. Did they wait for an invitation or did they enter and announce themselves? She glanced at the dwarf for guidance.

"Go on. It's as you said. He told me he's expecting you." He held the door of the tent open for them with a stubby hand. His smile bordered on a leer. She straightened her shoulders and strode into the tent.

The man inside looked nothing like a king. But in this place, he was as much a monarch as he needed to be. Rana knew power when she saw it. Even so, he smelled of last night's drink.

"I am *Serina Adivina*," she told him loftily. "I can shed light on your greatest desire."

He raised a bushy eyebrow. "What if I have more than one?"

"I can show you the paths that lead to them."

He stroked his beard, loosening a few crumbs. "And in return?"

"You pay our passage to the New World."

"A high price. Why the New World?"

"That's the path I must take to become rich."

He grunted as if that made sense. "Show me what you can do."

She made a calculated guess. "You want someone to love you and an easy way to gold."

"Like everyone. I'm not impressed."

"If you want specifics, I'll need a bird and a bowl."

"I can arrange it. Then what?"

"Then we'll see what there is to see."

"You're very sure of yourself."

"The water shows me."

He tucked his thumbs into his belt. Near his right hand, a bullwhip hung in thick black loops. She had no doubt about his ability to use it. He tapped his belt impatiently. "I need to see your face."

"You won't like it."

"I like to know with whom I'm dealing."

The sense of mystery she had hoped to create was lost. Unveiled, the welts would confirm she had dabbled in dark magic. He might kill her for coming into his presence, or he might hold her in cautious esteem. It depended on what kind of a man he was. She didn't think he scared easily.

She lifted the veil and regarded him with implacable black eyes. His face tightened. "How did you come by those welts?"

"Every *adivina* has her secrets. These, I don't talk about."

Silence descended. Even Tanya seemed too frightened to breathe.

"Tell Polvo I need a bird and a bowl," the *maestro* told Tanya without taking his eyes from Rana.

"Ppp...Polvo?"

"My manservant. The one who brought you here, you stupid girl."

Tanya fled without a word.

A short time later, Rana and the *maestro* sat opposite each other, between them a bowl of bloodied water and slaughtered doves. Rana studied the water. Her mouth had gone dry. It was altogether possible the ward had become stronger since Miriam had blocked her. She might see nothing. She couldn't lie well enough to fool him. Relief flooded through her as the blood coalesced.

"I see a woman," she said, wishing her heart would settle. To calm herself, she fingered the bone necklace about her throat. "She's older, about thirty. She bears a mole on her left cheek. She wears an unusual scarf...no, wait, not a scarf. She coils her hair about her throat, like a shawl."

Only one other in Rana's experience had ever worn her hair that way. The woman had nearly been strangled to death by her husband. The hair hid the bruises. Rana kept her eyes on the water knowing that any break in her concentration would make the image fade.

"Go on." The *maestro* shifted in his seat.

"She's standing beside a...a fence. There's a paddock...no, a bullring. A man practices inside it with a cape. He is smooth in his handling. There is no bull. The woman watches him."

"Where are they?"

Hills lay in the distance across a broad parched plain. "I don't know, exactly."

"You're a scryer."

"I need to see distinguishing landmarks. Most bullrings look the same, no matter where they are in Esbaña."

"Look harder."

She rolled the knuckle beads between her fingers. The bones gave her confidence. The image in the water broadened. A white-washed town nestled in the hills. Wherever they were, it was beyond the village. "I need more blood for a sharper picture."

"I'll arrange it. Just pinpoint where they are."

"She's your wife?"

He nodded.

"And the man in the ring?"

"My ex-partner. I have a surprise for them."

Rana had no doubt what the surprise was.

The blood in the water had turned. Her heart lurched as a tiger bared its long teeth, coiled its great body, and sprang for her with outstretched claws.

Chapter Thirty-Six: A Necessary Parting

"I refuse to dress as a woman!"

Miriam had never seen Ximen so upset. She and Joachin had chosen Zara to be their voice of reason.

"Be sensible, old man! You can't go where the patriarch is planning!"

"If you think I'm going to don a dress you're mistaken. I'll crawl into Qadis on my hands and knees if I have to!"

"Have you considered the patriarch needs you to accompany us to make sure we're safe? With that memory of yours, we won't run into trouble. You can tell us what we need to know!"

"Don't placate me, woman!"

"I am not placating! I am speaking sense! You're blind and sixty-four years old!"

"Sixty-two!"

"Fine! Climb the walls and break that stubborn old neck of yours!" Zara's chin trembled with emotion. She looked as if she were about to burst into tears.

"It's all right," Joachin said, coming between them. "Ximen will come with us. We'll figure something out."

"I am also going with Joachin." Inez met their eyes defiantly. "He's the father of my child. I am better off with him."

"No." Miriam stared her down. "If you go with him, the guards might mistake you for me."

"I look nothing like you."

"That isn't the point. You will do as I say."

"I answer to no one."

"She's a lying *puta* who would turn us in the minute she could," Zara muttered.

Inez overheard her. "And you're a dried out old hag."

"Enough!" Joachin was at his wit's end. "Inez, you will go with Miriam and the rest of the women, and you won't make trouble. If you do, you'll answer to me. I want no scenes or cat fights. Is that clear?"

She regarded him with surprise. It needled Miriam she reacted to him as if he were her husband enforcing control. She tilted her nose into the air, but Miriam caught the gleam of satisfaction in her eyes. "Very well, Joachin. If you insist."

"I do." He waited. After a moment, she walked over to stand with the women. Ximen remained where he was with the men.

Joachin turned to him. "I don't know how your memory works. Can you manage the wagon, by yourself? Barto, Iago, and I have to wrangle the horses."

Ximen lifted his chin. "I may be blind, but I don't need eyes. Even if the memory isn't mine, I still recall."

Miriam wondered how long he had been blind. If he saw the landscape as the Tribe remembered it, he would see the trail as it was, providing a landslide or some other disaster hadn't changed it. Fortunately, the path was clear.

The women's way was more hazardous. From the bluff on which they stood, a footpath dropped down a steep outcropping that ended at the beach. About a league distant, the sea walls paralleled the coast where they abutted the town. The men's route took them across a wide plain, where the track joined the main road.

Joachín drew alongside her. "The tide is on its way out." He surveyed the sea. "By the time you cross the delta, you'll run into the locals. I'll meet you tomorrow at the docks."

He said it as if he wanted to believe it. Was there something he wasn't telling her?

"Joachín, is there something—"

"The sooner you leave, the sooner we're together. Go, now. While there's time."

Had he a precognition? What if, after this moment, she never saw him again? The idea filled her with fear.

He gave her a squeeze. "Don't worry. We have the advantage. We know what Tomás is likely to do, and where he is looking." He glanced to where Ximen sat at the reins in the wagon. Two horses had been tied to the back of the rig. Iago and Barto held the reins of another three horses each. Fidel would lead them. Blanca stood panting with the women at the cliff's edge. Alonso had decided he would take his chances down the cliff face instead of riding with Ximen in the cart. "Looks like everyone's ready to go," Joachín said.

She studied his face. "What aren't you telling me?" she asked softly.

"That I adore you. That I love you. Always and forever." He kissed her.

"I love you, too, but—"

"Have faith. The goddess wants us in the New World. We are under her protection."

She made a face. "Lys's idea of protection leaves much to be desired. She could as easily send us there in chains."

He paled. "Don't say such things. You'll bring bad luck."

"You see? You have no more faith than I."

"Shhh. It's time to go. You've hours ahead, and I have to deal with the horses. I'll meet you in Qadis."

She wasn't sure about that, but they had come to this juncture. There were no other options except to stay where they were and cling to the rock like lichen. "Tomorrow, then. I love you, Joachín," she said, needing to say it again.

"I love you, too." They embraced and broke apart. Miriam waved at the women to proceed. Blanca waited at the edge of the cliff as the Tribe descended.

She turned to catch a glimpse of Joachín one last time. He sat mounted on Fidel, watching her as if he were of the same mind. She lifted her hand in farewell. A great weight settled about her heart, as if their parting was the beginning of a long absence. She fought the presentiment. They would see each other again, in the span of a day. She was being irrational.

But her heart still hammered as she turned and lost sight of him. She swallowed to keep from crying and set her hand into Blanca's ruff.

Alonso appeared, holding her hand. It was too much. Tears pooled in her eyes.

It's all right, he soothed, standing tall and shining before her. *I'm still here.*

Alonso! I am so sorry! For last night, for everything! Forgive me! I love him. I love you. I don't know what to do.

You don't have to do anything, Love. We're together. That's all that counts.

But this hurts you. It hurts me.

He shrugged. Whorls of energy emanated from him like heat mirages. *I made up my mind when I came back. I'll endure anything for you.*

I don't deserve you.

Hush now. You need to pay attention, so you don't trip. There's only so much Blanca can do to help. Careful, there's a drop ahead.

Tears slid down her face. She knuckled them away. He was right. Now was not the time for crying or losing her footing. *Do you think he'll be all right?* The question was in her head before she could stop it. How could she ask such a thing? She was being cruel.

He's as hard to kill as a cockroach. Not much chance of him being otherwise. The reference bothered her, but she was thankful for Alonso's tolerance. She didn't debate it. Alonso liked Joachín about as much as she liked Inez.

At least he had the sense to send you this way, he added. *Tomás won't be watching the beach. You should be able to get to the docks without a problem.*

Do you know where Tomás is?

On his way to Qadis, unfortunately. Riding with a skeleton troop, but he'll contact the town watch as soon as he's in residence. Don't worry. He can't be everywhere. I'll keep an eye out for him.

And you'll watch Joachín, too?

If I must.

They were halfway down the cliff-face. The delta divided itself into shallow rivulets heading for the sea. The tide was a long way out, leaving tidal pools sparkling in the sun. In the far distance, dots spread out from the sea walls in a slow moving fan. Determined to harvest the bounty of the sea, the women of Qadis marched.

Miriam squinted at them. *Is there any chance we might run into trouble with the locals?*

I don't think so. Why would you?

The market in Granad was a fiercely guarded enterprise. Every shopkeeper had his location. Stalls might stand in the same place for generations. If the women of Qadis were jealous of their interests....

Oh, I don't think anyone's going to quibble with you taking a few shells. It's not as if you're harvesting bushels.

I hope you're right, she said, but she remained unconvinced.

Chapter Thirty-Seven: A Settling of Scores

The worst part of the journey was across the open plain. They were vulnerable and easily seen. Joachin worried their timing was poor but once they reached the outskirts of Qadis, he relaxed. The town was a large port. There was only a slim chance they would encounter Torch Bearers here in the outer *barrio*.

"He looks to be of Barb or Arabi blood. I see no brands." The trader, with an eye for horse flesh, swept a hand over Fidel's flank.

Joachin had reconsidered selling him. "He's not for sale. Only the mares."

"Too bad. It's the coursers the army wants. How did you come by him?" It was unusual for someone of Joachin's status to own such a steed. Joachin had stolen him when he was a foal. He had broken him, too. Fidel was a warhorse, suited for battle or hunting.

"My business. How much for the mares?"

The trader tapped his chin. "You have thirteen? That's an unlucky number. You'd be better off selling this big fellow, too."

"I also need to part with those casks and the wagon."

The trader looked interested. "*Saca?* I'll have to sample it. The wagon's worth nothing. I'll give you twenty *soltars* for the lot."

"Fifty. The mares are worth two *soltars* apiece, the sherry about the same. At that, you'll have a solid profit."

"Impossible. Twenty-five."

"Look, you." Barto stabbed a finger at the trader. "We can take our business elsewhere. Give us a decent price or we leave."

The trader shrugged. "Fine, go. Unless you're willing to sell that horse with the rest, I don't need your business."

Joachín followed him. "Thirty-five."

"Including the stallion?"

"No. I told you. He's not part of the deal."

"Thirty, then. My final offer."

Joachín quelled his frustration. The price wasn't fair, but they had no time to quibble. Barto clenched and unclenched his fists. Iago looked as if he was ready to explode. No one liked the outcome, but they had little choice.

"Done." Joachín spit into his palm and met the dealer's hand, sealing the pact.

The trader smirked. "Wait here," he said. "I'll be back with your coin." He headed for a dilapidated shack sitting on the periphery of the compound. Joachín leaned against the paddock's fence.

"Well, that's done." As usual, Ximen put a positive spin on things.

"I was hoping for better." Joachín studied the passing traffic. A large black coach drawn by four black horses, careened around a corner. People scattered. The driver, dressed in red and black livery, snapped the reins. A footman balanced like an acrobat at the rear. The coat of arms—a triple-headed wolf—was emblazoned on the door. Joachín slapped Iago across the chest and turned his back as it rolled by, so as not to be recognized.

"Who is it?" Iago leaned against him.

"Don Lope."

"The vizconde who beat you in Marabel?"

"None other."

"Time to bust heads." Barto cracked his knuckles.

"That lacks a certain finesse, Barto," Joachín said lightly. "I have something much more entertaining in mind." He grinned and eyed Ximen. "Wouldn't you say, gentlemen, that given the right garb, our Rememberer here, might pass for a nobleman?"

"Maybe," Iago said, "but only from a distance."

Joachín smirked. "People make assumptions all the time." He looked at each of them in turn. "What we are about *do*, gentlemen, will be lauded for ages. Our sons will speak of it, and our sons' sons."

"You think so?" Ximen looked hopeful.

"Here's what I have in mind." He outlined his plan. The trader arrived with their coin, interrupting him. As Joachín counted the gold *soltars* to make sure they hadn't been duped, he whistled happily. The trader frowned. Iago picked his teeth while Ximen smiled. Barto continued to loom.

"It's all there," Joachín confirmed. "Let's go." Without another word, they headed after Don Lope's coach.

"You better not have cheated me!" the trader shouted after them.

Joachín peered around a corner. The coach was parked in front of a cheap brothel, as he had expected. Unlike the *bordello* in Marabel, the *Anchor* made no attempt at ostentation. Only a striped mermaid sign over the door indicated what kind of a premise it was. Don Lope's two toughs lounged against the coach's wheels.

Ximen staggered into the street. "Alms!" he cried. He held out his hands and stumbled in their direction. "Have you coin for a poor beggar? A *linares* or two? Sul blesses the gen...the gen'rous!"

"A *linares*?" The biggest guard scoffed. "He's got grand ideas."

"He's drunk. Get out of here, old man." The second waved him off. Ximen clung to him like a limpet, breathing into his face. "Ccc... copper, then. 'S'all I need."

Joachín pulled his hat low over his face and slipped into the *Anchor*.

"Get off!" The big guard threw Ximen into the street. He landed painfully on his knees. Swearing profusely, he climbed to his feet and gave them a wide berth. They eyed him with contempt.

Inside, Joachín waved a gold *soltar* at the madam who sat at the bottom of the stairs. "I'm looking for the nobleman," he muttered.

She held out her hand. "Second door, on the right." He held her glance to make sure she understood the threat he posed if she crossed him. The *soltar* was dear, but that much money meant he was a paid assassin. Which also meant he would silence any loose-tongued witnesses foolish enough to accuse him.

Joachín paused at the door to listen. A bed creaked repeatedly—the vizconde was taking his pleasure, enjoying himself. Joachín withdrew his knife and cracked open the door.

As the Don pumped, Joachín was across the room in an instant. He grabbed him by the scruff of his neck and settled the blade against his throat. "I wouldn't move, if I were you," he whispered.

The vizconde's eyes widened, first in outrage and then in recognition.

"All right, *Bonita?*" Joachín regarded the woman. "You're done. You can go." She nodded shakily and scrambled out from beneath the vizconde. She didn't bother to grab her dress.

"Good, she's gone," Joachín said. "Now, you. You're going to call off your men." He shook him like a terrier on a rat.

"I'll kill you!"

Joachín cut him. Don Lope gasped.

"Cross me again, and I'll slice you ear to ear. I don't care. Your choice." He dragged the terrified Don to the window.

The vizconde screamed. "Get away! Your service is over!"

The guards frowned up at him. "My Lord?" the smaller one asked.

"Be...be off before I set the constabulary on you!"

"What about our pay?" the big one demanded.

"How dare you question me! Guards!" Don Lope shrieked, losing his nerve.

Joachín cracked his head against the wall. The Don slithered to the floor. Joachín tossed another two gold coins from the window. "Here's your pay!" he screamed, in his best imitation of the vizconde in a temper. "Go!"

The guards picked the coins from the dirt. "Leave your uniforms!" he shouted.

Looking disgruntled, the guards tossed their livery onto the ground. The big one gestured obscenely at the window. As they strode off, Barto and Iago collected the doublets and set the hats upon their heads.

That leaves Ximen, Joachín thought.

The whore's dress lay in a heap upon the floor.

"I hope you like blue," he told Don Lope.

No one in the *bordello* uttered a word as Joachín made his way down the stairs with a body wrapped in a sheet. The vizconde's bare feet stuck out from the cloth, along with the blue hem of his dress. As they left the front door, a babble of voices followed them. Joachín headed for the coach. Barto, as driver, sat at the reins. Iago, as footman, opened the door. Joachín threw Don Lope at Ximen's feet. "Where to?" Barto asked.

"Main gates." Joachín climbed in and shut the door. "Put this on." He threw Don Lope's doublet at Ximen.

"That went well." Ximen smiled.

"We aren't done, yet."

"Will they stop us at the gates?"

"They'll see the coat of arms and wave us through." Joachín glanced at the lump at their feet. No one, other than Tomás, had ever robbed him of his dignity like Don Lope had.

"Is he dead?"

Joachín grinned hugely "Now where would the fun be in that?"

Barto ran the horses at the main gate without slowing them. The guards bellowed warnings. People scattered like geese. 'Don Lope' waved at the gatehouse as they rumbled by. Iago saluted as they passed through the gates.

The markets dwindled and the air cleared of fish. Barto drove the horses into a neighbourhood where the streets were broader. He parked the coach beside a small plaza dotted with orange trees. On every side of the square, expensive manors stood. None of the wealthier residents were about, although a number of their servants eyed the coach from windows. It was dusk.

Joachín propped the moaning Don Lope into a sitting position on the seat. Ximen stowed his doublet into a satchel.

"A trophy to show Zara?" Joachin asked.

The old man nodded.

Joachin retrieved the small casket he had seen stowed beneath Ximen's seat. It took only a few seconds to pry the lock. Inside lay the familiar roll of velum and its pouch of gold. He stuffed them into his shirt, and then he tossed the empty casket at Don Lope's feet. They had plenty of coin to establish themselves in Xaymaca now. The goddess had provided as he had claimed she would. His dreams were warnings, only. If he found Miriam in time, they would fail to take effect.

The servants of the local nobility would investigate the abandoned coach. They would talk. Don Lope would be ruined. Vengeance was his.

"Let's go," Joachin said, smiling.

Chapter Thirty-Eight: On the Move

"I want every cage mucked, every piece of *mierda* scoured from pelts and hides. I want costumes brushed and everyone smiling. If I see a smudge, I'll whip whoever is responsible for it."

Rana took in the tired, glum faces of the *maestro's* people. The sooner she and Tanya were gone, the better.

"Tonight, we perform for the Vizconde of Qadis. He is well-placed at court. If you impress him, we'll be welcomed everywhere. You have one hour before we strike."

The crowd dispersed. He beckoned to a copper-faced girl dressed in pantaloons and tunic. "This is Nivriti," he told Rana. "You will camp with her, as there is nowhere else. Before we move, I want you to scry again for my wife. As for tonight, you will entertain the vizconde personally. He'll be intrigued to know I have a bonafide *adivina* in my midst." He hailed a group of retreating men and exchanged words with them. They glanced her way and nodded.

Rana stiffened. He was having her watched! Did he suspect she would try to leave so soon? It wasn't beyond the realm of possibility that Tomás was also staying with the vizconde. Once they were past the gates, they had to run. She hoped Angél was already in Qadis.

Nivriti plucked at her sleeve. "This way."

She shivered as they made their way past the tiger. She was sure the vision she had seen in the bowl was not meant for her, but the beast was fearsome. Six men held it with iron chains. A thick collar encircled its neck. With a snarl of rage, it swiped a heavy paw at one of the handlers, but they brought it up short. Two workers scrubbed its cage with brushes and water. Tanya bumped into Rana, her eyes on the cat.

"Watch where you're going!" Rana shoved her aside. Tanya whimpered.

"It's only angry because it doesn't like being trapped," Nivriti said. "It wants to be free."

"Where are you taking us?" Rana demanded.

"My tent. I need to secure my pets."

"Pets?"

"Cobras. I'm a snake charmer."

Tanya turned white. They rounded a corner. The jester they had encountered approached them. Was he friend or foe? "My Lady," he said, bowing before Rana. "If I might have a word."

Nivriti frowned. "Did the *Maestro* send you? I haven't seen you before."

So Nivriti had been told to watch them, too.

"I'm a recent hire. There's been a change of plans. The *adivina* is to accompany me."

"Do I come, too?" Tanya looked hopeful.

Now that Rana had time to study him, she understood Nivriti's suspicion. The jester's clothes didn't fit him properly. His motley was too short in the arms and legs, and his expression was too serious for a fool.

"There you are!" Scowling, Polvo the dwarf, hastened toward them. He held a struggling chicken at arm's length. "Domanico said to give you this."

"Get it," Rana directed Tanya. She turned to speak with the jester. Once again, he had disappeared. Nivriti didn't pause to wonder, but led them to her tent. Half a dozen baskets were stacked around a central pole. A lantern rested on a wooden arm, providing a dull, yellow light. Near the baskets was a bed of rags.

"Don't worry," Nivriti said. "The master will provide blankets for you too, unless he moves you elsewhere."

Rana sniffed. Blankets were the last thing to worry about. She suspected the snakes were benign; either they were drugged or they had had their mouths sewn shut. Tanya still looked terrified. The place smelled. "How long have you been here?"

"Three years."

"And where were you before?"

"Pakesh."

"Where's your family?" Tanya blurted. "Did the snakes kill them?"

Nivriti shook her head. "My father sold me. He thought it would give me a better life." She scooped paint pots from a table.

"Has it?" Rana asked.

"It's not so bad. As long as you do what you're told."

"Have you ever tried to escape?"

"Only once." She refused to meet their eye. "A mistake."

Rana extracted the knife from her belt and set the point against the hen's breast. Nivriti watched without comment as she killed it. When it finally stopped jerking, she dribbled its blood into the water. She had no intention of finding Domanico's wife. *Show me Angél*, she willed.

As always, there was a chance the images would fail to form, that the goddess would intervene because she killed her creatures in order to scry. It was a forbidden magic she practiced, but without the Ancestors to advise her, she had no way of knowing what events might be. This was the only option left. *Angél!* she insisted.

The sluggish water shivered, rippled.

And suddenly he was there. Her heart quickened, she caught her breath. Still so handsome, even the water's image couldn't diminish that. She drank in his flashing eyes, his high cheek bones, the cleft of his chin. She wanted to kiss every inch of him. Their life together would have been perfect if not for that Medina *puta*....

The water clouded.

No! She imposed her will, hoping the strength of her desire would draw him back. *Where are you, my heart? Are you in Qadis?*

After a few frustrating seconds, his face reformed. She saw him clearly, speaking with a well-dressed merchant outside a chandler's shop. She knew the place. He was in Qadis, not far from *La Casa Gallina.* Once she was out of Domanico's clutches, they would be together, forever.

The vision faded. She sighed, satisfied with what she had seen. With luck, she and Tanya would be long gone before Nivriti reported them missing. Everything depended on how well she played her part, how smoothly she embellished so Domanico might not see the lie. "A word in your ear," she told him, shortly thereafter.

He quirked an eyebrow. "You found them?"

She nodded.

"Where?"

She set her hands on her hips. "We haven't discussed my pay, yet."

"Tell me first, and then we talk about coin."

"The gift doesn't work that way. You have to reciprocate. If you don't, the Ancestors reveal nothing."

"And if I beat you?"

"I've endured worse."

His eyes narrowed. "Very well. I'll have Polvo pay you. Where are they?"

"In Avila. I saw the ruins."

"They've run far."

"I would too, if I knew what you had in store for me." She glanced at the tiger meaningfully.

His lips twitched in amusement. "I'm glad we understand each other," he said.

Francisco trailed the circus from a distance. He had shed the motley. The menagerie people were too closely-knit. Everyone knew their role, and especially the dwarf. Polvo knew everything about everyone.

There was nothing for it, but to wait until nightfall when he might steal Rana Isadore away—unless she escaped herself. She was smart enough to know the circus was no refuge. All he could do was to wait for an opportunity to present itself.

You're not really cut out to be a spy, Francis, he thought. Espionage was mostly observing and planning how best to manipulate events. He hated waiting. The temptation to do something was always stronger. He repeated Pantalone's well-worn litany. *Do it by the book, Francis. By the book.*

Which was all very well and good if you were Lord Burley with an untarnishable reputation, and your head wasn't on the block.

Chapter Thirty-Nine: Murex and Other Things Purple

"Once we get through the gate," Miriam said, looking around at the women gathered at the base of the cliff, "we go in twos and threes to find the ship. Joachin has made arrangements with *Ser* Olivares for us to board the *Phoenix*."

"All of us?" Zara cast a gimlet eye at Inez.

She wished Zara hadn't said it. The *Phoenix's* captain had only allotted for their original number. Inez would have to stay behind.

Inez was quick to grasp it. "Better be," she replied.

"Let's go." Miriam refused to acknowledge her.

They spread out to avoid looking like a group. To her dismay, Inez, tagged along beside her. Blanca padded at Luci's and Casi's side.

"Go with Nadia," Miriam said stiffly.

"That baby makes too much noise. Besides, I need to talk to you. Woman to woman."

Luci sniffed with disgust. Miriam studied the distant sea gate. "We have nothing to discuss. Last night, you tried to have sex with my husband. You failed. He lay with you once, but that was the last."

Inez lifted her chin. "You think you're the only one with a special gift, Madelaina? I trust my instincts, and I am never wrong. He may love you, but you'll destroy him. If you love him, you need to let him go."

"Get away from me," She strode away from her.

Inez pursued her. "I don't know how it will happen, but it will. Here, in Qadis. He'll do something foolish. He's done something foolish, already. I can feel it. You don't want his death on your hands. Give him to me. I'll take care of him."

Miriam turned on her. "If you don't shut your mouth, I'll shut it for you! I don't care how pregnant you are, or whose baby you're carrying! I know something, too! I am leader of this Tribe! So is Joachin! Lys has ordained it!"

Inez sneered. "Fairy tales."

Miriam lifted her hand to strike her.

"Enough!" Luci came between them. "The locals are watching us. You're drawing attention."

Not far from them, clusters of women scooped shells into their skirts. Most of them were bent over at the waist, but a few eyed them surreptitiously. Miriam dropped her fist. Luci was right.

Inez clutched her skirt and reached into the water. "Stop gawking and do what I do, if you want to fit in."

Miriam ground her teeth.

Inez plucked a snail from the sand and held it up to the light. "Ah! So this is what they're after! Murex."

"I thought it was just a shell," Casi said.

Inez turned. "It is, but it's a special one."

"What's so special about it?"

Inez crooked an eyebrow as if inviting Miriam to explain. She had no idea why the shell was unique, except that it looked like a cream-coloured whelk with spines. Inez pursed her lips in amusement. "These make a purple dye. If we collect enough of them, they'll make us a lot of money. I suspect that's what the locals are harvesting."

"We're not here to make money," Miriam said. "We're here to look as inconspicuous as possible and to get through the gate."

"We might as well collect something. We'll be more out of place if we arrive empty-handed."

She was right. But it was also likely they were infringing on local harvesting grounds, especially if the Murex was valuable. Joachín mustn't have known. "Fine," she said. "But we take only clams or mussels."

"No reason why we can't collect Murex at the same time."

Miriam wanted to throttle her.

Behind them, the Tribe waded in small groups. Zara wandered close to the sea wall with Nadia and Carlotta in tow. Miriam frowned. What was Zara thinking? That close, anyone might see the differences between them and the Qadisi women. Zara bore the high cheekbones and black eyes that marked her as one of the People.

"Who are you and what are you doing, here?" A local fishwife, with her hair tied in a kerchief, confronted Inez. Her skirt was twisted into thick folds about her knees.

Inez met her glower with a glare of her own. "We're collecting, same as you."

"This is my plot."

"No one owns the sea."

"Take another one of my shells, and I'll drown you."

"We mean no harm." Miriam intervened. "We're not collecting Murex."

The woman pointed at the shells in Inez's skirt. "She's got at least a dozen of them!"

"Give them to her," Miriam told Inez.

"No. I know the law." Inez pointed at the woman's skirt. "You've taken more than your share. You have a bushel there, maybe more. If the buyers turn a blind eye to you, your neighbours won't." She indicated the nearby women who had paused to watch the confrontation.

The Murex collector sputtered. To Miriam's relief, she stepped back from them. "Not one shell more!" She shook her fist at them and retreated, wading away to express her opinions to a friend.

"That was close." Luci parroted Miriam's thoughts.

"One has to know how to deal with them," Inez said. "Lucky for you, I was here."

Miriam seethed.

Don't let her bother you. Blanca leaned against her side, but Alonso waded beside her. The dog's fur shifted in the ripples. A string of sea bracken floated from her tail.

I wish they'd come to blows.

It wouldn't have served any purpose.

It would have made me feel better.

Forget her. Just focus on getting the Tribe to the gate and then to the ship. Have you checked for the Guard, lately?

Not at the sea gate, but there's a lot of coming and going from the temple. The Solarium's stables are full.

Tomás' horses?

Hard to say. He left Bacalao with a smaller contingent, but he might be drafting from the local constabulary. We'll have to be careful. I could look again, but I'm worried about the dog. Every time I leave her, she starts to wander. If it weren't for Casi holding her back....

Why is she doing that?

She's old and confused. Sometimes, I get images of the girl.

Her previous owner?

I think so.

Have you looked in on Joachín?

No.

Would you? I'm worried.

I'm as fond of that low-life as you are of Inez. Let them have each other.

Please.

Oh, very well, he said sourly. *I'll go. But if it comes down to a choice between him or you, I'll sacrifice him to Tomás.* Without another word, he slipped away.

Pray to Lys it never comes to that, she thought.

Blanca paddled away from her side.

There were no further altercations with the local women as they made their way to the sea gate. By the time they reached it, the tide had turned and a crowd had formed. Women jostled baskets on their hips. Fishermen shoved past, shouldering glittering catches. At the market, hawkers shouted their wares, frantic to squeeze the last bit of coin from passersby. The air stank of sweat, fish, and garbage. Children ran underfoot, snatching whatever they could seize. Granad was busy, but its market was calm by comparison. Here, the people darted to and fro like schools of mad herring. They browsed, demanded, and haggled as if every hour were their last. Miriam could no longer keep track of the Tribe. As the women unloaded their meager burdens on whomever would take them, she hoped they had the sense not to linger or bargain.

I found him! Alonso's voice was overly loud as Blanca slammed into her thigh. *He's up to no good, in the worst place possible, with....*

The dog lurched away as if bit by a flea.

"Blanca!" Casi shouted. "Come back!"

The dog disappeared through a crush of people. Casi ran after her, calling. Miriam stared after them in alarm.

"Casi! No!" Luci pushed bodies out of the way. Miriam let her collection of clams fall to the cobbles and followed them.

She could still see Luci, weaving through the crowd. She squeezed past people, swerved around tables, and collided with a chair. Ahead, the tents thinned and warehouses appeared—two-storied buildings from their appearance. The crowds weren't as thick there, but the market gave way to dark alleys lined with shops and stalls that led deeper into the town.

She ran past the startled faces of a rug merchant and his customer. Blanca charged past a wall of stacked baskets, bringing curses down on Casi as she knocked them over. Luci stammered an apology and chased them into the sudden brilliance of a small, sunlit square. A group of merchants had set up booths there, but they seemed to be of a different sort. The dog ran full tilt at a group of people clustered about a wagon carrying great spindles of wool. To one side of the group, a little blonde girl stood. Blanca barked hoarsely and bounded straight for her.

"Lela!" the girl cried, overjoyed at seeing her. "Lela, is that really you?"

The dog threw herself at the girl's legs, became a frantic blur of white.

"*Madré!* Lela's back! She found me!" the girl said excitedly. She hugged the dog tightly. Blanca yelped, licked her face, and whined.

Miriam watched from the dusk of the alley. She was outside a chandler's shop. Casi had run into the square, but had stopped half-way, unsure of what to do. Luci caught up with her and pulled her away. Casi wailed, "But, she's mine!"

"I'll find you a new pet. Come away, now. Blanca was never ours to keep."

"Oh, no," Miriam muttered. It was obvious what had happened here. Blanca had found her first mistress at last. The dog's love was too great for Alonso to overcome. Nothing would wrench her away. Casi would have to find a new pet, and Alonso, a new host.

How long would they have to wait until he found a new one? She didn't have time to ponder it. A blow took her by the back of the head. She gave a thin whimper and crumpled to her knees. Unseen by Luci or Casi, her assailant was quick to drag her out of sight.

Chapter Forty: Tiger

"I will lead on the elephant, followed by the Joãos, First and Second, hauled on their cart. Then the tiger, and then you—"

"The Joãos? As in the kings of Portugal?" Rana asked.

"Yes, my little joke." Domanico meant the conjoined twins. "We call them that when we're in Esbaña. When we're in Portugel, we refer to them as Maria and Felipe. Sometimes, Joao Second dons breasts to make him look like Maria. It goes over well in Lispon."

Rana could well imagine.

"As for you, we're promoting you as The *Adivina of Delphi*. I'll get you a suitable robe. You mustn't go around in those rags."

"I can't be seen in the open. It diminishes the mystery."

"Don't worry about that. We will advertise you, but you aren't for the masses. Only for patrons who can afford you."

He missed the point. Still, if Tomás watched from the main gate, he would see her immediately. The circus had seemed like a good idea. She hadn't expected to be put on display.

"Before you, the tiger's cage and its tamers. You see how much I value you? Only the top spectacles, first."

With him in front and his men in back, it would be next to impossible for her and Tanya to escape.

"Ah. Here is Polvo with your gown." The dwarf carried an emerald green chiton in his arms. Atop it, a brooch of jade and gold shone. Rana suspected it was gilt and glass.

"Wear that, and you will look like a goddess," Domanico said.

"What about Tanya?" She pointed at her.

"She isn't important."

"She still needs a costume."

"She rides with Nivriti."

"She rides with me, or I won't go."

He said nothing for a moment. She knew it didn't matter what she wanted. She was a prisoner, but perhaps it might be better to concede on some things.

"Fine. Get her something," he told Polvo. "You have five minutes. Then we process."

As the parade approached the main gates, crowds hemmed it in on either side. From the elephant, Domanico boomed out invitations to the performance held in the main plaza. The *barrio* dwellers appreciated the excitement, but there was little chance they would attend the circus itself. Still, they shrieked with laughter, outran the elephant, and pelted the Joao's First and Second with fruit. Rana and Tanya swayed atop their wagon where rickety rails gave them a hold. Ahead of them, a team of nervous horses pulled the tiger in its cage. The beast roared and growled at the crowd. Cuffs had been bolted to its legs, but the animal wasn't secured by its chains. Inside the cage, it roamed free. One boy, braver than the rest, ran up to the bars and slammed a hand on the door. As the tiger lunged at him, Rana caught her breath. The peg securing its cage door loosened, but not enough to set the beast free. The crowd howled. Wranglers yelled at the youth, but no one was in earnest. It was all part of the display.

The main gates loomed. They had been thrown wide to allow the parade to enter. Along the upper walkways, both guards and priests watched. Rana paled. The tiger and its cage would hide her for only a moment. It didn't matter if Tomás were present. She would still be seen.

She grabbed Tanya by the wrist. "We have to jump."

"What?" Tanya went white. "I can't!"

Behind them, Domanico's riders followed on horseback. If they leapt, the crowd would catch them like trinkets. There was no place to go, but atop the tiger's cage.

Without thinking about it, Rana sprang from their cart and landed on the cage's roof. The cat lunged, causing the crowd to shriek. Domanico swore as he saw her balancing there. In their cart, Tanya froze, too frightened to move.

"Jump or die!" Rana screamed at her.

Tanya leapt.

As the tiger pounced for her, she shrieked and dodged its claws. Rana pulled the locking bolt from its place.

The door swung open.

The tiger vaulted from the cage, setting the horses and riders behind it into a frenzy. The crowd shrieked; this time from fear. Rana didn't wait to see who the tiger's unlucky victims were. She grabbed Tanya by the arm and jumped from the cage. Behind them, a dervish in orange and black attacked the throng. Blood spattered, the elephant trumpeted.

The crush from the panicking mass nearly trampled them. Tanya slipped and fell, but Rana hauled her to her feet and used her as a shield to plow their way through the mob. Somehow, they made it through the town gates. The Guard rushed past her, thrusting people out of the way. The priests remained where they were, unwilling to risk their necks. Rana felt for the knife and the *linares* Domanico had paid her. Still there. She and Tanya were too noticeable, dressed as they were. They needed a place to hide.

She pulled Tanya into a dark alley, knowing the further they ran, the safer they would be. Not everyone had witnessed the circus's procession, especially if they worked at the docks. An innkeeper might question her dress, but given enough coin, she could buy his silence.

"I can't run anymore!" Tanya clutched at her chest. "Stop!"

"We can't stop!"

"I don't care! I can't...."

Rana cuffed her across the ear, sending her sprawling to her knees. Tanya whimpered and clapped a hand to her face. Rana hauled her up by the arm. In seconds, they were running again.

Chapter Forty-One: Paramour

Within the blackness, she had the impression of eager hands pawing at her and the taint of lust seeping into her skin. A hot desperation spread through her pores, but it soon departed. The grasping fingers left her alone. The pulse in her head pounded an insistent beat, forcing her to wake. Her repulsion tattoo burned. She shivered with cold.

She had been propped against a brick wall like a discarded doll. She didn't recognize her surroundings and had to concentrate to recall where she was. Empty wine jugs lay at her feet. Someone had Someone had torn the top of her dress, exposing her breasts. The skirt had been pushed to her thighs where it billowed like a sail. She had been groped, but not raped, thank the gods. She was alone. She shouldn't be. Where were Luci and Casi? Where was Inez?

Gods! Inez had been right behind her. She must have done this, must have struck her across the back of the head and...sold her! The hands on her legs, the hot breath from more than one man—if not for her repulsion tattoo....

She covered her breasts. It hurt to move. She set a shaking hand to the wall and clambered to her feet. A wave of nausea swamped her. Her knees gave out and she crumpled to the cobblestones. She forced herself to breathe. How long had she lain here?

Either I make it to the main street or I pass out, she thought. Whoever found her might not leave her alone next time. The tattoo prevented unwanted coitus, but it didn't stop other types of violence.

She fought to regain her feet. Her vision greyed, but she tottered. When she finally emerged from the alley, she was too spent to call for help. She clung to a corner, terrified she might lose consciousness at any moment.

Shadows passed by her, people skirted past. Her throat was parched, too dry to swallow. A grey fog threatened the edges of her vision. She was a matriarch, a queen of her Tribe. Surely, this wasn't the end. Lys meant for her to survive, didn't she?

A man paused to regard her. She hugged the bricks a little tighter, not sure whether he represented friend or foe.

"Gods!" he said. What happened to you, my darling? Who did this?"

She knew that voice. Angél Ferrara's.

He pulled her free from the bricks. She had no more strength to prevent him than a kitten. "Speak to me, Miriam!"

"I...." was all she could manage.

"We must get you some help! When you didn't show up at *La Casa Gallina*, I thought I'd search for you at the *Phoenix*, but I hardly expected to find you in this state! Come, let's get you to the inn, where you can tell me what happened. I'll clap whoever did this in chains." He scooped her into his arms. She gagged at the sudden movement. "Please, don't...."

"Don't talk, *querida*. You're safe, now. We'll get to the bottom of this, and then I'll take you back to Tolede. Mother will be glad to see you. Father, too, I think, all things considered."

"No...." She had to find Joachin, had to reach the ship.

"Don't worry about Rana. She isn't my wife anymore."

"Alonso...." *Where are you? I need you!*

"Someone named Alonso did this to you? He'll pay for it. I have friends in high places in Qadis. They'll find him. When they do, he'll be sorry he ever set hands on you. He didn't...he didn't take advantage, did he?"

Anger cleared the fog. He was worried about her virtue? Clamping her jaw made her head pound harder, but the pain helped her form the words. "Where are you taking me?"

"To the inn, as you suggested."

Suggested?

"I'll have a doctor look at your head. After a bath and a rest, you'll feel better. Over supper, you can tell me what happened."

She didn't speak. She had to regain her strength, had to recover from what she suspected was a concussion. She had lost consciousness, couldn't remember much of what happened in the alley. It would be several hours before she could trust herself to reach the docks.

"Here we are!" He swept her through the doors of a bright and well-maintained inn. On one side of a sweeping staircase, wealthy patrons sat with their wives and partook of the afternoon *merienda*. On the other, men of commerce conducted business over cigars and sherry. There were no women for hire here. Everyone stopped mid-bite to stare. She wanted to die of embarrassment.

"My wife has been injured," Angél announced to them. The innkeeper, a stout, balding man, beetled toward them. "Fetch a doctor, at once," Angél said.

"Of course, *Ser* Ferrara." He nodded nervously. The onlookers muttered behind gloved hands.

"Everything is arranged as I requested?"

Miriam wished he would stop swinging her every which way.

"Everything is in readiness, *Ser*. I am sorry your wife has been brutalized on our streets. How did she become separated from her escort?"

"I'm not sure." Angél turned on his heel and carried her up the stairs.

The room smelled of roses. A large bouquet sat on a table. In a separate room beyond, a bathtub squatted. As Angél laid her on the bed, a knock came at their door. He ushered in a man with a long cloak. The doctor.

She closed her eyes, wanting them both to go away.

"What happened?" the doctor asked.

"She was struck over the head by something."

Competent hands fingered her scalp. Gorge rose up her throat.

"She needs to be treated with cold compresses over the next few hours. I can give you salve for that cut, as well as *sal ammoniac* to revive her."

"What's that?"

"A smelling concoction for clarity."

"Is she hurt anywhere else?"

"Give me a moment. You can wait over there."

"I'm her husband."

"Oh. I see."

Cool hands dabbed at the lump on her scalp. She smelled the pungency of agrimony and relaxed. The man knew what he was about. She startled with embarrassment as he opened her dress to examine her torso, then he glanced at her legs beneath the skirt. She was nearing the end of her monthly cycle. He would not miss the sodden rags. She wanted to curl into a ball and die.

"All seems normal. If there's anything more you need, the innkeeper knows where to find me. Keep her quiet and let her rest for the next few hours."

"I will, Doctor. Thank you." Angél ushered him to the door. Seconds later, the mattress creaked as he sat beside her.

"You have no idea how happy I was to get your letter." He leaned over her, trapping her between his arms. His face kept wavering.

"Letter?"

"Poor darling. That knock on your head has affected your memory." He stroked the hair from her eyes. "Yes, the note you sent me, telling me you loved me and that you didn't want to go to the New World. I left Tolede immediately, of course. I was overjoyed that you had escaped the fires in Elysir. How you did that, I have no idea. You must tell me when you're feeling better."

"I didn't...."

"Shhh, now. You're not supposed to talk. But I must admit, when I heard you survived, I worried that that low life Joachín de Rivera had something to do with it. I suppose I should be thankful if he did. Shall I undress you?"

She blinked, not sure she heard him correctly.

"You'll want a bath." He pulled at her dress.

"No...." She pushed his hands away. The room whirled. She had to get to the dock and find Joachín. What was the date? The twenty-first? The *Phoenix* set sail at dawn.

"Poor sweetheart!" He slid his hands along her legs. His fingers were hot. His desire pierced her like a spear to the gut.

"Angél, don't!" He meant to make love to her, for gods' sake! The repulsion tattoo had to stop him! The rags did first.

"Oh!" He removed his hands as if singed. "You're...it's your time. Why didn't you tell me?" He glared at her as if she had slapped him.

The utter arrogance, the assumption that she would satisfy him in spite of her condition.... Words failed her. Why had she ever found him attractive? He was an egotistical clod, selfish in the extreme.

"It's clear nothing can happen between us, now. I suppose I'll have to wait a few days." He glowered at her as if expecting an apology.

When she glared back, he softened and patted her on the thigh. "Well, don't worry about it. I know how it is. You women can't help it. You'll make it up to me when you can. Besides, you'll need a few days to recover from that bump on your head. Get some sleep. I have to go out and attend to some business. I'll be back in a few hours." He smiled indulgently. "When I return, we can eat."

She closed her eyes, thankful for the sound of his retreat. After he closed the door, she forced herself from the bed. Grey flooded her vision. She stood...and abruptly sat down again.

I must find Joachín. She was weak and faint, but she had no intention of remaining where she was. Joachín would be frantic. She had to reach him before he turned the town upside-down searching for her. The Tribe had no idea where she was. Their loyalty would make them forego their chance to sail to the New World.

Alonso, she thought sickly. *I need you!*

No disembodied voice responded to her. If he were with her, she had no way of knowing. He had yet to find a host. With shaking hands, she reached for the smelling salts. She fumbled with the stopper and took a deep sniff. The ammonia snagged her nose, but it cleared her head. She rose on unsteady feet and tottered for the door.

Chapter Forty-Two: Sacrificial Lamb

They had come to the warehouse district that lay adjacent to the docks. Rana paused in the shadow between two provisions houses.

"I can't!" Tanya slumped to the cobblestones.

Rana raised her fist to strike her again but saw the futility in it. Around the corner, women gutted and salted *bacalao* on an open promenade. Lines of drying cod hung from racks. Hundreds of ships lay at anchor on the water, many of which were docked at the wharf. If they ventured any further, they would be seen. A fool's choice.

She yanked Tanya to her feet and ignored her protests as they retraced their steps to a side entry of one of the warehouses. Rana pulled her inside.

The warehouse's interior was huge, dim, and lofty. The front doors lay open to the dock, where men rolled barrels onto carts. The last third of it was stacked with casks.

"They'll find us!" Tanya said.

"They won't, if we head for the back. They're busy on the quay. It'll give us a chance to catch our breaths."

"And then what?"

"And then...I do what I have to." She clutched the bone necklace about her throat.

"What?"

"Stop being a nervous ninny! I'll find us some proper clothes and a place to stay."

"I'm hungry, now. There's no food."

"We're surrounded by food. What do you think is in these casks?"

"Salted fish. Which makes me thirstier than ever."

"Just go." She pushed her ahead of her until they finally came to a small, dark alcove lined with barrels.

Tanya stumbled and rubbed her arm at the place where Rana had cut her previously. She pouted. "What now?"

Rana stood stock still. Only her veil fluttered slightly as it lifted and fell with each breath. Tanya shifted uncomfortably from foot to foot.

"We sit. We rest." She sat down abruptly and set her back to the wall.

Tanya frowned, and then followed suit. For a long moment, they sat side by side. Neither girl said anything.

"How long do we stay...?" Tanya began.

"Long enough. Get some sleep. I'll keep watch."

"I was so scared before. The circus and the tiger.... Thank the gods, we got away."

Rana shrugged.

"Do you think we'll escape the Grand Inquisitor?"

"Stop talking and close your eyes."

"Can I rest my head on your shoulder? I won't, if you don't want me to."

"I don't care. Suit yourself."

Tanya settled her head against Rana's arm. Rana endured it, girding her will. As they ran from the circus, it had occurred to her that there was only one way to break the Tribe's ward. It might not work, but fortune favoured the bold. The Medina bitch would pay for her banishment from the Tribe, for ruining her body and her face, for stealing Angél. It was too bad for Tanya, but Tanya was hers to do with as she pleased.

She slid her hand beneath her gown and found the handle of her blade.

"What is it?" Tanya murmured.

"Nothing. I'm getting comfortable."

"Oh."

Without warning, she twisted and plunged the stiletto into Tanya's gut. Tanya's eyes flew open and she gasped, her hands fumbling at the blade and then falling uselessly at her sides. Blood spilled from her lips. As her eyelids fluttered she choked her last, Rana pulled the knife free and carved an evil glyph across her belly.

Red obliterated Rana's vision. Power surged through her veins, heady and intoxicating. This sensation was followed by a revulsion so intense it threatened to overwhelm her. She ran from it as she might an angry parent. The wrathful presence receded, but it remained watchful. Rana ignored it and focused her will. She would break the tattooed chain Miriam Medina bore. At first, it seemed stronger than iron, but now it flaked away like so much rust.

She laughed, emboldened by her success. "Come," she whispered, beckoning with a bloodied hand.

In her mind's eye, she saw Miriam stumble down a cobbled street. She paused to lean against a stone wall. Rana knew the place. It was close to the inn where she had planned to meet Angél. Gods forbid he should run into her before her plans were put into place.

"No time to rest, little *bruja*," she whispered.

Blinking rapidly as if the fading day hurt her eyes, Miriam staggered in a new direction.

Rana shoved Tanya from her lap like a cast-off doll. Tanya had bloodied her chiton, but she ignored it. As long as she kept her concentration focused, the Medina bitch would come. How to finish her? Make it long and lingering, or dispose of her in one satisfying strike?

She clutched the bone necklace to steady herself. Soon, she would have her revenge. How it played out depended on Miriam Medina, what she would say, what she would do. Rana liked not knowing, even though the conclusion was set.

The thing to do was to act spontaneously.
Then to embrace the end when it came.

Chapter Forty-Three: In the Plaza de las Velas

"What do you mean, you *lost* her?" Joachin stared at Luci in fear and disbelief. The Tribe stood in a tight cluster on the quay. Beyond them, the *Phoenix* floated on calm waters. The crew loaded Fidel onboard in a sling.

"She was with us one moment and gone the next! We chased the dog...."

"That damned dog, again. Where were you, exactly?"

"In the Plaza de las Velas. She was right behind us."

"Do you think the dog is still with Miriam?"

"No." Luci lowered her voice. "Blanca found her first mistress. Alonso lost control."

Casi heard them anyway. Her face crumpled. She began to cry.

"Miriam's run off." Inez set her hands on her hips. "It's been known to happen. She's used to better living."

"You hope that, don't you? Last I saw, you were right behind her," Zara accused.

Inez read the suspicion in their eyes. "Oh, yes. Blame the outsider."

"No one's blaming you," Joachin replied.

"It sounds that way."

He ignored her. "I have to find Miriam." He gave *Ser* Olivares's ring and papers and Don Lope's pouch to Ximen. "Get everyone below decks. Tell the captain there will be two more coming." He regarded the women grimly. "Stay onboard. The town is crawling with inquisitors."

"Shall I come with you?" Iago asked.

"No. Stay with Barto and protect the women. I'm less noticeable if I go alone."

Inez set a hand on his arm. "I'm coming with you. I can show you where I last saw her."

"No. You'll be in the way." He was sure she had something to do with it.

He set off in the direction of the plaza, relieved to see Iago usher the women aboard. Inez protested as Barto pushed her up the gangplank.

He passed the fish market, less busy now than it had been earlier, and headed toward the first line of shops and warehouses. The narrow streets were growing dark, but the Plaza de las Velas still shone with a mellow light. In another half hour, the sun would dip beyond the horizon. After they had abandoned Don Lope, they had narrowly missed Tomás and his retinue passing by. The locals claimed the grand inquisitor would stay with the vizconde at his *palacio*. He wondered what arrangements Tomás had made if Don Lope were not in attendance.

He hesitated beside a chandler's shop to study the plaza. Two merchants spat into their palms to seal an agreement. Dogs scrounged in corners, eating refuse. Housewives gossiped by a fountain while their children ran rampant about it. A pair of sailors staggered from an inn. The wives cursed them as they relieved themselves in the fountain.

Joachin dismissed them all as unlikely sources of information. Perhaps the chandler had seen Miriam. He stepped into the shadowed confines of the shop. The chandler, a greasy man of wide girth and an oily expression, rested his hands on the countertop.

"I'm searching for my wife," Joachín said. "I was told she came by here today. She has the face of an angel, with black, wavy hair...."

"No one of that description came into my shop."

"Not into your shop, but outside your shop. She was with another woman."

"I might have seen her." He rubbed his thumb and forefinger together.

Joachín fished a copper from his pocket. He had expected as much, but had hoped a kinder soul might advise him without cost. "Would this make you sure?"

The chandler lifted his hands. "My memory isn't what it used to be."

He added another two coppers to the first. The chandler scooped them into his palm. "I may have seen them outside my shop. Early afternoon."

Someone entered the doorway, breathing hard. The chandler's eyes lifted. Joachín turned. Inez stood in the doorway.

"*Hola, Serina.*" The chandler smirked, as if enjoying a private joke.

Joachín escorted her from the shop. "What are you doing, here? I told you to stay on the ship."

"I know. I...I was worried."

"Why?"

"Because I thought you might be in danger!"

"You're lying. There's more to this than you're saying. Where is Miriam?"

"I don't know! How would I know?"

"Oy! *Chulo!*"

Joachín turned to see who had hailed him as a pimp. One of the sailors who had urinated in the fountain staggered toward them. "Your *puta* double crossed us!"

Joachín stepped in front of Inez. "What are you talking about?"

"She took our money and said we could have her sister. We tried, but we couldn't touch her!"

Inez pulled at him. "They're drunk. They don't know what they're talking about."

"Cheat!" the second drunk roared. "Give us our money, or we'll call the Watch on you!"

Joachín snagged Inez by the elbow. "This woman sold you another?"

"Whole ten coppers for the two of us. Give us our money!"

"Did you hurt her?" Joachín was ready to explode.

"Somebody'd already struck 'er 'cross the head."

It took all of his willpower to hold himself in check. "Where did you leave her?"

"Down there. Ay!" he yelled as Joachín bolted past him. The alley ended in a wall of dank, wet bricks. It was empty, save for broken wine jugs and a heap of trash.

Behind him, Inez screamed from the street. "Let me go!" One of the drunks had lifted her bodily from the cobblestones.

His partner pawed at her thighs. "Not 'till we get what we paid for!"

That earned him a kick to the gut. He landed on his backside. Inez bit the other one's hand. He dropped her immediately. "You stinking *puta!*" he shouted, shaking his wrist. With a growl, he regained his balance and lurched after her. Joachín grabbed him by the shoulders and redirected him into a brick wall. He collapsed as if poleaxed.

"Guards!" the second cried, sensing a similar fate. Joachín kicked him in the chin, leaving him senseless.

Inez clamped onto his arm. "Pigs!" She spat at them and then gazed at Joachín adoringly. "You were wonderful!"

"Get off me." He marched back into the chandler's shop and stabbed a forefinger in the man's face to show he meant business. "If I were you, I would tell me everything you know. Did you see my wife leave that alley?"

The chandler glanced at Inez. "I thought she was your wife."

"No. This one sold my wife to those two after striking her across the head, as you know. After she left the alley, where did she go?"

"She crossed the square and headed down that *avenida*. It leads to the Plaza del Sul."

He nodded. The sun plaza lay in the more affluent part of the city, which also included the Solarium and Don Lope's *palacio*. Miriam was walking headlong into Tomás and danger.

"Good luck!" the chandler called after them as if his well wishes might negate any bad blood remaining.

Chapter Forty-Four: Glamoury

She paused to smell the salts every few minutes. They helped her stay upright and moving. People avoided her and whispered as she passed. Either she was inebriated or opium-drugged, a scandalous thing in a respectable neighbourhood. Once or twice, shady looking characters stalked her, but they veered off. She looked too poor to be promising.

Her head pounded, her throat felt thick. Several times, she felt drawn down certain streets for no reason. If she chose one way, her feet took her another. Perhaps it only seemed she was travelling down paths she didn't intend. It hardly mattered. The road dropped seaward. She would soon reach the docks.

She came to a breach in the road. Two alleys set off in different directions. She sagged against a wall to catch her breath. The sun was setting. Although the sky was still rosy, the laneways lay in shadow.

This way.

She wasn't sure whether the voice was a man's or a woman's. It directed her to the right. That way fell between two large, block-like warehouses. A man loitered down the other, smoking a roll of *tabaco*, the latest fad from the New World. She lurched down the alleyway from which the voice had called.

"Alonso?" she muttered, hoping the voice was his.

No one answered her, but the shadows between the buildings grew less dim. A good sign—it meant she would soon come to the end of the warehouses and reach the quay. She could see how far she had to go before reaching Joachin and the *Phoenix*. She stumbled forward, but stopped beside an open door, overcome by sudden weakness. As she reached for her salts, a noise, like the snapping of pennants in a stiff breeze, made her look up. A white dove hurtled toward her on frantic wings, as if chased by a storm.

"Alonso!" She was sure it was him. As he reached her, a green blur lunged at her from the warehouse's side door. The thing was a nightmare—a blood-soaked corpse in a shroud. It knocked her off her feet. She landed badly on her side. A hand clamped itself about her hair. Pain bloomed across the back of her head. She scrabbled feebly at the flagstones as the thing dragged her into the warehouse.

A flash of white flew above her—Alonso, attacking her assailant. Abruptly, the thing loosened its grip and grabbed a piece of planking from atop a barrel. It swung at Alonso and missed. Alonso dove at its head a second time. She clutched at barrels to find her balance.

"No, you don't!" A heel slammed into her sternum, snuffing her breath. For a second, her vision went black. As she came to, gasping for air, the green thing struck the bird with the slat. The wood connected. Feathers exploded into dark space. Alonso's body sailed into the darkness and landed somewhere with a distant thump.

Her abductor dropped the board and snagged her by the hair again. Miriam clawed at its hands, knowing that if she didn't fight, it controlled her fate. Her exertions earned her a hard strike across the face. The blow dazed her. She fought to stay aware, knowing that if she didn't, she might never regain consciousness.

Finally, she was dumped beside a dead body—the butchered carcass of a girl. Her abductor straddled her.

"I don't know how you got that blow on the back of your head, but it served me well." The woman's voice was familiar. "Your power isn't as strong as I thought. Too bad for you."

She wore a veil. "Rana," Miriam whispered.

"Surprised? You shouldn't be."

She didn't reply. The Tribe's tattoo had failed. Something evil had broken it; it had to be the murdered girl at her side. Rana had tried to kill her once. She would try it again.

Her silence seemed to infuriate her. Rana grabbed her by the ear. "Do you know why you're here? Do you have you any idea? *This* is why, among other things!" With her free hand, she ripped the veil from her face. The welts from the *hymenoptera* were redder than ever and oozed pus. "*You* did this to me. You stole my place and my love! Now, you're going to pay."

She had to keep her talking, had to postpone whatever she had in mind, which could only be torture and death. "I didn't mean for any of that to happen to you, Rana."

"Shut up or I'll cut out your tongue." She set a knife at Miriam's throat. "Where to start?" she said softly as if relishing the moment. She pricked the soft flesh behind Miriam's jaw. Miriam flinched. Rana smiled.

"Do you know," she continued, drawing the blade lightly across her cheek, "that Tomás threatened me with gouging out an eye? Oh yes, after he raped me, he still wanted his precious sorceress, the one who escaped the stake in Elysir. He thinks you command the weather." She laughed bitterly. "He's also convinced you have the secret to eternal life. He'll do anything to learn it."

Miriam swallowed. "Why don't you turn me over to him, then?"

The blade pricked, drawing fresh blood. "I'll tell you why. Because I'm not that stupid. You reek of power. It clogs my nose—it's too cloying, too strong, too sweet. Like a bower of stinking roses."

She smelled nothing. No one had ever commented on it. Not even Anassa. "How do you smell it when I can't?"

"I don't know. But I hate it, and I hate you."

A psychic gift? Something that had come upon her after the *hymenoptera* had attacked her? Did wasps have an extraordinary sense of smell? She thought they did. "I'm sorry you hate me. I'm sorry for everything that's happened to you, Rana. If I could undo it, I would."

"Too late for that." Rana set the blade at her throat where her jugular lay. She didn't dare breathe. With one quick strike, Rana could drive the knife through her neck. Rana smiled, enjoying the fear she saw in Miriam's eyes.

"Not so strong now, are you?" she whispered.

Why didn't she strike? Why prolong it? Did she enjoy the play, the control she wielded over her? Terror made Miriam recede into herself. She still saw Rana looming over her, but she seemed a long ways off, as if they were separated by an invisible wall. She felt enclosed within a thick, protective bubble.

She's afraid. She knew it without knowing how. Rana had tried to kill her with the *hymenoptera* and had failed. Her escape from Elysir would have seemed miraculous. What would happen now, if Rana tried to kill her? Did she worry about unleashing worse demons than the one she had already suffered? There was madness in her eyes.

She is on the verge of doing it, a Voice warned her. *To live, you must make a sacrifice. It is the only way.*

Lys, it could only be. She didn't stop to question why the goddess intervened, now. *What does she want?*

Angél, more than anything.

How can I...?

The necklace about Rana's neck filled her vision.

"Goodbye, Miriam Medina," Rana said tiredly, as if her fire was finally spent.

"Wait! I can give you Angél!"

Rana paused. "How?"

She had no idea. "Anassa's necklace!"

Rana touched her throat. "My necklace!"

"As you say."

"*Puri* never should have bequeathed it to you." She sneered. "You don't even know the kind of power it wields."

"You're right. I don't."

"This connects me to every matriarch who ever ruled the Tribe. It protects me." A shadow crossed her face. How protected had she been, if she had been at Tomás's mercy? "It's a collection of holy relics, a knuckle from every matriarch who ever ruled the Tribe. This last one is Anassa's."

This unexpected confession sickened Miriam. Anassa's finger had been missing when she and the Tribe had set the old woman in her shroud. They had assumed Anassa had lost it while being murdered by Tomás's men. It had never occurred to her Rana had returned to the site afterwards, to cut the finger free. She hadn't bothered to perform the funeral rites for her grandmother. She had left her to rot in the dirt.

"When I die, my knuckle will grace it, and the necklace will pass to my daughter. The chain will be unbroken." She frowned and then her mouth fell open, as if she had come upon the answer to a riddle. She stared at Miriam. "So, *that's* why the necklace doesn't work for me! Because *Puri* passed it to you! So if I...but how would that bring him to me?" She chewed her lip.

Say nothing. She might still fall the other way.

Miriam held her breath.

"If I looked like you...but then I couldn't kill you, because if I did the glamoury would fail." She worked it through. "But if I had your looks, he wouldn't know differently." She nodded to herself. Open your mouth."

Miriam hesitated.

"I said open your wretched mouth!" Rana shouted. She pressed the knife into her neck. Fear made Miriam gasp. Rana stuffed the veil into her mouth, gagging her. The lack of air made her teeter at the edge of consciousness. A black pit sucked her down.

And then the blackness exploded as the blade severed her baby finger, cutting it free from the bone. The pain was excruciating. With her finger gone, her poor hand flopped like a bird without a head. Rana caught it and carved a glyph into her palm. The pain burned. She was on fire.

Rana laughed wildly. In wonder, she set her hands to her cheeks. "It's true," she said. "Beauty *is* only skin deep."

As the weight on her chest lifted, Miriam spiraled into darkness.

Chapter Forty-Five: Daven

It took Francisco all of thirty seconds to reason out where Rana Isadore might be headed in Qadis, much longer to actually find her. As he jogged through the town's narrow streets, he considered her motivations. What did she want? First and foremost, to avoid Tomás, but he also suspected she wanted to find Miriam Medina. Which led to the question, what did Miriam Medina want? The city was a main port to the New World. Chances were good she planned to leave Esbaña altogether.

One or both witches would be at the docks.

He stopped occasionally to question shopkeepers and passersby. A few confirmed they had seen two women in strange garb running past.

He smiled, recalling the chaos Rana had caused at the town's gate. Releasing the tiger into the crowd had taken nerve. She had been bold to the point of recklessness, but she had done it. No ordinary woman, that. Which was exactly what Ilysabeth needed, to pry her bloody sister from the Inglaisi throne.

If I were her, Francisco thought, *where would I go? Where could I watch the docks before boarding a ship?* Had Rana already made arrangements? Unlikely, considering she had been Tomás's captive, but on the other hand she had outwitted the Grand Inquisitor. Who could say what these Esbañish witches were capable of?

Ahead, the laneway branched two ways. A tavern lay in the alley to the right, a rough looking place. Halfway down the laneway on the left, a side door to a warehouse stood ajar.

Would she hide in a storehouse? It made a kind of sense. She might linger there until dark, and then come forth to find her ship.

A figure appeared in the doorway. He ducked beneath a shadowed overhang and didn't move.

She was young, female, about seventeen with wavy black hair and brown eyes. A beauty, as some Esbañish women were, but she walked as if she were hurt or drunk. She didn't look dazed. Instead, her face was joyful and fierce, as if she had just come from an assignation with a lover. Her dress suggested it. In places, the black skirt was sodden, but those damp places might not be male issue, but blood.

His back prickled as she walked by.

He had no reason to follow her. She wasn't his target. Yet his intuition screamed she was.

Could she be Miriam Medina? Did all powerful Esbañish witches have that effect? At the circus he had confronted Rana Isadore, but she hadn't affected him that way. Miriam Medina was said to be the stronger witch. Was it possible the woman who had just passed him left some clue as to her business in the warehouse? If he investigated quickly, he would still have time to retrace his steps and see where she went.

He ran into the storehouse. Inside, the place was stacked floor to ceiling with barrels. Which way to go? The dirt on the floor indicated someone had recently been dragged.

A cold certainty settled into his gut as he followed the tracks. He had no doubt something unpleasant awaited him at the end of his search. He paused when he saw legs sticking out from between two rows of barrels. A heap of green gauze lay beside them, heedlessly tossed. It looked like the chiton Rana Isadore had worn.

He leaned past the barrel stack. Rana Isadore lay unconscious on the ground, pockmarked and nude. Her tattooed breasts rose and fell slightly. She still breathed. Tanya, the maid beside her, did not. Both women were drenched in blood, although Rana less so. She was also missing the little finger on her right hand.

There was nothing he could do for the maid, but Rana was another matter. He had to get her out of here before they were found.

The closest place was the tavern, down the opposite laneway. Carrying a bleeding woman in a roll of sailcloth wasn't discrete, but he didn't have time for circumspection. One *linares* bought the barkeep's silence. Another purchased medical supplies and a dowdy dress—he didn't question from where they came. An icy look at the tavern's regulars ensured none were so foolish or drunk to challenge him. All eyes watched as he carried his prize up the stairs.

He washed and bound her hand as best he could. She came to as he finished dressing it.

"Joachin," she moaned.

"Sorry. He's not here. It's just me."

She cast a red-rimmed gaze upon him. "Who are you?"

"Francis Walington, at your service, *Serina*." He gave her a small bow. "In some circles, I am known as Fra Francisco. We've met. You don't recognize me?"

She paled. "You're a priest?"

"On occasion."

She struggled to rise and fell back onto the bed.

"I think you should lie still for a bit. I doctored your hand as best I could, but you've lost a lot of blood. I'm having broth and wine sent up. If you can stomach them, they'll give you strength."

"I have to go."

"You are in no condition to walk. Why are you in such a hurry?"

"I have to warn my people, get to my ship...."

"What ship?"

"The *Phoenix*...."

"I'll get word to them."

"That's kind, but I...."

"I think it's better if you stay."

She propped herself up on her elbows and glared at him. "Am I your prisoner, then? Is it your intention to keep me here?"

"No, but you are hurt. I'd like to be your friend, Rana Isadore."

"I am not Rana Isadore!"

Was she delusional? Concussed? "Who are you, then?"

"That does not concern you!"

He pursed his lips. How to handle her? Play along with her irrationality so as not to upset her further, or convince her she wasn't in her right mind? Either way, care was needed.

Someone knocked on their door. She stiffened.

"It's all right. Only the inn keeper, bringing food." He met the man and accepted a tray of wine and soup. After shutting the door behind him, he returned to the bed. "You should get something into that stomach of yours. Then we can decide what to do."

"You'll let me go?"

"Of course. I'm no kidnapper." At *least, not at the moment.*

"Why are you helping me?"

"I have a proposition for you. I'd like you to hear me out."

"Very well. But I don't guarantee I'll agree to it."

"Fair enough." He set the tray over her knees and poured her a cup of wine. "Eat first, and then I'll tell you."

She nodded and picked up her spoon. Her hand trembled; the bandages made it hard for her to hold. As she regarded her reflection in the broth, she froze. The spoon dropped as she touched her face. "No! Oh, gods...NO!"

Her hands became a blur as she clutched at her face and neck. She yanked up her sleeves. "Sweet heaven, what am I going to do?" she whimpered.

"What is it?" Her sudden change in mood was alarming.

"She's...she's *changed* me! I am her! She is me!"

"What are you saying?"

She stared at her bandaged hand. "This! THIS! She took my finger for the necklace! Look here!" She showed him her palm. An ugly collection of cuts criss-crossed it. "She's cut a new glyph! I don't know the tattoo, but it must complete the glamoury. She needed a token."

What better, than my finger! Oh, gods! She's exchanged places with me!"

"Places?"

"Our bodies! Our faces! How we appear to others!"

"Then you aren't the real Rana Isadore?"

"No! I am Miriam Medina!"

"Oh, my! I've wanted to meet you. But I never expected...why would Rana do this?"

"Because the man she loves doesn't want her the way she is." She lifted her pockmarked face to the ceiling. "Lys! How could you allow this? I am better off dead!"

She was talking to the goddess now, confirming she followed the forbidden faith. Before he had left for Esbaña, Ilysabeth had finally trusted him enough to confide that she did, too, but in deepest secrecy.

"So, she exchanged places with you? How can this be? I thought she was the weaker witch."

She stared at him in astonishment as if she couldn't quite understand his callousness. It was a self-serving and shallow thing to say. He regretted it immediately. The beauty who had passed him in the street—*that* was the real Rana Isadore. "I'm sorry," he said, meaning it. "Under the circumstances, what I said was unforgiveable."

She looked as if she were about to burst into tears. Her face, as revolting as it was, reflected a humility and strength he had never seen in Rana. Miriam clutched at the bed clothes, as if to stave off tears before they started.

"I...it doesn't matter. I am still myself. I will find a way to change it. I must find Joachín and the Tribe. I have to reach my ship."

"Can you walk?"

She nodded. From the determined expression on her face, nothing would keep her from her people. They meant more to her than life itself. He marvelled at her resilience. She was the stronger witch, after all.

"Here, let me help you." He drew the tray aside and offered her a veil to cover her face. "You might want to wear this."

She stared at the hateful thing but accepted it. As Rana, she was too recognizable as she was.

"What do you want from me?" She sounded tired, depleted.

"Your assistance. For the future queen of Inglais."

"Not the current one?"

"Hardly. I represent a small group who want to place her younger sister on the throne."

"So, I'm to participate in high treason."

"Yes, among other things."

"I don't murder. I won't do that."

"You needn't concern yourself. There are others better suited for it." He didn't think it wise to point out himself.

"How do you think I can help?"

"You're a powerful Esbañish witch. You can protect her."

"Hmph. At the moment, I can barely protect myself."

He offered her a hand to help her stand. "I have a sense about these things."

"You're a prophet then, as well as a spy?"

She was quick. "I wouldn't go so far as to say that. But I do get strong hunches from time to time."

"And you've had one about me."

"Yes. I can offer you and your people sanctuary in Inglais."

"Inglais is as bad as Esbaña for burning witches."

"At the moment. But we would keep you in secret until Her Royal Highness comes into power. She would welcome you with open arms. Give you an important position on her Council. She also practices the hidden faith."

"More the fool her, then."

"Will you consider it?"

"I'll consider it. But first, I must find my husband and my ship."

"Excellent. Columbine will be pleased."

"Columbine?"

"My pet name for the princess."

"You said your name was Francis?"

"Yes. In Papal circles, I am known as Fra Francisco." It was important to win her trust. Sharing a confidence was one way to earn it, but he also wanted her to trust him for himself. Her appearance was the stuff of nightmare, but there was something of the real Miriam Medina that shone through. She was a queen, as his Columbine was.

Francis knew greatness when he saw it.

Chapter Forty-Six: At the Docks

Angél was frustrated. At five o'clock, he had returned to *La Casa Gallina*, only to be told by the flustered *posadero* that his wife had left the premises and he had no idea where she had gone.

"Good gods, man!" Angél shouted at him. "She wasn't in her right mind! How could you have let her go?"

"Forgive me, *Ser* Ferrara, but she seemed so intent!" It wasn't the innkeeper's job to prevent rich patrons from leaving the inn if they so chose. Angél knew that, but it didn't stop him from clouting the fool over the head as he quit the inn.

Perhaps she's gone to the docks to say goodbye to the Tribe, he thought as he marched down the cobbled streets. He had been there earlier, arranging for arms to be sent to the military outpost at Vera Crucia via his own charter, *La Serina del Sol*. He hadn't seen Miriam, but there were many ways to reach the quay. Most of the locals dodged aside to let him pass. He shoved those who were too distracted by their own affairs, or too drunk to notice, out of the way. No one called him to account for his treatment. They saw him as a big, hard-muscled man in a temper. Which improved his mood a bit, but not much.

The ships bobbing at the wharf were black hulks. Their masts speared a burnished sky. Their sails caught the lingering rays of the sun. Halfway down the wharf, the *Phoenix* lay docked, a three-masted *nao* sitting low in the water. She was already loaded and ready to make sail. A gangplank extended from her to the wharf, awaiting most of the crew who were still ashore, making merry the night before departure.

"Hoy!" Angél shouted at the lone boy on watch. "Are there passengers on board?"

"Aye, *Ser*. Who wants to know?"

"I'm looking for a troop of Diaphani. I was told they bought passage on this ship."

The boy frowned, as if he had been warned against revealing too much.

"I know they are below decks," Angél continued. "I'm one of them. I need to speak to the one who has been left in charge." He congratulated himself on his cleverness. He had increased his chances of success by not referring to either a man or a woman.

"Ah, I see, *Ser*. Just a moment. I'll get her."

Angél snorted. How like the Tribe to put a woman in control. With luck, it would be Miriam. On the other hand, maybe not so lucky if she changed her mind.

After a moment of waiting impatiently, Zara appeared on deck. She glared at him when she saw who it was. "What do *you* want?" she asked without preamble.

"I'm looking for Miriam."

"Aren't we all?"

Luci and Casi appeared at her side. "He says he's looking for Miriam," she told them.

"How did you know to find us, here?" Luci asked.

"Miriam told me you were boarding this ship."

"She told you? When did she tell you?" Zara demanded.

"In a letter she sent me. I wondered if she had come by here to bid you goodbye."

"What nonsense is he talking?" Zara turned to Luci. "Miriam wouldn't have sent a letter...."

The comment made no sense, but a nasty suspicion occurred to Angél. "Are you holding her hostage? Keeping her from me?"

"Don't be absurd." Zara sneered at him. "The last person she'd want to be with is you."

He coloured. Protocol be damned, he would board the ship and search for her. He started up the gangplank when someone hailed him from behind.

"Angél!"

He turned. Miriam hurried toward them. She looked flushed and out of breath. "Here I am! It's all right! I looked for you at *La Casa Gallina*, but the innkeeper told me you'd already left!"

He tramped down the gangplank to meet her. "I told you to stay put."

"I know, I'm sorry, but everything's all right, now." She grabbed him by the waist. "We can start our life together."

"You look a mess. You shouldn't be seen in public like this." Her dress was smeared with blood. It was enough to make him lose his appetite.

"What's going on, here?" Zara demanded. "What are you doing, Miriam?"

Miriam drew herself up haughtily. "I've come to say goodbye. I'm not going with you to the New World. I intend to stay in Esbaña with Angél."

"You don't mean that!"

"I do. I know what I want, and I want him."

"But what about Joachín? He's gone to find you!"

"Tell him to forget me. I don't love him anymore. Come, Angél, it's getting dark. I'm hungry, and I want a bath. Let's return to *La Casa Gallina*."

"Miriam, you can't!" Zara clutched at the rail.

Casi tugged at Luci's skirt. "*Maré*, that isn't Miriam. She would never go with him!"

"What are you saying?" Luci glanced down at her and frowned.

"It looks like her, but it *isn't*!"

"Then who…?"

At that moment, riders erupted from a laneway and onto the promenade—the Inquisitional Guard, mounted in twos. Angél and Miriam were quickly surrounded. Angél glanced over his shoulder at the ship. Zara, Luci, and Casi had vanished. Only the cabin boy watched from his post atop the deck. As Angél protested his innocence, the guard split ranks to allow Tor Tomás to confront them.

"Miriam Medina," the Grand Inquisitor said, his face alight with victory, "we meet, once again. You are under arrest for heresy and witchcraft, as well as the attempted murder of myself, Grand Inquisitor and Confessor to their Royal Majesties, Maria and Felipe." He leered.

"No!" Miriam shrieked. Angél paled at her vehemence. He could understand her terror, but she wasn't acting as expected.

"Take them to the *cárcel*." Tomás was in the best of moods.

"There's been a mistake," Angél said quickly. Even if Miriam was the woman he desired more than any other, she wasn't worth this. "I was bringing her to you."

"Angél!" Miriam cried.

"Well, well, well, Angél Ferrara." Tomás finally recognized him. "Here you are, involved with yet another witch, and one even more dangerous than the last. Guards, arrest him." Soldiers clapped gloves on his shoulders.

Angél knocked them aside. "I am here, overseeing a large shipment of cannon and slaves on behalf of the Vizconde, Don Lope!"

Tomás paused. "I see. Well, it remains to be seen if the vizconde will vouch for you."

"He will!"

"Perhaps, perhaps not."

Angél stiffened. There was a chance the vizconde would seize his shipment of guns anyway, claiming he had already paid for it. In Qadis, his word was law. With Angél moldering in a dungeon, no one would gainsay him. On the other hand, it might profit the vizconde to not only claim the unpaid-for cannon, but to also expect Angél to buy his freedom. Angél glanced up at the Grand Inquisitor. Tomás wore a bemused look. He would expect a share, too. There was no point in confiscating goods when it meant a greater loss in money.

"Bring him," Tomás said, smiling.

Three hours had gone by, and Joachin still hadn't found Miriam. He had searched every tavern, every stinking alley that led to the waterfront. He had threatened those who looked as if they might have some knowledge of her and had come to blows nearly twice. The last time, only the approach of the Port Watch made him re-think exchanging compliments with his latest dance partner. Both of them slinked into opposite doorways as the contingent strode past.

Now, he and Inez headed back to the docks. She grabbed him by the sleeve. "She's gone, Joachin! You might as well accept it. I shouldn't have struck her, but I only forced what was going to happen. She isn't cut out for this life! She isn't good for you!"

Joachin lifted a hand to silence her. "I swear, if you don't shut your mouth, I'll shut it for you! It's because of you she's wandered off hurt or worse! I wish I'd never laid eyes on you!" He turned from her. Inez ran at his heels.

"But you did lay eyes on me and more. You loved me once, Joachin. I was the fool. I should have left Herradur when you asked." She grabbed him again.

"Get off me!"

"No! I will never leave you! If you persist in this wild hunt, the Guard will catch you. They may even have captured her, by now. If she tells them everything she knows, they'll search the docks and the ship. We have to think of our baby!"

"The child isn't mine."

"He is! He's yours!"

"Let Tomás catch me, then. If he does, I'll be closer to her."

"I'll...I'll stop you! I won't let that happen!"

He shook her. "What will you do, Inez? Forcibly restrain me from finding her? If she isn't aboard the *Phoenix* once we get there, that's where I'm going next—to the *cárcel*. I will find her and save her!"

"She isn't worth it!" She stopped in the middle of the street and burst into tears. He marched several feet ahead, before realizing she wasn't following him. He was tempted to leave her where she was, but the sight of her was too much to dismiss, in spite of what his better judgment said. She was crying. That wasn't a sham. She was also pregnant. Even if the child wasn't his, he couldn't abandon her in the street.

"Stop it," he said. "We have to reach the ship."

She shook her head. "I can't!"

"Calm yourself. You're drawing attention." It was true. People were stopping to stare.

She continued to weep. "You—" she said looking at him. Her face was mottled and red. "You don't know what it's like. To think that life holds nothing for you, and then someone blunders into it and you...you fall in love. I never believed in love before, but now...it is terrible! Love hurts so much! I love you, Joachín! I would die for you!"

"Don't say that. Think about your baby."

"*Our* baby!"

He said nothing, but set an arm about her shoulders to bring her along. Surprised to find herself in the crook of his arm, she allowed herself to be hurried down the alley. He felt guilty about making her think there was hope. It was a small token of compassion, a crumb, compared to the feast she wanted from him.

They turned a corner to reach the quay.

Twenty or so of the Inquisitional Guard surrounded a couple on the esplanade. Tomás was directing the guards to take them into custody. A horse shifted. He saw Angél Ferrara at the same moment that Angél saw him. "That's Joachín de Rivera!" Angél shouted, pointing in his direction.

He was about to bolt with Inez in tow, when he spotted Miriam. She swore as a guard hoisted her atop a horse. All thoughts of escape flew from his head. He had to reach her, to kill as many as possible before they took her away. He pulled his knife.

"Joachín! No!" Inez clawed at his arm.

With a sick understanding, he recognized his dream coming to life. Miriam, in custody, about to die in the torture chambers beneath the Solarium unless he reached her in time. His own hands had been in chains, but the dream hadn't shown him his fate. He threw Inez off and ran for the Guard. As he attacked the first rider barring his path, he caught sight of her briefly. Her face shifted between the one he knew and that of a hag. What dark magic was this? It confused him, but he had no time to ponder it. The guard fumbled with his sword.

Riders shouted as he drove his knife into the neck of his opponent. Other guards closed in. He fought them as best he could, but his knife was no match against longer steel. Soon, he was feinting and dodging. Behind him, Inez screamed. Horses reeled. He launched himself from a saddle, narrowly missing a strike to his thigh. Tomás shouted, "Take him alive!" He fought his way to Miriam, ducking beneath rearing horses and flailing hooves. Her guard held her tightly about the throat. He stabbed the man in the leg, finding the vulnerable spot between the rivets of his knee plate. The guard bellowed and released her. Miriam threw herself into his arms, but her face was wrong, it wavered along the edges as if she wore a mask. Her eyes were hard and hate-filled. Something blunt clouted him across the back of the head.

He fell to his knees. Guards in black and white fell upon him like vultures tearing a corpse. A hand hauled him up by the hair. Another fist drove into his gut. Nausea rose up his throat as he recognized its owner—Angél Ferrara.

"Half breed," Angél sneered as he leaned into his face. He turned to address Tomás, who waited upon his horse. "I have apprehended him for you, Radiance."

"Yes. Yet another example of your devotion to duty." Tomás smiled coldly. "Get them." He motioned to his guards.

Miriam struggled between two of Tomás's men. *I've failed her!* Joachín thought. *Goddess, help her! Take me, not my love!*

No miracle intervened on their behalf. He was hoisted atop a horse and clouted across the head again for good measure. Gorge rose into his throat. As Tomás's contingent made its way from the esplanade, he passed what looked like a heap of dirty rags lying in the street.

Inez lay on the cobbles without moving. Her back was bent at an odd angle; her face was smeared in blood. Cuts and bruises bore witness to what had happened. In the mêlée, she had been trampled.

He hadn't loved her; he had never believed she carried his child, but he still blamed himself for her death. If they hadn't dallied in Herradur, if she hadn't followed him from the al-Ma'dins'—if, if, if! Guilt burdened him heavily, told him he should be the one to die. He had failed Inez, and he had lost Miriam to gods knew what. They should have gone east, to Italia, instead of Qadis. His dream had shown him the risks, but he had ignored them. This was the result.

Goddess, he prayed, still holding onto what shreds remained of his faith. *Help us.* Surely, Lys would help them, wouldn't she? He and Miriam were patriarch and matriarch. That was their destiny.

For a moment, he felt the briefest touch of warmth, a tingling, not much more. And then that reassuring presence was gone, as if it were called elsewhere.

Chapter Forty-Seven: Reunion

"We have to go a different way." Francis stepped back from the corner. He looked tense. "The Guard is in the process of arresting several people at the end of the lane. I don't think either one of us wants to run into them."

As they hurried back up the alley, Miriam breathed deeply to clear her head. She still felt dizzy and weak. "You've encountered them before?"

"Oh, yes. Tomás would like nothing better than to see me dead."

The new route took them out of their way, down narrow streets that seemed little more than black, endless tunnels, but eventually they found themselves on the periphery of the wharf once more. The nightly curfew was now in effect. The townsfolk had quit their market stalls and fishing boats. All ships' crews were aboard for the night. The Port Watch was still a concern, but Francis assured Miriam that they only needed to wait a short while before they could cross the esplanade unseen. The guards would soon reach the limit of their patrols. Miriam's head pounded. Her hand throbbed. Hopefully,

Zara would have something for the pain. As she and Francis picked their way to the *Phoenix's* gangplank, she sighed in relief. The great three-masted ship seemed to doze on the water. Dull lanterns shone from its decks, fore and aft, as well as from the captain's quarters. A lone watchman in faded blue garb eyed them as they approached. Francis requested permission to board.

"Your names and purpose," the watchman said. He had a Low Countries accent.

"You don't need our names. As to our purpose, we're here to join the delegation on board. You know of whom I speak."

The sailor frowned, not liking being told his business.

"Our passage has been guaranteed by part-owner of this ship, Ser Olivares of Marabel," Miriam said.

"Very well. I was told to expect two more."

The deckhand assumed that she and Francis were those two. Which meant Joachin had not yet boarded. He was still searching for her.

As they stepped onto the waist, more crew appeared like phantoms from out of the dark. Their deckhand pointed to a low wooden door beneath the forecastle. "Down there," he said." As she and Francis crossed the deck, eyes bored into them. Sailors were a superstitious lot; it was bad enough that they harboured a group of Diaphani and mostly women. She was thankful for her veil. If the crew saw the pustules on her face, they would believe she had gained them through dark magic. They would not tolerate a witch among them.

She and Francis climbed down the companionway to the main deck. Between cannon, the crew watched, chatted, and from the stink of their vomit, slept off their drink. There was still no sign of the captain or his officers, but they were likely sequestered in their quarters beneath the poop. Talk died as she and Francis descended the ladder. All around them, sailors stared, their faces weather-worn and grim. No one bothered to direct them.

"Down two more, I think," Francis whispered, retrieving a lantern from a rafter. He nudged her toward a second stairway that descended to the lowest deck.

They passed the third deck which smelled of dung; half of it was devoted to livestock. Cattle, horses, and fowl shifted unhappily in stalls or cages. The other half was stocked from base to ceiling with bushels of straw and barrels of varying sizes—the ship's victuals. On the lowest deck and in a small niche that seemed to be created for that purpose, the Tribe huddled about someone on the floor. They turned as Miriam and Francis approached.

"Who are you?" Zara's tone suggested they should come no further. Luci, Casi, and the rest blocked whomever lay in the straw.

"It's me, Zara. Miriam," she said softly. "This is Francis. He helped me get here. He's a friend."

"You don't sound like Miriam." Iago fingered his knife.

"I've been hurt. Inez struck me across the head." The Tribe shared a look. "I wandered dazed about the town. Where is Joachín?"

"He's not here." Ximen looked unhappy. "We think...."

Zara cut him off. "Why are you wearing that veil?"

"I've been changed." With her good hand, she removed it from her face. The Tribe let out a collective gasp.

"You!" Zara said. "How dare you come here! What have you done with our matriarch?"

"It's me, Zara." Miriam held up her bandaged hand. "Rana did this. She took my little finger and evoked a glamoury. She thought it was the only way to fool Angél."

Barto hissed between his teeth. "Blood magic."

"Everything she says is true. This *is* the real Miriam," Francis said.

Zara pointed a finger. "How do we know you aren't here to turn us over to the authorities?"

Ximen set a hand on her arm. "Wouldn't they have already done that, if that was their plan?"

"I know nothing of the sort, old man! Maybe she wants something from us!"

Casi spoke up. "That *is* Miriam. I told you all before, but you wouldn't believe me. Even you weren't sure, were you *Maré?*" She eyed Luci accusingly. "I hear her thoughts, and I heard Rana's. She's furious that Tomás has found her again, especially now that she's fooled Angél."

"What are you talking about, Casi?" Zara demanded.

"I have a gift, Auntie. I hear people's thoughts."

Zara coloured. "How long have you been able to do that?"

"A while. That's how I know this is Miriam."

The Tribe shifted uneasily. Luci hadn't told them.

Casi regarded Miriam. "You should sit down, Miriam. Your head hurts. You aren't feeling so well."

Miriam brushed aside her concern. "Has Joachín shown up here?"

"He...."

A moan interrupted Ximen. The Tribe turned to gaze at the woman lying in the straw behind them. Miriam stiffened. Multiple cuts and bruises marred Inez's arms and legs. She was delirious; her skirt was soaked in blood. Luci set a hand to her brow. "She was trampled. We retrieved her after they left. She's lost the baby."

Miriam knelt beside Inez and set her hand to her face. In spite of the exhaustion that threatened her from all sides and the dizziness she fought from blood loss, her gift as a *sentidora* remained strong. Inez was hemorrhaging; Luci and Zara hadn't been able to staunch the flow.

Inez regarded her with pain-ridden eyes. Their brightness was dimming. A flicker of recognition passed across her bruised face. "I loved him so much," she whispered, as if seeing Miriam there, instead of the pockmarked stranger she was.

Miriam nodded.

Inez's pain, coupled with her own, was too much for her to endure. Inez was dying. Miriam drew her hands away. The break in contact eased her suffering a bit. She was able to hear Inez's last words.

"...but he only loved you."

Miriam's eyes filled. She had to say something, had to offer some comfort. In spite of the rivalry between them, she couldn't let Inez pass without some reassurance that her love for Joachín had not been a waste.

"He loved you, too." She wanted to believe it. Perhaps he had, for only a night. It wasn't in Joachín's nature to turn his back on love.

Inez's expression took on a trapped look as if she saw the specter of Death approaching. "Forgive me!" she whispered, "It...wasn't...." Her lips trembled. Without thinking, Miriam grabbed her hand so she might ease her passing—a mistake. The inevitability of Inez's death sucked her along with it. From a long way's off, she heard shouts of alarm. The world faded, disappeared. She and Inez stood in a bright space, as if in the midst of a cloud.

A figure approached them from out of the light. Inez whimpered in fear.

It's all right, Inez. Go. Alonso shone like the sun. His robe was brilliant, so white as to be painful to the eye. He had never looked so handsome, so vital, or so young.

Another shining figure stood behind him. "*Madré?*" Inez asked in wonder. The woman nodded and smiled. She held out her hands.

Inez hurried forward and then paused. She turned to Miriam one last time. Her face was a mixture of resignation and regret. Although her lips never moved, Miriam heard her thought. *In my next life, I want to be you.*

Miriam didn't know what to say. Alonso slipped an arm about her waist to steady her; his touch was distracting. Wonder of wonders, he wasn't a ghost. He had a mass. He was strong, solid, and whole!

Am I dying, Alonso? she asked him. It could only be. With him at her side, the prospect wasn't so terrifying.

I can't say yet, Love. He directed her attention back to Inez. In the moment since they had spoken, Inez had transformed. Her dress was no longer stained. Everything about her—her face, her skin, her clothes—shone. She seemed larger than life.

I lied, Miriam, came the thought. She looked wistful. *The baby wasn't Joachín's. More than anything, I wanted it to be his.*

Whose was it? She had to ask. It seemed important to know, as if the truth might shed light on Inez's reasons.

Inez smiled faintly. *My father's.* She and her mother joined hands and walked into the light until Miriam saw them no more.

A great weight pulled at her heart. Her eyes pricked; Inez had been born into a terrible, abusive life. She had had one fleeting moment of happiness—with Joachín. She had lied and done worse things to keep him. *How can I fault her?* Miriam wondered. A loveless life was a terrible thing. A life sacrificed for love was also heartbreaking. She leaned against Alonso, thankful he was there. He had died three times—the first and last time for her. *I was so afraid for you, Alonso... when you flew at Rana and she struck you.*

A short pain lasting only a moment. But I think I'll avoid doves in the future.

The future? You mean we have one? We can go...back? She meant the real world, where she lay unconscious aboard the *Phoenix*. Touching as they did, she wondered which place was more real.

His blue eyes encompassed her, as vast as the sky. *That, my cielo, is up to you.*

They could walk into the distance like Inez and her mother had done.

What awaits us, if we go? She stared at that place.

Unlimited potential, I think.

She believed him. If she went with him, she would die. He would complete his transition into the afterlife, and their mortality would end. Someone else—Zara—would become matriarch. Did it matter how one died if death led to a new existence? But how could she move on, knowing she would forsake Joachin, even if it meant being with Alonso?

She couldn't. Even Inez had understood that. She had confessed her sin and had cleared her conscience. Heaven, whatever and wherever it was, could only be reached through an honest and unfettered heart.

The light vanished, taking Alonso with it. With a cry, the door to that midway place closed and she found herself outside of it, tumbling through an inky sky. Terror seized her, but it was short-lived. Life jolted through her limbs. She landed with a crash. People shouted. Hands clutched her from all sides. Something inert and wet lay beneath her—Inez. The time she had spent with Alonso at that midpoint had been no time at all.

She felt as if she were going to be sick.

"Give her air!" It sounded like Francis, the Inglaisi spy.

Faces whirled in and out of focus. They solidified as the smell of ammonia struck her nose.

"Stop that! She doesn't need it!" Zara grabbed Francis's hand. "Leave her be!"

"I'm all right." She waved at them feebly. Her right hand throbbed. She struggled to sit. "I have to find Joachin."

"You aren't all right, and you're not going anywhere." Zara spoke for the Tribe. Everyone shifted uncomfortably.

A terrible suspicion settled upon her like a dead weight. "What's happened to him?"

"We're not sure, but we think...." Iago began.

"That's enough, Iago. He hasn't come back from looking for you, is all," Zara said dourly. "He's fine."

"Ximen?" Miriam glanced at him. If anyone knew where Joachín was, their Rememberer would. Ximen saw the past, seconds after the present had been.

He looked grim. "He's been arrested by Tomás. So has Rana Isadore. Tomás thinks she's you. At the moment, Joachín is in the Solarium's *cárcel.*"

"Gods! Is he hurt?"

"A bit. He was struck across the head."

Luci rounded on him. "Why didn't you tell us before?"

"Because we would have all run pell-mell to rescue him! Joachín doesn't want us to risk ourselves, and especially not Miriam! Fortunately for him, Tomás is too busy with Rana at the moment." He flushed hotly.

Miriam guessed at what he saw—if Rana lacked the protective tattoos she bore against sexual interference, Tomás would waste no time in taking his pleasure with her. He wouldn't understand why he was able to rape her now when the tattoo had prevented him before, but he would be conceited enough to think that the tattoo had failed, that he was the stronger. She wondered if Anassa's necklace provided a kind of safeguard. The necklace hadn't saved the old woman from death. Perhaps it offered only spiritual protection.

"You knew this when we retrieved Inez," Luci accused.

"Yes." Ximen didn't have the sense to look guilty.

Miriam struggled to rise. "It doesn't matter. We must rescue him."

Zara pressed a hand to her chest. "You're not going anywhere. Joachín will find a way to escape. The goddess will see to it." She eyed everyone in turn, daring them to contradict her.

"Miracles aside, I think I can help." All eyes turned to Francis. "I have connections with the Papacy. If I get word to the High Solar quickly, I can have Joachín transported to Italia before the Grand Inquisitor even knows he's gone."

"How?" Zara still didn't trust him.

"I'll say he must answer for his crimes against the Holy See."

"What crimes?"

"He stole the papal tiara—I don't know; I'll make up something. The point is I should be able to release him. If I act quickly, the Solarium will be confused."

"*Who* did you say you are?"

"A friend, *Sera*."

"Your accent—sometimes you sound Italia. At other times, Inglaisi."

"You have an excellent ear. I'd best be on my way. What is his full name?"

"Joachín de Rivera Montoya," Luci said.

He repeated it and trilled the 'r' for Zara's benefit. Then he saluted them and bounded up the ladder.

"Where did you find him?" Zara asked Miriam.

"He found me." She regarded them tiredly. "I don't like it. Francis may be able to arrange something, but it will take time. If Tomás is busy with Rana, he isn't watching Joachín. There's no better time to rescue him than now."

"Leave that up to your spy."

"Besides, it's no job for women." Iago nodded at Barto. "If your friend doesn't show up in half an hour with Joachín in tow, then Barto and I will get him."

"How?"

"I don't know how exactly, but we will."

"Have faith. The goddess will find a way," Zara said

Miriam turned to Ximen. "Will you keep me informed? Watch over Joachín, tell me what's happening?"

The Rememberer nodded, but his face gave away his true thoughts. He wouldn't tell her. He didn't think it possible to save Joachín. He thought Joachín was doomed. Ximen wanted the *Phoenix* to sail before Joachín blurted the truth of their whereabouts. He would honour Joachín's wishes to spare her and the Tribe.

She closed her eyes. She would ask Zara to re-bandage her hand and head, and then offer some excuse to climb above deck and leave. Zara was right. The goddess may have found a way to save Joachín, but there was only one person Tomás would allow near her husband, and that was his pet sorceress, Rana Isadore.

Chapter Forty-Eight: The Diabolical Mass

"How dare you assume the Grand Inquisitor tells you everything! You presume too much, old man!" Miriam drew herself to her full height and looked down her nose at the aging Luster monk. She had no idea who he was. The door warden had fetched him during the evening repast, which meant Tomás was still preoccupied elsewhere, likely with Rana. The monk had to be someone Tomás trusted, perhaps his majordomo.

"Forgive me, Fra Umberto, but she insisted on being taken to see the prisoner," the doorkeeper said, looking worried.

Fra Umberto lifted a spotty claw to silence him. "You leave without a word, *Serina*, and cause no end of irritation to his Radiance. I think it's safe to presume you ran away." He smiled nastily. He enjoyed this. In another second, he would order her placed in chains.

"Listen, you stupid fool. I left because there was no time to tell his Radiance what I found. I *had* to leave! Otherwise the opportunity would have been missed. You think I'd come back to suffer his wrath, if I had nothing to show for my efforts?"

"What opportunity?"

"That's for me and his Radiance to know."

"What does this have to do with the prisoner Rivera?"

"Why must I repeat myself? That is for the Grand Inquisitor's ears, only!"

"I am his eyes and ears. If you want access to the prisoner, you will tell me."

She stared him down, outwardly fuming but inwardly terrified he might throw her into a cell and leave her there until Tomás appeared. "Fine. I will tell you, but only in private." She glared at the doorkeeper who had been listening to them open-mouthed. Umberto dismissed him with a wave. The monk blinked rapidly, bowed obsequiously, and left.

"Well?" They stood alone in the vestibule. In the nave beyond, several monks toiled at the eternal flame. The rest of the community supped in the refectory. Soon, they would gather for Compline.

"You know what the Grand Inquisitor seeks."

"He seeks many things."

She paused for emphasis. "I have what he seeks *above* all."

Umberto narrowed his eyes, as if his scrutiny might expose the lie.

"If I succeed on his behalf, he will raise me above all women. He will make me his queen." She smiled, knowing he would see it beneath her veil. "And then, we shall see what happens to toadies who are unpleasant," she added.

His black eyes burned with hatred. He feared her, but he still wasn't convinced. "I am still required to ask," he said stiffly. His tone had lost some of its superiority.

"Rivera is key. I could sacrifice another, but the spell wouldn't be as potent. What better way to give Tomás what he wants, than through the downfall of his enemy? But we linger, here. Take me to Rivera. The sooner I begin, the sooner I bestow the gift of immortality on our master."

"Certainly. I will inform him of your intentions."

"You may, but he's still busy with the Medina woman. The process will take some time. There is no reason to disturb him."

Again, she had guessed correctly. Tomás would sate himself, rest, and then force himself upon Rana, again. He would relish every moment of it and be in no hurry to deal with Joachín, unless it occurred to him he might make Rana watch his torture. Miriam swallowed. Let it not come to that.

"This way," Umberto said sourly. He led her from the vestibule, away from the nave and down a long marble corridor. After a few turns, they came to a stairwell that lost its gilt and ostentation as they descended. At the bottom, one of the members of the Inquisitional Guard stood watch in a pool of torchlight. He gave a start as he recognized her, but stepped aside to allow her to pass. She and Umberto made their way down a dim corridor and came at last to a heavily boarded door. Through the grill, a half-naked figure hung suspended by chains from the ceiling. Iron cuffs bit into his wrists. His bare back was a crosshatch of welts. Miriam didn't breathe, knowing if she did she would not be able to stifle her cry. They had strung him up, facing the wall, so he might not see what next terrible thing they inflicted upon him. His head lay slumped against a shoulder. He appeared to be unconscious.

At her side, Umberto watched her closely. She met his glance with cold, unforgiving eyes. In that moment, she knew she would stop at nothing to free Joachín. Not even murder. "Release him."

"I am not releasing him!"

"Listen, you fool. You will release him and take him to the ancient chancel they have here. I can't perform the ceremony in this miserable place. It needs to be done on consecrated ground." She had to get Joachín out of the cell. Their chances of escape from the dungeon were next to none.

"Why? What are you going to do?"

Now was the time to weave a lie as she had never done. Were he conscious, Joachín would be proud. She curled her lip in disdain. "Apparently, you have never heard of the Diabolical Mass." Of course he hadn't heard of it. She had just invented it. The term suggested a dark potential.

Umberto would not be bested. "I am not ignorant! It's...it's a sacrifice to the dark goddess!"

Who was fabricating, now? "So you are not as stupid as I thought. Release the sacrifice. You will carry him to the chancel."

He sputtered. "I can't carry him!"

"Then have a guard do it! For Sul's sake, old man, must I think of everything?"

He hobbled to the door and bellowed at the guard to attend them. Then he set a large key into Joachin's cuffs. It took all of her willpower to do nothing as Joachin dropped to the filthy floor. He groaned as he came to. She thanked the goddess for it. With him conscious, they had a chance to escape.

A guard appeared at the door.

"Bring him," Umberto directed. "We are taking him to the east shrine."

She allowed Umberto to lead which proved to be convenient as she was not sure where the original chancel lay. She had guessed its location from the temple's exterior; it was a small, round tower that made up a section of the Solarium's earliest structure, but below ground, she lost her sense of direction. As they left the dungeon and ascended the steps, Joachin moaned before lapsing into stupor again. She ignored him as he dangled across the guard's back. Soon, they skirted the nave and followed an empty cloister to a little used wing of the temple. Umberto retrieved a torch from a wall sconce. At the end of the cloister, an unlit archway stood.

Umberto seemed loath to set his hand on the door.

He's afraid, Miriam thought. Had this shrine once been dedicated to Lys? That was possible. The stonework was old and crumbling. Newer portions of the temple were built adjacent to the old. As a rule, stonemasons refused to demolish any portion of a holy building. Was it because they feared the dark goddess? Miriam swept past Umberto and pushed on the door. It opened a crack, but no further. The wood had warped. The place had not been used in years.

"Set the prisoner down and open it," Miriam directed the guard. Their way to freedom lay through the shrine's outer exit. A yew tree sheltered the outside alcove, the stairs had been worn to grit, but the vestibule was still there. The guard lay Joachin down and set his shoulder to the wood.

It budged, but only slightly.

"Try the other one," Miriam said.

Perhaps the flagstones had settled more beneath the second door. In any event, it opened enough to grant them entry. Inside, the shrine was shrouded in darkness, but moonlight seeped through the high windows to illuminate a blocky altar at the far end.

"Put him there," Miriam said. Umberto's torch sent her shadow stretching towards the altar and the apse. The effect was not lost upon him. It gave her an aura of immense power. He swallowed as she took the torch from him. The guard set Joachín atop the altar. He lay there, unmoving.

"Now both of you, leave." Miriam ordered.

Umberto thrust his grizzled chin at her. "I will do no such thing!"

"Fine. It's your life at risk. But the guard must. Extra bodies will only tempt it."

"It?"

"I thought you understood what occurs in a Diabolical Mass." She pulled a knife from her waistband. Umberto flinched but stood his ground. The guard shifted uneasily, waiting for the monk's direction. Miriam pointed at Joachín, lying on the altar. "The sigil I'm about to carve invokes an arch-demon, one of the most diabolical in hell itself. Even with wards in place, it may blind you or do worse."

"The demon won't harm you?"

"It has already stolen my beauty. What more could it want?"

"Your soul?" Umberto's voice shook.

She despised him. It was likely he had supervised Joachín's flogging while Tomás took delight in forcing Rana. "My soul it has, already."

"By your leave, Fra Umberto, perhaps I should go. The Grand Inquisitor might have need of me." The guard looked white.

Umberto waved him off. The guard saluted and turned on his heel. His footfalls fell harshly, as he ran. Miriam smiled mockingly at Umberto. "This will be interesting. I shall enjoy watching a demon play with its food."

"You mean him, of course." Umberto nodded at Joachín.

"Do I?" She chuckled as she set the torch into a wall sconce. Ignoring him, she walked about the altar in a clockwise fashion, murmuring and carving the air with her knife.

Umberto stood rooted where he was. "What are you mumbling? I insist on hearing what you are saying!"

She saluted the east with her blade. Then she proceeded in a southerly direction and did the same.

Umberto took a step back. "Stop, at once! The Grand Inquisitor should be here to witness this proceeding!"

She shot him a dark look. West was similarly addressed, and then the north.

"The ward is complete!" she shouted, knowing Umberto would understand he stood unprotected outside of it. With her knife held high, she approached Joachin. She hoped with all her heart he wouldn't open his eyes to see the nightmare hovering over him. She prayed even harder her performance would send Umberto screaming from the chapel.

She whipped the veil from her face to reveal her pockmarked visage, and then held the point of the blade over Joachin's heart. She regarded Umberto with rage-filled eyes. "Al El Omigamatron! Belial Al El Alli!" she shrieked, raising the knife high. "I summon you! Take this mortal offering, and any others who linger here!"

The blade came down. It missed Joachin narrowly and stabbing the altar behind him.

Umberto squawked and fled. She kept screaming the bogus incantation over and over, until she was sure he had run far enough. She caught her breath and listened to the deathly silence. Then she grabbed Joachin by the chest.

"Oh, my love," she whimpered, "My *cielo*, I am here! It's me, Miriam! We have to go, now. You must wake up!"

She held him close and embraced him, hoping her kisses might ignite him to awareness. He drew in a sharp breath and moaned, stirring in her arms. They had to get back to the ship.

He whispered her name.

"Yes! I am here! But, Love, I must warn you. I don't look like myself. Rana amputated my little finger and cast a glamoury on me. She looks like me, and I look like her! Please, Lys," she murmured to the goddess. "Let him believe me."

He opened his eyes and let out a cry. He pushed at her feebly.

She stepped away from him, but only by a fraction. "Joachín, it *is* me!"

"Don't touch me!"

"I can prove it! The night of our wedding, you...you killed Alonso! He was a squirrel! And then there was Blanca and Inez! I'm sorry, Joachín. Inez is dead! And when you thought you were saving me from Tomás at the docks, that wasn't me! That was Rana! She stole my appearance! Dear Lys! What more can I say to you?"

He stared at her in horror. She wasn't sure what ran through his mind—whether he struggled to believe her, or whether he was sickened by what she was. She wanted to crumple into a heap beside him; she felt dizzy and sick. Every second they wasted was precious. If Umberto had run to find Tomás....

"I don't know how to turn myself back, but I'll find a way! I promise!" Tears welled in her eyes.

His lips trembled. He drew in a sharp breath. "Miriam, Gods!"

"Please believe me!"

Without thinking, he reached for her and gasped in pain. His arms fell back. He had reopened his welts. "I *do* believe you," he whispered feebly. "I do. Dream...makes...sense, now."

She had no idea what he was talking about. If he had dreamed Rana would do this to her, he hadn't mentioned it. If only he had! "Do you think you can stand if I wrap my arms about you?" she asked.

He nodded. "No choice. Have...to."

"There's a doorway leading out, a short way down the nave. After that, I'll...I'll steal a horse!"

"My Miri? Stealing a horse? Can't be...you."

"It *is* me!"

"Sshhh. S'a joke."

She wanted to laugh and cry at the same time. If he was making jokes, they had a chance of making it to the *Phoenix*.

Suddenly, she was assailed by vertigo. Reality bent and warped. Although she stooped over Joachín, she felt enclosed in a bubble, like a butterfly in glass. A presence, intimate and immediate, spoke. *Tomás is at the door.*

She set a finger to her lips to caution Joachín not to move. His eyes widened as she reached for the knife. She held it over him and glared at the door as Tomás stepped through it.

"So," he said, slipping into the chapel, but only by a few feet, "the pigeon returns to her roost. Umberto told me you were here."

She said nothing, but glared at him as she thought Rana would.

"He said he left you screaming an invocation to Belial. Odd choice for a sacrifice, considering he's the demon of fornication, wealth, and pollution of the sanctuary."

"Umberto's an old man. He is confused."

"Is he? Perhaps. Then again, perhaps he isn't." He took a few steps closer, as if checking for invisible barriers. "You ran away. Why?"

She ignored the question. "You're quite safe. The ward contains any fiends I invoke, while chasing busybodies away."

"You meant to scare him."

"I did. He's pathetic. He should be replaced."

"He has his purposes. That still doesn't explain why you left."

She had to embellish now, as she had never done before. There could be no hesitation, no faltering to suggest she misled him, that she was not whom she claimed to be. "I scryed. I saw Miriam Medina reading a grimoire, like the one in your possession. She focused on a particular spell."

"Yes?"

"You know the one."

He straightened, ever so slightly, his golden eyes as intent as ever. He waited for her to continue.

"A portion of the process was left out. When the sigils are sliced into the corpse, the demon wrests its soul from the afterlife. That essence can be bestowed on a recipient."

He sucked in a slow breath.

"There are two kinds of corpse that can provide for such a spell. Both need to be freshly dead, within forty-eight hours. The first type should be of someone of status—a priest who was high in the temple or a nobleman."

"And the other?"

She glanced down at Joachín. He had closed his eyes to play along with the ruse, but his breathing was rapid and shallow. "A sworn enemy."

Tomás stepped closer. "That would explain Miriam Medina's miraculous escapes and how she was able to command the weather. Of course. It makes perfect sense. She carved Alonso the first time to flee Granad. But that doesn't explain how she escaped me in Elysir." He halved the distance between them. "But Miriam is now in my power. She's my prisoner. How do you explain that?"

"The spell needs to be renewed periodically. The demon requires fresh food. She must have left it too long."

"Umberto said you intended sacrificing him for me. Is that the case? Or were you planning something else?"

Why was he being so accommodating, so polite? Was it the caution of a seasoned hunter, determining the strength of its prey?

She nodded at Joachín. "It's a good thing you didn't waste him. The sooner you receive his essence, the more powerful you will be."

"And if we, how shall I say it—if we harvest enough bodies, then...?"

"You will gain what you seek, Radiance. Eternity. It *is* possible to live forever."

He drew in a sharp breath, steepled his fingers, and held them to his lips. For a moment, he closed his eyes, savouring the thought. Then he pointed at her suspiciously. "Why have none of the Diaphani done this before?"

"Their faith stops them, but mostly, they lack the courage to do it. They think the deepest hell awaits them if they kill to attain eternal life. As well, the process becomes more difficult in time. The demons grow harder to control."

He nodded. "Only the fittest—of course. But I have no such reservations." He glanced at Joachín. "You will dispatch him, now? What am I required to do?"

"Bare yourself and stand before me. Carve yourself with the appropriate tattoo—I will show you—while I invoke the fiend. And then, once it appears...," she glanced at Joachín, "I will finish him. The effect should be immediate. You will sense the change immediately."

She prayed Joachín wouldn't move, that he trusted her, that he believed she was who she said, his Miriam. He had been weakened by the flogging. He was in no condition to fight. Her own strength was ebbing, but fear empowered her. She could still disable Tomás, providing he believed in the ruse. If Joachín reacted too soon, if he tried to defend them, the Grand Inquisitor would overpower them both. She hadn't forgotten Tomás's tattoo for speed and strength.

"Such fun!" Tomás undid his black cape and let it fall to the floor. Then he loosened his belt, letting it slide through his fingers. He pulled his white habit over his head, and stood naked before her. He wore a superior expression, as if he were proud of his form. His penis had lifted partially. Across his chest, the black tattoo gleamed like an oily python. He licked his lips. "Now what?"

"Now, you stand before me so I might show you the glyph."

Something dark passed behind his eyes—a shadow of disbelief or the heightening of lust? She wasn't sure what it was, but it was gone in a moment. She forced herself to stand firm and not shrink away from him. She would have one chance, only.

He closed the distance. Only an arm's length separated them. "Here I am," he said softly, standing before her like a lover.

She struck at him without a word. She aimed straight for his throat—and missed. Before she could react, he was beside her, seizing her wrist. She gasped and fought to keep possession of the knife. As they grappled, he leaned into her ear. She had the sense he was playing with her, that he enjoyed their fight. "I liked fucking you, Miriam Medina. But then it dawned on me—how could it be you, when something stopped me, before? I must give Rana credit. She has stronger magic than I thought. It must have upset you to find that you were her, and she, you."

He grabbed her by the breast and twisted it. She screamed in pain. It felt as if he meant to pull it free from her body. He could hurt her in any way he liked. The only thing he couldn't do was force coitus.

"I still think you're capable of giving me what I want, that you have the secret to eternal life. So, I'll tell you what," the knife inched toward her ear. She gasped and held it at bay. Her arms shook. "I'll save your *novio*, here. We'll find someone else to sacrifice. But you'll also let me fuck you in front of him, whenever I want."

She kicked him in the shin. She had hoped for his groin, but he had anticipated it. They collapsed in a heap on top of Joachín.

A blood slickened hand grabbed Tomás's wrist and yanked the blade free. The knife carved a line beneath Tomás's ear. Tomás bellowed and turned on Joachín like a gored bull. He lifted his fists, to ram him like horns. Joachín sliced at one of Tomás' arms, but he was too slow. Tomás ignored the blade and grabbed him by the throat, intent on throttling him. The force of his handling was too much for Joachín. The knife skittered into the darkness. Miriam was thrown aside. She narrowly missed knocking her head on the altar. As Tomás choked the life from Joachín, she grabbed the flaming torch from its sconce. With the last of her remaining strength, she swung it at Tomás's head.

There was a dull crack. Tomás fell back. He slithered down the side of the altar like a dead weight.

Whimpering, Miriam let the torch fall to the flagstones. She felt Joachín's throat, terrified Tomás had crushed his wind pipe. The cartilage was intact, but his pulse was erratic and faint. He wasn't breathing.

"Joachín, please, don't die on me! I can't bear it!" With a cry, she set her mouth on his to force air into him. His heart continued to stutter. Tears streamed down her ruined face as she worked. If he died, she would die herself, accept Tomás had won, find the knife wherever it had fallen and end her life before he came to. She had no doubt he would. A strange luck surrounded the Grand Inquisitor.

Finally, Joachín roused. His arms jerked feebly as a drowning man's might. He choked once, a harsh ragged sound, as he gasped for air.

"Thank Lys!" she whispered. At her feet, Tomás groaned. Her knees threatened to give out from beneath her. "Joachín, we have to get out of here! Now!" She couldn't fight Tomás, again. She didn't have the strength.

Joachín blinked feebly as if not understanding the ordeal they had come through. She slid an arm beneath his shoulders and bit her lip against his pain.

As quickly as she could, she hefted him into a sitting position. With her free hand, she nudged his legs over the side of the altar. As she struggled to set him on his feet, he collapsed into her arms. She held him tightly, aware her efforts were causing him hurt. It couldn't be helped; her arm was abrading the welts on his back. They stumbled for the side door, and then unexpectedly, the door burst open.

She whimpered in fear, sure Tomás had posted sentries outside, certain he had foreseen what she would do and take countermeasures to foil her attempt. After she had struck him, he hadn't had time to call for help, but it was likely help was close at hand. Two shadows crashed through the door. She cried out as she recognized them.

Barto and Iago had come to the rescue. Ximen had sent them.

Chapter Forty-Nine: From the Pot into the Coals

"Quickly!" Barto beckoned. Iago thrust his knife back into its sheath and ran to help Miriam.

"How did you know?" Miriam asked as he helped her prop Joachin from the other side.

"Ximen. When you didn't come below decks, he got suspicious. Thought you might try something on your own. He looked for you in that queer way he has. Told us where you were, and how we might reach you. He wanted to come too, but Zara wouldn't let him."

"Thank the gods he didn't."

"We have to be careful. The streets are crawling with Port Watch."

"Do we take out the trash, first?" Barto toed Tomás, who lay unmoving on the floor. Finishing him would prevent him from raising the alarm and sending the Guard to apprehend them. It would also throw the entire Solarium into turmoil.

The sound of many boots approaching interrupted them. "Gods!" Miriam cried. The Guard!"

"Radiance!" Umberto shouted from outside the chapel. "Are you all right? Do you need assistance?"

There was no time to kill Tomás as much as they might want. In seconds, the Guard would crash through the door and apprehend them. "Stay where you are!" Miriam shouted. "Enter now, and the demon will seize you!" Her voice had a panicked edge to it. She hoped Umberto didn't recognize it.

Barto collected Joachin from her and Iago. Without a concern for the stripes on his back, he threw him over his shoulder. The three of them bolted for the outside door.

"Why does his Radiance not answer?" Umberto shouted.

They ran out the door and into the night. Iago paused only briefly to close it, so as not to give away their path of escape. The ensuing confusion would buy them time. The Guard would be momentarily distracted by the condition of their leader. Soon, they raced down dark cobbled streets, breathing hard and listening for sounds of pursuit. Miriam's vision prickled to black. Her pulse hammered in her head. She stumbled.

Iago caught her as she fell. "Barto! She can't!" he called after the retreating giant. "We have to stop, if only for a moment!" Barto paused, an inky lump lurching about in the dark.

"Pick her up!" he bellowed.

"No," Miriam muttered. If Iago carried her, their progress would be slowed. Iago wasn't Barto. "I'm all right, now." She still felt faint.

Lights appeared from around the corner, lanterns held high to chase away the night. Their brilliance blinded her. She held up an arm to shield her eyes.

"Halt!" a harsh voice cried. "Who goes there?"

"Run!" Barto changed directions.

Iago snagged her by the arm and pulled her along, but too late, the clatter of hooves churned behind them. Soon they were surrounded by grim-looking men in naval regalia.

"You're under arrest for being at large after curfew! Identify yourselves!" A sergeant confronted them from atop his nervous, snorting horse. His tunic, emblazoned with the town's coat of arms—Hércules restraining two lions—confirmed who they were: members of the Port Authority.

"My brother's been hurt," Barto explained. He spread a hand for mercy. Joachín slipped off his shoulder. He shoved him back into place. "We had no choice."

"Wait a minute! These are the ones we've been searching for, Sergeant!" A foot soldier stepped forward. "The three of them, and especially that one on the big one's back. They fit the description! But instead of the blind man, they've picked up a whore!"

Miriam felt as if the world were closing in on her. This couldn't be happening. To come so close to escaping, only to be apprehended by the Port Authority? Was Tomás working in tandem with them? That made no sense. How did the Port Guard know about Ximen? Had the men done something illegal on their way into Qadis?

"Get the Vizconde. He'll confirm if it's them," the sergeant said.

She knew of only one vizconde—the vicious nobleman they had left in Marabel. Don Lope ruled here. But why would the vizconde think they were here? A sick certainty settled into her gut. Joachín had done something; he had avenged himself on Don Lope in some way.

"I knew we should have killed him when we had the chance," Iago muttered.

Without any regard for him, Barto threw Joachín at the closest guard. In moments, Miriam found herself in the middle of a brawl. There were too many men. As one of them shoved her out of the way, she tripped and fell over Joachín. She stayed there to cover and protect him. Barto roared and raged like a cornered bear until someone clouted him over the head with the butt of an axe. Iago did as much damage as he could with his knife, until another guard throttled him from behind.

In moments, Don Lope de Qadis appeared in their breathing, sweaty, cursing midst. He barely spared her a glance as a guard pulled her from Joachín. "It's him," he said, verifying Joachín's identity. He smiled nastily and kicked him in the ribs. "Take him away. Take them all away."

"Even her?" the guard asked.

Don Lope sneered. "No, not her, you idiot. You want her, take her. It's your cock."

Miriam clutched at the tunic of a retreating guard. He kicked her off. "Where are you taking them?" she cried, as the troop led Joachin, Barto, and Iago away.

"Listen to her," a guard said. "Crying for her lovers."

"Those old ones. They get sentimental," his comrade said, laughing.

They rounded the corner, leaving her alone. She hurt all over, as if every inch of her had been pummeled. She clawed her way along the cobblestones until she reached a stone wall. Around the corner, the Port Guard retreated in the distance. They had been on the periphery of the quay. Beyond the promenade, a familiar three-masted ship floated at anchor. The *Phoenix*.

She had to reach it, had to tell the Tribe what happened. Ximen would be able advise them about Joachin and the men. If Francis returned to the ship, perhaps he could use his influence to free them. There had to be something she could do to get them back. She had to get help. She couldn't free them on her own.

She stumbled for the ship, fearing she would pass out on the quay before she reached it, that the townsfolk would find her unconscious on the flagstones in the morning. The Tribe was below decks. Would Ximen have watched events as they unfolded? Surely, he had.

She held onto that lone hope as someone accosted her.

"You!" the stranger said through gritted teeth. He had come from out of nowhere. He must have watched her as she staggered around the corner. She let out a cry of pain as he grabbed her by the forearm. He shook her hard, as if he might rattle the life from her.

"I knew I'd find you here, you vengeful, jealousy-ridden witch! You're to blame for this! I should do the world a favour and drown you!"

She whimpered in fear. Angél had found her. From the look of loathing on his face, he believed she was Rana Isadore.

"And now the Grand Inquisitor has her in his clutches, you vile, stinking *puta*! I should have guessed something was wrong when she denied knowing about the letter. You sent it! Didn't you? DIDN'T YOU? "

"Let me go! I didn't...!"

"LIAR! You think I won't kill you? I should throw you in the drink, but drowning is too good for you! I'll finish you with my bare hands!"

His fists closed about her throat and squeezed the life from her. Her eyes bulged, she choked on her own tongue. The ground disappeared from beneath her feet. The world went black. A dark malevolence—Angél's rage—snagged her and pulled her down.

She was dying. Death was inevitable. She felt her life ebb. It was time to stop grasping, to stop trying.

From somewhere far away, she sensed her body drop to the ground as if released from the furious thing that held her. She floated apart from it. The vise about her throat was gone. She no longer breathed, but found she didn't have to. She felt nothing—no surprise, no worry, no fear. Except...that wasn't quite right. She still longed for someone, missed him. This place...it wasn't supposed to be dark. She should be surrounded by light. Alonso was in the light. He should be with her.

A voice drifted toward her like someone calling from the crown of a distant hill. The voice was scratchy and thin, as if it were shouting itself hoarse. "Come back! You can't die yet! I need you! They need you!" A man's voice. Not Alonso's. "Miriam! Don't go!"

She wavered, at the juncture. She could go either way—return to the life she had left behind, or...move on. She wanted to do that. Life was hard. It would be easier if she let someone else take care of...of whatever it was she had been taking care of. Alonso waited for her beyond the horizon. Ahead, a pinprick of light shone.

"I'll track them down!" The voice was so faint as to be hardly discernible. It verged on panic. "Was one of them Joachín? If he's in the *cárcel*, I'll have him released! Come back to me, Miriam!"

She hesitated. He was talking about Joachín.

"Not only that, but the Queen is pregnant! Ilysabeth is back at Hartfield, no longer considered a threat! Gods, don't die on me!"

Joachín, in jail? Memory of the immediate past swept through her like an icy rain. Tomás had caught them. They had escaped, only to be apprehended by the Port Guard. She had to find Joachín and rescue him. He wouldn't survive jail for long. She searched the dark landscape for the shepherd who had hailed her. The sky split open. Pain struck her in a bolt. She cracked open her eyes, dazed. A man cradled her in his arms.

"Thank the gods," Francis whispered.

He lifted her as gently as he could. It proved to be too much. She shuddered from the pain and knew no more.

Chapter Fifty: Hope Reigns

When she finally opened her eyes, it was to stare into the folds of a faded russet skirt. The cloth had once been bright, but the dress had lost much of its colour as if bleached by the sun. A fold fell over her right eye, blocking her vision. Someone had wrapped her head in bandages; her scalp itched. Her right hand, freshly bandaged, throbbed dully. She swallowed, overcome by thirst.

The russet skirt moved. "Sweet Lys, she's awake!"

A face filled her vision—Zara peering at her anxiously. Luci and Casi came into view, following suit. The floor rose and fell. Nausea assailed her.

"Give her some water," Zara looked concerned.

"I don't think I can." Her voice was a rasp.

"You must," Luci said soothingly. She slipped a hand beneath her neck and lifted her gently to drink from a cup. "You've been sleeping all day. We managed to get some into you, but if you don't take more, your body will fail."

A whole day? That meant they were....

"At sea. Yes, we are, Miriam," Casi said. "We all feel sick, but it's getting better. It helps if you're above decks, watching the horizon. Maré let me, 'cept I'm not allowed to talk to the sailors. Maré said I'll get in their way. She doesn't trust them."

"That's enough, Casi. Don't tire her out. Drink, Miriam."

She frowned, knowing she didn't have the strength to argue. As the water went down, her stomach revolted. She gagged, afraid it wouldn't stay there. After Francis had rescued her at the quay, she didn't think it was possible to feel any worse. She was wrong.

"Joachin...did Francis...?" she asked.

Their expressions gave them away. He hadn't been successful.

"They're alive, Miriam. That's all we know," Luci said. "Ximen confirmed it. They've been put aboard a carrack, bound for Nueva Esbaña. The ship has a stop-over in the Canarias, where it will pick up more slaves."

"Slaves?"

"Yes. Don Lope's intention for them, as Iago understands it."

"How are Iago and Barto?"

"They're on the slave ship too, a bit roughed up, but they are coping."

"And Joachin?"

Zara set a hand on Luci's wrist. Their reluctance to talk about him terrified her.

"Tell me!"

"Ximen hasn't been able to get a fix on Joachin. We think it's because he's unconscious. We know he's on board. Iago and Barto saw Don Lope's men carry him up the gangplank, but they didn't throw him into the slave pen with the others. Iago thinks he's been taken to the captain's quarters."

"Why?"

"We don't know."

The floor tilted as the ship rolled. She vomited up the water and lay in her sick. As Zara and Luci cleaned her up, she didn't think she could feel any more helpless. Why would the captain keep Joachin captive in his quarters? Her imagination supplied all sorts of reasons, none of them good. She moaned, clutching her stomach.

"Your Inglaisi spy thinks he can buy them at auction, once we reach Tenerifa. Let's hope," Zara said.

Hope. That was all she had. She had foiled Tomás, the Tribe was on its way to the New World, but things had not gone as planned. Loved ones were missing. "How did this happen?" she asked, at a loss. "Joachín and I escaped the Grand Inquisitor, Barto and Iago found us. I thought we were safe, but we fell into the hands of the Port Authority. How did Don Lope even know we were in Qadis?"

Zara's expression darkened. "I wondered about the same thing. I asked Ximen, and he finally confessed it. Male pride and stupidity is what it was." She drew herself up indignantly. "It seems that after the four of them left us, they couldn't leave well enough alone. They followed Don Lope to a brothel. Knocked him out cold over the head, kidnapped him, and then stole his coach to ride into Qadis in style. Worse, they trussed him up in some *puta's* dress and left him bound and gagged for anyone to find him. A great joke, to be sure!"

"Ximen was involved in this?" She couldn't believe it.

"He was the *worst* of them! Pretended to be Don Lope, himself! When I finally pried it out of him, I gave him the tongue-lashing of his life, I can tell you. Joachín is still young and foolish, but Ximen should have known better. If they only listened to us women, things would go smoothly. I suppose they can't help themselves."

Zara seemed to think they had suffered the worst of it. Although the men had been caught, everyone would be back together again, once they reached Tenerifa. Her faith in the goddess was unshakeable. But Don Lope was nearly as cruel as Tomás. He would find no end of ways to abuse and humiliate Joachín, providing Joachín recovered from what Tomás had already done to him.

"How long before we dock in the Canarias?" she asked.

"Another day or so, if the wind is with us."

Only a day. Let Joachín hang on. Let Francis have enough influence and money to buy them at auction.

"What of Inez?" It had dawned on her she lay exactly where Inez had died. They had disposed of the body, somehow.

"She was Tribe," Luci said simply. "Ximen told the captain one of our members had passed. We said prayers for her and surrendered her to Lys after we left Qadis, this morning."

Miriam remembered Joachin explaining Lys's elements were water and air. They had set Anassa in a scaffold. Here, they had surrendered Inez to the sea.

"You should rest, now." Luci laid a soft hand on her brow. The touch confirmed she lived in fear for both Iago and Joachin. She had already lost a husband. She wasn't sure she could cope with losing a nephew and a son. Miriam wasn't sure she could deal with that, either. What did she have to live for, if Joachin was lost to her? Alonso was no longer there. Despite the supportive company of the Tribe about her, she felt alone.

A few hours later, and after some sleep, more water, and a little food, she felt a bit better. Night had come. She wanted to stand on the spar deck of the *Phoenix* to look at the stars. It was better for her to remain out of sight during the day. Even now, she wore her veil to hide her face from hostile, superstitious eyes. As she climbed the last ladder to the ship's waist, she spotted two familiar figures standing by the rail. Ximen and Francis had their heads together and spoke quietly. The breeze was cool, sharp. Beyond the mizzenmast, members of the crew stood on watch, including the master at the wheel. Beyond, other seamen eyed them from the forecastle. The wind filled the sails, the yards creaked and groaned. Beneath her feet, the ship rolled, a creature of the sea and sky.

She wove her way unsteadily to Ximen and Francis. Ximen stiffened as she approached. Francis, in that way he had, excused himself and left, knowing she wished to speak with Ximen, alone.

"Rememberer," she said, acknowledging him.

"Matriarch," he replied.

He had withheld information from her when he shouldn't have. She couldn't permit him to do that, again. If they were to survive and bring each member of the Tribe back, he had to respect her leadership, believe in her ability to think and act rationally, even if she didn't entirely trust herself. "When did you know Joachin had been caught by the Grand Inquisitor?" she asked without preamble. He shifted his weight uncomfortably.

"The moment it passed."

"You had been watching him."

"Yes. In my defense, I didn't think it was possible to save him. I chose to save you."

"By keeping me in ignorance."

"I had to protect you."

"Your job isn't to protect me, Ximen. It's to advise. You once told me Matriarchs and Rememberers work as a team. We can't be equals if one of us is more equal than the other."

"You are young."

"Yes. I could say you are old and your faculties are failing." She held up a hand to stave off his indignation. "That isn't true. You're as clear-headed as ever. But let's not use age as an excuse."

He accepted her reasoning reluctantly. "I concede the point."

"Good. I'm glad you do. Can I rely on you to tell me everything you know about Joachín? No matter what happens?"

"I can't sense him at the moment."

"That isn't what I asked."

He set his jaw.

"You mustn't spare me, Ximen. I need to know everything. I must, for the sake of us all. How can I know what to do, if I don't have all the information at hand?"

"Some things aren't fit for a woman to hear."

He was an old man, set in his ways. She was tempted to walk away from him, frustrated with their lack of consensus. "I don't need brutal details," she said, softening. "I understand how hard it must be for you to see them. But I do need to understand what is happening. I need only enough detail to set my course. Anger doesn't slay me, it empowers me. It's a tool that prompts me to do what I might not ordinarily do." She thought of how she had tried to kill Tomás, of how she had lied to him to save Joachín. She would not hesitate to do that again. Only a month had passed since they had walked through the caves from Elysir. The Miriam who had done that had found the members of her Tribe wanting. She was a different woman, now. There were some things that were more important than thieving, lying, and murdering. She would stop at nothing to preserve her family and her Tribe.

She set a cool hand atop his. His emotions flitted through her like a flock of terns—embarrassment, protectiveness, and surprise in her growth and strength. "Very well," he said. "If you can bare it, I can too."

"Thank you."

"You know," he gazed at her with his milky-white eyes, "when I look at you, I don't see the pock marks. I know they are there, I know that's how others see you, but that's the strangest thing. I see the beauty you are, the grace that radiates from within."

His words brought a lump to her throat. There were no mirrors onboard the ship, or at least not in the hold where they were housed. She still missed her old self. That was vanity, yes. It seemed a lesser sin than most.

"I will search my memory. I am sure there is something I can retrieve from the past that will restore you."

She nodded. It was illogical, but she didn't want to waste her hopes on that, as if hope was a thing to be saved. Ximen stepped away from the rail. She had a feeling he intended to seek out Zara.

She stared out over the dark waves. Pale foam crowned each crest, as if capturing the light from the stars. Francis rejoined her at the rail.

"How are you feeling?" he asked.

"Sick."

"It passes. As for your other injuries, you seem to be healing well enough."

She drew in a deep breath. "In my old life, I was a healer."

"And now?"

"Still one, I suppose."

"I think you should know I had almost convinced the High Solar to have your husband released to me, when word came to us that Rana Isadore had returned. I had a devil of a time keeping out of Tomás's way after that. His guards broke into the shrine, informed the High Solar that you and Joachín had fled. Then, it was a race from the temple, only to find you in the middle of a brawl. I was about to intervene when that madman accosted you on the quay."

"Angél Ferrara."

"Yes. He thought you were the real Rana Isadore."

"Did you kill him?"

"No, I left him lying on the dock. I had more important things to deal with at the time. He wasn't there when we set sail." He eyed her soberly.

"Thank you for saving my life."

"You're welcome. Perhaps someday, you will save mine."

She smiled wanly. "I thought you wanted to take me away to Inglais."

"I do. But some of your people are missing, so we are taking a detour. Besides, I've always wanted to spend time at sea. Privateering is a lucrative business. I'm sure Ilysabeth will forgive me if I win her a prize or two."

"Ilysabeth? I thought you said something about her no longer being successor to the throne."

"You remember that? I'm surprised. Yes, I did say that. It comforts me greatly to know that for now, she is safe. On the other hand, I have a strange intuition about Maria's pregnancy. I'm not sure I believe it. It's almost as if it's something else."

"Perhaps you're also an empath, of a type."

The possibility startled him.

She rubbed her arms against the cold. Francis had big ideas and bigger plans. He was like Joachin in that way. She wanted her husband back, safe and sound. What was happening to him right now? Until Ximen advised her, she had no way of knowing. And what of Alonso? The last time they had been together, he had waited for her to accompany him into the light. She hadn't said goodbye. Did he watch her from beyond the stars? Would they ever be reunited again, in a better, happier place?

"I'll leave you to your thoughts," Francis said, retiring with a bow.

She didn't blame him. She was poor company.

She stared out over the dark, foaming sea. Eventually, she tired of it. Under different circumstances, she would have marvelled at the heaving waves and spangled night, but without Joachin or Alonso, she had lost her sense of wonder. Was it wrong to be so fickle? Was it a sin to love them both? Were the gods punishing her because she did?

Such an idea suggested the gods were punitive, but how could that be? Both men had brought her to where she was now. Both had contributed to her destiny. Joachín believed Lys had ordained they be together. Alonso had foresworn Sul on her behalf. If the gods endured their choices and their pains, didn't it mean that they allowed those decisions even when they were mistakes? And if the gods hoped for the best, didn't it mean man and god co-created, together?

Those were questions for the priests. And the only real priest who might answer them wasn't there.

Alonso, she thought feeling lost and alone, *I don't want you traversing the universe, uncovering its wonders. I want you here, with me.*

When he didn't respond, she made her way back to the hold with little notice from the crew. It was late. The watch bell rang out the third hour. A lone lantern hung from a post on the orlop deck. Her Tribe snored amid the water tuns and straw.

She settled beside Luci and Casi and tried to make herself comfortable. In the hold, the ship rocked less, but the sounds of creaking timbers and straining masts were hard to ignore, reminding her that only a sturdy hull of oak remained between her and the Great Ocean Sea. Beneath her was stone ballast, a keel, and then inky, bottomless depths. Casi murmured in her sleep, unaware of her fears.

The back of her head hurt. Her hand throbbed. She rolled onto her left side and cushioned her face with a patchy, scarred arm. She closed her eyes and thought of Joachín.

A rustling brought her back to alertness. Something disturbed the straw. She caught her breath as a rat appeared at her elbow.

It nosed the air and watched her, its whiskers twitching. Tears filled her eyes. She beckoned a finger to it to come. It crept onto her arm. Alonso sprang into existence, as large and as vital as he had ever been. His touch was little more than a soft puff of air, but she felt his arms slide about her. She held the rat to her breast and hugged it close. In her mind's eye, she held him.

Shhh, my love. I'm here. His voice filled her mind, her heart.

How? I thought....

He sighed. *After a while, it gets easier. I don't like being a rat, but I didn't have any choice considering where we are. This one may not last long. It'll serve us, for now.*

There are cows, horses....

Really, Miriam, a cow? As for the horses, they're too willful, although they won't be, after a few weeks.

If they missed hurricanes and dodged pirates, they would be at least six weeks at sea before reaching Nueva Esbaña. Her thoughts returned to the last time they were together, when Inez and her mother had walked into the light. *I thought you might go on, too,* she said softly.

And I thought you were coming with me.

Guilt infused her. *I...I couldn't Alonso. I wanted to! It would have been so much easier, but....*

But you still had the Tribe to think of. And you still love him.

She said nothing.

I was your first love. I was there before he was. You have no idea how many times I've wished things were different, Miriam. That we'd met under different circumstances. That I could be a man for you, as he is. If it is ever in my power, we will be together that way again.

She didn't know how it could be possible. He was bound to her in a limited way. She wasn't sure if loving him physically was possible in the afterlife. But the physical aspect was only one part of love. *I'm happy you're here, Alonso.*

You don't seem happy.

Comforted, then. I would be happier, if I could.

You're worried about him, aren't you?

Yes.

Would it make you feel better if I looked in on him?

You can do that? Over the water? She had heard once that ghosts couldn't travel over the sea. But then, he wasn't exactly a ghost.

Probably. I'll have to leave my host.

For the second time in a matter of seconds, relief swept through her. The first time was when he had reappeared, and now, as he was about to leave her to find Joachin. She was overcome with gratitude. She didn't deserve a love as great as his. *Alonso! I love you so much! Thank you!*

You may not thank me, once I report what kind of trouble he's in.

That was very likely to be true. *Then I must have faith everything will turn out for the best in the end.*

He looked sour but leaned in to kiss her on the forehead, anyway. She felt a brief warmth at the contact. *We need to find a way to return you to your former self, too,* he said, frowning slightly.

That's the least of my concerns.

She felt a slight pressure as he squeezed her. In the next moment, he was gone. The rat came to, dazed. She froze, fearing it might bite her, but it didn't appear to know where it was or how it had come to be there. She held her breath as it crawled away from her into a dark corner.

She lay without moving for some time, thankful Alonso had returned and knowing he would return again. With luck, Francis would buy the men's freedom once they docked in Tenerifa. She prayed Joachín would survive until then.

He has to, she thought. *Please, Lys,* she implored. She stared up at the ship's rafters. Her relationship with the goddess had always been a troublesome one. *Don't let him die. Protect him. Protect us. I love him.*

A snatch of memory came unbidden, catching her off-guard— Joachín in front of her as they rode to Marabel. His dark hair fell over his brow as the breeze tousled it.

Last night, I had a dream, he said. He looked so proud of himself. *I dreamt we had a son. You'd just given birth to him. He was beautiful, Miriam, with a mass of black hair and a strong pair of lungs. Zara handed him to me. I cradled him in my arms.*

She caught her breath, stunned by the poignancy of the memory and the hope it was true. She had forgotten it, had dismissed it as a dream of Inez's child. But now.... Was this Lys's way of telling her this was their eventual fate?

Something was not quite right about the memory. She frowned, trying to determine what it was.

He was beautiful, Miriam, with a mass of black hair....

In her memory, Joachín hadn't called her by name! She was sure of it. Which was why she had thought his dream had been of Inez! But in the way she remembered it now....

She let out a low cry. Lys had changed the past. She had altered it, but in such a fashion so as not to alter the present, except for this tiny bit of reassurance.

Tears streamed down Miriam's face. "Thank you," she whispered, grateful for the intervention.

There was no reply.

Miriam found she didn't need one. She had no doubt despite the trials awaiting them in the New World, she and Joachin would find each other again, they would be together, they would survive.

And Alonso, with them.

About the Author

SUSAN MACGREGOR IS an editor with *On Spec* magazine and edited the anthologies *Tesseracts Fifteen: A Case of Quite Curious Tales*, (Edge Books) and *Divine Realms* (Ravenstone Press). Her short fiction has appeared in a number of periodicals and anthologies, including *A Method to the Madness*, (Five Rivers) and *Urban Green Man* (Edge Books).

Her debut novel, *The Tattooed Witch*, the first in the trilogy of the same name, has been short-listed for an Aurora award through the Canadian Science Fiction and Fantasy Association, as has her blog, Suzenyms (http://suzenyms.blogspot.ca/).

Currently, she is working on the third book in the *Tattooed Witch* trilogy, *The Tattooed Rose*, which takes Miriam, Alonso, and Joachin to the New World of the Caribbean. There, after encountering piracy, voudou, and the long arm of the Inquisition, their intertwined destinies are finally resolved...

Books by Five Rivers

NON-FICTION

Al Capone: Chicago's King of Crime, by Nate Hendley

Crystal Death: North America's Most Dangerous Drug, by Nate Hendley

Dutch Schultz: Brazen Beer Baron of New York, by Nate Hendley

Motivate to Create: a guide for writers, by Nate Hendley

Shakespeare for Slackers: Romeo and Juliet, by Aaron Kite, Audrey Evans and Jade Brooke

The Organic Home Gardener, by Patrick Lima and John Scanlan

Elephant's Breath & London Smoke: historic colour names, definitions & uses, Deb Salisbury, editor

Stonehouse Cooks, by Lorina Stephens

John Lennon: Music, Myth and Madness, by Nate Hendley

Shakespeare for Readers' Theatre: Hamlet, Romeo & Juliet, Midsummer Night's Dream, by John Poulson

Stephen Truscott, Decades of Injustice by Nate Hendley

FICTION

Black Wine, by Candas Jane Dorsey

88, by M.E. Fletcher

Immunity to Strange Tales, by Susan J. Forest

The Legend of Sarah, by Leslie Gadallah

Growing Up Bronx, by H.A. Hargreaves

North by 2000+, a collection of short, speculative fiction, by H.A. Hargreaves

A Subtle Thing, Alicia Hendley

Downshift, a Sid Rafferty Thriller, by Matt Hughes

Old Growth, a Sid Rafferty Thriller by Matt Hughes

The Tattooed Witch, by Susan MacGregor

The Tattooed Seer, by Susan MacGregor

Kingmaker's Sword, Book 1: Rune Blades of Celi, by Ann Marston

Western King, Book 2: The Rune Blades of Celi, by Ann Marston

Broken Blade, Book 3: The Rune Blades of Celi, by Ann Marston

Cloudbearer's Shadow, Book 4: The Rune Blades of Celi, by Ann Marston
King of Shadows, Book 5: The Rune Blades of Celi, by Ann Marston
Indigo Time, by Sally McBride
Wasps at the Speed of Sound, by Derryl Murphy
A Method to Madness: A Guide to the Super Evil, edited by Michell Plested and Jeffery A. Hite
A Quiet Place, by J.W. Schnarr
Things Falling Apart, by J.W. Schnarr
And the Angels Sang: a collection of short speculative fiction, by Lorina Stephens
From Mountains of Ice, by Lorina Stephens
Memories, Mother and a Christmas Addiction, by Lorina Stephens
Shadow Song, by Lorina Stephens

YA FICTION

My Life as a Troll, by Susan Bohnet
The Runner and the Wizard, by Dave Duncan
The Runner and the Saint, by Dave Duncan
The Runner and the Kelpie, by Dave Duncan
A Touch of Poison, by Aaron Kite
Out of Time, by D.G. Laderoute
Mik Murdoch: Boy-Superhero, by Michell Plested
Mik Murdoch: The Power Within, by Michell Plested
Type, by Alicia Hendley

FICTION COMING SOON

Cat's Pawn, by Leslie Gadallah
Cat's Gambit, by Leslie Gadallah
The Tattooed Rose, by Susan MacGregor
Sword and Shadow, Book 6: The Rune Blades of Celi, by Ann Marston
Bane's Choice, Book 7: The Rune Blades of Celi, by Ann Marston
A Still and Bitter Grave, by Ann Marston
Diamonds in Black Sand, by Ann Marston

NON-FICTION COMING SOON

Annotated Henry Butte's Dry Dinner, by Michelle Enzinas

King Kwong, by Paula Johanson

Shakespeare for Slackers: Hamlet, by Aaron Kite and Audrey Evans

Shakespeare for Slackers: Macbeth, by Aaron Kite and Audrey Evans

Shakespeare for Reader's Theatre, Book 2: Shakespeare's Greatest Villains, The Merry Wives of Windsor; Othello, the Moor of Venice; Richard III; King Lear, by John Poulsen

YA NON-FICTION COMING SOON

The Prime Ministers of Canada Series:

Sir John A. Macdonald

Alexander Mackenzie

Sir John Abbott

Sir John Thompson

Sir Mackenzie Bowell

Sir Charles Tupper

Sir Wilfred Laurier

Sir Robert Borden

Arthur Meighen

William Lyon Mackenzie King

R. B. Bennett

Louis St. Laurent

John Diefenbaker

Lester B. Pearson

Pierre Trudeau

Joe Clark

John Turner

Brian Mulroney

Kim Campbell

Jean Chretien

Paul Martin

WWW.FIVERIVERSPUBLISHING.COM

Kingmaker's Sword
by Ann Marston
ISBN 9789127400126 $37.99
eISBN 9781927400173 $9.99

Kian dav Leydon brings the fabled Rune Blade Kingmaker back to the Isle of Celi after it was stolen, so the Isle will be ready when and if invasion comes.

Western King
by Ann Marston
ISBN 9781927400272 $37.99
eISBN 9781927400289 $9.99

Which of Red Kian's three sons will inherit the rune blade known as Kingmaker, in the face of Maeduni invasion?

Broken Blade
by Ann Marston
ISBN 9781927400470 $28.99
eISBN 9781927400487 $9.99

Brynda, daughter of Keylan, must teach her Rune Blade to sing death's song—or Maedun's Somber Riders will slay all Celi for their own!

Cloudbearer's Shadow
by Ann Marston
ISBN 9781927400579 $23.99
eISBN 9781927400586 $9.99

Gareth is the youngest and the last of the unfortunate lords of Skai. Called home from a lonely exile, he finds his father fallen into shadow. And worse.
For the Maedun conquest of Gareth's homeland is complete. The standing stones are silent, their webs of magic torn asunder. The Rune Blade called Bane has been lost forever to dark sorcery, and the somber riders rule the islands that were once home to Gareth's people.

King of Shadows
by Ann Marston
ISBN 9781927400616 $27.99
eISBN 9781927400128 $9.99

For generations, the Somber Riders have ruled the Calae lands. But this spring brings more than green buds, crying lambs, and sparkling burns. It brings new promise.

Destiny, that bold weaver, is pulling together three shining strands: A bheancora by blood, whose Rune Blade thirsts for justice; a brash young sovereign whose heart seeks vengeance; and a renegade Somber Rider, touched with Tyadda magic, who remembers a long-forgotten dream.

The Legend of Sarah
by Leslie Gadallah
ISBN 9781927400517 $23.99
eISBN 9781927400524 $4.99

Inspired by the storyteller's narratives, Sarah often conceives of her own life as the stuff of legend for some future troubadour.

Only, such daydreams could never have prepared her for becoming embroiled with a witchy Phile, an agent of the devil come seeking the Old People's places. How could Sarah have known picking the wrong pocket could strand her in the middle of a power-struggle between Brother Parker, the Governor, and the encroaching Phile spies?

The Runner and the Wizard
by Dave Duncan
ISBN 9781927400395 $11.99
eISBN 9781927400401 $4.99

Young Ivor dreams of being a swordsman like his nine older brothers, but until he can grow a beard he's limited to being a runner, carrying messages for their lord, Thane Carrak. That's usually boring, but this time Carrak has sent him on a long journey to summon the mysterious Rorie of Ytter. Rorie is reputed to be a wizard—or an outlaw, or maybe a saint—but the truth is far stranger, and Ivor suddenly finds himself caught up in a twisted magical intrigue that threatens Thane Carrak and could leave Ivor himself very dead.

The Runner and the Saint
by Dave Duncan
ISBN 9781927400531 $11.99
eISBN 9781927400548 $4.99

Earl Malcolm has reason to fear the ferocious Northmen raiders of the Western Isles are going to attack the land of Alba, so he sends Ivor on a desperate mission with a chest of silver to buy them off. But the situation Ivor finds when he reaches the Wolf's Lair is even worse than he was led to expect. Only a miracle can save him now.

The Runner and the Kelpie
by Dave Duncan
ISBN 9781927400654 $11.99
eISBN 9781927400661 $4.99

When the wyrd-woman warned Ivor he was going to meet a monster, he didn't believe her. He thought he had worse things to worry about. He was wrong about both.

The Tattooed Witch
by Susan MacGregor
ISBN 9781927400333 $25.99
eISBN 9781927400340 $4.99
Miriam Medina's only hope to proving her innocence is to ressurect
the high priest she's accused of murdering.

Indigo Time
by Sally McBride
ISBN 9781927400319 $24.99
eISBN 9781927400326 $4.99
Three women with rogue talents. If they meld, time will unwind, and
the universe collapse.

From Mountains of Ice
by Lorina Stephens
ISBN 9780973927856 $23.99
eISBN 9780986563027 $4.99
A mad prince, a reluctant hero and the dead who guide him.

Shadow Song
by Lorina Stephens
ISBN 9780973927818 $23.99
eISBN 9780986563041 $4.99
Danielle Michele Fleming, 10 year old daughter of a French aristocratic
mother, and the second son of English gentry, finds herself caught
in the economic ruin that surrounds the failure of the Bourbon
Monarchy. She finds herself aboard ship, destined for the Queen's
Bush of Upper Canada and a life with the catalyst of her doom, her
uncle, Edgar Fleming. Relentless in his hunt for her, her uncle has her
tracked not only by bounty hunters, but in the end through another
shaman of evil intent and a blood-debt to settle with Shadow Song..